# DESTINY
## OF THE
# DEAD

## BOOKS BY KEL KADE

SHROUD of
PROPHECY
Book Two

# DESTINY
## OF THE
# DEAD

## KEL KADE

**TOR**

**A TOM DOHERTY**
**ASSOCIATES BOOK**

NEW YORK

DESTINY OF THE DEAD

Copyright © 2022 by Dark Rover Publishing LLC

All rights reserved.

Map by Jennifer Hanover

A Tor Book
Published by Tom Doherty Associates
120 Broadway
New York, NY 10271

www.tor-forge.com

Tor® is a registered trademark of Macmillan Publishing Group, LLC.

Library of Congress Cataloging-in-Publication Data

Names: Kade, Kel, author.
Title: Destiny of the dead / Kel Kade.
Description: First edition. | New York, NY : Tor, a Tom Doherty
    Associates Book, 2021. | Series: SHROUD of PROPHECY ; book 2
Identifiers: LCCN 2021058914 (print) | LCCN 2021058915 (ebook) |
    ISBN 9781250293824 (hardcover) | ISBN 9781250293831 (ebook)
Classification: LCC PS3611.A287 D47 2021  (print) | LCC PS3611.
    A287 (ebook) | DDC 813/.6—dc23
LC record available at https://lccn.loc.gov/2021058914
LC ebook record available at https://lccn.loc.gov/2021058915

Our books may be purchased in bulk for promotional, educational, or business use. Please contact your local bookseller or the Macmillan Corporate and Premium Sales Department at 1-800-221-7945, extension 5442, or by email at MacmillanSpecialMarkets@macmillan.com.

First Edition: 2022

Printed in the United States of America

0 9 8 7 6 5 4 3 2 1

# CONTENTS

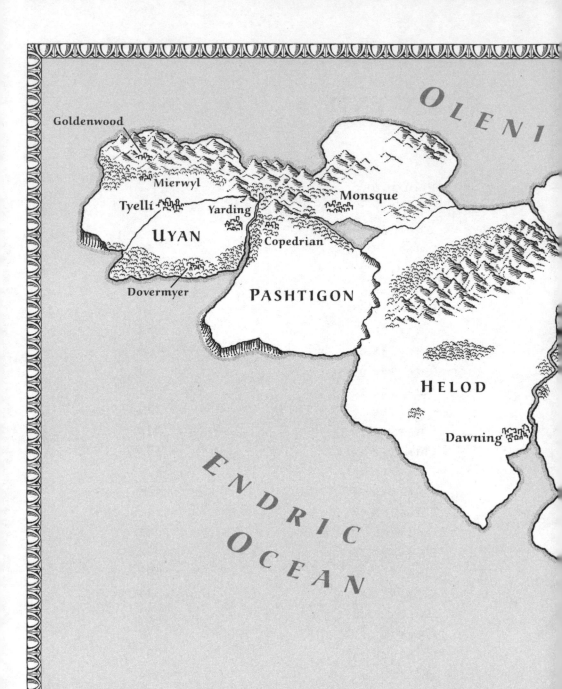

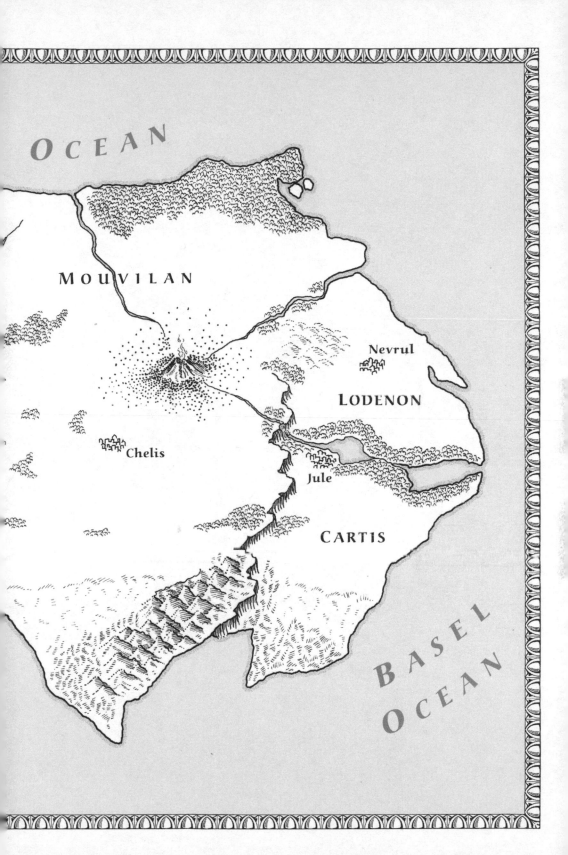

# DESTINY
## OF THE
# DEAD

# PROLOGUE

"What happened next?"

I looked down at young Corin. It was his first time listening to the story of the Grave War, and I could tell by his wide eyes and worried lips that he was upset yet enthralled. I remembered the first time I sat beside the hearth in the community house listening to my mother tell the story. It was an old one, one that would likely soon be forgotten by time; but it was our duty to keep it alive for as long as people were willing to listen.

Corin's brother, Maydon, turned to gaze in my direction. I was glad they had each other. Maydon kept vigil over his younger brother while their father was away. Their father had been gone for some time, and I wasn't yet ready to tell Corin that he probably wasn't coming back. Although the Grave War was long over, the world was far from safe.

I felt a tug at my sleeve and looked back down at Corin. "Leydah, what happened to the undead army? What did Axus do when the forester destroyed the giant tree monster?"

"Yeah," said Brenna, also a first-time listener. "I want to know what happened to Greylan and Rostus."

A few of the adults chuckled over the children's exuberance. I, too, was glad for their appreciation of our history. "Aren't you tired?" I said. "We can pick up the story tomorrow night."

"No," whined a dozen children in unison.

"Ple-e-ease," said Corin. He pointed toward the window as two ghostly figures passed by without a glance. "The wanderers are out there. Nothing's happening. We're safe here. Tell us what happened."

"Very well. Shortly after the Battle of Ruriton, the undead army Aaslo had raised fell back into the swamp, and Aaslo and his friends returned to the marquess's estate."

"That's it?" said Brenna. "The whole army just disappeared? That's not very exciting."

"That's where history differs from fairy tales, Brenna. Sometimes things just end, and it isn't very exciting. In this case, it was a good thing. You see, Aaslo didn't know what we know now. If he had continued pouring his power into those long-dead bodies, he would have been pulled down with them."

"But Greylan and Rostus were different," said Brenna. She lifted her chin and spoke with certitude. "They were different."

"That's right," I said. "But to know *why* they were different, you have to let me continue the story. You see, Aaslo and his friends were not the only ones who were trying to figure out what happened during the battle.

Aaslo had managed to do something perhaps even more intriguing than raise the dead. He had confused the gods."

Anxious chuckles flitted through the room from the older children, and the younger ones' eager stares implored me to explain. "A confused god is an angry god, especially when his plans have been foiled. Aaslo's interference had repercussions across all of Aldrea."

I leaned toward the young ones and with gravity said, "There were many who suffered fates worse than death. Aaslo's story is not complete without that of Cherrí."

# CHAPTER 1

"WHAT IS HE DOING HERE?" SAID A FEMININE VOICE THAT FLITTERED through Aaslo's mind like the forest song.

"I wanted to see this creature of yours. You think I cannot recognize the pride in your eyes, Arayallen?" The voice was deep and masculine yet melodic like the first. It, however, rang in sorrowful lament, resonating with the promise of freedom and rest.

"Of course, I'm proud, as I am with all my successful creations," said the female called Arayallen. "Do you feel threatened, Axus?"

Axus? Aaslo remembered Myra speaking that name. Was he in the presence of the *gods*?

"Ha ha!" rumbled the one named Axus. "*Me*? Threatened by *this*? Your pride has befuddled your sense. He is nothing. I could squash him beneath my foot right now."

Aaslo's heart leapt, but his mind was murky, and the fog did not clear from his vision. Bright, golden light shone through the haze as figures hovered over him. He couldn't move. He couldn't speak. But, as he struggled for full consciousness, he listened.

A third voice, that of a man, one who was accustomed to command and compliance, rumbled, "If you do that, I'll have to find another, and next time I won't tell you who it is."

Axus sighed. "Your games are tiresome, Trostili. Can we not be done with this?"

Glass clinked, then Aaslo heard the glug of liquid into a vessel.

Trostili said, "*Existence* is tiresome, Axus."

Axus's next words rolled off his tongue like the chill of a winter night. "You expect me to believe that *you* are suffering from ennui?"

"Not at all," said Trostili. "I have a purpose, a reason for being, and I intend to fulfill it. Besides, I have developed new techniques I'd like to try. It will make no difference to you. The prophecy guarantees the outcome. Leave the man alone and have some patience."

"Death waits for no man," Axus hissed.

"Don't be so melodramatic," said Arayallen. "Put him back. He doesn't belong here."

"I only brought him part of the way—"

"Solely because you're not strong enough to draw him fully into our realm," said a new voice. This one was deep and strong and carried with it the memory of warmth and security. The figures froze in place, then turned toward the third male voice. "Arayallen is right," he said. "What were you thinking, bringing a human here?"

"Disevy. I didn't expect you," said Axus.

"Obviously."

Axus's voice heated as he moved closer to Aaslo. *"This* creature has somehow acquired my power. I want to know how and to what extent."

"Has the ambrosia stolen your memory?" Arayallen said with a generous dose of mockery. "Who's playing games now? You hand out blessings, then claim no knowledge of it?"

"I assure you I had no hand in this," said Axus. "What do *you* know of it, Arayallen?"

"What do *I* know? I know he wasn't born this way. None of my creations bear power over the dead." Aaslo heard a grin in her voice as she said, "Except for *you*, of course."

Aaslo could hear the grinding as Axus gritted his teeth. "Must you remind me all the time?"

"Why?" she said sweetly, then with an audible pout, "Are you unhappy with your design?"

"Not at all," replied Axus. "In fact, you outdid yourself. Is your ego so fragile that you require me to repeat myself so often?"

"Enough," said Disevy. "Put the human back. You'd best hope he remembers none of this."

"Remembers? He's not even conscious. His mind is back on Aldrea. Give me some credit. I know the human mind is too weak to endure the power of Celestria."

"Strength is relative," said Disevy.

"What's that supposed to mean?" replied Axus.

"It means that the next time you try something like this, your punishment will be swift and effective."

"You threaten me, Disevy?"

"It has been a long time since I've put you in your place, Axus. You forget that *I* rule this pantheon. Your power may have grown, but I am still stronger than you."

"Are you so certain? While you expend your power on worthless creatures like *this*, I reclaim it. You can thank Arayallen for her so many design flaws and Trostili for pitting them against each other. In fact, all of you and your *blessings* are responsible for their inevitable demise and *my* rise."

*Whack!*

"Flaws?" shouted Arayallen. "How dare you! You understand nothing about life—about growth and evolution. The failure of one is necessary for the advancement of another. I may not always appreciate his methods, but Trostili understands this."

"Trostili's weakness is the leash you put around his neck during his creation."

"I did no such thing!"

"You go too far, Axus," said Trostili. "You should leave before I put that power of yours to the test."

"Of course, *brother*." Axus turned, and Aaslo could feel the god leaning over him. A chill suffused him, and somewhere very distant he felt a power so great it could have brought him to his knees. "You, *human*, will fail. Your soul and the souls of every pitiful creature in your world will belong to *me*. You are nothing. Aldrea is a grave." As the voice moved away, Aaslo heard it grumble, "He's not worth my time. Pithor will take care of him."

The other gods began speaking as if Axus were no longer present.

Trostili said, "I knew Axus was growing bolder, but I did not expect him to do *this*."

A figure shifted toward Aaslo, and Disevy's voice rumbled through him. "This is the one called Aaslo? I see the resemblance. It is quite the coincidence that *he* was the chosen one's friend."

"What are you saying?" said Trostili.

"Just an observation. What happened to his arm? They don't usually come like this."

Arayallen tittered. "Oh, just a little mishap with a dragon. The healer came up with quite the clever solution, don't you think? Humans can be so creative when pressed."

"A dragon on Aldrea? You have decided to help Axus?" said Disevy.

"Of course not. I care nothing for Axus's endeavors. I was just having a bit of fun with Trostili's pet."

"Is that so?"

Aaslo thought Disevy didn't sound convinced. Either way, he knew who he had to thank for the partial loss of his humanity. If they kept him there, he might even lose the rest. As if reading his mind, Arayallen asked, "Who's going to put him back?"

Trostili said, "Axus expended the energy to bring him here. He should return him."

"You think Axus spent that much power just to assuage his curiosity?" replied Disevy. Again, he sounded unconvinced.

"No, I don't," said Trostili, "but it's hardly important. They will all be dead soon enough, and I can move on to other annihilations."

"Touching," muttered Disevy. "I will return this one to his world. You two have somewhere to be, do you not?"

"Oh?" said Arayallen. "Is it that time already? How fantastic. I love new world unveilings. This one is going to be so pretty—so much like Aldrea, but different."

Two of the figures moved away until Aaslo could no longer feel their power. The remaining god stood beside him for a long while. Aaslo thought he could *feel* the god studying him. Finally, Disevy said, "You were never supposed to come here. We were never supposed to meet." Aaslo wondered if Disevy knew he could hear him. "I was not going to get involved in this project of Axus's, but the Fates seem to have decided otherwise. Listen carefully, Forester of Aldrea. Do not underestimate Pithor. He may be only human, but he is twice blessed by the gods of death and war. Your world will not survive him, and death follows in your wake. You may not be able to save Aldrea, but perhaps you can help Celestria."

Aaslo lurched upward and nearly fell from the settee. His head spun, and he was confused about how he'd gotten . . . wherever he was. More pressing, though, was his throbbing cheek. He blinked several times to clear his vision and met a pair of large, brown eyes.

"See, I told you it would work," said Teza.

Aaslo rubbed his face. "Wha—did you slap me?"

Teza smirked. "I'm a healer. It was therapeutic."

*"I must be a healer, too. I always felt better after slapping you around the practice yard."*

"Must you brag?"

"You're awake, aren't you?" she growled.

She stood back as Aaslo sat up and placed his feet on the floor. He winced when his claws dug into the soft fabric of the settee.

"What happened?" he asked.

She hooked a thumb over her shoulder toward Mory. "You collapsed. The boy said the reaper told him you weren't here anymore but that you weren't dead."

As if summoned by the mention of death, two figures ambled into the room. They silently crossed the overly furnished expanse to take up residence in the corner. Flickers of gold and orange firelight glistened off the milky-white haze that filled their otherwise empty eyes. Aaslo tried not to look at them, but his gaze was drawn regardless like a moth to flame. He was not alone in his discomfort. His companions stared at the *things* without blinking, their faces pale and eyes wide. Aaslo wondered who would be the first to flee—or become sick. A faint, salty breeze carrying the scent of ocean through the open sitting room might have been pleasant if not for the stench of death that pervaded it. While the blight had been destroyed, the once verdant marshland beyond the escarpment remained in a state of decay. It would likely be weeks before any significant signs of life returned.

Life.

With life came death. Usually.

Aaslo glanced toward the corpses again—the silent sentinels in the corner of the room.

"Well?" said Myra. "You need to say something, Aaslo."

He turned to find her suddenly sitting at his side. The reaper's insubstantial form did nothing to block the light of the hearth behind her. From the corner of his eye, he saw that Mory had turned to look at her as well. Aaslo figured that if Mory could also see her then he must not be completely crazy.

*"The absence of evidence is not proof of innocence."*

Aaslo clenched his teeth and inhaled sharply before releasing his breath. The voice had been silent since the battle in the marsh. Now that it was speaking again, he was both relieved and troubled.

"Crazy is not a crime," he muttered.

Everyone turned to look at him. The marquess pursed his lips as if he might argue the point. Beside him, Peck gripped Mory's shoulder as he looked at Aaslo with a hope-filled gaze. Standing over him, Teza tilted her head as if truly contemplating his assertion, and Ijen scribbled something in his book.

Myra sighed. "Say something *else*, Aaslo. You're making them nervous."

"*I'm* making them nervous?" He waved to the corpses of Greylan and Rostus in the corner. "*They're* the problem, not I."

"Are you talking to the reaper?" said Peck. "What did she say?"

"Never mind that." Teza's hand whipped out to snatch Aaslo's face by the jaw. She leaned over so that her face was mere inches from his own. "Where were you?" she said.

"*Yes, Aaslo, tell us. Where were you?*"

"Don't you know?" said Aaslo as he pried her fingers from his flesh.

Teza shouted, "If I knew, I wouldn't be asking!"

"No, not you. I thought . . . Never mind." Aaslo scratched the scruff along his sore jawline. "I must have been dreaming."

"No, Aaslo. A *reaper*, taker of the dead, said you weren't here. Your consciousness, part of your *soul* wasn't here anymore."

Aaslo stared into the air with a sightless gaze as he struggled to recall the foggy memory. "He said he didn't take my consciousness," he mumbled.

"Who? What are you talking about?" said Teza.

Aaslo jumped when a dark shadow caught his attention. He looked up and focused on Ijen, who was suddenly standing over him. The prophet's pen hovered over his book, and he was looking at Aaslo expectantly.

Aaslo frowned at the man. "Do *you* know what's going on?"

"Uh, no," said Ijen as he turned the book so that Aaslo could see its contents—or lack thereof. "This page is blank. I've been waiting to fill it."

Aaslo wavered as he abruptly stood. Teza and Ijen stepped back to give him space—or perhaps they were avoiding touching him. Maybe whatever was wrong with him was contagious. He noted that the marquess and Peck were leaning against the farthest wall from the corpses, and neither seemed inclined to move. Mory was huddled on the ground next to Peck with his arms around his knees. He blinked up at Aaslo as if he were seeing a ghost.

"I don't—I don't know where I was, but I think—I think I was with the gods."

"The gods?" said Teza as Ijen began scribbling.

"*You? Blessed to be in the presence of the gods?*"

"Not blessed—cursed," said Aaslo. "That foreign magus, Verus, was telling the truth. The gods want to destroy Aldrea. Axus, the one he called the God of Death, brought me to their realm against the others' wishes."

"You met Axus?" said Myra with alarm. "You saw the gods?"

Aaslo rubbed his chin. "I didn't exactly *see* them. I could hear them talking."

"How many were there?" said Ijen.

"I'm not sure. I think there were at least four. They were arguing. One of them told me not to underestimate Pithor."

The marquess pushed away from the wall and came to stand in front of Aaslo. "Who is Pithor? Another god?"

"No," said Myra. "He is called the *Deliverer of Grace, His Mighty Light*. He's human but blessed by the gods so that he may lead death's army."

After Aaslo relayed the reaper's message, the marquess released a heavy breath. "Good."

"Good?" said Aaslo.

"He's human. That means we have a chance. We defeat this Pithor, and we save Aldrea."

"With what army?" said Teza. "*Us?* An apprentice healer, a prophet, two thieves, a noble, and . . . whatever *he* is?" The last was said with a wave toward Aaslo. He internally cringed and wondered if she was referring to his mutated physique or abhorrent new powers.

The marquess turned back to Aaslo. "Were none of these gods sympathetic to our cause?"

Rubbing the scales that had grown around his neck, Aaslo said, "I don't know. It's a bit foggy. They seemed pretty confident in our demise." He looked to Myra, but she merely stared at him pensively.

"Well, that's disheartening," said the marquess.

*"Way to boost their spirits, Aaslo."*

"All the others—an entire *army* of the dead—fell back into the swamp," said Aaslo. He lifted a hand toward Greylan and Rostus. "Except these two. *Why?* What's different about them?"

*"They knew you?"*

"Why would that be significant?" said Aaslo.

"Why would *what* be significant?" asked the marquess.

"Never mind," Aaslo mumbled as his gaze flicked across the contours of the crown molding and tapestries that decorated two walls of the room. He had never taken the time to truly examine these surroundings. Whenever he had previously entered this room, more important matters had warranted his attention. Such was the case in that moment as well, but he didn't want to think about the current issue.

"So," said the marquess, "you are a necromancer."

There. Someone had finally said it. *Necromancer.*

"There's no such thing as necromancers," Aaslo growled.

The marquess and, well, everyone else stared at him pointedly. Aaslo could hear Mathias humming in the background. He covered his face with his hands, one of them covered in scales and bearing talons— another reminder of how much his life had changed since leaving the forest. He sank onto the settee and then looked up at the marquess. "Must we call it that?"

Ijen muttered absently as he thumbed through the pages of his book. "Calling it anything else does not change the truth of it."

*"He sounds like your father."*

Aaslo growled. *"Death,* she said. Magdelay told me that, down my path, the prophets had seen only death."

Ijen nodded his agreement.

Peck glanced toward the corpses, then leaned forward and whispered loudly. "Can't you make them, you know, *die* again?"

"Don't you think I would've if I knew *how*?"

"Just do the opposite of what you did before," said Peck.

"I don't know what I did before. I wasn't thinking about it. It just happened—like instinct. The rest of them went back to being dead, except these two. Why?" Aaslo looked around the room but was met with blank faces. His gaze settled on Ijen, who peered back at him without expression. The prophet either didn't know or wasn't telling.

"I didn't take their souls," said Myra.

Aaslo turned toward her. "What?"

*"You* did," she said. "When they died, I went to claim their souls, but you took them instead."

*"I* took their souls?"

"You killed them?" said the marquess, his voice heavy with accusation.

Aaslo scowled at him. "No, I told you, the blight killed them."

"Then what's this about taking souls?" said the marquess.

"The reaper says that after they died, I took their souls before she got to them."

Mory blurted, "You hear that, Peck? He's a thief, like us, except that he steals *souls.*"

"I'm not a thief," said Aaslo.

*"Except that you are, Soul Thief."*

"It makes sense," said Teza, who was gazing at the corpses thoughtfully. Of everyone in the room, she seemed the least offended by their existence. "There's a kind of magic that uses blood to generate power and gain control over other creatures—even people. It's outlawed in Uyan, of course. I imagine possessing a person's soul would have even greater potential."

Ijen said, "I've never heard of any being in this realm having the ability to steal souls—not even amongst the fae. This power could not have come from the creature you encountered."

"Well, where did it come from?" said Aaslo.

The prophet blinked at him. "How should I know?"

With a huff, Aaslo said, *"You're* the prophet. You have that book!"

Ijen tapped the book in question. "I assure you, there is nothing in here that will help. I only knew the result, not the how of it. But"—he tapped his lips with his pen—"you said the reaper fell into the power stream during the transfer. Perhaps you acquired some of *her* power."

Teza began to speak—or perhaps it was the marquess—but Aaslo wasn't listening. His gaze found the darkness of the night sky beyond the open wall. He yawned deeply, and his eyelids began to close of their own accord.

*"Go to bed, Aaslo. You'll sleep like the dead."*

His eyes popped open, and he glanced toward the still corpses. Then he noted that everyone was looking at him again.

"What?" he said.

"Are you unwell?" said the marquess.

"I'm just tired," Aaslo replied. "Can we pick this up in the morning?"

The marquess tugged at his collar. "Yes, I am sure you all are spent." With a nod toward Greylan and Rostus, he said, "But what about *them*?"

"You should lock them in a cell," said Peck. "I know you have one."

"You mean when you were caught skulking around the estate?"

Peck straightened and ran a hand down his velvet jacket. In what Aaslo presumed to be his best impression of a nobleman, the thief said, "We're respectable men. We don't *skulk*. We were, ah, testing the security of the premises on behalf of our master."

The marquess shook his head, then looked at Greylan and sighed heavily. He crossed the room to stand a few paces from the corpse. "Can you hear me? Are you still in there?"

Greylan said nothing as his milky gaze rested on the marquess.

"If you are truly dead, then I shall mourn your loss. We may not have seen eye to eye, but you were a good and loyal soldier to me and my father before me."

# CHAPTER 2

PITHOR TURNED AS THE TEAR IN THE VEIL CLOSED BEHIND THE FILTHY
creature. He hated engaging with the beasts of the Alterworld, but speaking with the vight was a small price to pay to receive the words of the gods. He strode across the dark octagonal room to the window and threw open the shutters. He smiled. Ascending the tower steps several times per day was worth the view. There, in the highest room of the palace, he was closest to the light, the light of the Almighty Bayalin, God of the Sun. Of course, Bayalin was not *his* god, but that hardly mattered. His dedication and loyalty to Axus would earn him a place among them.

The door opened, then closed behind him. Pithor turned to survey the room that was empty of all but its furnishings—a desk, a few bookcases, a long table, and several chairs. The floorboards resounded with the thud of his boots as he crossed to the desk that occupied the center of the sunlit chamber. He settled into the plush high-backed chair, crossing his fingers as he leaned his elbows on the desk. He said, "Thank you for coming. I have a task for you."

The empty air in front of him shifted then appeared to slide away to reveal a person. "Blessed be the Mighty Light," said the woman with a heavy dose of sarcasm.

Pithor ignored her tone and said, "Blessed be the Afterlife."

The woman took a seat in the chair across the desk. "So it is," she said.

Pithor studied her for a moment, and Sedi did not seem to mind. He imagined the magus was used to it after a few thousand years. The woman was short of stature, although she insisted that she had been considered tall in her day. Her face was thin with sharp features, her expression perpetually apathetic. The russet hues that streaked her dark brown hair complimented the deep orange that seemed to glow from within her otherwise brown irises. Pithor briefly wondered if the effect was due to the magus's unique power but then decided he didn't care.

"You have a new target," he said.

Sedi nodded as if she had expected nothing else. Perhaps she didn't, thought Pithor.

"This one should be easy, according to Axus."

"Is that so? You do not seem convinced." Her tone was almost playful in her taunt. Pithor knew better.

"I have no doubt this one is but a pebble beneath Axus's boot. *You* are not Axus, though."

"You doubt *my* abilities, then?"

Pithor ground his teeth. "No, I am fully aware of your efficacy. Sometimes the gods forget that not everyone is blessed with their grace."

"If you believe the target to be so dangerous, why do you not take care of him yourself?"

"I'm busy." He would not fall for her tactics. She was fishing for information, and he would not oblige.

She shrugged. "Very well. What is this one? A king? A general? One of these pitiful magi?"

"I was told he is a forester."

"A forester? That's it?"

"Axus was less than forthcoming about the man's powers, but it seems he has acquired some magical ability."

Sedi brushed nonexistent dust from her formfitting black-and-brown leather jacket, then rested one hand on her thigh. With the other, she created a small marble of white light and absently rolled it between her fingers. Pithor had seen her do this before, and he knew that it usually meant she was bored.

"Why do you think Axus would withhold information about this forester's ability?"

"I don't know, but I'm sure he would have told me if it were pertinent."

She snuffed the little light and leaned forward. "What if he doesn't know?"

"That's absurd. How could he not know?"

She leaned back and shrugged. "The forester didn't have any powers *before*, and now he does. Axus isn't omniscient. He probably hasn't figured it out yet."

"What do you know of this forester? You've been holding out on me?"

"It's no big deal. I did a little job for Trostili last month. I put together a team of idiots in Tyellí. They killed an old man, burned down a building. The idiots died, of course. Couldn't have them spreading rumors after the fact."

"What does this have to do with the forester?"

"I don't know, really. Trostili wanted me to drive the forester's former companions back to his side."

"To discern his location?"

"No, Trostili's messenger said nothing about following them."

Pithor gritted his teeth again. "Perhaps it was implied."

She leaned on the armrest and rested her chin on her fist. "If he wanted that, he should have said so. I don't have time to ponder the will of the gods."

"You have all the time in the world," Pithor growled.

"Precisely," she said. "And if we are successful, that time will be short."

"What do you mean, *if*? The prophecy—"

"Yes, yes. I know all about the prophecy. I've lived a long time—too long. I don't believe anything until I see it." She grinned. "Sometimes not even then."

Considering her power, he knew it to be a valid point. Still, the prophecy was clear. The Lightbane was dead, and he, Pithor, would lead Axus's army to victory. The infestation that was life would be wiped from the world so that the gods could begin their work anew.

Tired of looking at her smug face, Pithor elected to return to business. "Axus wants you to kill this forester and then his companions."

"Why doesn't Axus do it? Oh, right. He *can't*."

"He *is* doing it—through *you*."

"Are you sure that's what he wants?"

"He was quite clear."

"Hmm, don't you think that's strange?"

"What is?"

"That Trostili seems to favor the forester while Axus wants him dead. I thought they were on the same side."

"They are. Trostili just wants a war. Axus wants to win it. Besides, the forester killed Verus, and one of his companions killed Obriday."

"Ah, this is about vengeance."

"Axus would never be so petty. This is about fulfilling the prophecy. If you aren't up to it—"

"Don't patronize me. I'm only concerned that Axus may be overplaying his hand."

"You think you know better than a god?"

"You are young, Pithor. You still see them with the naiveté of a child."

"Young? I've not been called young in three decades, and I am far from naive."

"Regardless, Axus must prevail. If Trostili intends to interfere, it would be better to wait."

"That's not your call to make. You and I serve the same master. We do his bidding."

With resignation, she said, "Of course. Where is the forester now?"

"He was last seen in the March of Ruriton in southern Uyan."

She grimaced. "I hate the swamps. Perhaps I'll wait until he goes somewhere more pleasant."

"Just see that it's done."

The woman slinked from her chair, wrapping the light around her once more until she disappeared. Soft footsteps padded across the floorboards. The door opened and then closed seemingly of its own accord.

Pithor sat back and sighed. He hated dealing with Sedi, but he couldn't deny that she was his most valuable asset. He knew what she wanted and therefore knew that she would be ever faithful to Axus.

AASLO CRAWLED FROM HIS BED, HIS HEAD STILL FOGGY FROM THE DREAM. He couldn't remember the details, except for the end, of course. Always it was the same. Someone lost their head.

*"I think you lost yours when I lost mine."*

"I think you're right."

*"Brothers in all things."*

Aaslo held his dragon arm in front of him and flexed his claws. "Why?" he muttered.

*"Why what?"*

"Why are we brothers in all things? Why did we meet at all?"

*"I don't understand the question."*

"I can't help but wonder if we hadn't met, you'd still be alive, and the world wouldn't be doomed."

*"Or maybe I'd still be dead, and no one would bother to try."*

Aaslo stood and wavered as his vision swam. He was having trouble focusing and decided he must have slept too hard on one side. He didn't bother with a comb. He ran his claws through his hair a few times and then splashed water from the basin over his face. He cleaned his teeth, then dressed in a loose pair of brown pants and a green tunic. He strapped on his sword belt and the sack containing Mathias's head, then picked up the sword. He examined the beautifully adorned hilt, then sat back down on the bed with a groan.

*"Are you getting lazy?"*

"I want to go home."

A knock sounded at the door.

"Aaslo?" came Teza's muffled voice. "Are you awake?"

He sighed as he stood, then pulled the door open. She looked up at him, and her eyes widened.

"I'm almost ready."

She seemed frozen where she stood with her fist still poised to knock again. "Uh—"

"What?"

Shaking her head as if from a fog, she said, "I, um, I think maybe you should look in the mirror."

"I don't have one, and I hardly care if my hair is a mess."

"No, it's not that—"

"What now?" he growled.

Aaslo stomped out of the room and down the gaudy corridor that was lined with tapestries, vases, and busts of presumably historic figures but not a single mirror. Teza scurried up behind him as he turned the corner and entered the dining hall.

"It's not that bad," she said, but she didn't sound convinced. Neither did the others in the room, who had already taken their seats at the table to partake of the morning fare. The jabber and pleasantries ceased as everyone looked at him. Aaslo scowled in return then crossed the room to peer into the large mirror hanging between the sconces on the other side.

"What, by the gods, is this?" he shouted.

He leaned forward as if getting closer to the mirror might clarify things. It didn't. Staring back at him was his face but for his left eye, a bright fiery orange orb with a diamond-shaped pupil. It was the eye of a reptile—the eye of the creature that had nearly killed him. He turned to look at Teza. She wrung her hands and chewed her bottom lip as she returned his frenetic gaze.

"Um, how is your vision?" she asked tentatively.

"My vision? Look at me! I'm a monster."

*"Beastly. Maybe you* will *grow that tail."*

"Fix it!"

"I can't," she said as her curls bobbed around her face.

The marquess rose from his seat at the table and came to stand in front of Aaslo. He examined the foreign eye with a look of disturbed curiosity, then said, "How *is* your vision?"

Aaslo glanced at the others, then shoved past the marquess as he stormed over to Ijen. "What is going on? Tell me this isn't permanent."

Ijen stood and put a hand on Aaslo's shoulder. "I'm not surprised to see this. Actually, I was surprised *not* to see it when first we met. I had thought perhaps the path had changed, but I see now the timing was just a little off."

"You didn't answer my question."

Ijen sighed. "I'm afraid that your eye appears as it does now throughout the remainder of my visions."

"What about the rest?" said Aaslo. "Am I going to keep changing?"

Ijen spread his hands. "Not that I have seen."

Aaslo released a breath filled with relief and dread. "No tail," he muttered.

"Uh, no. Do you want a tail?" said Ijen.

"Of course not!"

*"You do seem quite preoccupied with the idea of having a tail."*

"Only because *you* keep bringing it up."

"I don't recall ever mentioning a tail," said Ijen. "How is your vision?"

Aaslo mussed his hair as he gripped it. "Why are you all so concerned about my vision?"

The marquess said, "Do we really need to point out that you have a dragon eye?"

"I can see that I have a dragon eye. The fact that I have one is what should be concerning you."

Mory reached over and poked Aaslo's scales. "You already had the arm. Why not an eye?"

Teza sounded unsure when she said, "It's better than being dead, right?"

Aaslo sank into the seat the marquess had vacated. "What am I becoming?"

*"You, Aaslo. You're just becoming you."*

"This is not me."

"It is now," said Ijen. "Have you considered that this may help you in your quest?"

"How is having a dragon eye going to help?"

Ijen shrugged. "That depends. How is your vision?"

# CHAPTER 3

SEDI STEPPED FROM THE FRESHLY CLEANED TILES OF THE LODENONIAN palace onto the decayed plant matter that covered Dovermyer and grimaced. The stench was overwhelming. She had thought that Ruriton couldn't have gotten worse than it already was, but she had been wrong. It seemed that a dead swamp was worse than a living one. She stepped onto the road that led to the marquess's estate and scuffed her scarlet boots across the gravel just to make sure she didn't carry any of the putridity with her. As she ascended the escarpment, the sea breeze wafted over her face, a welcome reprieve.

The marquess's estate looked different from how it had the last time she had visited. An encampment of shoddy huts and tents had been erected along the road, and it appeared to house the entire village—at least, what was left of it. Judging by the trail of wagons, carts, and pedestrians headed in the opposite direction, it appeared that many were abandoning the town. She didn't blame them. She wouldn't want to live in the swamp of death and decay either. She sidestepped so as not to collide with a man carrying a little girl in one arm and tugging the lead to his cart horse with the other.

"Papa, why do we have to leave? I want to go home," said the girl.

"The marquess may have stopped the blight, but he can't restore the land."

Sedi rolled her eyes. It was just like a secular to give credit to a noble for what a magus had done.

"What does that mean?" said the little girl.

"It means we have to find somewhere else to live—somewhere with food and work."

Sedi wouldn't miss them. If she got her way, she wouldn't be missing anything ever again. She approached the blockade that separated the hastily constructed town from the estate, but the guards couldn't see her. Of course they couldn't. People needed light to see, and light was hers to do with as she pleased. The days when she was vulnerable to the human gaze had long since passed, and people rarely honed their other senses. Her boot scuffed a rock as she passed the blockade, but she wasn't concerned. The guards looked confused, but like all seculars, they didn't believe what they couldn't see.

The marquess's estate was a beautiful construct, a rejection of the otherwise miserable surroundings—or perhaps it was a denial. Either way, she had always liked the open-air design. Nearly every exterior room had panels that could be opened to expose the interior to the refreshing sea breeze. As such, little stone was used in its construction. She supposed it was easier to import wood from the north than stone. Draperies of silk and linen billowed on the breeze like welcoming flags of color beckoning her to their abode. Soaring pillars cast shadows that stretched into the sheltered interior, and plush carpets cushioned her steps so that none would hear her pass. It was a shame she would have to burn it down.

Sedi stood within the strongest ray of the morning sun and dropped the guise of light that enveloped and hid her from prying eyes. Then she gathered the light around her, focusing it into a wall built upon the grace of the gods, a shining beacon of hope and beauty. She then propelled the wall of light forward with the mighty force of a hurricane.

THE ROOM SPLIT INTO IDENTICAL OVERLAPPING IMAGES. THEN ONE SIDE changed color as if he were looking through red glass. Aaslo sat on his bed and stared at the vases on the table across from him until they became one again. It seemed his eye hadn't finished changing. His vision was getting worse, but he knew there was nothing anyone could do about it. It was dizzying, and breakfast wasn't sitting well in his churning stomach. At least, he hoped a sour stomach was all it was.

He stood and stuffed the remainder of his provisions into his bag, then hefted it onto his back. It was noticeably heavier than when he had left the forest. The marquess had provided him with new clothes tailored to fit over his disfigured arm, and he carried with him the foreigners' book and wand in addition to his other supplies. He didn't want to depend on the availability of goods in the towns along his journey since he knew not the condition of the rest of the kingdom. Without the flow of information through the evergates, he couldn't know if the enemy had invaded in force.

*"Don't forget me."*

"How could I ever forget you? You're always nattering in my ear."

*"It's fun to hear the echo."*

"What's your problem now?"

*"Nothing. I just think this is a dumb idea."*

"Because it's mine?"

*"No, because it'll get you killed."*

"That didn't stop you."

*"And you see where it got me."*

"Look, this Pithor is apparently on the move. If we don't destroy the evergates, we could be inundated before we gather a semblance of a resistance."

*"You don't even know how to destroy them."*

"Which is why we are going to the citadel."

*"Assuming it's still standing."*

"You think the magi destroyed it?"

*"I wouldn't put it past them, if for no other reason than to keep ill-tempered ruffians from accessing their secrets. Grams probably knew you'd go looking eventually."*

"So now I'm an ill-tempered ruffian?"

*"You said it, not me."*

Suddenly, Aaslo was falling as the floor shifted beneath him. A cacophony ripped through the estate, and timbers toppled. Shards of debris pummeled him as two of the walls and part of the floor were ripped away. Then came the glowing inferno. A roiling colossus of flame billowed toward him, and without a second thought, he jumped into the dark abyss.

His landing was harder than he would have preferred. He wrenched his ankle when his feet struck the uneven rubble of the floor below his room, and then he fell hard onto his pack. Something jabbed him in the back, but he didn't have time to worry over it. The ceiling was about to come down on top of him. Aaslo surveyed the darkness for an exit and realized he must have fallen into a storage room that unfortunately had no windows. Broken boards had fallen in front of the door, and he struggled to remove them as more fell into the small room behind him. He gripped the largest one with his clawed hand and threw his weight into it. Just as it shifted, the door blasted into him as another explosion rocked the estate.

*"Aaslo, wake up."*

He groaned, roused by the voice. He wanted only to stay asleep within the warm embrace of the darkness.

*"Aaslo, you're going to die, and as much as I'd like to see you, I don't think it's your time."*

"Shut up," he grumped, but his lips were dry and cracked, and his chest hurt. Actually, everything hurt—and he couldn't breathe. He began to cough as smoke filled his lungs, and his eyes burned with tears.

*"Stop being a selfish, stubborn mule. You have my destiny to fulfill."*

Aaslo wheezed as he pushed the debris off him and rolled over. "How can I be selfish for not fulfilling *your* destiny?"

*"What else would you be doing! Puttering around in the forest, waiting to die!"*

He rubbed grit from his eyes and tried to focus. Abruptly, what was once impenetrable black became red, and he could make out all the shapes in the rubble. The doorway was only partially blocked, and he was sure he could squeeze through the opening.

"At least the forest doesn't try to kill me," he mumbled as he crawled forward.

*"Of course it does. Remember when that storm came through—"*

"That wasn't the forest. That was the wind."

*"All right, what about the wolves?"*

"They keep to themselves so long as they have enough to eat."

*"And that bear?"*

"Was only trying to protect her cubs."

*"So, it's okay if it tries to kill you as long as you understand it."*

Aaslo worked his way toward a bright crack in the darkness. He mulled over Mathias's words to keep his mind off his many pains. "I guess you're right. I never thought about it like that."

He peered through the crack into the bright light of the day. The grass beside the estate was strewn with rubble, and people ran about in a frenzy. Aaslo shouted as he tried to pull off his pack. Whatever had been poking him in the back was stuck, and his mind was too muddled to figure out what it was. He shook his bag until it came free, then shoved it through what looked to have once been a window. His head had just cleared the hole when rough hands grabbed his arms and pulled him the rest of the way through.

"Healer! We're needin' the healer!" shouted the man who had grabbed him.

"No, I'm okay," Aaslo mumbled.

"Ya just had a building fall atop ya, and ya've got an axe in your back. Ain't nothin' is okay 'bout that."

Aaslo tried to look over his shoulder. "Wha—"

"Aaslo!" cried Teza as she rushed to his side. "You're alive! I'm so relieved."

"Not for long," said the man. Aaslo blinked up to see an older man with a greying beard and sun-darkened skin. He wore the uniform of a soldier.

Teza ran a hand down Aaslo's dragon arm. "No, he always looks like this."

"Yeah, I seen him afore. I ain't talkin' 'bout his monster half. I'm re-ferrin' to that axe in his back."

"What!" Teza shouted as she jerked him forward.

Aaslo couldn't help the growl that escaped as his back was wrenched. To his pained ears it sounded less than human.

*"Even your own axe is trying to kill you."*

"Oh, thank the gods," said Teza. "It's stuck in your scales. It didn't go very deep. Roll onto your stomach."

Aaslo didn't so much lay down as crash into the dirt. His head swam as two distinct images drowned his vision. One was a smoky world of sunlit chaos, while the other was shaded in red with the figures of men and women lined in black and glowing white at the center. Teza placed her foot on his back and tugged the axe until it came free with the sound of grinding metal. Aaslo shouted and inhaled deeply so that the scent of grass, dirt, and smoke filled his lungs. A tingling numbness suffused his back while Teza stood over him casting her healing spell. He swallowed hard and focused on the image delivered to him by his human eye. Once the red had faded and he could see clearly, he sat up and gripped her small hand with his monstrous fingers.

"Thank you," he said.

She patted his scales. "You're welcome. I'm just glad you made it out of there. I thought for sure you were dead."

"I may be working on death, but it's coming to me slowly," he replied.

*"I wonder how long dragons live."*

"I'm not a dragon. I'm a man."

*"Are you sure?"*

Teza peered into his eyes as she wiped blood from his temple. "It would be pretty amazing if you sprouted wings."

*"Wings? Why would I want wings?"*

"I don't know," she said with a shrug. "I've always wanted to be able to fly."

Aaslo looked up at the stranger who had found him. He got to his feet and said, "Thank you for pulling me out."

"Weren't no problem, Sir Forester. Glad I could help." He held out a hand in greeting. "People call me Bear—on account of my thick pelt." He stroked a bushy beard that didn't stop at his chin. Thick curls sprouted from his torn uniform so much so that Aaslo wondered if the man's whole body was covered in fur.

*"Oh, I've got one. A bear and a dragon walk into a bar—"*

"Please, stop," said Aaslo. Bear looked at him as if trying to decide if he should be offended. "Call me Aaslo, I mean."

The man grinned, his white teeth shining past the dirt and hair that covered his face.

Since his head had finally stopped spinning, Aaslo abruptly remembered that they were in the middle of a disaster. He turned and finally surveyed the damage. Dovermyer had been blown apart. The rubble and what little was left standing was a blazing inferno. He noticed that Teza and Bear didn't seem to be in a hurry.

"Where is everyone? Peck, Mory? The marquess?"

"They're fine," said Teza. "Mory, Peck, and I were out in the stables preparing the horses when the blast occurred. The marquess was in the barracks talking to his men. I don't know where Ijen was, but he's fine, too. Unfortunately, there were a number of casualties among the household staff. A few people are still missing."

"How do you know all this?" said Aaslo. "The blast just happened."

Teza grabbed his face and stared into his eyes. Her fingers roved his scalp rather roughly, and her frown deepened.

"I don't see any signs of damage."

"What are you talking about?" he said while swatting away her hands.

"Aaslo, the estate exploded over an hour ago. I thought you were dead."

"That's not possible. I remember every second."

"Look around. Does it look like it just happened?"

He blinked dust from his eyes as he turned his gaze toward the chaos—except that it wasn't chaos as he had originally thought. People were scurrying about but with purpose. A tent had been erected about thirty yards from where they stood. The canvas sides were rolled up to allow people to come and go, and a number of injured lay moaning on makeshift cots. He looked back at the estate. While a few small fires still burned in the difficult-to-reach areas, most of the structure was naught but rubble and ash.

Aaslo searched his mind trying to reconcile what he had just endured with the current state of affairs. There was no other explanation. He was missing time.

"I must have been unconscious."

"Does your head hurt? Do you feel dizzy or sick?" said Teza.

"No, except—except when my vision turns red."

Bear's gruff voice interrupted their exchange. "Pardon me, Mage Teza, but the marquess's orders were to inform him soon as Sir Forester was found."

"Right." She grabbed Aaslo's arm, but he could barely feel her hands pressing against the hard scales that covered it. Bear walked at his other side, not touching him but seemingly prepared to catch him should he fall.

Aaslo didn't feel unstable, though. Since his vision had returned to normal, he felt fine—not at all like he had just had an axe in his back or been trapped under a burning building.

To Teza, he muttered, "You're a good healer."

She squeezed his scaly arm. "I have my moments."

*"It seems the two of you are having a moment."*

"That's ridiculous. Have you seen this disaster area?"

*"Uh, no, I've been stuck in a bag—and I'm dead."*

"Well, I have healed a number of people, but I just don't have the energy or expertise to help everyone," said Teza.

Aaslo grumbled, "You wouldn't have that problem if you had waited for me."

*"Waited for you? I had a destiny. I had no idea you intended to come with me."*

Teza said, "Right, if I had waited for you, I'd have been smashed under the rubble, too."

"You thought I wouldn't come for you? How could you think that? Have I ever abandoned you?"

*"Well, there was that time you left me trapped in a tree for nearly half a day."*

"Wait, you're upset because I didn't wait for you and therefore *didn't* get blown up?"

Aaslo frowned down at her. He had been so wrapped up in his conversation with Mathias that he hadn't been paying attention to what she had been saying. "What? Of course not. I'm glad you weren't there."

"Then what are you talking about?"

"Mathias got stuck in a tree."

Teza pulled him to a stop, grabbed his head, and started feeling around again. Aaslo pulled her hands away.

"I'm fine. I was just thinking of a time when we were kids, and Mathias got stuck in a tree. I left him there all morning. I told him that he got himself up there, he should get himself down."

"What does that have to do with this?"

"I'm not sure. He brought it up. I ultimately had to go back and get him. He wouldn't speak with me for over a week."

Teza snickered. "I bet he never climbed a tree again."

"No, he did. Many. After that, I taught him how to do it properly without getting hurt."

Bear said, "It sounds like ya taught yer friend a valuable lesson. Don't get yerself caught up a tree without the know-how to get yerself out." The man pointed to a second tent that had been hidden by the first and said, "Here's the command center."

"Thank you," Aaslo said as he stepped into the shade of the tent. His vision flashed red so that he could see what lay within and then became normal as his eyes adjusted. He was abruptly jostled from the side as Mory flung his arms around him.

"Aaslo, you're alive! I was so worried. I haven't seen Myra. I thought maybe she took you away."

Aaslo met the marquess's relieved gaze as he untangled himself from Mory's grip. "I'm fine now. Teza healed my injuries."

"My mind may be at ease knowing that our hero is well," said the marquess.

*"Ha! He called you a hero."*

"I'm no hero. I'm just a man doing a job"—he waved toward the soldiers digging through the wreckage—"like any of them."

The marquess's expression sobered as he looked back over the remnants of his estate. "They still search for those we've lost. The fact that you survived gives me hope." He paused, then said, "My brother is in there somewhere."

"I'm sorry to hear that. Do we know what happened?"

"Some kind of attack. The prophet said it was of the magical sort. I have men looking into it."

"Is there anything I can do?"

"Yes, you can figure out how to destroy those gates and stop any more of the enemy from coming through."

"I—" Aaslo paused as the wind whispered across his ear. It was a voice—a memory, but his struggles to capture it only caused the words to become more elusive. "I'll look into it."

The marquess nodded and then exited the tent to join the men who were searching for the missing. He was joined by Greylan—or what used to be Greylan, but it seemed the marquess was lacking the energy to show his disdain for the undead.

"Why does he do that?" said Peck. "Why does he follow the marquess around all the time?"

"Because that's what he would have done in life," said Aaslo.

"So, what, they just go back to work as usual?"

*"Sounds like a plan to me. No use sitting around rotting."*

"I don't know. Perhaps the dead need purpose, too. You said you haven't seen Myra?"

Mory shook his head. "No, but I see the others."

"The others?" said Teza.

The boy gave the estate a sidelong glance. "The other reapers. I thought it might be best to not let them know I see them."

Aaslo followed the boy's gaze. "I don't see anyone."

"They're gone now."

Aaslo considered the implications and decided it was unlikely the marquess's brother lived. He turned to Teza. "We need to go to the Citadel of Magi."

"Why? No one is there."

"Perhaps, but if there is any information on how to destroy the evergates, it should be there."

"It's a long way, Aaslo."

"I'm a magus now. I should be able to use the evergates, right?"

"That is debatable," said Ijen as he entered the command center.

"What do you mean?"

Ijen rocked back on his heels as he held his book tight to his chest. "I am glad to see you are well, although I expected as much. There were few paths where you were killed in the attack. In answer to your question, the nature of your power is unclear. I cannot say how the evergates would connect with you."

Aaslo narrowed his eyes at the prophet. "Is this another of those situations where you don't like the outcome, so you try to discourage me?"

Ijen frowned. "I have always been honest with you, if somewhat aloof."

*"Aloof, he says. He's less obvious than I am, and I'm dead."*

"You admit it, then?"

*"It's what you want to hear, isn't it?"*

"I have always told you that your decisions are yours to make."

"I've never wanted to hear that."

*"You've never been one to reject reality in favor of a dream."*

"You may not like to hear it," said Ijen, "but it's how it must be. Besides, I cannot see *you* willingly submitting to the Fates."

"The only design that I want from the Fates is one that involves me in the forest," Aaslo grumped. "What outcome are *you* hoping for, Ijen? Are you one of Axus's and Pithor's zealots?"

Ijen lifted his chin. "I may have little experience living in the *real* world, but I still wish to preserve it. I have dedicated my life to the cause—*your* cause."

"We'll see," mumbled Aaslo. He turned to Teza. "So, about the evergates. The closest are in Tyellí and Yarding, yes?"

She pursed her lips and said, "Yes, but I wouldn't suggest going to Tyellí."

"Why not?"

"I don't imagine the gates in the center of the capital would be left unguarded. They've either been taken by the enemy or protected by the king. It didn't seem to me that the royal guard cared much for you."

"She has a point," said Peck. "But you're friends with the queen, aren't you?"

"I wouldn't say *friends*," muttered Aaslo. "And my association with her does not simplify matters. Besides, the enemy attacked us there already. It's best to try for Yarding."

"Where *is* this enemy?" said Peck.

"What do you mean?" replied Aaslo. "We don't yet know where they are."

"That's exactly what I mean." Peck pointed to the smoldering ruins. "Everyone knows that if you're going to attack the enemy, you make sure to get them all. Otherwise, it'll come back to bite you later. If this was an attack, where are they? Why aren't they still attacking? We're a mess. They could come in and kill all of us right now and we wouldn't be able to defend ourselves."

"I see your point," said Aaslo. "What do *you* think is going on?"

"Well, if this was a fight between thieves' guilds, I'd say it was a targeted attack by a small force. They probably left because they thought they succeeded."

"Targeted?"

"*You, Aaslo. He's saying you were the target.*"

"Me?"

Peck nodded. "If they stuck around, they would have seen that the marquess and the magi survived. They didn't attack again, so it's unlikely they were the targets. *You* were missing for over an hour. We all thought you were dead."

Aaslo knew that what Peck said had merit, but he was loath to admit it. An entire estate and the lives within it were destroyed just to get to him. "When did you get to be such a strategist?"

Peck grinned. "I didn't survive the streets with my good looks alone."

SEDI LEANED AGAINST A TREE, IF ONE COULD CALL IT THAT. IT SEEMED more like an overgrown bush, but it and its few companions were the best cover she could find on the escarpment that were close enough for her to view the estate—or what was left of it. She pried open the hard shell of a roasted pistachio and popped the green-and-purple seed into her mouth. After flicking the shell to the ground, she pulled another from her sack and started the process again. She was disappointed that she had failed to kill the forester, but a small part of her was relieved. He was too interesting, and she wasn't done playing with him yet.

In the scope of things, she figured anything she did or didn't do wouldn't really matter. Life on Aldrea was destined to die, so she wasn't in any hurry to dispatch this one tiny hitch in the plan. She thought Pithor was overreacting anyway, but at least it gave her something to do while she waited for the blessed end.

She lounged in the miniscule shade of the tree as the forester and his companions searched the wreckage; she watched as they formulated plans and issued orders; and she paced when they finally mounted up a few hours after the sun had passed its zenith. Anyone else might have been bored, but Sedi had spent the majority of her very long life waiting. People were slow, and, at least for her, death was even slower. It seemed the forester was afflicted with a similar problem. He seemed none the worse for wear and was harder to kill than she had anticipated. This pleased her.

Sedi smiled as she mounted her stolen horse. Riding wasn't her preferred method of travel, but it would be the easiest way to follow her prey. Sedi liked horses, though. She had come to feel a sort of kinship with the animals. The lucky, wild creatures had nothing more to do than eat, breed, and run. The captive beasts had only to serve their masters. Horses had few natural predators in this part of the world, and they could become no greater than they already were. Essentially, they too were just *waiting*—waiting to die.

As she took to the road, the forester, the healer, and the prophet rode ahead of her. Two soldiers followed in their wake.

# CHAPTER 4

In his periphery, Aaslo saw Teza turn in her saddle *again*. She looked for only a few seconds before turning back with a disgruntled frown.

"What is it?" Aaslo said.

Teza didn't respond. She simply glanced over her shoulder again.

"Tell me," he said.

"I don't like them," she replied.

Aaslo turned and looked back at the dead men. They were riding horses as well as any living man. Their milky gazes stared forward until Aaslo acknowledged them, and then they turned their attention toward him as if waiting for something. Aaslo faced the road ahead and mumbled, "I don't think you need to worry. They're just doing their jobs."

"Their *jobs*? They're dead! They don't have jobs."

*"Work never ends."*

Aaslo and Teza were both jostled as their horses jerked to avoid Greylan's, which had suddenly surged forward. Aaslo became alarmed as the animated corpse rode ahead, but Dolt refused to pick up his pace.

"He's getting away!" shouted Teza. "Do something! You can't let the dead roam free."

Aaslo dug his heels into the ornery horse's sides but ultimately failed to induce pursuit. The thought to dismount and take one of the other horses had just crossed his mind when Greylan abruptly stopped about fifty yards ahead of them. The corpse's head turned as he surveyed the brush and rocks. He looked back at them and croaked, "Enemy."

Aaslo took a moment to process his shock over hearing the dead man speak, but Ijen seemed less surprised as he tucked his book into his tunic and dismounted. The prophet strolled over to stand in the middle of the road between them and the haunting guardsman. He stood with his arms crossed behind his back and tilted his head back as if sniffing the air. Disharmonious sounds finally reached Aaslo's ears. The grunts and snarls carried on the light breeze seemed to be growing closer. A ghastly scream shattered the air, and a man's gurgling rumble cried, "Run, Traydan, run!"

Aaslo and Teza scrambled down from their horses as a boy of about thirteen came thrashing through the bushes. His face was pale and eyes were wild as he stumbled into the road. He didn't acknowledge their presence as he gasped and continued running into the brush on the other side, seemingly oblivious to the bloody tears on his arms and clothes.

Aaslo had just turned back to peer into the bushes from which the boy had emerged when the creatures appeared—the same grey, humanoid abominations he knew to belong to the enemy. The monsters brutally shoved and tripped one another as each tried to take the lead. Some were still ripping through the fleshy limbs of a freshly dismembered person with their teeth as they ran. Aaslo took quick count.

"At least twenty," he muttered, and their hazy gazes turned.

*"Now you've done it. They see you. Must you say everything aloud?"*

The monsters seemed to forget the boy as they salivated over the larger prey of people and horses. The creatures changed direction as one, a fluidity of order within chaos, like flocking birds.

A handful of the creatures reached them before a shield ward snapped into existence between them and the horde. Aaslo was reaching for his axe when Rostus rushed past, sword in hand, to join Greylan, who had already bared his blade. The two corpse-guards fought against the enemy creatures, taking down two at a time, dispatching them so quickly that Aaslo barely had to bloody his axe. The other monstrous creatures crowded the ward, banging against it, tripping and climbing atop each other in a rabid attempt to reach their newfound quarry.

Teza's voice quavered as she reached for her pack. "I-I think there's more than twenty, Aaslo!"

She was right. More came storming through the brush, and Aaslo sprinted toward Ijen. "How long can you hold that ward?"

Ijen pursed his lips. "How long do you need me to?"

With another perusal of the enemy's numbers, Aaslo said, "That depends. How many can you kill?"

"Isn't that *your* job?" said the prophet.

*"No, it's mine; but thanks to you, Aaslo, I don't have a sword—or hands, for that matter—so you'll have to pick up the slack."*

"How did this become *my* fault?" Aaslo growled.

"I never said it was," replied Ijen, "but it *is* your problem."

"What are you going to do?" said a voice from right beside him. Aaslo jumped and turned.

"Myra! Where have you been?"

She frowned at the horde of monsters. "I left to check on you and ended up with a long list of errands. A moment ago, I was summoned to take a soul just over there," she said with a lift of her chin toward the bushes. "Imagine my surprise when I found *you* here."

"That seems like a big coincidence," said Aaslo.

Teza abruptly shoved him as she stormed past. "Will you stop talking to yourself? We're in the middle of a battle." She stopped a few paces in front of him and reached into the air. In her grip was a short metal rod with a fist-sized, green sparkling orb clutched in its claws. A bright green light appeared on the other side of the ward over the monsters' heads. She dropped her arm in a ripping motion, and the light shot toward the ground, crashing into the creatures and causing them to scatter. Ijen's ward dropped, and Greylan and Rostus began fighting anew.

"We'll have to talk later," Aaslo said to Myra as he raised his axe and rushed forward.

With two hands on the haft, Aaslo dropped the axe to one side, then whipped it upward, tearing through the torso of the closest creature. Its guts spilled over Aaslo's boots, yet it lunged at him. He brought the axe back down to lop off its head. Before he turned to face the next fiend, he noted that the slain monster wore clothes akin to those of a farmer. A small tinge of guilt struck him as the thought flitted through his mind that this may have once been a human being. He shook off the feeling and turned to thrust his axe into the back of a creature that had grabbed Teza from behind and pulled her off the ground. Aaslo's blow produced a mushy thud, then a *schlopp*, as he pulled it free. Still in the monster's unrelenting grip, Teza kicked a creature advancing at her front before her feet finally struck the dirt. She smashed the brightly glowing orb into the forward creature's face. It howled but continued to lunge at her until she drew her dagger with her free hand and sank it into the monster's burnt and bubbling eye socket.

As Aaslo pried Teza from her captor's grip, alarm struck. Several of the monsters were converging on his and Teza's horses. Their mounts stomped and huffed, then with Dolt in the lead, smashed through the brush and disappeared. The monsters tried to follow, but Teza swirled the small scepter in the air above her head and cast a dome ward. It blocked the creatures from pursuit of the horses but effectively caged Aaslo and his companions inside with them. The frustrated creatures kicked and clawed at the ward as Aaslo attacked from behind, dispatching them with relative ease while they were distracted.

When he and Teza turned back to the scene, Aaslo realized the remainder of the creatures had been felled. Ijen was breathing heavily, bent over with his hands on his knees. The prophet's tunic was torn, and blood ran down his face from a cut at his temple. Aaslo had been too preoccupied during the battle to see how the prophet had fought, but it must have been effective since a ring of shredded body parts surrounded him and his ever-stoic horse.

Greylan and Rostus had dispatched at least eight creatures and looked none the worse for wear—for dead men. They both stood unperturbed and silent. Unfortunately, their horses, having been at the head of the fray, had not been so lucky. One was clearly deceased while the other lay on his side kicking as he suffered the throes of death.

"Damn it!" shouted Teza. She threw her arms up and rounded on Aaslo. "How am I without a horse *again*?"

Aaslo shook his head and looked in the direction their horses had run. Dolt had finally abandoned him. "Perhaps they didn't go far."

Myra suddenly appeared beside the guards' horses, the second of which had succumbed to its injuries.

*"There go your rides."*

"No!" blurted Aaslo.

Myra looked up at him and blinked. "What?"

"Don't take the horses. We need them."

"They're *dead*," said Teza.

"So are they," he said, pointing toward the guards.

"I'm not here for the horses," replied Myra, holding up a small bluish-green orb on a string.

*"Uh-oh. Who's going to join me?"*

Aaslo looked to Ijen and Teza, then examined himself. No one appeared to have any life-threatening injuries. Then he looked into the brush. "The boy?"

Myra nodded solemnly.

"And the creature that killed him?"

"Looks to have been trampled. It's dead—again."

Just then, Dolt came tromping onto the roadway, appearing very proud of himself. He held the reins of Teza's mount between his teeth, and the mare trotted beside him.

Teza said, "Your horse is weird, but I think I love him."

"I hate to interrupt," said Ijen, "but we're still two horses short, and we're getting off schedule." The man patted the bulge beneath his tunic with one hand as he held a handkerchief to his temple with the other.

"There is no schedule," Aaslo complained as he stalked toward the dead horses.

"I must disagree. We're on a deadline. It is pertinent that we reach the citadel on time if we want things to go our way."

Aaslo turned back to the prophet. "What are you talking about? You never said anything about a deadline."

"That's because we didn't have one before. The boy died, though."

"So, if we had saved the boy, we wouldn't be in a hurry?"

"Was he someone important?" said Teza.

Ijen looked at her oddly. "I like to think everyone is important. But, in this context, no. The boy, himself, had no bearing on the outcome. His death is simply an indicator of which path we currently tread."

Aaslo sighed. "Okay, what happens if we don't get to the citadel on time?"

"I can't say."

"Well, how long do we have?"

"I can't tell you that either."

"Then what *can* you tell us?"

"That we are in a hurry, and we are two horses short."

Aaslo glared at the prophet, and something shifted inside him. It was as though worms were crawling under his skin. The mesmerizing gaze of Ina, the marshland fae creature, swam across his vision. Something dark within him roared. Ina smirked, then turned away. Aaslo struggled to breathe. It felt as though he were submerged beneath the murky depths of the swamp once again. Black tendrils snaked out of his fingers toward the horses that lay dead on either side of him. A memory of strange words filled his mind, and then a question. He grappled for an answer, then realized he was not expected to provide one. The response came from the horses. They were willing.

When Aaslo's vision cleared, he was staring into Teza's startled gaze.

She abruptly raised her hand to her mouth and ran to the side of the road before retching into the bushes. She wiped the spittle from her mouth and murmured, "Gods, that's disgusting."

Aaslo turned to see what had made her ill and found himself face-to-face with two horrors. The dead horses were standing beside their equally dead riders. Both creatures bore the bloody cuts and gouges of the battle, but he knew those weren't what made Teza sick. Rostus's horse might have passed for alive if not for the entrails hanging from its belly to drag the ground. Greylan's horse, however, was grotesque with the flesh torn from half its face to reveal previously hidden bone and muscle.

*"What unusual mounts, Aaslo. Your breeding program leaves much to be desired."*

Aaslo groaned. "I didn't mean to do that."

"Didn't you?" said Myra.

Ijen cleared his throat. The prophet looked a bit pale. "We required two more horses, and you acquired them. It seems you did exactly what you felt was necessary."

"Is raising the dead really necessary?" Aaslo said. "How are they any different from these creatures we've been killing?"

He was surprised to hear the answer come from Myra. "The grey creatures aren't human." Upon seeing his questioning gaze, she continued. "Um, they're called *lyksvight.*"

Aaslo relayed her message, and Teza said, "But they're dressed like people."

"Yes, the bodies were once human, but they're not anymore. They've been changed."

"How?" said Aaslo.

"I don't understand how it's done. It's some kind of magic that Axus gave to the magi from Berru—the people you call the enemy."

*"Why?"* said Aaslo.

"They wanted to use the evergates to bring their armies here quickly—at least, the forward troops. The rest are coming by sea."

"Why didn't you tell us this before?"

Myra shrugged. "I haven't had time. What difference does it make? The prophecy is certain."

"Tell us what?" said Teza. "What's she saying?"

Aaslo clenched his jaw but decided it was best to keep the reaper talking while she was willing rather than to berate her and have her disappear again. He relayed the message to Teza and Ijen, then said, "Why make these creatures?"

Teza moaned with dreaded realization. "Because they can't take living seculars through the evergates."

Myra looked at Aaslo and said, "She's right. They kill people—some of their own, some from here—and move their corpses through the evergates. Then, they perform a ritual that draws the essence of a creature from the Alterworld."

Rubbing his temples in an attempt to relieve the building pressure, Aaslo said, "The Alterworld?"

"It's another realm—a realm of creatures that revel in pain, destruction, and death. From what I understand, it takes a lot of power to draw the creatures fully into this realm. Instead, the Berru capture their essence inside a human corpse. It's basically the vight's soul—if you could call it that."

Teza stepped into the space between him and Myra, nearly walking straight through the reaper, and looked at him expectantly. He repeated Myra's message while Ijen scribbled in his book.

"So, let me get this straight," said Teza. "*We're* living people with human souls"—she pointed toward Greylan and Rostus—"they're dead people with human souls"—pointing toward a dead lyksvight—"and they're dead people possessed by these vights."

Ijen snapped his book shut with a definitive *thump*. "Now that we have that figured out, we need to be going—unless you *want* to lose the only advantage you might have."

Without additional prompting, Greylan and Rostus mounted their undead horses. Greylan's gelding swung its head around to peer at them with half a face and a vacant, hazy gaze. Aaslo cringed.

"Very well, but we must be vigilant," he said. "This does not appear to be a targeted attack, and I didn't see a magus with these lyksvight to keep them in check. It seems they're roaming the countryside freely now."

Myropa shivered but not from the cold that pervaded her veins. The dead men were disconcerting, but she was used to seeing dead people. The slaughtered horses, however, were outright disturbing. Somehow, they looked both empty and more aware than your typical horse. It was as if death had given them more to think about. It had certainly given *her* much to consider.

She propped herself on the back of the prophet's horse as they rode. Since she wasn't actually *riding* the horse, it made no difference how she sat; so, with her legs pulled up to her chest, she kept an eye on the road behind them. Her thoughts were a muddled mess. Although it had been a few days in Aldrea since she had seen Aaslo, it had been only minutes in Celestria. Time was fickle between the realms—sometimes faster, other times slower. It never seemed to bother the gods, though. They somehow planned accordingly.

Abruptly, she felt the call of a departing soul, a message from the Fates. She would have sighed if she'd had breath; but as it was, she simply said, "I'm sorry, Aaslo. I must go."

"But you just got here."

"I know, but I have a soul to reap."

With alarm, he said, "Where? Nearby?"

"I don't know. I won't know until I'm on my way. I'll return as soon as I can."

Myropa opened herself to the pull of the Fates and followed the shimmering cord that bound her to her quarry. In a blink, she was standing in a room unlike any she had before seen, and it was a disaster. Blood soaked the elaborate carpet beneath her feet. More was sprayed across the walls, and still more dripped from the decorative tassels and tapestries that hung from the angled ceiling. Shreds of flesh and shards of bone were strewn among the numerous cushions and pillows that encircled a short, knee-height table in the center. The fine silver and porcelain tableware was in disarray.

The scene did not cause Myropa's stomach to churn as it might have if she had been alive. She had seen enough death to render her numb where even the cold hadn't. What did give her pause, though, was that which was missing—bodies. She had been called there to collect souls, but it seemed there was nothing to collect *from*. Looking past the bloody gore, she reassessed the room and realized she was actually in a very large heptagonal tent. The tether connecting her to her charge directed her through one of the tent's canvas sides. When she emerged, she found herself standing beneath stars dotting the night sky, and the silvery moonlight was all that illuminated the encampment.

Following the tether through multiple tents, most of which were in similar condition to the first, she came upon one that had collapsed. The tether stopped there. Somewhere beneath the bloody mess of canvas was a soul that needed to be collected. Myropa surveyed the area. For as far as she could see in the moonlit darkness there were tents, but no sounds could be heard from within, and there was not a single human movement between them.

The thread led Myropa to a mound on the far side of the tent. It appeared that the central beam had fallen atop something hard. As she neared, the thread split into two. Myropa decided she didn't want to see whatever mess lay beneath the canvas, so she tugged the souls to her. Her heart clenched upon realizing why the souls had not been standing in wait. They were infants.

# CHAPTER 5

CHERRÍ AWOKE WITH A START. SHE MUST HAVE CRIED HERSELF TO SLEEP, she thought, and then her panic began to rise again. She slammed her fist against the side of the trunk and shouted for help. Her voice was hoarse and barely made a whisper. Salty tears once again dribbled down her cheeks as she kicked the lid. She knew the trunk wasn't locked, but something was blocking it from opening. She squeezed the small bundles that lay atop her chest, but her failure to elicit cries only intensified her own. She was trapped. Effectively buried alive. She briefly considered that she should have taken her chances with the monsters.

She pressed her palms against her eyes and took several deep breaths to calm herself. She needed to think. She would not die trapped in a wooden trunk with two dead babes. Her chest seized, and for a moment she thought perhaps it was fitting. She could go with them to the Afterlife and be at peace. But the trunk was not airtight, or she would have suffocated already, and waiting to die of thirst or starvation seemed worse than being eaten alive.

With another deep inhale, she drew her knees back as far as they would go, summoned what little strength she had left, and kicked. If she couldn't open the lid, she would have to go out the side. The trunk shook, but the wood held strong. Cherrí repeated the process over and again. When she was tired, she rested, but not for long. The air in the trunk gradually warmed, and she began to sweat. Still, she kicked. Just when despair tightened its grip, there was an abrupt *crack*, and the wood shifted beneath her throbbing feet. Cherrí's heart leapt with hope, and her efforts were renewed.

After several more kicks, the wood gave way. Her right foot plunged through the cracked side panel, and she yelped with the glorious pain. She laughed and did not stop laughing until the side had been smashed away so that she could inch her way out of the horrible trunk. She frantically clawed at the canvas that covered her, then stabbed it with a piece of splintered wood before ripping it apart. The bright light of the late-morning sun enveloped her, yet her sweat-drenched skin froze in the cold breeze. She inhaled, then coughed violently as her dry throat and lungs protested against the frigid air.

Cherrí's chest ached with great heaving sobs, but she had no tears left to cry. She fumbled beneath the canvas to retrieve the two bundles, then slowly gained her footing. Her right foot throbbed, and a quick inspection revealed several gashes and a large splinter nearly the size of her pinkie.

"I wish I had been wearing shoes," she muttered. She chuckled, a discordant sound among the destruction. *What a ridiculous thing to say,* she thought.

She blinked several times to wet her eyes, then gazed across the encampment. Here and there canvas flapped in the breeze, but there was otherwise no movement. A lump formed in her throat as she considered that she might be the only survivor. She squeezed the two bundles tightly, then stumbled over the collapsed tent until her feet met the crunchy, dried grass. The tent beside hers had belonged to Minea and Leyin, an older couple who had been great mentors for her and Runi. She knew they were dead. She had heard their screams as she cowered in the dark with the babes.

Stumbling into Minea's tent, Cherrí nearly dropped Leyla, the youngest of her and Runi's daughters by nearly a month. Ueni had died first, and although she was slightly older, she had been the smaller of the two. It no longer mattered, she supposed. Neither of them would be getting any bigger.

A blessedly undisturbed pitcher of water was on the table where Minea and Leyin had been eating dinner when the attack occurred. She remembered the moment when the two older ladies had run outside to discover the reason for the screams. She had seen them because she and Runi had done the same. Runi had grabbed her scimitar and told Cherrí to hide with the babes in the trunk. Cherrí had not questioned Runi. She had never questioned Runi. Runi had always known what was best. But Runi had not come back for her, so she knew Runi was dead.

Cherrí laid the babes on a cushion, then drank deeply before splashing a bit of the icy water on her face and cuts. She hissed as the stinging water washed away the blood and grime. Then she used one of Minea's thin scarves as a bandage. A pair of shoes that had to have belonged to Leyin were beside one of the beds. Minea had been taller and broader of form than the petite Leyin, who was closer to Cherrí's size. Cherrí discarded the sweat-soaked dress she had been wearing and donned a blouse and pair of loose wool slacks from Leyin's trunk. She slipped the fleece-lined, soft doeskin shoes onto her feet and pulled the laces tight. They were slightly large but fit well enough over the bandage.

A travel bag hung from the hook beside Leyin's hunting gear. Cherrí took it down and stuffed it full of clothes and food. Then she claimed a bow and quiver along with a knife and rope and a few other necessities. Cherrí had never traveled alone, but Runi had taken her hunting several times before the babes were born. Mostly, she thought Runi liked to show off her prowess with a bow. A memory flashed through her mind. Runi, in all her glory, knelt beside the riverbank over her kill. The sun reflected off her golden hair and glinted in her amber eyes as she looked over her shoulder with her lips turned up in a smug grin.

Cherrí thought she should be crying with the memory, but she had no more tears. She was empty, cold, and numb inside. She donned a fleece-lined leather jacket and collected the babes before heading out of the tent. Again, she looked for movement, for any sign of life, but there was none. Her gaze roved the treetops and grey sky. The sun was obscured by the haze, but she knew midday was nearly upon her. She saw no sign of smoke, which meant all the fires had died with her people—people whose spirits would never be freed by the pyre. She would not allow that to happen to her babes. They would not be eaten by savage, unnatural creatures.

Each of the tents she passed on her way toward the center of the encampment were devoid of people but not of their blood and flesh. The scent of iron hung in the air, but the decay of the small bits left behind in the cold had not yet begun. She briefly wondered why there were no scavengers. This much carnage should have had the vultures and rats feasting. Bears, lions, and wild dogs should have been tearing through the tents with abandon. Although it was disquieting, she was glad they hadn't made it into the camp. Not only was it safer for her, she didn't have to watch as the tiny remnants of her friends and family were consumed.

In the center of the encampment was a large pit where a fire burned day and night in honor of Everon, the fire spirit. Her clanswomen often cooked meals there and danced and told stories. It was a place of joy, hospitality, replenishment, and worship. Cherrí laid the babes down gently as she knelt beside the pit and used the pole to stir the coals. Although the flames had died, the coals were still hot, and those underneath glowed with the strength of Everon. She picked up her babes, one by one, and kissed each on their foreheads. Then, she laid Leyla and Ueni gently on the coals. She covered them with dried kindling to stoke the flames then retrieved wood from the massive pile beside the elders' tent. Eventually, she had a sizable roaring fire that was so hot she had to move several paces from the pit. She could not see her daughters burn, but she knew that Everon would carry their spirits to the Afterlife.

Cherrí stared into the flames, her eyes too dry to shed mourning tears. "Everon, Great Spirit of the Flame, I give to you my babes, those in whom my heart resides, and beg you to carry my heart with them. I give to you all that is left of my people and ask that you grant me the strength to live in this world without them."

With a torch lit in the fire of Everon, Cherrí limped among the tents of her fallen clanswomen and set the world aflame. When she reached the edge of the encampment, she turned back to watch as it was consumed in its entirety. Smoke filled the sky, and Cherrí blinked. In her weary stupor, the flames began to take shape. They stretched toward her in the form of a giant serpent. She thought she should run, but she had no energy. The thought crossed her mind that if Everon wanted to take her, he could have her. The serpent towered over her, its tongue flicking out to taste the air, and it stared into her eyes.

"I accept your sacrifice," it hissed. "In return, I grant you this gift."

The serpent suddenly reared back, then struck faster than Cherrí could scream.

Cherrí awoke with a start to the dark. Her first thought was that she was again in the box, and she kicked out in a panic. Her feet struck nothing, and she sat up. Then she remembered the serpent of fire. Her hands flew to her chest and face, but nothing seemed to be burned. A light flickered behind her, and she turned. What was left of the encampment was awash in moonlight. Only a few small fires remained to consume the final morsels.

Cherrí dragged herself to her feet. She did not remember falling asleep but could not fault herself. Her dream of the fire serpent had seemed terrifyingly real, though, and she could not shake the feeling that she had been in the presence of divinity.

THE ROAD TO YARDING HAD SEEMED LONGER THAN IT HAD THE FIRST TIME Aaslo had traveled it. It seemed as though their eagerness to get there on time had caused it to stretch. They had encountered a few roving clutches of lyksvight on the journey, but none so large as the first. The presence of so many smaller bands was a darker omen than the one large group. They were diluted but covered more ground. Although he was sad for the initial loss of life, guilt no longer suffused him for killing the creatures. No, there was only one battle on the road to Yarding that truly tormented him.

*"Stop thinking about it."*

"I can't."

Teza gave him a sidelong glance.

*"You didn't have a choice."*

"Didn't I?"

*"Well, if you didn't, they'd be dead soon enough anyway."*

"I'm a monster."

Teza huffed. "No, the lyksvight are monsters. You're, well, you're . . ."

"What?" said Aaslo as he met her gaze with the eye of a reptile.

"Different." Aaslo gave her a dubious look. With a sigh, she said, "Okay, you're a monster. But not all monsters are bad."

"You know all about monsters now, do you?"

"Well, no, just what I've read in the stories—same as anyone."

"Name one story about a monster who isn't terrible."

*"Let's see . . . there's the mitrite—no, they eat their young; the ban-shees—no, they eat people; the fae—no, they curse people with evil power . . ."*

"I'm not evil!"

"I didn't say you were evil," said Teza. "It's just, I can't think of any good monsters right now, but I'm sure there are plenty. I mean, if you look at it from *their* perspectives, they're not evil. Most of them are merely trying to survive."

*"We* aren't them," said Aaslo. *"We* are human."

*"You're not."*

Aaslo's anger roiled at Mathias's jibe, but he ignored it. "We must look at it from a human perspective, and in that sense, I am a monster—not because of this"—he held up his claw then pointed behind them—"but because of what happened back there."

Teza's expression fell, and she blinked away tears. "That wasn't your fault. Those people attacked us—"

"Because they thought we were the enemy. And *why* did they think that? Because my terrible power raised horrific cadavers to serve as our guards. How am I any different from the Berru?"

"For one, you don't kill people to make your monsters. You raise those who died valiantly in battle, those who died for our cause, the *victims* of the monsters. You give them back some semblance of life that allows them to fight back against their killers—a chance they wouldn't have had in death."

Aaslo motioned toward Rostus, who had taken the lead. "Where is the *life* in that? Is there actually a *person* in there?"

He jumped when something gripped his shoulder. He turned to find Greylan riding beside him. The corpse's foggy gaze followed his own, and Aaslo again wondered how it could see if not through its own eyes. The fallen guardsman squeezed Aaslo's shoulder, then released him before falling back to the rear.

Aaslo turned to meet Teza's startled gaze. Neither said anything for several minutes as they continued riding.

*"At least he seems to like you now."*

"He's probably just messing with my head."

"You think?" said Teza.

"He wants me to know he's more aware than I thought so that I can worry over all the things he's planning to do to me."

Teza laughed. "I said he had some life. I didn't say he was a mastermind."

"He might be."

*"And you're worried a dead man might outsmart you. I guess you should be used to it by now. I always win."*

"Not always."

"You think he's aware sometimes but not others?" said Teza.

"I don't know what to think." He motioned ahead with a thrust of his chin. "There."

"Woot! Finally!" cried Teza. "I'm so tired of riding, and the scenery was just as boring as the first time. Maybe we should have asked the marquess for a coach."

"A coach would have been too obvious and difficult to defend in an ambush."

Out of the blue, Ijen said, "The paths in which we rode in a coach were ugly. You would not have enjoyed them."

*"Now* you're willing to share?" Teza said. She pointed toward the city looming on the horizon. "Now that we're already there?"

Ijen shrugged. "We're here. Taking a coach is no longer an option."

"I'm pretty sure it stopped being an option over a week ago," she snapped.

"Hey, you two, look," said Aaslo. "Something's not right."

They both followed his gaze toward Yarding, or what was left of it, and somehow it felt as if even Mathias was staring at the destruction. The party remained silent and vigilant until it reached the edge of what was formerly a border town busy with merchant caravans, taverns, inns, and auction houses.

After observing an unofficial moment of silence, Teza said, "What could possibly have happened here?"

"I don't know," said Aaslo. "The entire city is naught but rubble."

"Just like the marquess's estate," she said. "Where are all the people?"

Ijen said, "Perhaps the survivors gathered somewhere farther into the city."

Aaslo wanted to ask the prophet what he knew about it but figured he wouldn't get an answer. If the prophet wanted him to know something, he would say it. Such was a forester's way. A grim smile threatened his lips, but he overcame the urge. Even thoughts of his father and the glorious, verdant forest would not lighten his mood among the utter decimation through which they rode.

Aaslo met Ijen's gaze. "We may not have time to search for people, but what do I know? I'm just a forester."

*"Oooo, sarcasm looks good on you, Aaslo. So un-forester-ish."*

He then looked toward Teza. "The evergate is our priority. Lead the way."

"Yes, he's right. We should hurry," replied Ijen.

Teza said, "Why? Is this another cryptic warning?"

"No," replied the prophet as he raised a finger toward the sky. "It's starting to rain."

Just then, a drop of water struck Aaslo's cheek. He really didn't feel like being wet and especially didn't want to be caught in the rain during an attack. He glanced around for shelter, but not a single structure in sight was standing.

Upon reaching an area slightly north of the city's center, they dismounted.

"Where is it?" he said.

"I don't know, okay? I'm trying," replied Teza. "Nothing looks the same."

Aaslo squinted as droplets dripped from his lashes, threatening to cloud his vision. "I know. I'm sorry. I didn't mean to sound curt."

*"Are you sure? There's been a lot of it lately."*

"*You're* part of the problem," Aaslo grumbled.

Teza turned on him, leaning into his face as she thrust her hands onto her hips. "If I'm such a problem, why don't you get Ijen to find it for you? Is this about the duck? Because that wasn't my fault."

"No," Aaslo said. He turned and gripped her shoulders, careful not to scratch her with his claws. The duck incident had been upsetting, but it hardly weighed on him. The potential implications of those events, however, stuck with him. "This isn't about the duck. I wasn't talking to you. You're great." Teza smirked. When he saw the playful glint in her eye, he quickly said, "I mean, it's great that you're here."

*"Smooth."*

She eyed him suspiciously, then relaxed. "Well, okay, then. As long as you remember how great I am." She turned and pointed toward the crumbled pile of stone blocks and pillars. "I think it's in there."

Aaslo surveyed the building's remnants. It certainly looked like it had been important, but it was hardly the kind of place he would have thought to find an evergate. Having never seen one, their manifestations in his mind had always been strange and mystical. This appeared to have been a grand building, but a mere building, nonetheless. The pillars along the front had fallen, and part of the roof had collapsed. Even so, the remains were taller than the others in Yarding. Most of them were naught but small piles of colorful rubble.

"Are you sure?"

"No, I'm not sure," snapped Teza. "That's why I said *I think.*"

*"Yeah, Aaslo, you need to listen more carefully."* The snide remark was followed by distant, hollow laughter.

Aaslo raised his hands. "Okay. We'll just have to check it out."

"Where do you suppose all the people went?" Teza said with a sniff. "I haven't seen any bodies. You would think if there were a bunch of rotting corpses, it would smell bad."

"I don't know," replied Aaslo. "Maybe they evacuated."

"But *why?*" said Ijen.

Teza looked at the prophet like he was crazy. "What do you mean? Obviously, someone or something attacked the city. It's in ruins!"

Ijen's voice was flat as he looked at her and said, "Yes, I can see that. But there are no bodies—not of the people of Yarding *nor* of the enemy. There are no remnants of weapons, and we have seen no armies. Why did the people leave, and why are all the buildings collapsed?"

With a scowl, Teza said, "*You're* the one who is supposed to be giving *us* the answers. Isn't it in your precious book?"

"No, I'm afraid not. I only knew that the city would eventually be destroyed, not the how or why of it—not even the *when.*"

*"He's pretty useless for a prophet."*

Mathias's comment seemed to echo Aaslo's thoughts. He knew it was unfair, though. The prophet had other skills, even if his information was cryptic and suspect.

*"He's probably working for the enemy to confuse and spy on you."*

"Is that the opinion of the chosen one or the cynicism of a dead man?"

Ijen shifted in his saddle. "I would say I'm neither."

"I wasn't talking to you," Aaslo muttered. "Let's see if there's an entrance in the back. It's not safe to remain in the open."

Greylan and Rostus led the way. Aaslo didn't like having the corpses at his back, and he figured it wouldn't be a terrible loss if they were attacked first.

*"You have no concern for the dead. I see how you discriminate against us."*

"I'm just saying, they're already dead. What difference does it make?" Aaslo muttered.

*"They unquestioningly serve you, Aaslo. Doesn't that carry value?"*

"Of course. That's not what I meant."

*"What exactly did you mean?"*

"I—" Aaslo suddenly noticed Teza staring at him. "What?"

"You're arguing with yourself again."

"I'm just trying to figure out how they"—he nodded toward the guards—"fit into everything."

"Why don't you ask them?" said Teza.

"Ask them? They're dead."

"They're *undead*. And we know they can talk. You could at least try."

The thought of talking to dead people sent a shiver up Aaslo's spine.

*"You should be used to it."*

"Perhaps I will, but not now."

The rear of the building appeared as if nothing untoward had happened. Water splashed over a pair of marble lovers in the central fountain of the courtyard. It was surrounded by beds of purple and red flowers, and two smaller fountains graced the sides. An hourglass-shaped staircase led to the back doors, which stood open to reveal a parlor filled with elegant furnishings, sculptures, and a glistening chandelier. If not for the rubble of the surrounding buildings, it would have felt serene.

The party dismounted, leaving their horses to drink from the fountain. The dead horses followed the living ones to the fountain's edge but did not drink. Dolt snorted at the closest one, then rounded the fountain to drink from the other side. When Aaslo started to walk away, Dolt tried to follow him up the stairs.

Aaslo stopped and turned Dolt's muzzle back the other way. "No, you stay here, you stubborn mule." He turned again to ascend the stairs, and Dolt followed.

"You'll have to tie him up," said Teza.

"It won't do any good," Aaslo muttered. "He'll just hurt himself trying to get free."

"We may want to take them with us," said Ijen.

Aaslo looked over to see the prophet staring vacantly across the courtyard as if he were seeing something else in its stead. Aaslo said, "Are you speaking now as a prophet?"

"Do I ever speak as anything else?"

*"Sometimes I speak as a pirate. Do you think he can speak as a pirate?"*

"He's not speaking as a pirate," Aaslo grumbled. "Fine, bring the horses with us. We wouldn't want to come back to find them eaten."

*"Do you think the lyksvight would eat undead horses?"*

"They seem to eat everything else."

*"What do the undead eat?"*

"So far, I haven't seen them eat anything."

*"Hmm, maybe they're like reptiles and only need to eat once a week or something."*

Aaslo clenched his clawed hand. Sometimes he wondered if he was more reptile than man. Although the majority of his body remained human, there were times when it felt as if his mind were something else.

As they led the horses into the parlor, Aaslo sidled up to Ijen and asked, "Are dragons reptiles?"

Ijen's gaze swept over the scales on Aaslo's neck. "I don't know. They *appear* to be related, but they could be something else altogether. Is that significant?"

"No, I suppose not. I was just wondering. Which way to the evergate?"

"Since none of us have been here before, your guess is as good as mine."

Aaslo looked at both Teza and Ijen. "You're both magi. If you were to put an evergate in this building, where would you put it?"

"I don't think it worked that way," said Teza. "The evergate was far older than the building. It would have been built around the evergate."

"All right, then the evergate would have been seated on the ground when the building was constructed."

"I suppose so," said Teza. "Unless it was in a cave or something."

"I am not aware of any caves in this region," said Ijen. "But, of course, I haven't gotten out much."

Aaslo said, "Assuming it isn't in a cave, it should be on the ground floor. Since we ascended the stairs, we are probably one level above it."

They all turned to examine the room. A set of double doors was on the far side, but the space between them was filled with debris from the partially collapsed structure. An extensive stone mosaic of the sun and moon decorated the floor, and a few carpets lay between the sofas and chairs grouped along the sides.

"I don't see any doors besides the one that's blocked," said Teza. "What if we can't get to the gate? What if it's been buried or destroyed?"

*"Ah, well, there's no evergate. Time to go home."*

"We aren't going home," said Aaslo. "If the enemy wants to bring more troops through the evergates, they wouldn't destroy them—especially since the rest of the magi left."

"Perhaps the former residents of Yarding collapsed the building to prevent the enemy from using it," said Ijen.

"Why only half of the building?" said Aaslo. "It looks like all the other structures in Yarding were completely leveled except this one. If it takes as much power as you said to destroy an evergate, doesn't that mean they're protected in some way? What if the presence of the evergate is what prevented this part of the building from falling?"

"You think we're standing on top of the gate?" said Ijen.

Aaslo walked forward, and Dolt followed on his heels like a dog. Teza and Ijen seemed to understand what he was thinking because they, too, followed. The three of them searched the floor around the mosaic for anything unusual.

"Oh!" said Teza. "It's a lift."

"A lift?" said Aaslo.

"Yes, it's a platform that's enchanted to rise and descend when triggered. It's easier to load and unload goods this way." She motioned to the outline of the mosaic. "See? It can fit at least two wagons."

"You can make it work?" said Aaslo.

"I think so, unless it's locked."

"Let's hope the magi didn't lock it behind them when they left."

Aaslo instructed Greylan and Rostus to bring their horses onto the lift. The undead soldiers complied, as usual, and Aaslo abruptly realized what had been bothering him about the undead horses—aside from their torn flesh and hazy eyes. They made no sounds or motion besides those necessary to carry out his orders. Not a snort, neigh, or hoof stomp. Not a swish of their tails, twitch of skin, or blink.

*"It seems lonely."*

"Lonely?"

*"To be without the comfort of your own movement—like your mind is trapped inside an empty wagon waiting for someone else to push it."*

"Is that how you feel?"

Ijen said, "I suppose I do sometimes. It's not easy living in a world that hasn't happened yet."

*"Of course not. I'm carrying you."*

"You mean *I'm* carrying *you.*"

*"Are you sure about that?"*

Ijen tapped his book. "I've been carrying you much longer."

"Well, neither of you would have gotten this far without me," said Teza. "So, it looks like *I'm* carrying both of you."

Aaslo glanced at the two of them, not sure what had just happened. Somehow, everyone had concluded that he needed them—and they were right. He wondered if he was the leader or the servant.

"Here goes," Teza said as she cast a spell. Her face scrunched with the effort. She suddenly yelped and began hopping in a circle while shaking her hands.

"What?" said Aaslo. "Are you okay?"

"I got shocked. I don't think it wants to let me activate it."

"Ah," said Ijen. "You were never raised to magus, and you are still under the binding spell."

"So?"

"Some enchantments are locked so that fledglings or bound magi cannot use them."

"You have got to be kidding me!" Teza hollered. "You could have told me that *before* I got shocked! The magi are gone. I should be free to do as I please."

"I may be able to help, but it'll have to wait. I'll activate the lift."

Aaslo rocked as the floor beneath him began to move. Ijen's horse was calm as usual, but Teza's became agitated. Dolt clamped his teeth onto

Aaslo's pack and began pulling as if to divest him of the burden. One particularly hard jerk nearly dropped Aaslo to the floor.

The platform descended into a room of the same dimensions as the one above. This room was empty, though, with bare walls and no furnishings. In the wall, directly beneath where the double doors stood above, was the evergate. Runes decorated each of the stones that formed a keyhole-like opening that glowed with shimmering iridescence. The light illuminated the empty chamber with a tranquil glow.

Aaslo approached the structure but did not dare touch it. He looked back at Ijen. "What are the chances I can use this safely?"

Ijen shrugged. "Probably about the same as successfully bonding with the arm of a dragon."

Teza said, "Those are terrible odds. I had no idea if that would work. The only reason I risked it was because I figured he would probably die anyway."

"Precisely," said Ijen. "Aaslo is a mixture of human, dragon, fae, and perhaps even *death*. The latter three are not native to this realm, nor are any of them from the *same* realm, as far as I know. There's no telling how the gate will respond to him."

"What about the horses?" said Aaslo. "We can't take them, can we?"

Ijen tapped his book but said nothing.

Aaslo turned to him. "Well?" But Ijen's lips were sealed.

Aaslo sighed and looked at Teza, but she was staring at Ijen crossly. When she turned to Aaslo, she said, "What? Everyone knows it's not possible. I don't know what his problem is."

*"At least you won't have a problem taking me, since I'm dead and all."*

"But they're not dead," he grumbled. He looked at Greylan and Rostus and their horses. "What about them? They're dead but presumably have souls."

"Do they?" said Ijen as if he already knew the answer.

Aaslo clenched his dragon claw and released an inhuman growl that startled even him. "Prophet, be straight! What are you trying to say?"

*"I'm* not saying anything. Remember, I didn't even want to be on this path of the prophecy."

Teza tapped her lips thoughtfully. "You told me that the reaper said *you* took their souls."

Aaslo nodded. "Yes, but she also said they still have their souls." He, Ijen, and Teza all turned to stare at Greylan and Rostus, who didn't seem to mind. "So, I somehow took them and then put them back? Why didn't they just come back to life like normal people? And why do they do my bidding?"

Teza shrugged. "Maybe they're still connected to you?"

*"Have you looked at them? I don't care how many souls you stuff into them. Those bodies could not possibly sustain life."*

Aaslo pondered Mathias's assertion. He was right. "Maybe . . . maybe

I'm maintaining the connection between their souls and their bodies because their bodies *can't* hold the souls." He looked at Dolt. "These horses are perfectly well." He turned back to Ijen and Teza. "The Berru move dead bodies through the evergates and then fill them with those *vights.* What if I could take the live horses' souls, rendering them dead, move them through the evergate, then put their souls back into their bodies?"

Teza's voice echoed throughout the empty chamber. "You want to *kill* the horses?"

*"You monster."*

"I don't *want* to kill the horses, but it would work, right?"

"Aaslo, you're talking about stealing *souls*!"

Aaslo repressed a shiver as he remembered the Berru's horrid creatures that slaughtered and ate his countrymen. He wondered if doing what he was proposing would create something just as horrid. Dolt had been a pain, but he had been loyal—of a sort. Aaslo didn't want to see any real harm come to the wily animal.

*"Could you put my soul back?"*

"You don't have a body."

"I most certainly do," said Teza. "And I'm pretty sure I've caught you looking at it a few times."

Aaslo scowled at her. He had a bigger issue to contend with than silly romances. Besides, the last one he pursued had failed miserably.

*"Maybe Teza could attach my head to another body."*

"That's disgusting. And I don't have your soul."

*"I'm* disgusting?" Teza huffed. She raised a finger to his face. "Don't you ever *think* of taking my soul. I'd rather the reaper have it!" She stormed across the room all the while muttering something about stupid, stubborn foresters. She sank to the floor in the corner, then pulled an apple and a chunk of hard cheese from her pack.

Aaslo decided to deal with her later. They had all been on edge since entering Yarding—longer than that, if he thought about it. The journey had been harrowing with sporadic attacks from lyksvights. It seemed the creatures had been given free rein over the countryside. Most of the farms they had passed had either been overrun or abandoned, and there was no indication of where the people had gone. Those few they had encountered on the road and towns were scared. The first few who had seen him and the undead guards had either attacked or run screaming that the enemy was upon them.

He and his companions had avoided one heavily guarded caravan headed toward Tyellí. Aaslo hoped the capital city was in better order than Yarding when they arrived. One horrific incident had led them to kill off most of the fighting members of a caravan in defense of themselves. Not only had they taken innocent lives, they had left the remaining travelers unprotected and vulnerable, not to mention terrified. Afterward, Aaslo had ordered Greylan and Rostus to remain far enough from the road to be inscrutable, and he had covered his dragon arm with his coat. With his hood shading his face and a patch over his eye, he looked passably human. Still, the other travelers had been skittish. It seemed no one was trusting of anyone anymore.

Aaslo looked into the luminescent barrier of the evergate and considered his options. They could leave the horses behind; they could take them as they were and most likely lose them in the pathways; or he could kill them and try to bring them back from the dead.

*"Desperate times—"*

"I get it. Let's do this."

# CHAPTER 6

MORY OBSERVED THE PROCEEDINGS FROM HIS PERCH ATOP A TOPPLED wall. Peck wouldn't let him participate, which, to him, made no sense. He was just as likely to get killed by the greys as anyone. He watched as one of the soldiers swiped the legs from beneath a new recruit. The recruit was a young woman, shorter and thinner than he. Mory decided that Peck was wrong. He needed to be training with the rest of them.

He scrambled down from the rubble, slipping once on the wet stones. A storm was rolling in, and the light drizzle had just begun. The marquess had already announced that there would be no break for the storm. The enemy, he said, would not care if they got wet, so neither should they. Mory thought the marquess seemed like a smart man. Not smart like Peck. The marquess knew about books and history and politics. He knew about battles that had been fought and why. The marquess wasn't a soldier, though. He trained with his guards, but by the number of times he lost, Mory thought him a mediocre fighter at best. Not that he knew much about fighting. Peck had said *no*. But he was about to change that.

Water dripped from Mory's hair into his eyes, and he pulled up his hood. The ground was not yet soaked, but he knew it would quickly become a muddy mess. He traversed the training grounds, dodging between bodies with the practiced ease of a street rat, then ducked into the recruiting tent.

He approached the rickety table that had been thrown together with wooden debris from the estate's wreckage and waited for someone to acknowledge him. The three men who sat on the other side were busy discussing numbers and training schedules. Mory cleared his throat, but the men didn't greet him.

"Excuse me," he said. "I need to get trained to fight."

The men finally looked, and the closest turned to face him. Mory had never seen a man with so much body hair. The man squinted. "Don't I know you?"

"Uh, I don't think so."

The man sat back. "Yeah, I do. Yer the forester's boy."

"Um—I guess, but I'm not a boy. I'm fourteen."

"Hmm, mayhap yer not a boy, but ya ain't a man neither. Gotta be sixteen to join the guard."

"I don't need to be sixteen to be eaten by a grey."

The man made a sucking noise through his teeth and nodded. "Ya got a point there. I was told ya might show up. Yer brother said to turn ya away if I did."

Mory's blood heated. "Peck's wrong! I need to learn to protect myself. I need to help Aaslo."

The man glanced back at the others, neither of whom expressed an opinion beyond a casual shrug. Mory's gaze followed the man's face as it rose to tower over him. The man was practically a giant.

"The name's Bear," said the man.

"Mory."

"I'll let ya train, Mory, but not as a regular recruit, okay? It's jus' fer survival. You can join up when yer sixteen like the rest."

A memory—a dark alley, his body lying broken on the steps of an apothecary, of Peck crying over his lifeless form—flashed through his mind. Then he thought about the line of innocent prisoners in the camp north of Ruriton getting their throats slit, of the men and horses being swallowed by the blight in the swamps, of the terrible screams when the estate burned and fell. Mory swallowed hard and muttered, "If we live that long."

"Yer too young to be a cynic. Best to keep a positive attitude," said Bear. "Otherwise, what life ya got ain't worth livin'. Come on. I'll get ya set up." Mory followed the massive Bear out of the tent into a full-on downpour. "Take off yer hood," said the burly man.

"But it's raining."

"It narrows yer field of view—can't see in your peripheral." Mory's head suddenly jerked forward when Bear walloped him from behind. "If ya weren't wearing that hood, ya mighta seen that comin'."

Mory lowered his hood and immediately dodged a second attempt to pop him in the head.

"Ya see?"

"Yeah, I get it, okay?"

Bear grinned as if pleased to have imparted some ancient knowledge. "So, what do ya think of him?" he asked.

"Of who?"

"The forester."

"Um . . . he's a good man, I think. He's a bit grumpy, but I guess he's got plenty of cause to be."

Bear grunted. "Don't we all. But what do ya think about him bein' kind of, ya know, not human?"

"Oh, I knew him before that happened. I don't see that it's changed him much—his personality, I mean. I thought he was kinda scary to begin with—back when I thought he was an assassin. I guess if I didn't know him, I'd think he was pretty terrifying. He's good, though. He helps people."

"The marquess seems to respect him."

"I can't say I understand their relationship," said Mory. "I can't figure out who works for who."

Bear didn't say anything more, but he seemed deep in thought as they rounded the practice field toward another tent. It had been constructed of a patchwork of canvas, drapes, and tapestries that had only partially escaped the fire. The poles that held the structure began to tilt as the material became heavy with rain. Mory wondered how long it would be before the entire structure collapsed.

"Hey, you," said Bear, motioning to a plain-faced man with an equally plain expression. "The kid, here, is gonna need some armor. Not too heavy. No, not that one. The leather plate should suffice."

The man dropped the brigandine in Mory's arms, and Mory thought he might drop it even before the greaves, vambraces, and other parts were piled atop. "This is the lighter armor?" he said as he struggled not to crumble under the weight.

"That's yer first assignment. Get used to it," said Bear.

"What do you mean?"

"I mean, you're gonna wear that armor day and night. You'll go about yer chores—and ya *will* have chores—wearin' that armor."

"How's that going to teach me to fight?" said Mory.

"It's not. It's gonna make ya fit enough to live. When ya can wear that armor as easy as ya don't, you'll be ready to start learnin' the sword."

"I'd kinda like to learn the bow," said Mory.

"You'll learn that, too. Ya don't always get to pick what yer good at, so we'll see where yer strengths are."

"So, um, are you like the general or something?"

Bear laughed heartily. "Me? A general? Nah, kid, I'm the training master. Commander was Greylan when he weren't too busy with the marquess, but he's gone and gotten himself undead."

The undead soldiers didn't bother Mory the way they did the others. He had seen death firsthand. The walking corpses weren't nearly as frightening as the reapers. Myra had been nice, delaying the taking of his soul until he could be saved, but he had watched the others as they had wandered among the ruins of the marquess's estate. It seemed a terrible power to be able to simply pull the soul right out of a person's body.

Bear trudged back into the rain, and Mory followed him toward the edge of the encampment. "So, um, what am I supposed to do?" he said as he struggled to keep pace. He breathed heavily with his arms threatening to give out and worried that if he stood in place too long, he might sink into the mud.

They stopped where the road turned down the hill, and Bear turned to him. "When I tell you to do somethin', ya say, 'Yes, sir.' When I ask if yer tired, ya say, 'No, sir.' You got it?"

"Yeah, I mean, yes, sir."

"Good, now let's get this armor on ya. Hmm, yer gonna need better boots. Those won't do. I'll check around the storehouse and barracks to see if we got any extras that'll fit. In the meantime, yer job is ta walk down this hill. When ya get to the bottom, you'll drop and give me fifty push-ups. Then, you'll walk back up the hill fast as ya can. At the top, you'll give me fifty sit-ups."

"In the mud?"

"The mud ain't gonna kill ya."

Mory muttered, "You haven't seen the kind of mud I've seen."

Bear paused, and Mory thought his look might have been one of sympathy. "I keep forgettin' ya went with 'em against the blight. But, as ya know, Sir Forester's taken care of that. Ain't no reason to dwell on it, and if ya do see somethin' like that again, you'll know to stay away from it. Now go on. You'll keep this up till chow time."

"Yes, sir."

As Bear walked away, Mory blinked droplets from his lashes and looked down the hill. He knew what the master trainer was doing. Peck had made him climb walls and crawl under tunnels of crates and tables for months. He hadn't let up until Mory could do it fast enough and quiet enough not to get caught by the merchants or guards. But Peck had been trying to make him quick and agile. Bear wanted him to get strong.

Mory took a deep breath, then began his descent. He followed Bear's directions and didn't skip any of the parts even though no one was supervising him. After all, he figured, he did want to get stronger. Cheating wouldn't do him any good. He was trudging the last few steps to the top of the hill when the bell rang, signaling time for the midday meal. He bent over with his hands on his knees, trying to catch his breath without inhaling rain. Water dripped from his nose into the muddy stream at his feet. He finally succumbed to the shaking in his legs and collapsed to his knees. Then he fell to the side and rolled onto his back to stare into the grey sky, blinking with each droplet that fell into his eyes. He closed his lids and heard only the rushing water slipping past his ears down the hill.

A thunderous pounding broke through the lulling shower, and he was suddenly jostled. Then there was a sharp pain at his ribs.

"Ow!" he opened his eyes to see his assailant standing over him. "Did you kick me?"

"What do you think you're doing?" said Peck. "I've been looking for you for over an hour. Why are you wearing that? I told you, you're too young to join the guard."

Mory blew water from his lips and said, "I know that. They wouldn't let me join. Bear said he'll teach me how to defend myself, though. I don't want to get eaten by monsters."

Peck frowned, then deflated. "I get that. It's time to eat. Get up."

"I can't."

"What's wrong with you? Are you hurt?"

"My armor's soaked. It's too heavy. I probably couldn't lift my body *without* it at this point."

"They made sausages with pan-fried cakes."

Mory abruptly rolled over and hauled himself to his feet. His stomach cheered him on, and he grinned. "Do you think they have any syrup?"

Peck threw an arm around Mory's shoulders, nearly causing his knees to buckle again. He said, "I don't know. I guess we're just lucky this was an old manor and the kitchen wasn't attached. Otherwise, we'd be eating whatever grass hadn't rotted in the blight."

"How's the investigation going?"

"Seems dead. No one can figure out how it happened or who did it. There's no trace. It's like the place just exploded on its own. We think we got all the bodies out, though. The marquess wants to hold a memorial service."

"His brother?"

"Dead."

"Too bad Aaslo isn't here to bring him back."

Peck cringed. "He wasn't in any state to be walking around."

"I suppose it's too late anyway, since his soul's already gone."

Peck looked at him from the corner of his eye. "Can you really see them? The souls?"

Mory didn't like it when Peck looked at him like that. He didn't want Peck to fear him, and he certainly didn't want his judgment. "Only when the reapers take them. I mean, I can't just look inside you and see your soul."

"Are you sure?"

"Uh, well, I've never tried, but I don't think so."

Peck was quiet as they approached the awning that extended from the kitchen over the eating area. Before they joined the others, though, he pulled Mory to a stop and looked at him with a severe expression. "I don't think I want to know what my soul looks like."

"Why?"

"It's just—you know—I've done some bad things."

"It's like you said before. We're not bad people. We were just desperate people. You're a good person, Peck."

Peck patted the side of his face. "Thanks. Maybe I've not always done right, but I've done what I thought was necessary."

"Yeah, Peck, it's not like we're getting rich. We're just trying to survive."

"I hope that matters."

"As far as I can tell, the reapers come for you either way. I don't know what happens after that. But I guess if Aaslo claims you, you don't have to go with them."

Mory knew that look—the one Peck was giving him in that moment. Peck had an idea. Peck always had ideas, but the spark in his gaze told Mory this one was something special.

Peck and Mory both turned when someone called out. It was the marquess, and he was waving to them. He wasn't under the awning with the rest of the men. He was standing in the doorway of the kitchen. Mory shared a look with Peck, then followed him into the kitchen. As soon as they entered, the chef squawked and began yammering to his helpers to rid his kitchen of the muddy mess.

Although secretly relieved, Mory still protested as one young man, perhaps a couple of years younger than Mory, began untying the laces of his armor. "Hey! I'm supposed to wear that."

"Not in my kitchen, you won't!" said the chef. "It looks like you dug it out of a pigsty." He waved the young man away. "Go clean that up so the leaf'll quit his flapping."

"*Leaf?*" said Mory.

"That's what they're calling us," said Peck. "You and me. We're the forester's men, so they're calling us *leaves.*"

"Huh. I suppose it's better than *thieves.*"

"That was the intent," said the marquess from the doorway that led into the servants' eating quarters. "We can't very well go around calling our savior's men *thieves,* can we?"

"No, I suppose not—even if it's what we are."

"No longer," said the marquess. "Now, you are scouts and procurers of resources."

Peck turned to face Mory and tapped a patch that had been hastily stitched onto his tunic. "Our leaves are brown. There's a different color for each division." He traced the edge with his finger. "My leaf has five points because I'm second in charge of the scouts. Daniga has seven. She's the leader." He dug into his pocket, then handed Mory a scrap of fabric. "Yours has three points because of your experience. New recruits get only one point."

"What is this? Some kind of new military system?"

Peck shrugged. "We're the Forester's Army."

"You said I wasn't old enough—"

"To fight. You're plenty skilled to be a scout."

Mory took the fabric leaf. It was rough and unimpressive, but it was possibly the most significant thing he had ever owned. He felt a surge of pride, of belonging. He was no longer a thief. He was in service to the forester. He was a leaf.

"Congratulations," said the marquess. "Now, come sit with us. Eat. We have much to discuss."

Mory had been so engrossed in the discussion of leaves that he hadn't noticed the others sitting around the table. Daniga was a slight woman with a severe countenance. She always looked angry, but he thought that was just the way her face was designed. Most of her tiny, black braids were wound atop her head, while a few dangled freely with small, intricately carved clasps at the ends. Her tunic, woven of green, gold, and brown thread, blended perfectly with the long grasses of the plains, and her formfitting pants lacked for even the slightest rustle. For a woman who spent much of her time skulking in the shadows and crawling through trenches, she never looked less than perfect.

Across from Daniga was Bear, grinning at him like a cat that caught the mouse. "Hey, boy, where's that armor? Day and night, I said."

"Y-yes, sir. It's just that chef—"

"You gonna let a cook tell ya what ta do? I thought you were a warrior."

"I am. I mean, I will be. But chef said—"

Bear barked a heavy laugh. "Sit down, kid. I'm just messin' with ya. One thing a soldier knows is to never piss off the cook."

Mory released a nervous chuckle and took the charred seat that Bear indicated—right beside him. Peck sat across the table next to Daniga, straight-backed with his chest puffed out so that his patch was plain to see. He grinned. Mory smiled back, but only because he liked seeing Peck with such pride. Peck had always talked big, going on about his plans and how they'd be set one day. Mory wondered if what Peck had really wanted all those years was to be a part of something important.

The marquess stood at the end of the table with his arms crossed behind his back. His fancy clothes looked to have seen better days, and the dark circles around his eyes bared his fatigue. "We are preparing to move out," he said. "If we stay here, we will run out of resources. In addition, the enemy has already struck a major blow here. We need a securer location."

The four of them stared at the marquess, waiting to hear the rest of the plan. It didn't come.

Daniga leaned forward and said, "Where shall we go?"

"That is for you all to figure out," said the marquess.

The woman leaned back in her chair. "I see."

The marquess stared at his feet. When he looked up, it was as if his fatigue had poured from his eyes to drench his face. "The truth is, I have no idea what to do, where to go. We don't know where the enemy is located, we don't know the status of the rest of the kingdom—or the other kingdoms, for that matter—and we don't know how Aaslo fares. I need more information if I am to make decisions."

"Mayhap we should be thinkin' 'bout what we *do* know," said Bear. "You'll always want for more information, but if ya keep waitin', you'll never make any decisions."

"That is a fair point," said the marquess. "My first instinct would be to go to Tyellí and join with the king's forces. According to the latest arrivals, though, the king has dismissed the army. There are no forces, no staging ground."

"We should go there anyway," said Bear. "Tyellí is already designed to house an army. We could recruit the soldiers who haven't left and use the supplies."

"Yes, but the palace was not designed to withstand battle. It was built for aesthetics. Most of its defenses were created to keep out assassins and the like, and the magi are no longer here to maintain them. Plus, it could be overrun any moment via the evergate. It possibly already has been."

"Maybe we should just stay here until we hear back from Aaslo," said Peck. Mory thought he looked anxious and imagined Peck was thinking about Jago back in Tyellí.

"We don't know when or *if* we'll hear from Aaslo," said the marquess. "Without use of the evergates, it will be nearly impossible to communicate."

"But if we leave, he won't know where to find us," said Peck.

Mory said, "Too bad we don't have a fortress—like from the old days before the magi." Suddenly, everyone was looking at him, and he worried he had made a mistake. "Uh, sorry, was I not supposed to say anything?"

Daniga turned her dark gaze toward the ceiling and muttered a prayer, then said, "Tohl Gueron."

"The ruins?" said the marquess, and Mory's heart pounded harder.

Bear nodded. "We could make it work."

"The *cursed* ruins?" said Peck, his voice echoing Mory's distress.

With a grin, Bear said, "You believe in curses?"

"You should not mock the spirits," said Daniga, "else the curse will befall *you*."

"I don't want to be cursed!" said Mory.

The marquess looked at him. "Some might say you already are." Mory shrank back, and the marquess continued. "Our hero talks to himself and raises the dead. I can't see how taking up residence with the spirits could be worse."

"They're *evil* spirits," said Peck.

"I think perhaps they are not evil," said Daniga, "only angry."

"What difference does it make?" replied Peck. "Either way, they'll kill us or possess us or cause some other terrible fate."

Bear said, "If the prophecy has its way, we're gonna die anyhow. At least at Tohl Gueron we won't be alone."

"That's not funny," said Peck, and Mory had to agree. "Besides, according to the legend, it's not just the spirits you have to worry about."

"Bah, come now. It's not cursed. That was probably made up by bandits to keep people away from their hideout."

"You don't believe in curses?" said Mory.

"Ain't never seen a one that turned out to be true."

Peck threw up his hands. "You never saw a walking dead person before either, had you? Doesn't mean it can't happen."

The marquess ran a hand over his face and said, "Fine. We'll go to Tohl Gueron. It's probably unknown to the foreigners and far enough from any towns and evergates that it's unlikely they'll happen across it. We'll send out riders with a call to arms. With sufficient people, we may be able to reconstruct enough of the fortress to make it defensible."

"Have you been there?" said Mory.

"No, and I don't know anyone who has, but the story's well known. People will have a general idea of where it's located. The scouts can roam the area and guide lost recruits."

"What about the curse?" said Peck.

The marquess shrugged. "We will deal with that when we get there. Hopefully, it is as Bear says."

# CHAPTER 7

THE SEA TOSSED ABOUT VIOLENTLY, SLOSHING AS SMALL WAVES CRASHED against each other. Myropa had never seen it in such a state. Its typical serenity had been frustrated, and she knew not how. She stepped out of one of her slippers and dipped a toe in the frothy tide. The water-that-was-not-water surged toward her in colorful streaks, then climbed up her shin. At once, she was assailed with feelings of alarm, sadness, and loss. She knew the feelings were not hers, but they struck her in the gut so deeply that she would have cried had she been capable of it.

She took several steps back to rid herself of the intrusion, then retrieved her shoe and hurried from the shore's edge. Disevy would want to know of the drastic change. Myropa pictured the pond beside his temple in the forest and willed herself through the veil into Celestria. When she arrived, she was immediately struck by warmth around her frozen feet. She looked down to find herself standing in the water up to her ankles.

"Oh, for Transcendence's sake," she grumbled as she ascended the steps that led from the pond. Her slippers sloshed and left wet tread marks on the stone. She had never before made such a blunder when passing between realms. She chided herself as she imagined accidentally stepping through the veil and right off a cliff.

"Disevy," she called. "Where are you?"

Her brow furrowed as she searched for his energy. His temple was saturated with it, and she could not seem to place him. She walked down the corridor calling for him. "Disevy? Are you here? I have news."

"Is that so?" said a dark, melodious voice. Myropa's frigid heart thundered in her chest. Axus stepped from behind a pillar into the corridor directly into her path. "What news is this?"

Myropa's mouth soundlessly moved as she tried to take a breath that she knew she didn't need. Axus grinned, and air finally stole into her lungs. The feeling of suffocating to death receded, and Myropa's head spun with the influx of oxygen. It always disturbed her how Axus could make her feel alive only so long as she also felt the grip of death.

"It's a message for Disevy."

"Come now, Reaper. What message could you possibly have for Disevy that you cannot also impart on me? You serve *me*, after all."

"I serve Trostili," she said a little too quickly.

Axus's gaze glowed with power as he leaned down to look her in the eyes. "You are a reaper. Whether or not the Fates assigned you to Trostili, you still belong to me. Either way, you have no business reporting to Disevy."

Myropa's muscles shook so hard she thought she might collapse. Her words were barely a whisper as she said, "Disevy ordered it so. Trostili is aware."

Axus straightened to his towering height and turned to pace the corridor, power radiating from him in his fury. "They plot behind my back!" He rounded on her and yelled, "Do they seek to steal my power?"

His voice roared like thunder, and Myropa's knees met the hard stone as she crumpled under the weight of his power.

"Tell me! What is this news?"

Myropa knew she could not lie to Axus, but she *could* choose which truth she told. "Th-the human resistance was attacked. The forester was buried under the collapsed estate, and lyksvight are running freely across the countryside."

Axus paused then smiled proudly as his power was withdrawn. It was dreadful and enticing, and it was all Myropa could do not to follow it into his embrace.

"So, things are proceeding as planned," he said. "Why does Disevy desire this information?"

She didn't know if Disevy would have any interest in what she had told Axus, but Axus wanted an answer, and she was obliged to provide one. "I am neither worthy nor blessed to know the will of a god."

"Of course you aren't," he snapped. "You are only a pitiful little reaper. Why am I wasting my time on you? Disevy isn't here. Scurry off and find him. When you do, tell him I am looking for him. And take a message to Pithor. It is time to flood the gates."

Myropa still could not stand on her shaking legs, so she crawled toward the steps and then tumbled down them to land in the pond. By the time she righted herself, Axus's power was gone, and she was thoroughly soaked. She pulled herself from the water and sloshed across the stone path toward the other side of the pond, tugging at her wet dress where it clung to her legs. Then, she stood and searched within her for Disevy's power. It was strong in the direction of his temple, but she could not sense the spike that would indicate his presence. She cast her senses outward and still could not find it. Never had she been unable to locate one of the gods.

A flutter of worry swirled in her stomach. What if something had happened to him? What if he was in trouble? She willfully dismissed the idea. A god as powerful as Disevy could not possibly need help. She decided that Disevy must have a place that was protected from the reapers' ability to sense his power.

She wondered if she should tell Trostili or Arayallen about the disquiet in the Sea of Transcendence, but neither had ever expressed much interest in the Sea. Myropa had no desire to visit Pithor but knew that Axus would not suffer a delay. She closed her eyes, inhaled the breath of life, and walked through the veil to Pithor's side.

He was lying on a table in an empty room, stiff and pale. His vacant gaze stared into the darkness that filled the rafters above him, and his breath was silent. Myropa searched for any sign of life, and just when she thought him dead, he blinked.

"Pithor."

He blinked again and furrowed his brow. Then he turned his gaze in the direction of her voice. He squinted, and Myropa knew that even had the room been well lit, he would not have seen her clearly. Pithor, like the incendias that served him, was blessed by Axus to be able to see and hear her—and, presumably, the other reapers.

"Myropa," he said, then coughed. His voice sounded dry, like he had not used it in a while. He sat up, and the single length of red fabric he had wrapped around himself nearly fell from his otherwise naked form.

"Are you unwell?" she said.

He cleared his throat. "No, I've been in prayer for two days awaiting word from the almighty Axus."

"Did he answer?" she said without bothering to disguise her mockery.

"As always. You are here, aren't you?"

"I seriously doubt that has anything to do with your prayers. Axus does what he wants when he wants, regardless of your desires."

"As he should. He is a god, after all."

"But not the only one."

"Perhaps not, but he *is* the one who answered my call, who blessed me with his guidance and, dare I say, power."

"Power? I have felt the power of the gods. Your pitiful spells and rituals are nothing by comparison."

"Of course not. I have yet to prove myself worthy. But I *am* the Almighty Light, Deliverer of Grace. Do you know what that means? It means *his* grace. And when I have completed my task, I will ascend to the realm of the gods and be granted true power so that I may serve at Axus's side." He stood and took a step toward her. "And you, Reaper, will serve *me*."

"You get ahead of yourself, Pithor. I am here only to deliver a message."

"Very well. What have you to say?"

"Axus says it is time to flood the gates."

For the first time, Pithor looked shaken. He swallowed hard, then turned to the uniform draped across the chair at the end of the table. As he began to dress, he said, "Are you sure? Are those his exact words?"

Myropa was secretly pleased to see him upset, even if she didn't know what had caused it. "Yes, exactly."

"I, um—when?"

"I got the impression he meant *now*."

"Which ones?" he said as he pulled up his pants.

"I'm sure all of them. The message was pretty clear, Pithor. What has you so rattled?"

He shrugged into his jacket but failed to button it before he turned to her. "It's just that—well, we are not ready."

Myropa smirked as she sidled closer to him. "You mean *you* aren't ready."

"The magi haven't deciphered all of the evergate keys."

With a shrug, Myropa said, "That isn't my problem. I've delivered the message."

She turned to go—a completely unnecessary gesture—and he said, "Wait, wait. Tell Axus we need more time."

She turned back and smiled. "Why don't you *pray* for it?"

"Do not mock me. I do Axus's bidding. If he could but share a bit more power—"

"You want *me* to go to Axus and not only ask for more time but more power as well?"

"I seek only that which is necessary to carry out his will."

"How long?"

"I, um—six months."

She laughed and turned again.

"No, no—four! I am certain they can do it in four."

She tilted her head. "Are you so certain?" She closed the distance between them and raked a frozen finger across his cheek. "Request denied."

"What? You cannot do that. You are only a reaper." He tried to grab her arm, but his hand passed straight through her.

She said, "*I* serve the gods directly. I was tasked with delivering a message *to* you. I am not required to carry one *for* you. The great and powerful Axus has given you a command. You will carry it out or risk his wrath."

"But you must tell him that it cannot be done!"

The echo of her own laughter resonated through the room as she stepped through the veil.

PITHOR PACED THE ROOM WRINGING HIS HANDS AND CHIDING HIMSELF for his loss of self-control. He had sounded like a blubbering idiot in front of the reaper. He was the Mighty Light, Deliverer of Grace, blessed by the power of Axus, God of Death. No one should be able to make him feel so feeble. The reaper was nothing but a minion, he knew, yet she held power of her own, power he didn't understand. It was her confidence that gave him pause. Without the slightest hesitation, she had rejected his request, and he didn't know whether to be offended or grateful. If *she* saw him as weak, what would Axus think?

"You don't look well, Pithor," said a soft yet scathing voice from behind him.

He straightened and turned to peer into the dark corners. Shadows and light slipped from around her like the wispy scarves of the Achmerian dancers of the Berru Royal Court. "Sedi."

She grinned as she swept across the room to perch on the edge of the table. Her feet dangled over the floor as she leaned back to prop herself up with her hands. "You look pale, like you've seen a ghost."

"Maybe I have," he muttered.

Sedi casually kicked her feet with childlike playfulness. "An emissary of the gods?"

"Hardly. Just a reaper."

"*Just* a reaper? It sounds like a dreadful creature. Do they really have the power to steal men's souls?"

"I wouldn't know. Axus uses her to deliver messages."

"I see. It makes perfect sense now."

As usual, Sedi was grating on his nerves. "What sense? What are you going on about?"

"You said *her*."

"You know nothing about me."

She laughed. Never before had he heard her truly laugh, yet she had the nerve to laugh in his face. "You think yourself special? I've been around a *long* time. I've seen every kind of man there is, and you are no different. Your only value is that one of the gods has decided to use you."

"You think your words hurtful, yet I am not offended. To be chosen by a god is to be divine. Now, what of your task? Is it finished?"

She tilted her head and issued a lighthearted "No."

It was not what he had been expecting to hear. Sedi was disrespectful and difficult, but she was also dangerous. She *always* completed her missions. "What do you mean *no*?"

"Oh, I tried. I blew up an entire estate with him in it—dropped the whole burning thing on top of him." With a glowing smile, she said, "He survived."

"This pleases you?" he growled.

"It amuses me."

"I said you were to kill him! He should be dead, beholden to Axus's mercy by now."

Sedi rolled her eyes and hopped off the table. "*He* is different. I've never seen anything like him. It'll be interesting to see what he can survive. Don't worry over it. He'll be dead soon enough."

"*Now*, Sedi."

"What's the hurry? It's not like it'll make any difference. The Lightbane is dead." She waved a hand toward him and mockingly said, "The *Deliverer of Grace* will rid the world of life, and I will finally have peace."

Pithor closed his eyes and counted to ten. When he opened them again, she was standing in front of him with crossed arms and a drab expression. He rubbed the ache at his temple and said, "If you are not here to report on the success of your mission, what do you want?"

"I wish to speak with the empress."

"About what?"

"That is none of your business, Pithor, and I need not ask your permission. It will only take a few minutes. Give me the Amulet of Anthiyh."

"Fine," he said begrudgingly as he pulled the heavy chain from his neck. He handed the amulet to Sedi with the reverence it deserved. She snatched it from his fingers and twirled it through the air before hopping back onto the table.

Sedi held the obsidian sphere in front of her face as if she were looking into a mirror. She then rotated the rune-bearing gold rings that encircled it into the correct position and waited. After several seconds nothing happened. She tapped the sphere with her fingernail and said, "Is it broken?"

"If it is, it's your fault," he replied.

Just then, the orb pulsed with a faint glow, and Pithor heard the empress's voice. He was glad he could not see her face from his vantage. She was a rather disturbing creature to behold. Her appreciation of death was expressed in every nuance. He imagined she was wearing one of her many gossamer, grey robes whose ends were tattered such that they fluttered with the slightest movement or breeze. Her long black hair would be braided and partially wound atop her head, and her pale skin would be powdered to appear as ash. Her eyelids and lips would be painted black, and her black-lacquered fingernails would be grown so long and pointed as to render her hands useless.

"Sedi, my sweet," she purred. "What fortune brings you to me?"

"I'm glad to see you, Lysia. You look well."

Pithor clenched his jaw as disgust filled the pit in his stomach. He told himself it was distaste for Sedi's disrespectful use of the empress's name, but he knew his feelings were truly wrought of envy. As her general, he had never been given leave to do so. Even the empress's own consort was not permitted use of her name.

"As do you, Sedi," she said.

Pithor could hear the smile in the empress's voice. Her teeth were shaped and capped with razor-sharp points, even more so than his own, which caused most of her words to escape with a hiss.

"What is that gleam in your eye?" said the empress. "Have you found something interesting?"

"Indeed, I have," said Sedi. "You would like this one. He is a man but not a man."

"Hmm, that does sound interesting. Tell me."

"Part of his body is different—like a reptile's."

"I wonder how that happened," said the empress. "I've never seen a reptile large enough to bond to a man. It's difficult to believe he could survive such a pairing regardless. As you know, we have had little success bonding humans to other creatures. Bring this man to me."

"Would that I could," said Sedi. "Pithor said that Axus wants him dead."

The empress sounded amused. "Axus wants *everyone* dead."

Sedi sighed. "Yes, but Pithor ordered him killed *now*."

"Pithor is ever so impatient."

His voice barely above a whisper, Pithor said, "Sedi, please tell the empress the decision was not mine."

Before Sedi could say anything, the empress said, "No, Axus must have his due. Although it pains me to prematurely dispel such a unique creature, we must comply. Still, it is curious. With the Lightbane dead, the prophecy will be fulfilled. I wonder over the significance of this lizard-man. Find out for me, Sedi—*before* you kill him."

"You would have her delay Axus's orders?" said Pithor.

The empress hissed and said, "Does that man dare question me?"

"Forgive me, Empress," Pithor said. "I only seek to serve Axus's will, as is my duty as his chosen disciple."

"No one is questioning that *or* Axus's orders," said the empress. "I simply wish to know about this strange man before he is destroyed. Perhaps he can serve me in the Afterlife."

Sedi gave Pithor a scathing look. "Will you stay out of this? We're trying to have a conversation." She smiled back at the empress and said, "I intend to play with him awhile. I'll let you know." Sedi ended the link without so much as a farewell, much less a dismissal from the empress.

Pithor was disgusted with the lack of decorum but ultimately decided that Sedi's relationship with the empress was insignificant, as was Sedi. She had never been blessed by Axus. In fact, she was cursed to walk Aldrea for all time, untouched by Axus's grace. Pithor might have pitied her had he cared.

As she walked past him, she handed back the Amulet of Anthiyh, dangling it carelessly into his grasp. "Sedi, you must—"

But she was already gone—disappeared before his eyes. For a brief moment, he wondered if she truly walked the world of the living. Her powers were mysterious and formidable, and it grated on him that he didn't know what she truly was.

He ensured that he was composed and dressed for his station before leaving the meditation room. The corridor beyond was filled with white and grey gossamer scarves that hung from the ceiling to dance in the breeze that wafted through the arrow slits. The fresh décor was a small bit of home that made the campaign more bearable. The hideous militaristic tapestries and artifacts of the Lodenonites had been burned, cut, or melted down for use in other, more industrious applications. The palace's former residents and staff had been repurposed as well. The new lyksvight had been set free to rampage through the city. Most had eventually been dispatched by the people of Nevrul. The city itself was still a war zone. Pockets of resistance clashed with the remaining lyksvight and Berruvian magi daily. Although his people still had not been able to find the Nevrulis' warren, he doubted there were enough living to cause any real trouble.

The doors at the end of the corridor swung open as he approached. The chamber of magic was a glorious affair. It was obvious that the Lodenonite magi had been revered, and their hasty departure had not diminished that fact. Shelves of bottles, ingredients, and elixirs lined the walls between bookcases filled with tomes and scrolls. Tables with glassware and other alchemical equipment were arranged in two rows of six, and several cauldrons stood empty beside the open windows. Chests, cabinets, and drawers were filled with magical artifacts, both natural and created, and spell forms hung from the ceiling. The former queen had ordered her subjects to maintain the room as though the magi would return at any moment, and no doubt they had hoped it would be so. The magi did not return, though, and the queen was dead. Even her lyksvight had been slaughtered and dismembered by her own people. Pithor grinned at the thought of the ironic twist of fate.

"Your Grace, it is good to see you again. Have you news from Axus?"

Pithor frowned and placed a hand on his friend's shoulder. "I do, Cobin, and I am afraid you will not like it. He has ordered us to flood the evergates—immediately."

Cobin was a small, middle-aged man with a pointed nose and narrow jaw. His mussed hair and muddy brown eyes did nothing to improve his appearance, but he at least had a healthy complexion—usually. At that moment, though, his face had drained to the color of milk.

"B-but we are not ready," he protested, and the six other magi under his charge stopped in their tasks to anxiously watch the exchange.

"I know," said Pithor as he led Cobin toward the other side of the room.

"I've tried. You know I've tried. It's just that keying the gates is difficult work. If we had more power—"

"We don't," Pithor snapped, then regretted it when Cobin jumped. "I am sorry, my friend. I did not mean to sound cross. I know you are doing your best."

"But d-does Axus know?"

Pithor steadied his voice to seem calm and reassuring as he spoke to Cobin. The man was brilliant and powerful—the greatest magus in Berru, but he was sensitive. When placed under too much pressure, he tended to freeze, and they could not afford the delay. "I'm sure Axus is aware of your dedication, Cobin. We must work harder, though. Axus has greater priorities than our small world, and time is different for the gods. Perhaps he will not notice a small delay, but if we wait too long, he may become angry. It is not advisable to incense the God of Death."

"No, I should say not."

"Don't worry about Axus. As his chosen, I will deal with him. You just worry about the evergates."

"Very well, Your Grace. I will see what we can do. We're close to another key, but we won't know which one until we open it."

"Good. I must check in with Margus now."

"Of course. I'm sure he will have better news."

"You've spoken to him?"

"No," said Cobin, blinking up at him from behind his spectacles. With a silly grin, he said, "I was just being hopeful."

Pithor patted Cobin on the back, then left the chamber of magic to find his general seculari. The man was, of course, in the training yard. Pithor approached the brawny man who was lounging in a reclined wicker chair in the shade of a red umbrella. Several retainers were serving him drink and food as he squinted into the sun to watch the recruits. "How goes the training?"

"Ah, Your Grace, please join me," Margus said as he waved to another of the chairs.

Pithor was about to reject the invitation when his stomach grumbled, reminding him that he hadn't eaten in two days. He sat down at Margus's side and propped his feet up on the ottoman in front of them. The servants brought a goblet of fresh water and platter with a number of small bowls containing local dishes for him to try.

Margus pointed to one of the bowls and said, "Try the green one. It starts out sweet and ends with a kick."

"What is it?" said Pithor.

Margus chuckled. "I've found it's better not to ask."

"So—the training?"

Margus waved a dismissive hand toward the recruits—local boys and girls old enough to hold a sword but too young to rebel. "These Lodenonites have a penchant for war. The young ones'll fight for anybody. I doubt any of them will make it through their first battle, but at least it puts bodies on the field."

"Good, as long as we can overwhelm them with numbers. We are lucky it is Axus's grace we bear. It's easier to wage a war when it doesn't matter if your troops live or die."

"True enough," said Margus. "Still, the fact that we must fight the war must mean something. It seems like it would be easy for the God of Death to just wipe us from the world."

Pithor elected not to mention Trostili or any of the other gods, for that matter. He thought it best to keep all his people focused on one god— *their* god. He had not even told the empress what little he knew about the deals Axus had made with the others. The fact that Axus had to make deals might make him appear weak in the eyes of the Berruvians. It was absurd, of course, but his people valued strength above all else. The empress didn't make deals. She did whatever she wanted.

He paused as a disdainful smirk crossed his mind. Sedi didn't make deals either. She was impertinent and stubborn, and no one would tell her to act otherwise. He had wondered at that a number of times. Her strength was incontrovertible, but she had never taken an active role in politics, nor had she sought any other position of power besides her mere existence. Although he had never cared much for her, he could not deny her magnificence.

"You're smiling."

Pithor roused himself from his thoughts. "What?"

Margus grinned at him. "I said you're smiling. It's not a look I'm accustomed to seeing on you. Is it a woman?"

Pithor scoffed. "That's absurd."

"It's a woman," Margus said with a chuckle.

"It's not a woman," Pithor snapped. "I was simply thinking about power."

"If you say so."

"I do. Now tell me about the troops. What news have you?"

Margus shrugged. "It looks like they're at least a month out, maybe two or three."

"Couldn't they narrow it down even a little?"

"Nah, there's storms in the south. It's hurricane season, you know. They're wary of sending the ships."

"They knew what to expect before this started. How did the timetable get so far off?"

"It was the blight—or lack thereof. It was supposed to have consumed half the west by now. We weren't expecting to need the ground troops for another six months."

"When I heard that the Endricsian magi had evacuated, I expected an easier win. I still don't understand how that secular destroyed the blight."

"Too bad Verus didn't survive. Would've been nice to get a report."

Pithor sighed. "So, the ships won't be arriving anytime soon, and we still don't have the evergate keys. Is anything going *right*?"

"The lyksvight in Cartis have made progress."

"How long until we have more?"

"Well, that's another problem."

"What now?" said Pithor.

"We were expecting to have Endricsian magi to sacrifice in the ritual. They're gone, though. We could sacrifice our own, but then we wouldn't have the upper hand."

"Hmm, we may not need our magi now that the Endricsian magi are gone."

"I've considered that, but what if it's a ruse? What if they come back? The only way to prevent that from happening is to destroy the evergates."

Pithor groaned. "Which we can't do because we need them to disseminate the lyksvight and supplies. That's why Axus wanted to flood them."

"He wants what?"

"He wants us to move the troops through *now*. The Endricsians must be planning to destroy the evergates now that their magi are gone."

"How would they do that?"

"I'm not sure. Find out from Cobin."

"Yes, Your Grace."

# CHAPTER 8

CHERRÍ STUMBLED ON A LOOSE STONE AND CAUGHT HERSELF WITH THE walking staff she had fashioned from a piece of driftwood. A dark blanket had covered the sky over the Basel Ocean, and she could see showers in the distance obscuring the harsh grey waves of the churning sea. Lightning crackled through the clouds that had begun to turn, then it streaked toward the water. She pulled her scarf tighter over her head and covered her face so that the windblown sand could not reach her skin; but, still, her eyes stung. She ran her tongue over cracked lips and blinked, searching for even the smallest hovel that might be somewhere down the beach. She hoped dearly to find a fisherman's shack before the storm reached her.

She saw nothing, so she dropped her gaze toward the ground to keep sand from her eyes and kept walking. Never had she been on the beach alone, although she had lived upon it most of her life. Her people were fishermen during the sea's calm months, and they moved inland when the storms arrived to hunt and seek refuge among the trees and valleys. They moved as a clan, and they had always been with her. Until now. She bent to pick up a sand dollar. She ran her finger over the flowerlike pattern and smiled. Runi would have rejoiced to find one whole. She would have begged Cherrí to string it with beads and then worn it always until it broke.

Cherrí continued walking, and in her heart, Runi walked beside her. She couldn't remember how long she had been walking. Her eyes closed of their own accord as she took the next step, and she could feel herself drifting. She started to tip over and caught herself. Her hand tightened on the staff, and she opened her eyes. She was tired, she knew, but she did not expect the nightmare to visit her while awake. For a moment, she thought she *had* fallen asleep on the beach. Her heart jumped, and she rubbed her eyes. With every wave that washed toward her feet came red. As her gaze traveled the shoreline in front of her, she was struck with dread.

Blood streamed into the water and saturated the sand where body parts were strewn haphazardly across the beachfront. Bloated corpses bobbed in the water, where they were pulled into the sea, then thrust back upon the shore farther down the beach. Seabirds and crabs scampered over the carnage in frenzied glee, pecking the flesh from within tattered clothes.

Cherrí took a tentative step forward, then another. The scavengers were so elated with their feast that they didn't bother to scatter. Strangely, a number of the animals were dead beside their hungry brethren. She wondered if they had died fighting and why they would feel the need.

There was plenty for all. Her gaze was drawn to one of the more intact corpses—the torso of a man. It was missing its arms and everything below the waist, and it stared at the sky with one milk-white eye, the other having been plucked. Its skin was grey and sagging, it had no hair, and, in place of blood, milky white liquid oozed from its wounds. She had seen dead bodies before. She had even seen a woman found drowned. But she had never seen anything like this. It barely looked human.

It blinked.

Cherrí jumped. She calmed her racing heart, knowing the thing could not possibly be alive. She took a cautious step, and its head suddenly turned toward her. It released a shrill cry that ended in a growl, and Cherrí screamed in return. In her panic, she stabbed the butt of her staff through the creature's face, then stumbled backward before tripping over a severed limb. Her rear had barely hit the sand before she was up and running.

Her mind was spinning as she fled. She hadn't seen what had attacked her encampment, but she had heard the sounds—the sounds of her babes crying on her chest, and the sounds of those horrid creatures. It was those things that had killed her people.

Her weary legs gave out, and Cherrí fell to her knees in the sand. She clung to the staff as the rain began to fall. Her chest heaved, and she realized it was not just the rain that had wetted her face. She began to cry in earnest, finally releasing the horrible pain she had carried with her for days. She cried for her people, for her babes, and for Runi. The thought of Runi being killed and eaten by those . . . *things* was more than she could bear.

When Cherrí looked up again, she was not alone. In fact, she was surrounded. She sobbed even harder, dropped her staff, and held out her arms. The ring of armed warriors who were poised to attack relaxed their stances, and one man, broad of shoulder and sun-dark, came forward to kneel in the sand with her. His strong arms embraced her, and he said nothing as she cried into his chest. After several minutes, she pulled back and looked into his grey eyes.

"They're dead," she said. "They're all dead."

He gripped her shoulders as if she would otherwise fall—and perhaps she would have—and said, "From which clan do you hail?"

With quivering lips, she whispered, "Fire Serpent."

A chatter rose within the group. A woman said, "The clan of our mothers is dead?"

Cherrí nodded. "Yes—the elders, the hunters, the babes—I am the last."

The man helped Cherrí to her feet. She gripped her staff for strength and comfort, and as they walked, the group huddled around them. She noticed that they were on constant alert, and she was thankful for it.

The man said, "Relax, young Mother. We will protect you now." Cherrí's shoulders dropped, but she couldn't relax. She had seen what those creatures could do to an entire armed encampment, and she knew a dozen hunters wouldn't stand a chance if they were attacked in force. He said, "I am Natu, Clan Father of the Black Rock."

"But you are so young," she said. She had never seen a clan leader without grey in his or her hair. With his dark hair, muscular build, and chiseled face free of the ravages of time, Natu could not have been over thirty-five.

"Few of us are left. I am the oldest now," he said. He must have caught her glance toward the others, for he added, "These are not the Black Rock— not *only* Black Rock, anyway. We are all like you, survivors from other clans. I suppose we were lucky, though. Our clans were able to defeat the attackers but at heavy cost. We have banded together to strengthen our numbers. Our encampment is not far."

"I am glad to hear it. I don't think I could have walked much longer. I'm worried about the storm. It looks to be a bad one."

"We have taken refuge in the charnel. We will be safe."

Cherrí swallowed hard. The last thing she wanted was to be surrounded by more death, but the charnel would certainly be safer than the tents. For hundreds of years, the people of Cartis had been entombing their dead in the caves and building stone tunnels above them. The other clans would visit the charnel a few times per year to inter the mummified remains of the dead they carried with them. Her clan did not bury their dead, though, so she had never been to the charnel.

The group led her away from the shore and over the dunes. The serrated, sticky plant leaves tugged at her clothes, and scaling the loose sand of the mounds taxed her already overburdened muscles. She was glad to finally step onto a hard surface, even if the jagged rocks did stab into her feet. The shrub-dotted landscape began to rise steeply, but they had only a short way to go before the first of their party stepped down into a hidden crevasse. The split in the rock was narrow, barely wider than Cherrí's shoulders. The ground was not level either, and Cherrí endured a number of cuts and scrapes to her fingers and palms. The opening to the sky gradually narrowed until she struggled to see those in the lead.

Cherrí paused and her breath hitched. She was trapped in the dark. The cry of a babe, a haunting echo, reached her ears. Her hand shot out to her side and her staff smacked into the wall. After dropping the staff, she began clawing at the other side. She turned in a panic, searching for a way out, and lost all sense of direction. Strong hands grabbed her wrists, and she screamed. The hands fell away, and suddenly her head was in a grip with one hand covering her mouth.

"Shhh," the creature hissed.

Cherrí's heart pounded as though it would thrust itself from her chest, and she felt as if she couldn't breathe.

"You are safe," said a deep voice. The voice sounded familiar, but she could only imagine one of those horrible creatures with its claws wrapped around her. "Cherrí, it's okay. You're safe. It's me—Natu. I've got you."

Cherrí stopped fighting him but continued struggling for breath. Her fingers followed his arms past his shoulders, over his face, and into his hair. There was no sagging skin, no sharp teeth, and no bald scalp. She pulled his hand from her mouth. "Natu?" she whispered.

"Yes, we are nearly there." He turned her but kept his hands on her shoulders. "Look there. A light is around the corner."

Cherrí blinked. She realized she could see the faint glow of a light somewhere ahead of her. She started to run toward it but immediately collided with another person. A second set of hands grabbed her arms. The hands were smaller but still firm.

"I am Aria. I will guide you," said a female voice. Cherrí recognized it as the voice of the woman who had questioned her on the beach.

"O-okay," said Cherrí. "I'm okay now. Just, please, I need to see the light."

Aria released her shoulders and took her hand. She led Cherrí the rest of the way through the narrow cave and around the bend, where they were finally met with torchlight. At first, it was only a single torch and then a second farther down. After a few more minutes of walking, the passage opened into a huge cavern filled with enough candles and torches to light every nook.

Cherrí's chest loosened, and she could breathe again. Once her mind settled, she began to notice the people. They were everywhere. Little pockets of men, women, and children gathered around small fires, cooking meals, and chatting quietly. A baby cried. A woman rocked a swaddling while humming a soothing tune. The scent of food reached Cherrí's stomach, and it grumbled with desire.

Aria turned and smiled at her. "Come, we will get you some food. Then you may rest."

Some members of the patrol left to join other groups, but a few, including Aria and Natu, gathered with her beside a firepit. Some of them perched on the smooth rock formations, while others sat on pillows or blankets. Cherrí set her pack behind her, leaned back, elated to finally rest. Natu laid Cherrí's staff in front of her, and she was relieved.

Someone handed her a plate of potatoes, leeks, radishes, and fish. Cherrí began shoveling the food into her mouth without waiting for a spoon. Natu and Aria sat across the fire from her, each wearing a mournful smile. She knew what they were thinking because she knew she would feel the same in their place.

Cherrí drank deeply from the cup of nectar that had appeared in front of her, then said, "Why don't we go to the city? I've been walking for days. Port Loess must not be far."

"Port Loess is not safe. Much has failed since the magi left, and it is there that the lyksvight came through the evergate."

"Lyksvight?"

"The creatures you saw on the beach."

"Is that what they're called?" Cherrí said as her empty plate was collected and replaced by a full one.

"That's what the Berruvian magi said."

"Who are the Berruvians? I've never heard of them."

"There is another continent to the south of Endrica called Berru, home of the Berruvian Empire. It is they who have been attacking us."

"Why?"

Natu shrugged. "They say they are here to enact the will of the gods. There is a prophecy about an evil enemy from our land called the Lightbane. This Lightbane was the only one who could have succeeded in defeating the Berruvians, but they killed him. Now, we are all meant to serve under the Deliverer of Grace, Pithor."

"That doesn't make sense," said Cherrí. "How are we supposed to serve them if we are dead?" Natu nodded and stared into the fire as if he too had pondered the question. "How do you know all this?" she asked.

Aria said, "The lyksvight kill everyone when they are left alone, but sometimes they are accompanied by a Berruvian magus. The magus keeps them from killing some of the boys and girls. They take them to be trained in their army. One of the girls escaped. Onlí." She nodded toward a girl who looked to be about twelve. She was sitting quietly with another group, but she seemed to be in her own world. "Onlí made it to the city of Koyra, but it was already overrun. She was found by the White Tusk Clan when they fled and brought her here."

"The others that were taken?"

"We don't know," said Aria. "I'm sorry to bring this up, but we need to know what happened to the Fire Serpent Clan."

Cherrí set her plate on the ground beside her and wrapped her arms around her knees. "We were traveling inland from Loess to Mynor. Our hunting camp was in the Ident Valley. We had been there for six days when we were attacked. Before we knew what was happening, Runi told me to take our babes and hide in a trunk. During the battle, our tent collapsed, and the babes and I were trapped. I never saw the creatures, but I listened to my people's dying screams. When I finally escaped, everyone was dead. There were no bodies—only parts. I burned the encampment."

"The whole thing?"

"Yes, it is our way. At least, it was the best I could do given the circumstances."

"You said you were trapped with your children. What happened to them?"

Cherrí swallowed hard as her eyes filled with tears. "Yes, mine and Runi's. They had both been sick with fever and were having trouble breathing. We tried to see a healer before we left Loess, but they were all gone. Ueni was a month older than Leyla. She died first. Leyla went shortly after, as if she knew Ueni was gone. I lay there terrified and trapped in a trunk for hours with my dead babes."

They were quiet for a while, then Natu said, "I am truly sorry for your loss and the terrible ordeal you suffered. I understand, now, why you were so upset in the cave. If I had known, I would have better prepared you."

"It's not your fault," said Cherrí. "I am thankful you all found me."

"You are safe with us—for now. I'm afraid this terror has only just begun."

"WHAT IS THIS?" SAID MYRA, HER VOICE FILLED WITH ACCUSATION.

Aaslo glanced up. "Um—"

*"Go on, Aaslo. Tell her you're a horse killer."*

Myra's gaze was drawn to the strange vortex of colors that surrounded them. It looked like shattered glass. "Are we inside an evergate?"

"Yes."

"I've never been in one of these." She leaned over Dolt who was sprawled in an awkward lump on the ground where he had fallen. "I don't see any injuries. How did he die?"

"I'm not exactly sure he *is* dead," said Aaslo.

*"I recognize dead when I see it."*

"You can't see anything," Aaslo muttered.

"You're right," said Myra. "His soul is gone."

"What do you mean, he's not dead?" said Teza. "I'm looking right at him, and he looks dead to me."

*"That stubborn horse can't even die right."*

Ijen stared at the horse, but his pen was still, as if he was unsure what to write.

"Okay, look. I sort of *borrowed* his soul—I think. I'm holding it for him until we activate the evergate. Once we're on the other side, I'll put it back into his body, and he'll be good as new."

"You don't seem certain of that," said Teza. "What makes you think it will work?"

"Mory."

"Mory? What does Mory have to do with this?"

Aaslo patted Dolt's neck, then stood. "I thought this through, and I think it'll work."

*"Of course you do, or you wouldn't have done it."*

"That's right," Aaslo snapped. He ran a hand through his hair that had come loose and then tied it back again. It had grown too long since he had left the forest, and he hadn't gotten around to taking care of it. "Think of this. Peck said the boy was dead. Myra, however, refused to take his soul. She waited with him until the apothecary had treated his wounds and gave him some kind of lifesaving elixir. Then, his soul went back into his body, and he was alive again—not like Greylan and Rostus, but *actually* alive. What was the difference?"

Teza's curls bounced as she shook her head. "I don't know."

"The difference was that Mory's body was healed—at least, healed enough to harbor life once it was filled with a soul."

Myra said, "You think that so long as the body is fine, you can just put a soul back in and everything is normal again?"

"How do you know what happened with Greylan and Rostus wasn't a result of your power?" said Teza. "*You* didn't bring Mory back."

Aaslo sighed. "I don't. I'm just guessing here, but I think this might work."

Teza gave him a pointed look. "We really don't want a repeat of the duck incident. What if this doesn't work?"

"Then I suppose I have a dead horse."

Crossing her arms, Teza said, "No, we all will have dead horses."

*"If he's dead, that makes him mine, right?"*

"You wouldn't want him," Aaslo growled.

*"He's presently the most accommodating he's ever been."*

Aaslo didn't disagree. He looked at the other two horses, then glanced between Ijen and Teza for approval. They didn't appear excited for the idea, but neither did they protest. He approached Teza's horse first. He stroked its soft muzzle, then turned to Teza.

"It would probably be best if you make them lie down. You saw what happened to Dolt."

They both glanced at the not-dead horse who looked like he had splattered onto the ground from a rooftop. Aaslo hoped Dolt wasn't injured but had confidence that Teza could fix him if he were—probably.

Teza's lips twisted with concern. "Have Ijen do it. He knows how to bespell horses."

Aaslo glanced to Ijen, who was simply watching their exchange. The prophet met his gaze but said nothing.

"Ijen?" said Aaslo.

"Yes?"

"Will you bespell the horses so they'll lie down?"

Ijen appeared genuinely confused. "Why would I do that?"

"Have you not been paying attention?" barked Teza.

With a nod, Ijen said, "I am quite familiar with this part of the story."

"Then do it," Teza snapped.

"But they weren't lying down in the story—"

*"Oh, I'm going to like this story."*

"They'll be lying down *now*," grumped Aaslo. "And it's *not* a story!"

Ijen appeared unsure but finally relented. He muttered and waved his hand so that the horses followed his fingers down to the floor where they lay still. He frowned as he stared at them, then muttered, "I don't like it."

"Why not?" said Teza.

"Because I don't know how this will affect the story."

Aaslo said, "What difference does it make to you if they're standing or lying? What's the point in risking injury in a fall?"

Ijen tapped his book, then shrugged. "Maybe none. Maybe it will change the outcome of the war. Who knows?"

*"Well, that's a little dramatic. I hardly think the position of a couple of horses is going to have a greater effect than my death."*

"Getting a little full of yourself?" said Aaslo.

"Not at all," said Ijen. "It's the way things work. Sometimes the slightest incident can cause the greatest change."

*"Like the tragic death of a hero from Goldenwood."*

Aaslo muttered, "Now who's being dramatic?"

"It's not drama," said Ijen. "It's prophecy."

"Let's get on with this," Aaslo said as he moved to stand between the horses.

"How do you do it?" said Teza.

"I'm not exactly sure."

"It's kind of disturbing that you can just steal souls right out of living beings."

"I don't *steal* them." He opened his mind as he spoke and allowed the strange words to fill him. The powers that struggled inside of him—that struggled *against* each other—twisted and surged like serpents competing for their prey. He grappled the one he sought—the dark and enticing silk that whispered promises of peaceful rest—and shoved the others down. Then he cast his power toward the prone horses. He said, "They don't *want* to leave. I sort of invite them, coerce them. It's like something inside me speaks to them, and I offer them a deal. When they accept, they come to me."

Myra said, "What happens to them once you have them?"

"I carry them within me, wrapped in the power like a little ball."

Myra held up several of the orbs that dangled from her belt. "Like these?"

Aaslo glanced toward her. "Something like that, I suppose, except they're on the inside."

"Like what? Wait, who are you talking to now?" said Teza.

"Myra."

"The reaper? No. Make her leave. She'll take the souls, and you won't be able to put them back. We'll have no horses."

"She can't take them. I've already claimed them," said Aaslo.

Teza and Ijen looked at the horses. They were no longer breathing. Each looked as dead as Dolt.

"Great," said Teza. "Now we have three dead horses and two *undead*. Can we go now?"

"Yes, we should go quickly. We'll want to minimize any damage death might cause."

*"That's true. I lost an unhealthy amount of weight after my death."*

"Activate the evergate," said Aaslo.

Myra said, "I've never tried to travel by evergate. I'm not sure I'm compatible with its power. You're going to the Citadel of Magi, right? I'll meet you there."

She was gone before Aaslo could reply, and Teza had already started talking.

"First, we all need to connect our power to this rune here, the one that looks like two rivers crossed by an arrow. It's the one for the citadel. This is what will keep us from getting lost in the paths. Try it."

"How?"

Teza started to answer, then paused. She said, "I'm not sure how your power works."

Ijen said, "I imagine it's much like what you used on the horses. You reached your power toward them, yes? You made a connection?"

"Okay, but which power do I use?"

"You have more than one power?" said Teza.

Aaslo frowned. "It feels like it—like there's more than one, and they're fighting against each other."

Ijen said, "That would have been good to explore *before* you killed the horses and we started activating the evergate."

*"That's not a very nice way of talking to the hero of Goldenwood."*

"Are you talking about you or me?" said Aaslo.

*"I'm starting to wonder if there's a difference."*

Aaslo had often wondered that as well. He hated to think that it might be true, because that would mean he'd gone mad.

*"You can keep your madness to yourself. I've got my head on straight."*

"How can you tell? You don't have a body."

*"Which means every way is straight."*

"Are you done?" said Ijen. "We're supposed to be in a hurry, remember?"

"Right," said Aaslo.

"I suggest you use the power the fae being lent to you. It should be most like that of the magi."

Aaslo reached inside himself again, this time searching for the power of Ina. It felt markedly different from the power that he had used on the horses. That one had been enticing and seemingly selfish—as if it wanted nothing more than to *take*. The power of Ina felt generous and giving. It made him feel as if he could make anything happen.

*"Careful, Aaslo. Delusions of grandeur are a sign of an unhealthy mind."*

"I suppose you know all about the mind, do you?"

*"It's all I've got."*

Aaslo ignored the twinge of guilt caused by Mathias's jab and used Ina's power to reach toward the rune. It was a struggle to keep the *other* powers from escaping with it. They clawed at him as if angered they weren't invited to the party. Ina's power slid over the rune like water lapping at the shore. He tried again. The power sluiced across the stone, happily caressing the rune, then slipped away.

"It won't stick," he grumbled as he tried a third time.

Ijen said, "It's unclear how the power of the original magi worked. It's said they didn't need the evergates to travel. Therefore, they wouldn't have needed the runes. Later generations of magi created them to give their power guidance. Ina's power probably doesn't recognize it. Try telling it what the rune means."

Aaslo wondered how he was supposed to *tell* power anything but didn't argue with the prophet. He held the power over the rune as he explained to himself what it was he was trying to do. The power churned in confusion. In that moment, it felt as if the power were really alive. He imagined standing in one location and then in another. He had never been to the citadel, though, so he couldn't picture how it would look when he got there. Then he realized he didn't need to tell the power where to go, he only needed it to connect to the rune. The evergate was supposed to open the portal to the right place, so as long as he was connected to it, he would go there, too. At least, he hoped that was how it worked. With that realization, Ina's power latched onto the rune as if it feared being left behind.

"It's done," he said.

Teza and Ijen presumably went through a similar process to tether their powers to the not-quite-dead and *undead* horses and guards. Then someone activated the gate. Aaslo wasn't sure which one had done it, since his mind abruptly began to swirl. No, he decided, it was the room that was swirling. The shards of color contracted and expanded and began moving around him in disjointed chaos. Just when he began to think that something had gone terribly wrong, it all stopped, and he fell to his knees. With closed eyes, he inhaled deeply and exhaled slowly hoping to settle his churning stomach. When he opened them again, he could see that the colorful shards were gone, and everything had turned red. A moment later, a bright light appeared to his side, and his vision began to shift. He blinked several times as his eyes adjusted.

"You'll get used to it," said Teza with a pat to his back. "Everyone feels that way the first time. You made it through, though. To be honest, I was kind of worried you wouldn't."

"You didn't think I would make it, but you let me go through with it anyway?"

"It didn't seem you would take *no* for an answer," she said as she stood and walked through an open doorway.

Aaslo glanced around the room and saw Ijen watching him but giving nothing away of his thoughts. Greylan, Rostus, and the horses were all exactly as they had been before activating the evergate. Teza called from somewhere in the corridor beyond the room.

"Hurry up and bring those horses back. I don't want to sit around the receiving room all day."

Aaslo was about to protest that it wasn't so easy bringing creatures back from the dead, but then he realized it was—at least, it was when *he* held the souls. It did seem as though the achievement deserved a bit more fanfare, though.

*"Is the forester frustrated with the lack of pomp? Do you need an award?"*

"Of course not," Aaslo grumped as he stood. "I was thinking of the souls. It seems like they're deserving of more respect."

*"You barely respect people when they're alive. Why should it be different when they're dead?"*

"I respect people—those who are deserving of respect, anyway."

*"We'll have to agree to disagree."*

Frustrated, Aaslo wrangled the souls he was carrying and shoved them back into the horses' bodies. Although he wasn't gentle, he was careful to make sure the correct souls went into their respective vessels. Dolt's soul was being ornery, as was to be expected, and didn't seem to want to leave him. When it finally relented, it tried to enter Ijen instead. Aaslo snatched it back and thrust it into the horse's ugly self.

Dolt abruptly rolled to his feet, then snapped at Aaslo. Aaslo didn't know if the horses remembered being dead, but the stubborn steed certainly awoke in a foul mood. Aaslo was thankful that he awoke at all.

"Hmm, I see your plan worked," said Ijen. "I suppose I must prepare myself for the events to come."

"What events?"

"Those that you will cause," said Ijen.

Aaslo raised a finger to the prophet. "Look, I am not the *cause* of any of this. I am only trying to fulfill Mathias's role in the prophecy as best I can."

Ijen met his gaze and with unusual clarity said, "*He* was the chosen one. *You* are not. I'd say you will fail and that you are doomed, but the two states are not necessarily mutual."

"That makes no sense," Aaslo grumbled as he grabbed Dolt's reins and led him through the doorway to join Teza in the corridor. He stopped at her side as his gaze roved the soaring lancet arches of the ceiling, then dropped down to the polished floor. He was amazed by the majesty of the structure that was far more impressive than the palace in Tyellí. There was not a tree or plant in sight, yet somehow it still appealed to him.

"You feel it, don't you?" said Teza.

"Feel what?"

"Like it's alive—like it wants to know you." She held her arms out and tipped her head back. "Ah! It feels so good to be here again."

"If you liked it so much, why didn't you go back?"

She dropped her arms and scowled at him. "You know why. *They* were here. They're not here now, though, and I am—so I guess I won."

"I wasn't aware it was a competition," said Ijen.

"More like a battle," muttered Teza. "When was the last time you were here?"

"I've only been here a few times—once, when I first came into my power, and twice for evaluation. They kept the students of prophecy sequestered in a sort of monastery in the far reaches of Mouvilan so that we couldn't *disturb* others with our insight."

"Huh, that makes sense."

"Yes, many share your abhorrence."

"I'm sorry. I didn't mean it like that. It's just—you know how I feel about prophecy."

"I am aware. After I received the status of magus, I avoided coming to the citadel. I had rather hoped people would forget about me since I was hiding the true nature of my prophecies."

*"It seems like all his prophecies relied on my being dead."*

"This way," said Teza. She stopped in front of an open archway that led into a courtyard. It was paved with smooth stones and dotted with small garden plots about the perimeter. A circular lawn in the center surrounded a fountain designed to look like a waterfall flowing over a cliff from a mountaintop. "We can put the horses here for now. I don't think any of the plants are poisonous. I know of no stables here."

"The Citadel of Magi has no stables? How can that be?" said Aaslo.

"Everyone comes by evergate. How would the horses get here, and where would we ride them?"

"You said there was a way to get here without using the evergate."

"Truthfully, I don't know if there is," she said without meeting his pointed stare.

*"Ha ha! I was right. She was lying all along."*

Aaslo clenched his jaw and stared at her as he considered the best way to respond without fully unloading his anger and frustration on her.

"Don't look at me like that," she said. "I was going to bring you here—at least as far as I could. I've never seen a secular in the citadel. Seculars needing to meet with the magi on official business go to the embassy outside Copedrian. The magi held court there, so to speak."

"You were taking me to this embassy?" said Aaslo.

Teza's curls bobbed as she nodded. "Yes, it was the best I could do."

"The best anyone could do," said Ijen.

Aaslo thought to ask her why she hadn't told him that in the first place but decided he already knew the answer. She was afraid he would find the embassy on his own and leave her behind.

*"You were considering kidnapping her."*

"That was *your* idea," Aaslo grumbled.

"Yes," replied Teza. "I'm sorry. I should have been honest with you."

Aaslo took a few deep breaths to calm himself, then growled, "An ivy left to grow wild cannot be reshaped without destroying what has already grown—so we'll leave it as it is."

"I don't understand," said Teza.

"Never mind," replied Aaslo. He turned to Greylan. "You and Rostus tend to the horses in the courtyard. Stay there until we have returned. If you see anyone besides one of us, come find me."

The undead guardsmen said nothing as they collected the horses' reins and led them into the courtyard. As soon as Dolt saw the fountain, he pulled away from the guard and trotted over to splash in its spray.

"He really likes water," mused Teza. Then with levity, she said, "Are you sure we can trust them with the horses?"

"I'm not sure of anything," Aaslo muttered. "Please lead us to this spell chamber or library or whatever it is you think might have some answers."

She offered a mock salute, then turned on her heel and continued down the corridor. As they followed, Aaslo said to Ijen, "Did Mathias live in any of your prophecies?"

Ijen stared straight ahead and said, "No."

"*All* your prophecies were about what would happen if he failed."

"Yes."

"And in none of those was the enemy defeated."

The prophet turned his head only enough to catch Aaslo's gaze. "Every path I have ever followed ended in death."

Aaslo considered what it must have been like for a man who experienced none of life and only visions of a future drowned in death. "That sounds like a miserable existence."

"It is the existence I was provided."

"Death isn't so bad," said an unexpected voice.

"Myra, you startled me," Aaslo said as he stopped short. Teza and Ijen continued walking but paused upon realizing he wasn't with them.

"I apologize. That was not my intent," said Myra.

"It's not your fault. Why are you here?" he said.

"I told you I would meet you."

"Yes, but *why?*"

"Am I not welcome?" she said with a feigned pout. Then her lips turned upward as though she were teasing.

Teza stormed up to him and examined the air where Myra was standing. "What is it? Is the reaper here? Make her leave."

"Why?" said Aaslo.

"Because she works for the enemy! She can't be trusted. She's a spy."

Myra's smile fell. "What she says is true, but I also would like to help you."

"Why would you help us?" he said.

"I don't agree with Axus's designs, but there is nothing I can do to stop it. And I must serve Trostili. I have no choice in the matter. I still have some amount of free will, though. Believe it or not, I do care about you— about life. I used to be a part of your world, after all. It was my home."

"So, you'll be a double agent?"

"If you'll let me."

"No. Absolutely not," said Teza. "It's a trap. She seeks to gain your trust, then lead you to your death." Teza turned to Ijen. "What does your book say about this? What about the reaper?"

Ijen tapped his book thoughtfully. "Unfortunately, none of the paths mention a reaper. I'd never even heard of them until Aaslo found her."

"*The prophet's prophecies meant I had to die, and the reaper doesn't even exist.*"

"Perhaps this is a good thing," said Aaslo. "If Myra wasn't on any of your paths, then perhaps she's part of one you haven't seen. Maybe it will lead to victory."

"I doubt that," said Myra.

"I'm afraid not," said Ijen. "I was unable to see her in my prophecy, but that doesn't mean she wasn't there."

Aaslo was frustrated with everyone's lack of hope and confidence, but he knew he should have been used to it by then.

*"Why did you wait until I died to become an optimist?"*

"I'm not an optimist. I'm a realist. If we don't try, then we might as well already be dead."

*"Are you saying that I, the chosen one, am not trying?"*

"You *are* dead. The only thing you're *trying* is my nerves." Aaslo realized that Ijen, Teza, and Myra were all staring at him with concern. He turned to Myra. "Please tell me why you're here."

She appeared anxious but graced him with a faint smile anyway. She said, "I feel that I must tell you something, but I really shouldn't."

"You must have already decided to tell me, or you wouldn't be here."

"Quite so," she said. "Axus has ordered Pithor to send the lyksvight and magus army through the evergates *now*."

Aaslo's heart lurched. It was too soon. Things were happening too fast. "Why now?"

"I don't know. He doesn't confide in me."

"What did she say?" said Teza, apparently picking up on his alarm.

Aaslo relayed the message.

"Then it's over," said Teza. "Ijen was right when he said we had to hurry. We only just got here. There's no time to destroy the gates."

"Not quite," said Myra. "Pithor isn't ready. They don't have the keys yet."

"How long do we have?" said Aaslo.

"I don't know. He wanted me to ask Axus for more time, but I refused."

"You refused? If you're truly intent on helping us, why would you do that?"

"Because Pithor believes that he *must* flood the gates now or he will anger Axus—which is true. He's more likely to make a mistake. His plans will not go well if he tries to follow through now. He'll send through the evergates a trickle of lyksvight that he currently has instead of a flood through all of them at once. Don't you see? People will have a fighting chance."

"I hear what you're saying. The problem is, there's no one to fight them. Not in Uyan anyway. King Rakith disbanded the army."

"What of your friend the marquess? Is he not amassing one?"

"That's the plan. I don't know what's truly happening there. We have no way of communicating."

Myra smiled happily. "I can help with that. I'll be your messenger."

"How?" said Aaslo. "No one else can see or speak with you."

"Mory can."

Aaslo had nearly forgotten that Mory knew Myra. He wasn't sure, though, that he could trust an agent of the enemy to deliver messages. Besides her nostalgia, she had not given him a good reason for betraying the gods.

Myra stepped forward but didn't reach out. "Please, Aaslo, let me help you."

*"She's hiding things. Never trust the dead."*

"Oh, never?" Aaslo grumbled.

*"Except me, of course."*

"How do I know you won't report everything to this Pithor or Axus?"

"I hold no love for either of them. I hate that I must help them, but I figure it doesn't really matter. The world is already doomed, and I'm afraid your efforts will be for naught; but your willingness to fight has earned my respect and admiration. I'd like to help your cause, even if I don't expect you to succeed."

Aaslo glanced at Teza, who was judging him with her eyes, and Ijen, who was poised to begin writing in his book. The prophet seemed to have little opinion about anything, and Teza had already made hers clear. Aaslo retreated to a corner where he could think without the burden of demanding gazes. He dearly wished Mathias were there. He had always been better at reading people.

*"I like her."*

Aaslo frowned. "You said not to trust her."

*"I didn't say you should trust her, only that I like her. You don't have to trust a person to use her, though."*

"I've never heard you speak of using people. That's awfully harsh."

*"She's not really a person, is she? She's dead."*

"Maybe, but she clearly has feelings."

*"You're the leader of a rebellion, Aaslo. You're expected to use people. It's your job."*

"My *job* is to be a forester."

*"Think of them as your trees. Cultivate them, then put them to good use."*

Aaslo sighed. He knew he wasn't cut out for the position of the chosen one, but it would do no good to complain about what couldn't be changed. He returned to his companions, who stood silently awaiting his decision. Myra was apart from the others, although she needn't have bothered. They couldn't even see her.

"Very well," he said. "Myra can deliver messages to Mory, who will hopefully be able to get them to the appropriate people."

"Excellent," she said. "Where should I begin?"

"Tell them we have reached the citadel, then inform them of Pithor's plans. Find out where they're going and how the recruitment and training is coming along."

"Is there anything else?"

"Have you heard news regarding the destruction of Dovermyer? Do you know who attacked?"

"I'm afraid not."

"Then that will do for now. Are you sure you don't mind?"

"It's my pleasure."

*"I think she means that, but why?"*

Aaslo tried to ignore Mathias's comment that echoed his own thoughts. He said, "Thank you, Myra. Hopefully, we will see you again soon."

Myra smiled, then vanished. He muttered, "Remind me to ask her how she does that."

"Does what?" said Teza.

"Travels between places like that. She's gone."

Teza narrowed her eyes at the air in front of Aaslo. "What if she's a spy?"

"What if she is?" said Aaslo as he motioned for Teza to continue leading the way down the corridor. As they walked, he said, "It's not like we can do anything about it. No one can see her but me, and there's no guarantee of that. She could be watching us at any time."

Ijen said, "Even if she's not, that doesn't mean there aren't others."

*"Good point."*

"We've always been at a disadvantage," replied Aaslo. "Perhaps it is our one saving grace that the Berru and Axus don't see us as a genuine threat. The fact that we are destined by prophecy to lose may cause them to extend little effort in trying to stop us."

"Yet they will still win," said Ijen.

They paused outside an unusual door with a dark wood trim and multiple shades of wooden inlays that looked like books and scrolls resting in a bookcase. Before entering, Aaslo turned to Ijen and said, "If you feel that way, why are you with us?"

"As I told you. It's in the story." Aaslo opened his mouth to protest again, but Ijen held up a hand. "I know, I know," he said, "it's not a story. We all have our roles to play, and mine is with you. At least I will get to live an adventure before my end."

Aaslo knew Ijen's words were supposed to be placating, but they only burrowed deeper under his skin. He said, "Hear this, Prophet. A man who plants a tree expecting it to die will not give it the care it needs, and his assumption is destined to be proven correct."

"I am well acquainted with the notion of the self-fulfilling prophecy."

"This isn't about prophecy," said Aaslo. "It's about spirit and hope. Cromley said that a man who goes into battle believing he has nothing to live for is unlikely to survive."

"Even a man who wants to live can die," said Ijen.

"Yes, but he will fight to live and has a greater chance of succeeding."

"That's not applicable where prophecy is concerned."

"I'm not willing to accept that."

Ijen tilted his head and looked at Aaslo curiously. "It's strange. Everything I know about you points to you being a practical man, yet you choose not to believe what is set out clearly before you."

"I do not see these prophecies, so I have only the claims of others that they are true. I'd rather not stake my life—or that of everyone and everything else—on their validity."

Aaslo pulled the door open and stormed into the dark room. It had no windows, and if there were lamps or torches, he could not see them. For an instant, the room flashed red, and he could see the shapes of tables, scroll racks, and bookshelves. Just as light bloomed from glowing stones set into the walls and ceiling, Teza's arm abruptly slipped through the air and whacked him in his scaly shoulder.

"Oops," she said mockingly. "I was lighting the stones and didn't see you there."

Aaslo frowned at her and grumbled, "Probably hurt you more than me."

By the way she clenched and shook her hand, he knew he was right. She lifted her chin and strutted through the room pointing at things. "These are the historical references, here are the few prophetic scrolls the students were permitted to study, and over there are books on spells and enchantments. In the back are a number of tomes on science and engineering." She pointed to a loft accessible via a winding staircase. "Up there you will find books on philosophy, culture, languages, and even a few tales of fiction."

Aaslo surveyed the room as his vision adjusted to the light. "This is the student library? I don't think we will find what we need in here. There must be another library accessible only to the magi."

"There is. You're standing on it."

Aaslo looked down to see that he was in the center of a mosaic similar to the one in Yarding that had descended into the sublevel to the evergate. "Great. Come here and activate it."

"I can't," she said. "I was never raised to full magus."

Aaslo looked to Ijen.

"I doubt it will respond to me since I neither studied nor was raised to magus here, but I will try." They gathered together on top of the mosaic and waited. After a minute of watching Ijen stare at the floor, he looked up at them and said, "I can't unlock it."

"*How* do we gain access? How does it know if you are an authorized magus?"

Teza said, "There's a ceremony. I've seen it a few times when a fledgling was raised to magus. A plinth stands in the center of the citadel. Everyone gathers around it and focuses their power on the runes carved into the sides. Once it is sufficiently powered, a fire ignites atop the plinth. Then the high sorceress does some kind of spell that I don't know, and the person being raised casts a similar spell into the flame. The enchantments on the citadel and those connected to it will then recognize the new magus."

"Is this something we can perform?" said Aaslo.

"It requires the power of many," said Teza. "Plus, I don't know the spells."

"I know the spells," said Ijen. "I performed them during my time at the Hall of Prophets. It would still require immense power, though—much more than a couple of magi could provide." He eyed Aaslo speculatively. "Or perhaps we need only one."

"What do you mean?" said Aaslo.

"If you possess the power of the original magi, yours could be sufficient to perform the ritual."

*"I was supposed to be a powerful magus."*

"I didn't ask for this," said Aaslo.

Ijen raised an eyebrow. "Technically, you did."

"That's not what I meant. Maybe we could find some tools and smash through the floor. Can either of you use your power to blast a hole through it?"

"Brute force will not open this door," said Ijen. "It's protected against such things. If you try, it will strike back and likely kill you."

*"You've become part of a dangerous world. Even the doors want to kill you."*

"It's always been a dangerous world. Foresters are well acquainted with the dangers. *You* were sheltered."

"Yes, perhaps I was," said Ijen, "but only from physical danger." He tapped his temple. "I watched the terrors of the future in here."

*"He's always so cheerful."*

Aaslo turned to Teza. "Where's this plinth?"

"This way," she said as she sauntered out of the room.

As they walked through the labyrinth of corridors and took what Teza said were shortcuts through rooms, Aaslo committed to memory as much detail about his surroundings as possible. He decided that either the citadel was much larger than he had expected, or Teza was intentionally trying to confuse him. They took stairs up and then down again and made multiple right turns followed by the same number of left turns, but when he finally recognized a room through which they had already passed, he stopped her. "Where are you taking us?"

Teza smiled. "To the dining hall, of course."

"Why would you take us there?"

"Because that's where we're going, isn't it? Truthfully, I've been a little confused. At first, I was taking you to the dormitories, then I remembered you wanted to see the spell chambers. As soon as we got there, I realized it wasn't the spell chambers you wanted to see but the library. Halfway there, I remembered we had already seen the library and thought you'd like to get dinner."

"Dinner? Look around, Teza. No one is here. They won't be serving dinner. You're supposed to be taking us to the plinth."

Teza scrunched her face and blinked several times. "I *am* taking you to the plinth."

"You just said—"

"Never mind that," said Ijen. "I know what's happening. The plinth is protected from students and visitors who would seek it without permission. The more we search for it, the more confused we become."

"I didn't feel confused," said Aaslo. "At least, not about where we were *supposed* to be going."

"You were merely following Teza. *She* was the one looking for it."

Ijen began waving his hands in the air and muttering something unintelligible. Aaslo had seen him do the same while casting other spells, and he wondered if the words actually meant anything. Teza rarely said anything when casting spells. After a moment, a glowing web of symbols and lines appeared in front of Aaslo's eyes. It was shaped like a small dome or cap. Ijen placed the cap over Teza's head as she looked at him anxiously. As soon as he released the cap, it disappeared, and Teza shivered.

"That should protect your mind from most of the plinth spell's effects. You must remain focused on your destination or you will get confused again. We'll help remind you."

"Um, thank you. It's not going to damage my brain, is it?"

"No, it's simply a shield from mental attacks."

"I'd think you'd want to wear that all the time," said Aaslo.

"It's not practical most of the time. It prevents most spells from getting into your head—even the ones you want. In addition to a number of other limitations, it will prevent her from being able to see anything written in spell script, and mind speak will be impossible. The former would be a severe setback, especially for a healer, but I suppose the latter is no longer important since the magi who might use it are gone."

"Mind speak?" said Aaslo.

"A spell used to communicate directly from mind to mind without the use of sound. Fledglings are not taught the spell for obvious reasons."

"Can you remove the shield?" said Teza.

"It will dissolve on its own, usually in less than an hour, so we'd best be going."

"Right this way," she said and then paused. "Where are we going again?"

# CHAPTER 9

MYROPA WAS PERPLEXED WHEN SHE FIRST APPEARED AT THE MARQUESS'S estate. Not a soul was in sight, all the tents were missing or collapsed, and the shelters were abandoned. She spied a vight atop the rubble of the mansion. It's taut black skin and wild hair seemed to absorb the last rays of sunlight as it searched for something. It glanced up and hissed at her, then bounded down the far side and disappeared.

She wondered why a vight had been sent to that place. Without any people to kill or torment, it served no purpose. Perhaps it had arrived, as she had, expecting to find the marquess's camp. The vight was not familiar with that world, though, and would have little chance of tracking them on its own. She knew people, though, and people took roads. It was harder for her to find living people without the help of the Fates, but the closer she got, the more she could sense them. Some individuals, those whose souls were familiar, were easier for her to find. She knew Mory's soul.

She took a step and was a few miles down the road. When she saw that they were not there, she stepped a few more miles. With such a large caravan that also consisted of families with children, they would not be traveling fast; but as the sun was close to setting, she figured they had probably already stopped to prepare for the night. She continued snapping down the road a few miles at a time until she finally felt a tug. It was Mory. Somehow his soul still called for her to take him. It was faint, a whisper, but it was there.

Myropa snapped to Mory's side. He was washing his face and hands in a creek and didn't sense her at first. She waited until he was finished before she spoke.

"Hello, Mory."

The boy abruptly tumbled forward, his palms digging into the river stones as he became submerged up to his shoulders. He coughed and sputtered while pulling himself out of the water. It took more than a little effort on the slick, muddy bank. He raised his filthy hands to look at them, then plunged them back into the water and scrubbed vigorously.

"H-hi, Myra. You startled me."

"I'm sorry. I didn't mean to."

"No, I know. It's not your fault."

"I'm beginning to think that's not true. This is the second time today that I have startled someone, and that's quite a lot since few people can see me."

Mory abruptly stood and took a few eager steps toward her as he wiped his hands on his pants. "You've seen Aaslo?"

"Yes, a short time ago."

"Thank the gods, he's alive."

"I doubt they have anything to do with it. They're working toward the opposite effect."

"Right. Of course. I forgot. I still have trouble believing the gods want us dead. I mean, we're taught to revere the gods, to do as they command. Now they say *die*, and what are we to do?"

Myropa wanted to wrap her arms around the boy, but she settled for a nod. "It is confusing if you see them as worthy of worship."

"You don't?"

"I know them now—at least to some extent—and I know that they are often vain and greedy and flawed, just as we are."

"I didn't realize—"

"How could you? It's politics. Their realm is much like our own in that regard."

"Their realm? Do you not live there?"

Myropa's gaze fell beyond the few short trees and shrubs to where the caravan of guards, newly enlisted soldiers, and refugees had set up camp for the night. "No, I do not live there. I do not live at all. I never sleep, never eat, never rest my feet. Sometimes . . . sometimes time slips away when I'm not looking. I think maybe I forget to exist." She shook herself out of her morbid reverie and looked at him again. "I came to give you a message."

"You have a message for *me*?"

"Not you, exactly. I suppose it's for the marquess, but he can't see me. I need you to speak for me."

"I'm not sure if he'll see the likes of me. Is it a message from Aaslo?"

"Yes, I have volunteered to carry messages between you."

Mory looked at her with skepticism. "I like you, Myra. I do. But aren't you working for the gods?"

"Please, Mory. I want to help."

He stared at her a moment longer, then sighed. "All right. I suppose it's not up to me anyway. I'll go to the marquess for you."

Myropa watched with curiosity as Mory picked up a brigandine and strapped it over his torso. It was too large, and he groaned under the weight of it. Next, he grabbed a thick wooden stick cleaned of bark and cut to the length of a sword. As they walked, he swung the stick back and forth, then switched hands and did the same. She said, "I didn't think you were old enough to enlist."

"I'm not, but I don't want to die neither. Bear says I have to do this to get strong enough to use a sword."

"Everyone must die someday," she said.

Mory offered her a lopsided grin that didn't reach his haunted eyes. "I want to live first. I survived death once. I doubt I'll have such luck again. Mayhap next time some other reaper will come for me. They might not possess your kindness."

"I don't know if it was kindness," said Myropa. "A quick death might have been better than the things to come."

Mory said nothing as they walked into the camp. It was well guarded around the perimeter, organized, and decently stocked. It appeared that the seaside town near Dovermyer, once abandoned during the blight, had been raided for anything that could be carried. People went about the business of survival, plucking small birds, skinning rabbits, and using whatever materials could be found to construct temporary shelters. Since wood was scarce on the plains, campfires were small and only used for cooking. Dogs sniffed around the wagons for scraps that might have fallen to the ground, men and women laughed and teased each other, and a group of children ran through the tall grass on the other side of the road. It was an oddly peaceful scene.

A guard stood at the entrance of one of the few tents in the camp. He was a big, burly man with entirely too much body hair but a pleasant smile. Mory stopped swinging his stick and propped it on his shoulder. "Hi, Bear," he said. "I need to see the marquess."

"Oh? What business does a fawn have with a stag?"

Mory's face screwed up in adolescent protest. "Stop treating me like a child. My life's been hard, and my death was harder."

Bear's smile faded. "Be that as it may, I'd like to keep you from death fer as long as possible. The marquess is in a mood. You'd best not be botherin' him right now."

"This is important," Mory whined.

"Be gone with you, boy, before I add more chores to yer list."

"You don't understand. I have a message from Aaslo."

"How would *you* be gettin' a message from the forester? He's gone far to the east."

"I just do. Trust me. The marquess will want to hear it."

A glowing tether abruptly snapped into place at Myropa's core. The Fates were calling her away, and she had yet to deliver her message. "Mory, hurry," she said. "I must go."

"I'm *trying*. He won't let me pass."

"Who you be talkin' to, boy?"

"Please, Bear. It's urgent."

Bear sighed. "All right, but it'll be yer head if the marquess gets angry."

"The marquess isn't like that. He's a good man."

Bear stepped aside and pulled back the canvas flap. "Even good men have their bad days."

A voice lashed out from inside the dark tent. "What is it? Close the flap!"

"Yes, my lord. Sorry, my lord. The boy's sayin' he has a message from the forester."

A cot creaked as a shadowy figure sat up and turned up the miniscule flame in the oil lamp that hung at the side. "I doubt that, but come in already, and close that flap!" The marquess squinted up at Mory, and it was obvious he was in pain. "You have a message, you say?"

"Well, not me, exactly. Myra is here."

"Myra? Oh, right. The reaper. You say she's here? She'd best not be coming for me."

"Are you unwell?" said Mory.

"It's this blasted headache—feels like my skull is set to explode. I can't even sleep."

"I'm sorry. I can see if anyone has some feverfew or valerian."

"What do you know of such things?"

"Peck was friends with this girl—"

"Never you mind. My manservant Vigold has already gone to check. Seems he's been gone an age. If he takes any longer, I'll see that the reaper carries him with her."

"It's that bad?"

The marquess rubbed his temples. "I apologize for my brusque tone. If the reaper is really here, perhaps she should deliver her message already."

Mory looked at Myropa expectantly. She told him of the deal she had made with Aaslo to deliver messages and of the forester's progress. After Mory relayed the message, the marquess sat in silence. Myropa began to wonder if the man had fallen asleep when the tether tugged at her again, this time more urgently. She knew if she didn't heed its call soon, she would be pulled away regardless. Such travels were rather painful when forced.

The marquess finally roused and said, "These messages are to come from an agent of the enemy through the lips of a boy, a thief, no less."

"I'm no longer a thief," said Mory. "And I didn't choose this. I'm the only one besides Aaslo who can see her. She says she has no choice in serving the enemy, but she *wants* to assist us."

The marquess lay back down on the cot and placed his arm over his eyes. "Beggars cannot be choosers, as the saying goes."

"She says that Aaslo wants to know where we've decided to go."

"So she can arrange for an ambush?" he snapped. "No, I think not. Aaslo can know once we've arrived."

Mory glanced at Myropa apologetically, then said, "She can travel at will. She could be spying on us at any time. There's no point in trying to keep it from her."

"Maybe she knows, maybe she doesn't. I don't have to *help* her cause. If she desires to spy on us, she can bloody well work for it." The man groaned, then sighed. "Please forgive me. I should not use such language, especially in front of a lady—assuming she's really here, that is, and that she really *is* a lady. I only have your word for it."

"And Aaslo's," said Mory.

"Right," the marquess grumbled. "A forester who left his forest, carries a head in a bag, raises the dead, and speaks to invisible people."

"You doubt Aaslo now?" Mory sounded as shocked as Myropa felt.

"No, no. I am not myself. He has my support as always. Ignore my ill-bred ramblings. Reaper, if you can hear me, tell Aaslo that we should arrive at our destination within the month. Travel is slow with this many people. We are recruiting along the way."

Myropa was about to speak when she was suddenly ripped through the veil. It was as if she had been torn asunder—with every piece of her body traveling separately. Although she arrived at her destination instantly, it felt like hours. She inhaled sharply, a breath she didn't need. It was an instinct held over from her past life, a failed effort to alleviate her torment.

"What took you so long?" snapped the familiar voice of an irritated goddess. "I've been waiting forever."

Myropa surveyed her surroundings as she panted through the pain. She was standing on a rocky bluff covered in snow. Far below, the sea failed to crash upon the rocks as might be expected. It was a frozen sheet of ice for as far as she could see. At her feet was a body—or what was left of it. She looked up at the goddess who glowed with golden light, a beacon in an otherwise bleak landscape.

Arayallen pointed to the body and said, "Bring him out. I have questions. Find out what killed him."

The tether at Myropa's core tugged again. It was connected to the savaged remains at her feet. She searched the goddess's dispassionate expression for any indication as to why she might care about an old man—a human—and how he had died in the middle of nowhere. She turned to the body and beckoned the man's soul to join her with unspoken promises of a glorious afterlife. It responded with gusto. Those who perished in pain usually did.

"Wh-where am I? What happened?" said the old man who had just vacated his body. Myropa gazed at him with compassion, then motioned for him to look down. The man recoiled. "What is *that*?"

She said, "I'm sorry, sir, but that is you."

"What! Am I dead?"

"You were killed. Do you remember?"

"No, I—wait, yes. Yes, I do remember. It was horrible. There was so much pain."

His eyes abruptly widened, and he surged forward, passing through her in a chilling instance that was always disturbing. He stopped after several paces. Although his clothes had been shredded and his boots were missing, she knew he wouldn't feel the cold. In truth, his appearance was merely an illusion. She briefly wondered if it was likewise true of her own.

The man's gaze searched the snowy landscape with fervor. "My family. Where are they? Did they survive?"

Myropa appeared at his side, examined his strained features, then turned her attention to the frigid plain. Rubbly mounds of black rock extruded through the otherwise undisturbed snow. A sharp wind carried flurries across the landscape in a rolling tide of white. The icy sea breeze might have been torturous had they been capable of feeling it.

"Survive what?"

"I don't know," said the man, turning to her. His pale blue eyes were stricken with terror. "I've never seen the like—a demon from the hells it was. It was the size of a horse and black, at first, with the body of a snake. It had spines like swords down its back and long, thin arms that ended in sharp claws. It had a mouth big enough to swallow a dog and rows of pointed teeth that seemed to never end. The worst was its eyes, though. They were the eyes of a man, I swear."

"What happened?"

"My wife, our young daughter and infant son, and I were traveling with friends." In a sudden panic, he said, "Where are they?"

"I don't see them," said Myropa. "Perhaps I'll find them when we're finished."

"Who are you?"

Myropa glanced toward Arayallen, who made it obvious that her patience was wearing thin. "We'll get to that in a minute. You are no longer in danger, though. Tell me what happened to you."

The man glanced back at his ravaged body. "No, I suppose I'm not. The bay froze early this year, and we were hoping to get farther inland before the storms came. It's easy to get lost out here. There's no way to orient yourself, you see? It's best to follow the coast to the river, then turn inland. We were huddling in our coats, our hoods pulled tight against the snow and wind. That's probably why we didn't see it right away. Josen and Lobat saw it first. The *thing* came up the cliff. They yelled for the women and children to run. Its belly turned bright blue when it attacked. It was vicious. We tried to hold it off, but I knew we were going to die. Our knives and spears weren't nearly enough. You'd need an army to kill that thing. In the fight, Josen went over the cliff. I guess I died next. I don't know what happened to Lobat."

Myropa looked around again. There was no sign of the passing of people. No clothes or supplies. No dead horses or livestock. And no bodies besides the one belonging to this man.

"Are you sure the attack took place *here*?" she said.

The man seemed to take her meaning. His brow furrowed as he surveyed the area. "I don't know. It all looks the same."

"I've heard enough," said Arayallen. "You can take him now. At least the trip wasn't a *complete* waste."

While the man was preoccupied with his thoughts, Myropa placed one of her spheres into the stream of the tether that bound them. The man disappeared, and the sphere began to glow with a pale orange light. Arayallen looked at her curiously but said nothing.

Myropa said, "You came here on your own?"

The goddess huffed. "Yes, no thanks to you." She held out her hand. A large iridescent beetle rested in her palm. "You forgot this in the swamp. Don't lose it again." The beetle unfurled its wings and flew to Myropa's shoulder. "I should not have had to expend so much energy just to visit this little world."

"Why did you?" said Myropa.

"I had a suspicion. I needed to know what killed this man."

"Why? I mean, why do you care about this one human?"

"I don't. I care about what killed him."

"What was it? It sounds like a terrible creature."

"It does, doesn't it? The things humans come up with. Hmm, maybe I'll design something like it."

"Are you saying he was lying?"

"No, I'm saying we have no idea how he *actually* died."

"But he just told us—"

"He told us what he remembers. You recall my gallery?"

"How could I forget?"

Arayallen smiled fondly. "Yes, it is quite unforgettable." Then her expression soured. "One of my prototypes is missing. I believe it was responsible for that man's demise, but it was never meant to exist in this world. It shouldn't have lived at all. I designed it for a different realm, one where the rules of reality don't work like they do here. You wouldn't understand. Regardless, I decided it was too advanced for that world. It would have thrown the entire realm out of balance."

"But you said the man wasn't killed by the creature."

"He wasn't killed by the creature he *described*. Oh, for Celestria's sake. Will you give it a name already so we can stop calling it *the creature*?"

"Me?"

"We've gone over this, Reaper. Do you see anyone else here to name it?"

"Uh—"

Arayallen stared at her expectantly as Myropa's mind drew a complete blank. She glanced around her for a source of inspiration. Rocks. Ice. Wind. Dead man. She looked back to the goddess, but her mind had provided nothing. The wind released a howl as it swept up the cliff. "Wind," Myropa mindlessly muttered.

"Wind?" said Arayallen with disdain. "You can't call it *wind*. Wind is already a thing."

Myropa glanced toward the dead man. "Uh . . . de-e-man."

"Wind demon?" Arayallen tapped her perfect lips with a slender finger. "That's oddly fitting. Very well. The wind demon lives in the space *between* reality. You see, there's the reality of things you know and the reality of things you don't know."

"I don't understand."

"Of course you don't. Look there." She pointed toward the sea. "You know there are fish in the sea. There could be one fish or millions of fish. The wind demon lives in the space where both could be true."

"O-k-a-a-y . . ."

"It communicates with its mind. Its thoughts become your thoughts. Therefore, it can make you perceive either reality or anything in between."

"So, this wind demon can make you see things that aren't really there?"

"See, hear, feel, taste—it makes all of it true to your mind. Do you see?"

"I think so. You said it lives between what you know and don't know. Does that mean it can't change what you know to be true?"

"Yes, but you must be careful in your assumption about what you know. For example, you know that I am beautiful. The wind demon cannot make you see me as less. However, you also know that I can change my form. You don't know which forms I might take. Therefore, it could make you see me as something else because you don't know that it cannot be true."

"So, the man whose soul I just took, we don't know what actually happened to him, but we do know the wind demon was involved?"

"Yes."

"How do you know?"

"Because I have never created a creature like the one the man described."

"How did you know to come here? And how did you know that *I* would reap his soul?"

"I didn't know it would be you. It is an odd coincidence, though, since you are the only one with whom I've actually spoken. As far as coming here, I felt when my creation received a soul. As I said, it was a prototype. It had no soul prior to coming to this world."

"You felt when it was born?"

"Yes, I suppose you could put it that way. But since I was not the one who placed it here, I don't know how that came to pass."

"How long has it been missing?"

Arayallen pursed her lips. "I don't know. I last walked that hall about two weeks ago, but that was in Celestria. I wasn't paying attention to the time. It could have been days or months here."

"Do you know where it is now?"

"Unfortunately, no—which means it now resonates with the energy of *this* world. The only way that can be so is if it was born to a creature of this world." The goddess growled with frustration. "Axus goes too far once again. He is not satisfied with the power of death, so he seeks to usurp the power of birth as well?"

"You think this is Axus's doing?"

"Who else? What better way to wreak havoc than to release a wind demon into the world?"

"How do we find it? What does it look like?"

"I don't know on both accounts. It will look like whatever creature birthed it."

"So, it could be *anything*? It'll be an infant, though."

"Not necessarily. It may look like a creature familiar to this world, but it is not one. It exists within its own reality. It will be of the age it considers itself to be."

"You said it has a soul. Where did the soul come from?"

"Where does any soul come from?"

Myropa felt it odd that the goddess stared at her as if she might actually hold the answer. "I don't know," she said.

"Well, neither do I. I've wondered, though—Axus gains his power when souls pass through the veil. That means power is released—or generated—in the process. What if souls are simply a piece of the veil that is torn away when a being is brought from our realm to another?"

"I—"

"No, I don't expect you to answer. It's just a hypothesis. In truth, none of us really knows. I've done what I came here to do. Now, it's time I returned to Celestria."

"Wait," said Myropa. "Aren't you here to take back the wind demon?"

"I would if I could, but I cannot."

"Then why did you come here?"

"So that you would know."

"But *why*?"

"I know you're helping the forester. You can tell him what you've discovered. Now, give me a lift back to Celestria so I don't have to expend more energy."

"How am I—" Myropa jumped when the beetle she had forgotten on her shoulder buzzed its wings. "Oh."

Myropa closed her eyes and released the breath of life that held her in Aldrea. She slipped through the veil unhindered and stepped onto smooth marble. As soon as they were back in the fifth palace, Arayallen acted as though Myropa no longer existed. She sauntered toward Trostili's quarters without so much as a farewell. She paused and turned back to look at Myropa. Myropa momentarily thought the goddess might grace her with the simple courtesy of a farewell.

"When you see Disevy, tell him I need to speak with him," she said.

Myropa was confused. She had no plans to meet with Disevy. "I haven't seen him. Last I went to his temple, he wasn't there."

"Hmm, I wonder where he's gotten to. I haven't seen him in a while." She shrugged.

"Seen who?" said Trostili as he stepped from his room wearing a splendid silver-and-blue set of armor. He effortlessly plucked Arayallen from her feet and spun her around before pressing his lips to hers.

Arayallen passionately returned the kiss, then playfully pushed him away. "Disevy. I need to speak with him."

Trostili pulled her back into his arms to nuzzle her neck. "I don't care for you to say his name while my kiss still wets your lips."

"Are you jealous? Would you rather I call out his name once your kiss is dried and forgotten?"

He brushed a thumb over Arayallen's plumped lips and said, "Dried, perhaps—never forgotten."

Arayallen tilted her head and grinned. "No, never forgotten."

He growled with pleasure, then said, "I haven't seen him. Perhaps he decided to be done with us all and left to play with his reaper."

Myropa's cheeks would have flushed if they hadn't been frozen.

"I doubt it," said Arayallen, "since she's right here."

Trostili's gaze followed Arayallen's to land on Myropa. "Ah, you're here. Good. I have a task for you."

"Of course," said Myropa as a gush of power swept over her.

"I've inspired a human to create the most interesting suit of armor. I need you to make sure that forester finds it."

"Why would you want him to have it?" said Myropa.

Trostili's eyes grew wide, and he looked at Arayallen with awe. "Did my ears deceive me? Does the reaper dare question *me*?"

The ice in Myropa's veins began to crackle as she shivered in fear of the consequences of her folly.

Arayallen patted Trostili on the chest and offered him a playful smile. "You know these humans. They're so inquisitive. It makes them easier to inspire, does it not? Come, let's relax together in the pool." She took his hand and began leading him back through the doorway.

Trostili paused and called back to Myropa. "He can find the smith in the human city of Chelis. His name is . . . ah . . . Bordeshi, Bondeski— something like that."

As the two disappeared, Myropa frowned. Chelis was in Mouvilan, nowhere near Uyan. She wondered how she was to get Aaslo to Chelis and if she should follow through with Trostili's orders at all. She was bound by the Fates to serve him, but he was in league with Axus. She couldn't help but wonder why he would provide Aaslo with armor designed by the God of War, himself.

# CHAPTER 10

THE CEREMONIAL CHAMBER WAS SMALL COMPARED TO MOST OF THE rooms in the citadel. Aaslo couldn't imagine more than forty or fifty people fitting into the room, much less the entirety of the former population of the place. There was no furniture or décor besides the rune carvings on the stone walls. A plinth stood in the center of the room. It was about waist height and had only a small platform just wide enough for a single person to stand. The stones in the floor were arranged so as to define concentric rings of alternating colors that radiated from the plinth's base to the walls.

Teza pointed to the rings. "The participants stand on the rings. The person being raised to magus stands there on the inner ring, and the high sorceress stands on the same ring on the opposite side. The spells are cast at the runes carved along the circumference of the plinth."

"All right. You want me to cast this spell at the plinth, then?"

"Yes," said Ijen. "Unfortunately, you are the only person here with the power to do so—we hope."

*"My power."*

"Your power would have been different," mumbled Aaslo.

"Yes, and that may be an issue," said Ijen. "We'll have to see. You'll also need to cast the high sorceress's spell *and* the receiving spell if you want to gain access to the doors for yourself."

"You're saying I have to figure out *how* to cast a spell, then cast three very powerful ones in unison?"

"Essentially, yes."

*"A task worthy of the stubborn fortitude of a forester."*

"I'm not stubborn, I'm determined."

"Good," said Ijen. "Then you will not despair."

"I didn't say that," Aaslo grumbled.

*"Despair is a forester's lifeblood."*

"It's no such thing. We're perfectly happy in our forests."

Ijen and Teza shared a glance.

Teza said, "Uh, is the reaper back?"

"No, why do you ask?"

"Because you're talking nonsense."

*"Nonsense is a forester's second language."*

"Will you be quiet?" Aaslo snapped.

"Excuse me?" said Teza as she took a step toward him with her fists clenched.

Aaslo held up his hands. "I wasn't talking to you. Calm down."

She crossed her arms. "Is he giving you trouble again?"

Aaslo swallowed his embarrassment as he looked at her, then glanced toward Ijen. The prophet's gaze was on the sack dangling from Aaslo's belt. "Never mind that."

"Why don't you get rid of it? You don't need it anymore," she said.

*"Yeah, Aaslo. Toss me aside. Bury me in the ground like my body or throw me back in the river."*

"I lost him once. I can't bear to lose him again. He may be dead, but he is always with me. Wouldn't you do the same if it were someone you loved?"

"I—I never cared about anyone that much," said Teza, "but I definitely wouldn't carry my best friend's head everywhere I went."

Ijen said, "I never had anyone to care about. The life of a prophet is not a sentimental one."

"Well, this was his task," said Aaslo, "and he's either going to complete it with me or I'll join him."

"Fine," said Teza. "But if I die, I don't want you carrying around any of my body parts. Got it?"

Aaslo grunted, "I wouldn't dream of it," and somehow, she looked both relieved and offended.

*"You'll never win with her."*

"Don't I know."

Teza narrowed her eyes, no doubt wondering what Mathias was saying this time. She huffed and said, "Let's get on with this. Prophet Ijen, please teach Aaslo the spells."

The spells were not unlike those rituals and poems taught to him by Magdelay over the years. He learned quickly. He knew the skill was not in the formation of the spells, but rather in the casting of them. Ijen explained that fledglings and inexperienced magi often had trouble holding the spells in place while powering them. The greater the power, the harder they were to hold.

"And I'm expected to wield the power of dozens of magi while holding *three* of these spells?" he said.

Ijen spread his hands. "It is the only way this will work."

"That's like asking a single man to lift a fully grown fallen oak."

"It'll be much more difficult than that."

"Wonderful," muttered Aaslo. "Should we do it now?"

Ijen tilted his head. "Perhaps it would be best to wait until you are rested. It has been a long time since any of us slept well."

"Or had a bath, for that matter," said Teza as she sniffed her own shirt.

"We should take advantage of the facilities while we are here. There are plenty of beds and washrooms, and I am sure the larder is still full."

Aaslo felt a wash of fatigue settle over him. They had initially hoped to rest in Yarding, but the city had been devastated. "What of our urgency?" he said.

Ijen shrugged. "I doubt one night will matter much."

"Are you saying that as a weary traveler or a prophet?"

"Both, I suppose. In truth, I prefer the path that occurs after a good night's rest."

"I thought you intended to leave those decisions to me."

Ijen brushed nonexistent lint from his tunic, then looked at Aaslo as if he hadn't spoken.

*"Do you trust him to lead you down the right path?"*

Aaslo paced to the other side of the room as he thought. He whispered, "I should do what I think is best."

*"But now your decision is tainted by his claims. You may do as he says and find him to be a liar, or you may do the opposite and find that he was telling the truth."*

"You're right. The outcome isn't of consequence. It's only a matter of trust."

*"That's not what I was saying."*

"Yes, you were. Both paths have equal probability of being the wrong one; and, once taken, we couldn't know if we had made the correct choice because we would never know what might have happened on the other path. Therefore, the best choice is the one that proves faith in our companions."

*"Faith? In people? Now I know you've lost your mind."*

Aaslo looked up to find Dolt staring at him from the doorway. He blinked several times to clear the hallucination, but the horse remained. He leaned over to peer around the frustrating horse only to find that the other horses had apparently decided to follow him. None were saddled, and their leads dangled freely from their halters. Aaslo didn't see Greylan or Rostus anywhere.

Teza, who stood between Aaslo and Dolt, seemed to think he was looking at her. "What?" she said. Aaslo shook his head and pointed. Ijen and Teza both turned to see the horses that had snuck up on them.

"What are *they* doing here?" exclaimed Ijen. "How did we not hear them coming?"

"More importantly, how did they find us?" said Teza. "We had a hard enough time finding the room."

"I'm more concerned about *why* they came to us. Dolt knows how to find trouble."

A bright light flashed in the corridor, and the horses suddenly spooked as if something were attacking from behind. They stormed into the small room, and Dolt headed straight for Aaslo. Aaslo yelled, "Stop!" to no avail. The horse's mismatched eyes rolled wildly as he reared and then crashed into Aaslo, knocking him to the ground. Aaslo's head struck the stone, and he momentarily lost sight. His stomach churned when the room swam back into focus. Bile swept up his esophagus, but as he rolled over to expel it, he saw another bright light surge toward him. He rolled out of the way, but the edge of the beam caught his left side. It singed his shirtsleeve but did no damage to his scales.

Aaslo tried to gain his feet, but he tipped to one side as his mind and body struggled for balance. Just as he stumbled, another beam of light swept past his head. He stumbled into a wall that hadn't existed a moment before. It was practically invisible with a faint bluish hue. He peered through it to see the room in chaos. Horses were running everywhere, and Ijen and Teza couldn't cast their spells fast enough so were forced to run and dodge. Above the clamor of hooves, snorts, and shouts, a woman's laughter echoed through the chamber. Another streak of light splashed into the ward surrounding Aaslo. The ward wavered briefly before bursting like a bubble.

Exposed once again, Aaslo muttered words and drew symbols in the air without thought for what he was doing. He activated the spell, and the room was cast into complete darkness. His vision snapped from the black emptiness to red, and Aaslo could see bright white where the horses, Ijen, and Teza stumbled in the dark. Without their sight, the horses seemed to calm. Aaslo's hackles rose as he realized another figure was in the dark—one he had not been able to see in the light. He ran toward it, and it chuckled.

"Clever boy," she sang.

Then the figure disappeared. Vanished.

"Who's there?" shouted Teza as a ball of light appeared in her palm. "Show yourself."

Aaslo said, "She's gone."

"Who's gone?" said Ijen as he grabbed the lead rope of his own horse.

"I don't know," he said. "A woman, I think. I didn't get a good look at her."

Teza walked up to him, holding the ball of light. Aaslo's vision shifted between his normal vision and the red night vision the dragon eye provided. The constant switching did nothing for his already shaky stomach and poor balance. "What makes you think she's gone?" said Teza.

"I saw her disappear."

*"You don't know what you saw."*

"I know I saw a figure. She was there—laughing—then she was gone."

Teza said, "How could you see *anything*? It was pitch black in here."

Aaslo raised a clawed finger to his left eye. "This. It allows me to see in the dark."

*"You monster."*

Aaslo tried to ignore Mathias's taunt, but the thought had already echoed through his own mind numerous times. "The vision isn't the same as in the light, though. I couldn't see her features."

*"You* made the lights go out?" said Teza.

"I didn't mean to. At least, I don't think I did. I can't really remember what I was doing. I hit my head."

Teza reached up to examine the back of his head, and her fingers came away bloody. "I'll say you did. Did she manage to hit you with that light?"

"No. Dolt ran me over. He's deranged."

*"Takes one to know one."*

"Sounds like he did you a favor. The horses are singed. That light was really hot. I'm guessing a direct hit could kill a man."

"Then why aren't we all dead?" said Aaslo.

Ijen joined them after collecting the rest of the leads. He said, "She seemed to be targeting you. None of the light bursts were directed at us. I'm sorry. I was only able to get the one ward formed in the chaos."

"That was you? Thank you. I think you saved my life," said Aaslo.

"Perhaps." He looked down at Aaslo's singed sleeve. "It seems you have some protection of your own."

Teza elbowed Ijen in the arm and grinned. "Thanks to *me*."

Aaslo started toward Dolt, who was standing with his head in the corner on the other side of the room. Aaslo took a step and turned his ankle on a large rock that nearly sent him sprawling on the ground again. He caught himself but looked down in confusion. There hadn't been any loose rocks on the floor before the attack. He grabbed Teza's hand that held the glowing orb and followed the rubble to a pile in the center of the room. Ijen cast another spell that reactivated the lights on the walls, and the extent of the damage became apparent. The plinth was gone. All that stood in its place was a scattered mound of broken stone.

"What do we do now?" said Teza.

Aaslo realized, suddenly, how very tired he was. It had been a long time since he had slept more than a few straight hours, and despite his concussion-induced nausea, he was hungry.

"Every step we take forward seems to set us back," he mumbled.

*"Maybe that's why I was the chosen one. My stride was larger."*

Aaslo appreciated the reminder of his inferiority about as much as a splinter in his foot. He turned to Ijen. "I think it's time we take your suggestion and rest."

"Rest?" said Teza. "How can we rest now? That woman got in here with no problem. How did she do that?"

Ijen pushed away one of the horses that was sniffing his hair. He said, "She could have used the evergate after we arrived, or she may have already been here."

"Well, she attacked us, destroyed the plinth, and then disappeared. How do we know she's not still here? She could be right around the corner waiting for us to let our guards down. People don't just disappear into thin air."

"We don't have the numbers to carry out a decent search," said Aaslo, "nor can we risk splitting up. We also can't simply stop what we're doing because of her. We'll keep going and deal with her if she shows up again."

*"That doesn't sound like a plan for survival."*

"What would you do?" grumbled Aaslo, but Mathias was silent.

"I guess you're right. There's nothing we can do about her right now," said Teza, "but I'm not going to be able to sleep a wink, and I'll constantly be looking over my shoulder."

"Then you'll become overtired and careless. We need to stay alert."

"We will watch," said a grating voice from the doorway. Teza jumped, and they all turned to see Greylan and Rostus spying on them with milky eyes.

"By the gods, they'll give me a heart attack," said Teza. "Why do you keep them around?"

Ijen said, "I believe they're offering to guard us in our sleep."

"And that's supposed to be *better*?" she said. "They're walking corpses! *Undead.*"

Aaslo closed the distance between them slowly. His balance was still a little off, and he didn't want to trip on the debris, especially since he wasn't sure he could catch himself. He looked into Greylan's eerie eyes and said, "Why are you here? Why do you walk among the living?"

"You called," said the dead man.

"But what do you *want*?"

Aaslo thought he wouldn't answer, but Greylan eventually said, "Our service is not finished. We will not go without a fight."

"Who do you serve?" said Aaslo.

Both corpses looked at him and said, "You."

"Why me?"

"It was the deal," said Greylan.

Aaslo thought back to the horror of the marshland. He had been drowning, trapped in the murk of the swamp. He had opened his eyes to see Rostus and Greylan staring into the Afterlife with sightless gazes. They hovered there in the water, their deaths oddly peaceful. Words had erupted from Aaslo's lips—strange words that he had never before spoken nor heard. A deep, dark power within him had given life to those words—life that Greylan and Rostus had accepted. It *had* been a deal. A promise of a fight—of vengeance—in return for service.

"So it was," Aaslo said. "You will keep watch while we sleep."

Both men nodded once. Teza wasn't having it, though.

"No! We can't trust them. They're dead, Aaslo."

"Which means they have more reason than any of us to despise the Berru."

"They don't have feelings. They're *dead*!"

*"Hey now, that's uncalled for. We're dead, not heartless. Well, I am, but that's not my fault."*

The familiar twinge of guilt struck Aaslo, as it did every time he thought about chopping off Mathias's head. He turned to Teza. "Their bodies are dead, but their souls live. They're here because they want to fight."

"Then we should let them," said Ijen.

Aaslo and Teza both turned to look at the prophet, who suddenly had an opinion. He wanted to question the man further, but Aaslo doubted Ijen would be more forthcoming. The prophet seemed satisfied to drop them a crumb every once in a while, perhaps only to watch the resulting ripples.

"A Mascede indeed," Aaslo said.

"What is that supposed to mean?" said Ijen.

Teza jumped at the chance to needle the prophet. "It means that you're toying with us. You continually spout that you can't tell us anything, then suddenly you have an opinion that you won't explain."

"Am I to cease talking altogether? I do have a personal interest in this war, you know. If I am to suffer the coming storm, I would like to at least live as long as possible."

*"He won't explain that ominous statement either."*

"This discussion is going nowhere," said Aaslo. "We'll sleep tonight, then figure out how to destroy the evergates in the morning."

# CHAPTER 11

NIGHT BROUGHT THE NIGHTMARES. AGAIN, AND AGAIN, PEOPLE LOST their heads. Every time, Aaslo awoke in a sweat, his heart racing. When Teza found him the next morning, he wasn't surprised to learn that he had overslept. The night seemed to have lasted a lifetime. She threw open the drapes to allow the late-morning light into the room. Aaslo rubbed his temples then begrudgingly pushed the blankets off of himself, exposing his bare skin to a chill. He realized it was much cooler where the citadel was located than it had been in southern Uyan. He rose and walked to the window. It had been too dark the previous night to see anything, and the scene using his dragon eye had been confusing. Now he understood why.

"We're in a forest," he said, relief washing over him like he had never before felt.

Teza grabbed his chin and turned his head toward her. She surveyed his face but didn't appear to really see *him*. "You look terrible," she said. "What's wrong? Are you sick?"

Aaslo ran a hand down his face, then used his fingers to comb his hair. He considered asking Teza to cut it for him, and again he balked at the idea of *her* wielding scissors near his head.

"You're a healer," he said as his gaze was drawn back to the glorious greenery beyond the window. "Do you know any spells to drive away nightmares?"

"I wish I did. I would have used it on myself weeks ago. You know, I had to write an essay about dreams when I was taking a class called *Realms*. Magus Logan was a strange man, but I kind of liked the class. He believed that the mind visits another realm during sleep. He said that our deepest feelings—love, fear, desire, guilt—design the sleep realms. He called them *Sopora*. According to him, we live within the Sopora while we sleep to help us understand and deal with those feelings."

"Sounds like Magus Logan had a whole lot of branches without a trunk."

Her brow furrowed as she looked at him. "You have the strangest sayings. Anyway, maybe if you tell me your dreams, I can help you figure out what's bothering you."

*"It's not that difficult to figure out. You miss me."*

Aaslo crossed back to the bed, picked up the sack from the floor, and held it in his lap. "Most of the time, it's pretty straightforward. There's a battle, and someone's head gets removed from his shoulders." Teza's gaze fell to the sack on his lap. He said, "Last night was worse, though. It was strange. Every time I fell asleep, I heard this voice. It was a dark whisper in my mind that it was *my* fault the Lightbane was dead. I kept hearing how I should have done more to save him. I should have asked him to wait for me. I should have run faster. I should have stayed closer." He grabbed his head and hunched forward. "So many *should haves.*"

Teza came to sit in quiet contemplation next to him. After a minute, she said, "This voice—it said *Lightbane*? Not *the chosen one*?"

Aaslo lifted his head and frowned at her. "Yes. Why would my mind use that phrase? I've never thought of Mathias in that way."

"Hmm. What if it wasn't your mind that was speaking to you?"

"Then who? How could someone get into my mind?"

She shrugged. "Some magi use mind speak. I've also heard there is a way to view others' dreams. Maybe it's some combination of the two?"

"But who? And how would someone get close enough to use the spell without me knowing?"

"I don't know. Different spells require different proximities. Maybe they know a way to do it from afar."

"Why?"

"Maybe they're trying to drive you crazy."

*"Too late. He did that on his own."*

"If I am crazy, it's *your* fault," Aaslo muttered.

"Mine?" blurted Teza. "What did *I* do?"

Aaslo scratched the scales on his neck, causing a few to flake away. "You've done plenty, but I wasn't talking to you. If the Berru don't see us as a threat, why are they bothering to attack us here? Maybe we should talk to Ijen."

"Why? He won't tell us anything."

"Perhaps, but he's a magus and might know something besides what's in the prophecy."

"Fine. I'll let you get dressed. Meet us in the kitchen. Do you remember how to get there?"

"Yes, but—is there a way to go out there?" he said with a nod toward the window.

"Of course. We weren't prisoners. I'll tell you what. I'll make us lunch, and we can eat under the trees—like a picnic."

"I've never heard a better idea in my life."

Teza grinned, then bounced out of the room with the carefree spirit of someone who wasn't deep into a battle for the preservation of all life. Aaslo dressed, then met her in the kitchen. Beyond it was a small butler pantry with a second door that led into a larger storeroom. Another door opened to the outside. Ijen and Greylan waited in the yard that contained a meat shed, silo, water tower, and numerous animal pens and chicken coops.

Aaslo hadn't considered where the residents of the citadel had obtained their food. He supposed he had assumed they imported everything through the evergates. The pens were all empty, which he figured was a blessing since the magi had been gone for several weeks. He didn't see any livestock besides some geese and a few chickens that pecked around the yard as though they had nowhere better to be. What caught his attention was the chipmunk. It had stuffed its cheeks full before scurrying across the open expanse to ascend the thick trunk of an evergreen. It was a beautiful sight.

As they walked toward the forest, Teza pointed to the pens. "I used to have to come down here every morning to take care of the animals."

"The magi didn't have servants to do that?"

"The fledglings *were* the servants. Students of healing were told that if we couldn't take care of an animal, we couldn't be trusted to take care of a person. Truthfully, I liked the animals better than the people. Sometimes, if they were injured or sick, I got to practice healing them."

"Why didn't you just work with animals, then?"

She looked at him aghast. "Only magi who can't make it as healers go into caring for animals."

"So, it was a matter of pride."

Teza lifted her chin. "I was too good for that. Besides, my mother would never have allowed it."

"Not everyone agrees with that sentiment," said Ijen as if he were scolding a pupil. "Animals can be harder to treat than humans. They can't tell you where it hurts."

"What do you know of it, *Prophet*?" snapped Teza.

"I may have lived a secluded life, but you are hardly the first healer I've known. There are some, like you, who prefer animals to humans. You should have done what you like rather than what you were expected to do."

"Are you serious?" said Teza. "You do remember that *I* was the one expelled for going against the administration."

"You were expelled for cheating, not for being an activist."

"You know what? I didn't invite you on this picnic. Why don't you go back to the citadel, where you can focus on your prophecies, since that's obviously all *you* care to do?"

"I meant no offense," said Ijen. "I have never had a choice about what I do. I am a prophet. Despite the darkness in my prophecies, I like being a prophet; but it could not be escaped even if I so desired. I was only suggesting that you had a chance to be a happier person."

"How could I be happier being ridiculed for failing as a healer and being forced to work with animals?"

"I didn't realize you cared so much about what others think."

Teza huffed. "I don't, but I still want respect."

"Will you two please be quiet?" said Aaslo. "I'd like to enjoy the forest while I can, and you're scaring away all the animals."

Teza replied, "I get that you're a forester, but I don't see what's the big deal about a bunch of trees."

"Why did you come?" said Aaslo. "I could have come out here on my own."

"Right, and have you disappear?"

"Why would I disappear?"

"Maybe you'll decide not to come back," said Teza.

*"She's really gotten to know you."*

Aaslo growled, an inhuman rumble he knew came from the *other* inside him. "You doubt my commitment?"

"I think Healer Teza was merely expressing her concern that you might be attacked by our mystery magus or the lyksvight," said Ijen. "We can't be too careful."

Teza glanced at the prophet sideways, then pointed ahead. "There's a nice overlook up here. We can sit on the rocks and view the valley."

"Valley?" said Aaslo.

"We're nearly at the top of a mountain. You'll be able to see the peak once we reach the overlook."

The granite outcrop at the mountain's edge was a dream come true—if Aaslo's dreams had been pleasant. Nothing but trees and mountains raked the landscape for as far as he could see. He released a breath—one he had been holding since stepping from the shade of the Efestrian Forest to walk beneath the unbroken sky. He lowered himself onto a rock and leaned against a tree as he ate the sandwich Teza had prepared. Teza and Ijen were blessedly silent, and even Greylan's vacant gaze could not disturb Aaslo's peace.

*"When the Berru have their way, all of this will be destroyed."*

Aaslo sighed. Of course, Mathias could be counted on to redirect his attention back to the turmoil of gods and men.

"What's wrong?" said Teza. "Don't you like the forest?"

"More than you can imagine. The Berru would have it all destroyed, though, and for what? For promises of some great fortune in the Afterlife? Do they even consider that the gods could be lying?"

*"Exactly. Death could look like the inside of a sack."*

"They're gods. Do gods lie?"

"Myra says they aren't much different from us in their politics. Where there's politics, there are lies." He looked to Ijen. "Are the Berru truly fanatics? Is it everyone in their country or just the leaders?"

Ijen pondered for a moment, then opened his book. He was perched on a boulder that didn't match the rock of the outcrop. Although the book of prophecy lay open on his lap, he wasn't looking at it. His gaze seemed lost in the trees of the mountain that stood across the valley. It appeared as though his mind were elsewhere as he spoke.

"The Berru are a strict religious society led by an empress. Officially, their patron god is the God of Death known as Axus. A heathen sect secretly worships a different god. I do not know which one. When a heathen is discovered, he or she is burned to death in offering to Axus." The prophet shivered then turned to Aaslo. "It is a most disturbing death. The scent of burning flesh and bone wafts through the city as a warning to all who sympathize with the heathens."

Aaslo said, "You saw all that in your mind? You could smell it?"

*"And I thought you were creepy."*

"It is as though I am there—like in a dream."

"How many are there? How big is their empire?"

"It is massive—perhaps as large as the entirety of the known lands."

Teza said, "How is that possible? How is it that no one has found it in the thousands of years since people have been sailing?"

"They kill anyone who ventures within sight of their borders, and they have many, many magi—strong magi."

Aaslo abruptly stood and kicked a stump in frustration. "How are we supposed to fight an enemy so massive—and one aligned with a god, no less?"

"Perhaps we can kill the leaders," said Teza.

"I doubt it would matter," said Aaslo. "You kill one spider, and a dozen more are waiting to take its place."

"True. It's too bad we can't kill the god—"

Aaslo held up a hand to forestall any further discussion. He whispered, "The sounds of the forest have changed. Someone is here."

"Yeah, us," said Teza.

He waved his hand and shushed her. "I mean someone *else*."

Suddenly, a clapping echoed around them, followed by a light, feminine cackle. All three of them searched for the source of the sound but could find no one.

"There," said Aaslo, pointing toward a tree whose image seemed to waver as if part of it was underwater.

"I don't see anything," said Teza.

"Nor do I," added Ijen.

*"You're hearing voices again, only this time it's contagious."*

Aaslo raised his voice. "Show yourself!"

"Why should I?" said a voice filled with laughter. It sounded as though it were coming from behind him.

Aaslo spun around to see only the sheer drop of the cliff. He suddenly felt a hand on his shoulder. Jumping back, he swatted at the invisible woman. His claws swept through the empty air, striking nothing. Teza and Ijen both stood poised to defend themselves as soon as they could see their foe. Aaslo felt his torso cave as a massive force struck him, and then he was abruptly flying through the air. His spine popped, and the little wind he had left was knocked from his lungs when he collided with a tree. He fell to the ground with a miserable thud.

Through the moisture in his eyes, he saw Teza rushing to his side. She was at least five paces away when he felt his hair being yanked. The *other* inside him roared as he lashed out, striking something he couldn't see. More laughter reached him from farther away. He raised his head and blinked toward the sound. His vision rapidly shifted from human to dragon, and he closed his eyes to allow it to settle. When he opened them again, he could clearly see the outline of a woman among the trees.

"I see you!" he shouted.

"Do you now? My, my, you *are* interesting."

She vanished again, only this time he thought she was truly gone. Aaslo felt himself being jostled, and someone was yelling. He turned his head and realized it was Teza, and she was yelling at *him*. Ijen was right beside her, his face bearing more expression than Aaslo had ever seen on the man.

Aaslo tried to push Teza's hands away as he struggled to right himself. "Stop, just stop," he said. "What's wrong with you?"

*"I've asked myself that same question about you so many times."*

"Aaslo, you just took a direct hit from that light beam power and were blasted a good ten yards before the tree stopped you. You're lucky if your back isn't broken."

"I don't think luck had anything to do with it," he said as he ran a hand down the scales that covered half his torso. He abruptly realized his chest was bare and he had only a few pieces of rag hanging from his shoulders. "What happened to my shirt?"

Teza stood and crossed her arms as the concern drained from her face. "The same thing that would have happened to the rest of you if not for my handiwork. You owe me for saving your life *again*."

"I can't keep owing you every time I *don't* die from an attack just because you forced my body to grow armor. Does a knight thank the smith every time he doesn't die in battle?"

"He *should*," said Teza. "And since when are you a knight?"

Aaslo scowled at her as he gained his feet. "I'm not. I was just saying—oh, never mind. Let's get back to the citadel and do what we came here to do. There's no telling when that woman will show up again."

Teza and Ijen collected the items from their spoiled picnic while Aaslo gathered the shreds of evidence that used to be his shirt. Greylan followed him around the picnic area so closely that Aaslo finally turned to confront him. "What are you doing?"

"Protect."

"Why didn't you do anything while that woman was *attacking*?"

"My sight was empty."

Aaslo grunted. "You couldn't see her either." A sudden thought occurred to him. "Can you see the reaper?"

Greylan blinked in what appeared to be a forced motion. "Yes, the reaper."

Aaslo almost asked if the undead man could hear Mathias but decided to wait until they were alone. Instead, he said, "That means the woman who attacked us bears a different kind of power. She's not a reaper. She's probably not even dead." He looked to Teza and Ijen. "Could she be a magus?"

They glanced at each other, but neither seemed to know the answer. Ijen said, "If she is, she's far more powerful than either of us. Perhaps she's fae."

Teza said, "Maybe she's a goddess."

The thought sent a chill through Aaslo. He had been in the presence of the gods once—at least his mind had—and once was enough. "I hope not," he said. "If she's fae, perhaps we can bargain with her—get her on our side."

"It seems like she's already chosen a side," said Teza.

Ijen said, "My understanding of the fae is that the only side they choose is their own."

Aaslo mentally ran through his limited knowledge of the fae. "That reminds me of something Ina said. She couldn't interfere directly. The woman who attacked us was definitely direct."

"Which means she's probably either a magus or a goddess," said Teza.

*"Or something else entirely."*

They entered the citadel through the same door they had used to exit. Aaslo was deep in thought as he led the way back to the room with the destroyed plinth. When they arrived, it looked just as they had left it.

Teza said, "How did you find it so easily? I was getting completely confused about where we were going."

"I wasn't thinking about it," said Aaslo. "My mind was elsewhere."

Ijen said, "It seems you've discovered the secret."

Aaslo grunted and motioned to the plinth. "If only I knew the secret of how to fix this."

"Technically, we don't need to rebuild it. The power isn't in the plinth. It's only directed by the runes. It would have been possible for the ancients to direct the spell without the runes."

*"That's you, in case you didn't know."*

"Yes, I get it. I have no idea how to do that, though."

Teza said, "You've used your power before without any training."

"I had training—by the high sorceress. I just didn't know I was being trained. But this—this was not in my studies. Perhaps she taught Mathias."

*"You only wish you knew half of what I knew."*

"I can't argue that," muttered Aaslo.

*"Quit whining and get to work. Just do it already."*

It was a very forester thing to say. Mathias knew him well. "Fine," said Aaslo.

"Fine, what?" said Teza.

Aaslo mumbled, "You're the hero. What do I do?"

*"This is* your *quest now. Not mine. You have to figure out how to use your own power."*

Aaslo closed his eyes and searched inside himself for the foreign power—the *other* that seemed to want to take over so often. An ancient power leapt at him. It was visceral, driven by instinct, salivating for the hunt. It felt wrong. It clawed and hissed at him as he pushed it aside to wrangle another power. Dark and insidious, it taunted and tempted. It called to him, a seductress with a promise, a desperate desire to infinitely bond in the abyss. Aaslo knew it would have been all too easy to fall prey to its allure.

The dark power tried to wrap around him as he pushed through. Buried deep beneath the first two was a brighter, subtler power. It was the power of growth and fertility. The soft scent of jasmine and honeysuckle drew him in with its natural simplicity. Since the fateful day when a lone rider was dragged into his village, he had not felt such serenity. Aaslo didn't completely understand the nature of the various powers he felt, but he was certain that if he wanted to grace the world with anything it would be *this* power.

As he reached out, it leapt at him, latching on with unexpected strength. His first instinct was to draw back, but it held strong as more tendrils snapped around him. They threatened to drag him in, to consume him completely. He struggled against them, grasping for anything to help pull him free. From somewhere far away, the beast's roar echoed through his mind. Sharp claws dug into him as they tried to rip him from the sweet enchantress. The light power loosened its hold, as did the claws, but neither released him. Aaslo suddenly felt balanced, in control. It was as though each power were snarling at the other as they pouted and waited to be called upon.

He opened his eyes. Around him, he could hear people murmuring—or were they shouting? It didn't matter. He ignored them. Teza had said the pillar required a spell that produced fire over it. The beast purred its pleasure at the prospect of producing an inferno. Aaslo remembered, however, that fire wasn't the goal. It was a means to an end. He needed to create a bond with the power of the magi—a way for the spells and enchantments they had created to recognize him. Memories of struggling with his fellow foresters to protect the most sensitive parts of the forest from the destruction of fire flashed through his mind. Fire didn't create bonds. It destroyed them. He asked himself how the fire on the plinth could then create such a bond, and he realized it wasn't a fire at all. It was power—pure, unadulterated power. It was the bright light he had seen deep inside him—the one that threatened to consume him. It was the power of Ina, the power of the fae, the same power wielded by magi over the millennia.

It made sense, then, why the spell required so many present-day magi to power it. Individually, they simply didn't have enough at their call. He did, though. He could feel it. Ina's power whispered to him. It begged to be set free. Then he realized it had been listening to him. It knew he wanted to use it, and it was simply waiting for him to pull the stopper. Worries began to twist in his mind. If he did release the power, how could he be sure it did what he wanted? And once released, could he make it stop? Would he become a slave to the power? Would it consume him? Destroy him?

"No," he said.

Someone outside of himself said something, but it was as though the sound were passing through water. All he could hear was the beckoning whisper in his mind.

*"Let me be free."*

It wasn't Mathias's voice he heard. It was a new one, a sultry but gentle murmur.

"You are mine," he said.

*"Are you sure? Perhaps you are* mine." He recognized the voice. It was Ina.

"No, you are lent to me," he said. "The deal was made. I followed through. You will do as I command."

*"Mine cost was paid, 'tis true, but others wait to receive their due."* A beastly roar accented by a sizzle of dark power filled the empty space in his mind. A growl escaped his own throat as he gripped his head. The seductive voice said, *"I can help—for a price."*

Aaslo's stomach churned as he realized he had truly received more than one power, and the others would exact payment in their own way. He didn't have time to consider it, and he certainly wasn't going to make another deal with Ina. Her power had already tried to consume him once. If he gave in, he would likely lose himself forever.

"I will deal with them. You will serve me now."

*"I will not offer again."*

"I will not ask."

It giggled. *"We'll see. What do you ask of me?"*

Aaslo didn't know how to explain what he needed since he wasn't sure how the spells were supposed to work. The voice of Ina seemed capable of knowing his thoughts, though, so he imagined his goals. Then he began performing the first spell that Ijen had taught him the previous evening. Before he was even finished, Ina laughed, and power shot out of him toward the plinth.

Abruptly, Aaslo was vividly aware of his surroundings. Teza screamed, and Greylan was at his side—entirely too close—looking as if he were trying to figure out how to protect him. Ijen scribbled rapidly as his gaze bounced between his book and the plinth. A bright pillar of light reached from the rubble of the plinth to the ceiling. Glistening eddies churned within the pillar, and it pulsed with a fire-like flicker.

"What did you do?" shouted Teza.

"I, um, lit the plinth," said Aaslo.

*"It's a bit big. Overcompensating?"*

Aaslo growled, but he was glad to hear that Mathias's voice had not been permanently replaced by Ina's.

"Hey, I'm not complaining," said Teza. "It's just, I've never seen one so big."

Mathias cackled as if from afar. *"I'll just say I told you so."*

"Look, I wasn't *trying* to make it that big. It was my first time."

Teza took a few steps forward and peered at the ceiling. The light had shot straight through the wood and stone and continued into the room above them. "I'd say your first time was rather explosive."

Mathias laughed again but thankfully held his tongue.

"I've never seen anyone connect with their power so quickly," said Teza.

Ijen looked up from his book. "He didn't even finish the spell."

Teza looked at Aaslo with suspicion. "How did he cast the spell if he didn't finish it?"

"Don't look at me like that," Aaslo grumbled. "I did what you wanted. Now do what you need to do to gain access."

Ijen snapped his book shut and tucked it into his shirt. "Perhaps I should as well while we're here."

He raised his hands in preparation to cast a spell, but Teza leapt forward and knocked them down.

"Oh no, you don't. We still don't know if you're trustworthy. You could be one of the Berru pretending to be a Mascede."

Ijen blinked at her in surprise. "I knew you didn't care for prophets and that you didn't much trust me, but I never realized you thought I might be one of the enemy—at least, not anymore. We've been traveling together for some time now."

"Not long enough," said Teza.

Aaslo crossed his arms and watched the exchange with disinterest. His companions could argue all they wanted, and it still wouldn't change the facts. "Both of you, stop it," he said. "Either Ijen is or isn't Berruvian. Since Ijen wouldn't confess if he were, we can't possibly glean the answer right now."

"I can," said Ijen.

Aaslo scowled at the prophet. "What I am saying is, there is no reason to argue over it. What's important is to determine whether the benefits of allowing you access to the enchantments of the magi outweigh the threat of the Berru gaining access." Aaslo looked to Teza. "Can the Berru gain access on their own?"

She looked dumbfounded but hesitantly said, "I don't know. The plinth is destroyed. Technically, no one should be able to cast the spell without the runes to guide it. They would have to reconstruct the plinth, they'd have to know the correct spells, and they'd need to have enough power."

"So, the person who attacked us actually did us a favor in destroying the plinth," mused Aaslo.

"I suppose, since *you* were still able to light the fire without it. The Berru could do it if they also have someone like you."

*"There's no one like Aaslo."*

"Very well. We will assume for now that it will take the Berru a while to gain access unless we give it to them. Therefore, Ijen should not have access."

Ijen gave him a disgruntled look but didn't argue. Teza grinned with satisfaction and said, "Great, then it's just you and me."

"*Me?*" said Aaslo.

Teza rolled her eyes. "Of course. You lit the fire. Somehow, you connected *yourself.*"

*"Look at you, just taking what you want and not even apologizing for it."*

Aaslo waved at the shining pillar of light. "Just get on with it."

Teza nodded excitedly and turned to cast the spell, but this time Ijen stopped *her*. "What are you doing, *Prophet?*" she snapped.

He lifted his chin and looked down his nose at her. "Fledgling Teza, doing this will raise you to the status of magus. It should not be taken lightly, and it should be done with ceremony."

"Who has time for that garbage?" said Teza.

"It isn't garbage," said Ijen. "It's what you worked many years to achieve. Surely that means something to you."

Teza's expression fell, and she looked uncertain. She glanced toward Aaslo.

Aaslo started to argue the need for pointless pomp and ceremony, but Mathias interrupted his thoughts.

*"Cultures—traditions—are the products of life that you struggle to preserve."*

Aaslo muttered, "There have been hundreds of cultures and thousands of traditions. What difference does one ceremony make?"

Ijen said, "This is *our* tradition, the tradition of *your* people."

"*My* people? You mean the magi who left before I even gained any power?"

"No, I mean *her*"—he nodded toward Teza—"and me."

*"And me!"*

Aaslo was surprised to hear Mathias chime in. He was the chosen one, after all. It should have been the other way around. "You're one of my people?" Aaslo said.

*"Of course. Brothers in all things."*

Ijen said, "Despite what Fledgling Teza thinks, I am not Berruvian. I have spent my life awaiting the time when I would stand beside you, and I will continue to do so until my end."

Aaslo glanced between Ijen and Teza, who were both apparently awaiting his decision. It was in that moment that he realized he had truly become their leader. He was no longer a simple secular living among the trees. His gaze turned toward the light streaming from the rubble of the plinth, the light he had created, and he knew. He was the leader of the magi.

"All right. What do we do?"

Ijen slipped a page from his book and handed it to Aaslo. It was a list of instructions on how to raise a magus—specifically, a healing mage.

"You knew this was going to happen?" he said.

Ijen grinned. It was a silly lopsided thing that Aaslo had never before seen on the stoic prophet. "It's in the story," he said.

# CHAPTER 12

THE DARKNESS OF THE CAVES STILL DISTRESSED CHERRÍ. THE BODIES ENtombed there, many of which were reduced to skeletons, weren't the worst of what troubled her. Every time she turned a corner, the meager light dimmed. She felt as though she were back in that horrible trunk, trapped, struggling to breathe through the stifling torment of the breathless babes pressed against her chest. There, in the catacombs, it was as if she could hear the passage of their souls. A hollow whisper slipped past her ears, then disappeared into the glowing torchlight of the tunnel behind her. She shivered. Even the buried and lost souls of the crypts sought the light of Everon.

She wiped a cold sweat from her brow and shook her head. *It's merely a breeze*, she thought. Her fingers slid from the stone to brush against something soft. She looked over and immediately regretted it. The partially mummified remains of a woman had been stuffed into a recess that should not have been large enough to hold her. She had been bent and twisted to fit, and worse, she was wrapped around a young child. Cherrí swallowed a whimper. That could have been her.

She quickly stepped past the alcove and continued her trek toward the surface. She didn't use the main entrance. The guards would not have allowed her to pass. Only those with official business on the surface were permitted to leave for fear of discovery. Aria had shown Cherrí another way out, though, and Cherrí desperately needed *out*. The mixed clans had been good to her. Hers had been one of the few that were not at war with any other clans. Fire Serpent had been a clan of mothers—women who chose to live apart. A woman had to be brave to join the Fire Serpent Clan. They were expected to bear children, provide for their families, hunt, and protect the clan—all without the assistance of men. Cherrí didn't feel brave in that moment, though. She felt trapped.

She came to a split in the passage and had just taken a step toward the right when something latched onto her arm. Her mouth opened, but a second hand caught her scream.

"Quiet," whispered Aria. "I told you to go to the left. That way would have taken you down to the next level—*deeper* into the catacombs."

Aria's hand fell away. Cherrí could barely make out the other woman's form in the insufficient light that still reached them. She said, "I'm glad you caught me, but I thought you were going to meet me at the exit."

Light glinted off the white of Aria's teeth as she smiled. "I knew you'd go the wrong way. Come, it's not far now."

They came to a place where the crypts had partially collapsed spewing rubble into the passage. Loose rocks rose to the ceiling at a steep incline.

The going was made all the more difficult by the near absence of light, but Cherrí was undeterred. It was dark, but it was the way *out*. Her confidence grew. She was not without talent. Runi had been the better hunter, but Cherrí had been a good scout. She knew how to climb and how to do so quietly.

Aria, on the other hand, was not quite so nimble. Hers had been a militant clan from Jule called the Great Oryx. They were hunters and renowned fighters. They were also mercenaries. Other clans paid Aria's for protection; or, if not, they often became prey. It was not unusual to find Great Oryxes fighting on *both* sides of a battle. For them, though, it was merely a game.

At the top of the rubble, on one side, was a burial alcove. If a body had been laid to rest there, it was long gone. Cherrí crawled into the alcove and shimmied through a crack that had presumably opened during the cave-in. Fresh air struck Cherrí in the face. It felt like the first breath she had taken in a long while. It was cool and crisp and smelled of soil and snow. Cherrí pulled herself through the crack with haste, nearly tumbling down a slope after tripping on a log in her path. Aria stepped out behind her with the same result, just as Cherrí said, "Watch out for the log."

"What? There was no log here before," said Aria. "What is that?"

They both leaned over the lump on the ground. It was a moonless night, and most of the stars were obscured by a thick covering of clouds that preceded the impending storm. A flash of distant lightning gave them their first good view.

"Oh no! It's Lockry," said Aria as she knelt beside the man.

"Lockry? Of the Salt Wave Clan?"

"Yes," said Aria as she tugged at his clothes. She found his neck and paused. "He's dead."

A chill went up Cherrí's spine. "What? How?"

"I can't tell. It's too dark."

"He isn't torn apart, so it can't be the lyksvight, right?"

Aria's fingers prodded the body, then Cherrí followed the other woman's gaze up the cliff through which they had exited. Lightning illuminated the clouds again, and she could see that it was at least fifty feet high.

"I think he fell," said Aria. "It feels like his neck is broken and perhaps a few other bones."

Cherrí was relieved. Although she couldn't imagine the terror of falling to one's death, some deaths were better than others. Death by lyksvight had to be the worst. "What was he doing up there?"

"He was assigned sentry duty. You should go back into the cave while I investigate."

Cherrí froze at the thought of reentering the tomb. She was sure that if she did, it would become her final resting place.

"Go," said Aria.

As Cherrí turned to squeeze back through the crack, a bloodcurdling sound reached her ears. Her heart pounded, and it was as if the darkness had wrapped her in its sightless shroud. She was trapped, again, listening to the screams of her friends and family. Only this time she had no family, and she barely knew the people with whom she had found refuge. The sounds that echoed through the tunnels were no less terrifying, though. Death wails struck her countless times as they escaped from the very fissure through which she had fled the tombs.

Aria grabbed Cherrí's arm, nearly knocking her down the talus slope again. "Move," she said. "We're under attack. I must get in there to fight."

"No!" said Cherrí. "If you go in there, you will die, too."

"I must. Our people are in there."

"Our people are dead already," said Cherrí. "Listen."

The sounds of tormented men, women, and children had been replaced by the growls, hoots, and grunts with which Cherrí was all too familiar.

"No," said Aria. "They must have escaped. The patrol. Natu was leading it tonight. He would have seen the enemy coming. He was probably leading everyone to another exit when they were attacked from behind. I'm sure most of them made it out alive."

Cherrí had heard the screams, though. Many, many screams. Too many. "I don't—"

Aria took her hand and said, "Come on. We'll search for the others, but first we need weapons and supplies."

"We can't go back in there," said Cherrí, her heart thumping against her ribs so hard she thought it might break through.

"No, we have a few secret stashes, just in case."

Cherrí thought *just in case* had come too soon. She had only been with the combined clans for a week, and already they were gone. Aria believed others survived—or perhaps merely wished it to be so—but Cherrí knew better.

They cautiously trudged across the talus where it met the cliff face, then began climbing a section of solid rock with decent hand- and footholds. They lacked the fingerless gloves and climbing shoes that would have made the going easier, and the brief flashes of light from the encroaching storm were hardly sufficient. It was a difficult climb, and Cherrí hoped Aria had the necessary experience. She didn't think she could handle being left alone again, the sole survivor of a horrible slaughter.

She scampered over the top ledge, then reached down to help Aria the rest of the way. They stayed low as they surveyed the dark expanse, looking for any movement or man-shaped silhouettes in the intermittent flashes of light. The wind raked across the plateau, and Cherrí was no longer thrilled with the chill air. She hadn't planned to be outside long and had grappled with the idea of bringing a coat. Luckily, sense had won, and her warm, fur-lined hood was tight over her head. Aria was equally equipped for the weather—until the rain began.

It started with a drizzle but quickly escalated to a downpour. The rain came at them sideways, slapping Cherrí in the face as they headed into the wind. Her scarf was tucked inside her jacket, and a few good tugs didn't loosen it enough to cover her face. She figured it wouldn't help much after it was soaked anyway. It was best to keep it dry until they could get out of the rain.

Cherrí and Aria were alert, scanning the plateau for danger before moving to their next position. Neither saw anything large enough to be a person or lyksvight, so they hurried toward a shallow crevice for cover. It was barely deep and wide enough to hide their crouching forms. Aria rolled a boulder aside, then dug through the wet chunks of rubble to uncover a small cask. Cherrí's fingers were already stiffening from the cold as she helped Aria pry off the lid. Inside was a full pack, waterskin, and hunting knife. Aria pushed the pack and waterskin into Cherrí's arms and took the knife.

"Come. Another stash is hidden not far from here," she said.

Cherrí nodded, and they both poked their heads out of their hole. When it appeared that all was clear, they darted across the plateau to hide behind a few small boulders. Aria inched forward and peered over the lip of a massive crevasse. Until that moment, Cherrí had been turned around in the dark and hadn't been sure of her location. She could see now that they had made it to the main entrance of their subterranean haven. It was a haven no longer.

Screeches and growls escaped the entrance, but they weren't accompanied by anything sounding the least bit human. About thirty paces from the opening, two balls of subtle, glowing light hovered in the air, casting an eerie glow into the chasm. Beneath them, a couple of women appeared to be waiting. They silently stood in puddles of blood surrounded by corpses.

"No," said Aria, her voice nearly drowned out by the rain. "This is wrong."

Cherrí didn't know the clan members well enough to be able to recognize their savaged bodies in the dark, but she could tell by her companion's distress that Aria did. "Who is it?" she asked.

"It's the patrol." Aria pointed to a dismembered torso. "There's Natu. They must have seen the Berru coming and tried to get back to warn us."

"You think they led the Berru here?"

Aria slid away from the edge and lay on her back. Cherrí knew the rain was probably obscuring the woman's tears.

"No," said Aria. "Natu was smarter than that. He was selfless and brave. Those foreign magi had likely already found us. Natu and the others were probably trying to hold them off while everyone inside evacuated."

"You cared about him," said Cherrí.

"He would have made a good husband. I never told him how I felt because he was in mourning."

Cherrí was unexpectedly struck with guilt—and envy. She had not had the opportunity to mourn her losses. Her wife and babes had not been properly remembered, and she was the only one left who knew them. She still did not have the luxury, if mourning the dead could be called such. It would have to wait—again.

"We should see if we can find the survivors," she said, hoping to rouse Aria from her despair.

Aria rolled over and looked back into the crevasse. "I know where they would have exited. More supplies can be found there as well, but it's pretty far. We'll have to move slowly. The rain and dark of night will cover us, but we'll be exposed if anyone happens to look our way when the sky is lit."

"Okay, I'll follow you," said Cherrí as she tied the small pack to her back and tucked the waterskin under her coat.

The plateau was flat and easy to traverse so long as they watched for the occasional fissure. They paused behind the few outcrops and shrubs in their path to collect their breaths and check for pursuit. They didn't speak during their miserable trek. It was all Cherrí could do to keep her teeth from chattering. Her heart pumped rapidly, and the strain kept her mind sharp. They finally came to a ravine that was larger than the others. It was a thirty-foot drop to a raging river of runoff from the plateau and distant mountains.

Aria paused at the cliff's edge. Cherrí didn't fancy going into the ravine but knew staying on the plateau wasn't safe either. After a few minutes, she nudged her companion. "Where to?"

"I'm not sure. I'm trying to find it, but I can't see the markers. We might not even be in the right place."

"Should we go up- or downstream?"

"I don't know," Aria growled in exasperation. "I'm sorry. I've practiced this so many times—"

"Don't blame yourself," said Cherrí. "These conditions—they're impossible. How about we find a place to shelter for the night and look for survivors in the morning?"

"No," said Aria. "What if they're injured? What if they wander away in the dark and we never find them? It's our duty to help these people."

Cherrí put a hand on Aria's shoulder. "No, it's not. We're just like them. *We* need help, too. We're drenched and freezing, and we can't see where we're going. We'll be no good to anyone if we fall into the river or catch ill."

Aria stood tense for a moment but finally shook her head. "You're right. We need to care for ourselves before we can help others. We can't shelter here, though. Those creatures may have followed the survivors, or they might find the exit on their own. The Towering Tree Clan was camped a couple of hours to the northwest when the Berru found them. They left their belongings when they fled. Since the camp was already destroyed, it's unlikely they'll be looking for anyone there."

Cherrí hadn't thought to make another daunting journey so soon, but it wasn't her worst experience. At least she wasn't alone. Aria had been kind to Cherrí since they met, but she didn't talk about herself and seemed glad to do most of the questioning. In fact, her abrupt confession regarding her feelings for Natu had been the first personal detail Aria had shared with Cherrí. Still, Cherrí's greatest dread at that point was losing Aria.

In just a few weeks' time, death had become so commonplace that Cherrí wondered if she would ever feel anything but fear again. Before her people were slaughtered, death had been an inevitability, a rite of passage into the Afterlife. The elderly, the sick, and the unlucky took a single step into the next phase of their existence, and although their loss was mourned, their journey had been celebrated. Cherrí no longer felt the ability to celebrate. She had grown to despise death. She *hated* it, and yet it was insubstantial. It was not something she could fight or punish, and she was helpless against it.

MYROPA STOOD IN THE GUSHING WATERS, UNTOUCHED BY THE CURRENT. She could feel the tether getting shorter, which meant her target was coming toward her. Lightning briefly illuminated the black storm clouds of the night, and she was able to see a man upstream. He flailed and then was gone. As his body rushed past her, she snagged his soul, sending it straight into an orb without greeting or ceremony. The river was not the place for conversation.

She didn't know where she was. The landscape was foreign to her. It was raining, and patches of snow painted the rocks white. Although she couldn't feel it, she figured the river was probably as cold as the ice in her veins. She wondered if perhaps she had returned to the region where she had met Arayallen to question the old man. The thought of the wind demon might have disturbed her if her nerves hadn't been too frozen to shiver. *This* man's death was not a murder, though. He had merely drowned. She had collected other victims of drowning in her time as a reaper, and they had all said the same thing. It was terrifying until they succumbed, at which point they died in peace.

Myropa opened her mouth to release the breath of the living but stopped when she noticed movement upon the ridge. Flashes in the clouds illuminated two figures running along the ravine. Her first thought was that this man might have been murdered after all. Then she realized he had floated toward her. The runners were moving upstream, so they could not have pushed him off the cliff. She wondered, then, if they had known the man. Perhaps they were looking for him. She was sad that they would not find him. Once again, she wished she could communicate with the living—to tell them the man was gone, and they need no longer look.

With a thought, she was floating alongside the runners. The two women looked haggard yet determined, brave yet frightened. They continuously surveyed their surroundings, and the shorter woman in back often turned to search behind her. She could see that the desperation on the woman's face was accompanied by something else. Anger. Myropa saw no one else in the area. She wondered what could be lurking in the dark and hoped it wasn't the creature Arayallen was missing. Could she find a way to warn them? Even if she could, would it be useful? She knew nothing of the creature's whereabouts *or* motivations. Did it have motive, or was it driven by instinct? Was it even a threat to these people? Was it a threat to *her*?

Myropa decided to see what information she might glean from following the women. She could at least discover the name of the kingdom. She floated along as the women ran. They continued at a brisk pace for a couple of hours, stopping only for short breaks, during which they rested in silence. Myropa knew that had she been alive, she would not have been able to keep up with them. The rain became sleet, and by the time the two reached what looked to be an abandoned encampment, they were enduring a blizzard.

The wind whipped at the tents, a few of which were still standing, although no fires glowed in or around them. Myropa followed the women as they ducked into the first tent that looked like it would withstand the weather. Both women were crusted in ice and snow, their clothes frozen stiff as they struggled to shuck them. The women moaned and shivered as they grabbed any clothes and blankets they could find in the tent and huddled beneath them.

"W-we n-need a f-f-fire," said the shorter woman through chattering teeth.

The second woman picked up a small tinderbox from beside the dark firepit, then dropped it. She fumbled for the tinderbox as she stuttered, "My f-fingers are f-frozen."

Myropa could relate. She was always frozen, but her body rarely shook anymore. These women looked like they wouldn't make it through the rest of the night if they didn't get warm soon. She wondered, if she waited long enough, might a tether snap to one or both of them? If she did collect them, she'd have the chance to ask questions. Guilt over the callous and selfish thought drove her gaze to the tinderbox. She wished she could help them, but they were on their own.

The shorter woman reached for the tinderbox as she said, "P-please, Everon, help us start this fire."

A brilliant red-orange light flashed in the woman's eyes, and steam started to roll off her skin. The partially charred wood in the firepit began to smolder. The flame within the wood grew until it was too large to be supported by the few pieces in the pit. The taller woman quickly fed it with a couple of fresh logs from the pile behind her, then looked at her companion in awe.

"Why didn't you tell me you were a magus?" said the taller one.

"I'm not," said the shorter. "I prayed to Everon, and I guess he answered."

"Your clan could do this?"

"No, I've never seen this happen before, but I will not question it. Everon has blessed us. He wishes us to survive."

They were silent for a moment as they both huddled by the fire, enjoying what appeared to be the blessing of someone named Everon. Myropa had never heard of him. She didn't think he was one of the gods, but there were so many she could not say for sure. Eventually, the taller woman said, "Our clan did not worship Everon. We didn't worship any spirits. I thought they weren't real."

"If you did not believe in the spirits, what did you believe in?"

The taller woman shrugged. "I don't know. Ourselves, I guess. I didn't think about it much."

"Do you believe now?"

The woman held her hands to the fire and sighed. "If Everon has blessed us with this fire, then he has my gratitude. I will not doubt him."

Again, both women fell quiet before the shorter one said, "Where do we go now? Is there another group we can join?"

"Not as far as I know. Look, Cherrí, I don't have all the answers. I'm just as lost as you."

The shorter woman named Cherrí said, "Perhaps we should go to a city. It might be safer and easier than trying to find one of the migrating clans."

"I don't know. People get trapped in the cities. Everybody is concentrated in one place. They're easier to kill, and these lyksvight aren't like humans. They kill indiscriminately and don't pause to question their actions. I don't think they even sleep. Besides that, there are no magi left in the cities to protect them from the Berruvian magi."

"Then we should head toward Mouvilan. They must have heard word of the invasion. They should be amassing their army along the border. Perhaps they'll give us asylum in exchange for what we know."

"What of *our* people?"

"Our people are dying, Aria. If it's this bad here in the frozen south, just think what it's like in Jule. For all we know, the army has already lost. Besides, we can warn any clans we encounter on the way."

"So, we just abandon them?" said Aria.

Cherrí looked uncertain for a moment, then her expression hardened. "No," she said. "We'll go to the Cartisian embassy in Chelis and plead our case. We'll convince the ambassador to seek aid from the Mouvilanian parliament."

Myropa finally had a location—southern Cartis.

"Chelis is too far. By the time we get there, our people will be dead. Besides, I'm sure the ambassador already knows."

The anger Myropa had seen on Cherrí's face while on the ridge returned. The woman said, "Fine. If we cannot save them, then we shall seek vengeance. If the Berru love death so much, they should join him. With Everon as my witness, I'll not stop until every death-worshipping, hate-monger is dead or I am."

"*What* are you doing here?"

Myropa jumped as the voice thundered in her ear. She scrambled to her feet and spun to find Arayallen standing over her with crossed arms and pursed lips. The goddess glowed with power yet somehow restrained it enough that Myropa wasn't crushed under its weight.

"I, uh, had a collection—"

Arayallen waved a dismissive hand. "Never mind that. I don't care. I've been calling you for *forever.*"

Words eluded her as Myropa struggled to tell the goddess that she had received no such call. She shivered when an urgent summons suddenly reached her.

"See?" said Arayallen.

"But I only just received it—"

Arayallen said, "Time dilation is no excuse. I expect an immediate response when I call."

"Time dilation?"

"Do I have to explain everything to you? Time dilation is the difference in time between Celestria and another realm or world."

Myropa had no trouble ignoring the Cartisian women's conversation to focus on the goddess. Arayallen's energy suffused the tent, and Myropa wondered if she was doing it intentionally. An errant chill crackled through her veins as Myropa considered the possibility that she wasn't. An unhinged Arayallen worried her more than an irate one.

"I need to speak with Disevy *now,*" said Arayallen with a pointed look.

Myropa stared at her a moment, then said, "You think *I* know where he is?"

Arayallen narrowed her eyes at Myropa. "If anyone does, it's you."

"But I don't," Myropa said emphatically.

"You can find him, can't you? Sense him somehow? I know you can. You always seem to find us when you want."

"It doesn't work like that."

"Then how does it work?" Arayallen said as she leaned over Myropa and released a small burst of energy.

"Don't you know?" Myropa blurted in haste. Immediately, she wished she hadn't. She expected to be overwhelmed by the goddess's power. To her surprise, though, Arayallen straightened and looked at her as one may study a squashed bug.

"What *I* know is not important here. It's what *you* know. Explain to me why you can't do this miniscule task for me."

"Of course. I mean, I'll try. I'm not sure I understand it completely. I can find Trostili in Celestria."

Arayallen looked skeptical. "Only Trostili?"

"Um, yes and no. I can sense the direction of his power and follow it to him. It depends on how much he's releasing, though. He doesn't restrain it as much as you and Disevy."

With a smirk, Arayallen said, "Of course not. He's still young. It's like he doesn't even try sometimes."

Myropa struggled to wrap her mind around the notion that a god who was probably billions of years old was young. She swallowed the questions that danced on her tongue and said, "I can feel the power of the other gods, but it's, um, more diffuse. It's everywhere, and I can't really tell who it belongs to. Sometimes I can follow it, sometimes not. It's weaker here. Disevy, though—he has almost no power bleed at all."

Arayallen tapped her lips with a brilliant red fingernail. Her power retreated, and Myropa noticed the goddess's appearance for the first time. She was wearing a skintight, black leather body suit that covered everything from her chin to her wrists and down to her black boots. A red leather whip was wound and attached to the belt at her waist, and over her heart was a glowing emblem of red flame. The most striking change, though, was her hair. Arayallen's usual wavy, blonde mane was tied into a high ponytail that rested over her shoulder, and it was bloodred from roots to shoulders where it gradually transitioned to black. Myropa had never seen anything of the like.

"So," Arayallen said, waking Myropa from her daze, "you think you can't find him. I believe that you believe that, but I disagree. When you find him, tell him I need to speak with him immediately. No, best not to waste precious time. Tell him the depraved have been taken."

"The depraved?"

"He will understand. Do not, under any circumstances, mention this to Axus—or Trostili, for that matter. Actually, don't mention it to *anyone* except Disevy. Go. *Now.*"

Myropa's perpetually empty stomach twisted and the ice in her veins snapped as she was suddenly thrust from that little tent on Aldrea into the infinite ether.

CHERRÍ SHIVERED AND PULLED THE BLANKET TIGHTER AROUND HER shoulders as the frozen air inside the tent stirred. The fire rustled, and tiny sparks spiraled on a rushing eddy toward the small opening at the pinnacle. They glowed brighter with the fresh supply of air, then thankfully winked out before they could set the canvas alight.

Aria shivered and said, "What was that? The tent flap is secure."

Cherrí's gaze dropped back to the fire where she found reassurance and comfort in knowing that Everon had not only heard her prayers but had blessed them with the fiery warmth of his embrace. Her hands and feet felt a different kind of burn. Thousands of tiny pinpricks spread across her flesh as it thawed. She sucked in a breath and held it, grateful for the pain and thankful that she would not be losing any of her toes or fingers.

"We should rest," she said as her eyelids grew heavier.

Aria lifted her chin toward the edge of the tent where firelight glinted off metal. "Hand me that spear. I'll keep first watch."

Although her hands no longer shook, her fingers were still stiff as she closed them around the spearhead. She pulled the rest of the weapon into the tent only to find that nearly a quarter of the shaft was missing. She handed the broken spear to Aria and said, "Take it, but sleep. We are frozen and exhausted. Night has fallen. If we are attacked now, we're dead. It would be better to risk sleeping now so that we are both rested later."

Aria looked as if she wanted to argue, but the yawn that followed must have decided it for her. "I suppose that makes sense. I'm too tired to think." As she reclined on the pile of clothes and pillows beside her, she said, "Hopefully, we don't die."

Cherrí was not surprised to see the other woman's breathing slow to the steady rhythm of sleep as soon as her eyelids closed. Soon enough, hers did the same.

# CHAPTER 13

CHERRÍ STRUGGLED TO WAKE. SOMETHING HAD DRAWN HER FROM DEEP in slumber, but her lids wouldn't part to reveal what it was. She wiped a salty crust from her lashes, and her fingers came away wet. She realized she had been crying in her sleep. The skin around her eyes was puffy, and her chest was still tight.

"I wasn't sure if I should wake you," said Aria as she handed Cherrí a waterskin and rag.

The cold water spilled over the rag. Its fresh chill was soothing against her raw face. She pressed the pads of her fingers against her cheek and forehead. Her skin felt fevered and sensitive.

"You're windburnt," said Aria, motioning to her own red face. "It doesn't look serious—no frostbite."

Cherrí sat up and swished the water around her mouth before allowing it to slide down her parched throat. "Thank you. I'm sorry if I woke you."

"You didn't. I've been up for a while. It's already past midday."

"Really? I don't recall ever sleeping so long." Her stomach punctuated the statement with a rumble.

Aria nodded. "I thought it might have something to do with *that*," she said.

Cherrí followed her gaze to the firepit, then looked back to Aria. "What about it?" Her fingers immediately sought her face again. "Did it burn me?"

"No, nothing like that. It's just—it's been burning all night and day, and I've never fed it more wood. When you were dreaming and seemed upset, it flickered a lot. Besides that, it's never changed size."

Cherrí stretched her feet out, then reached for the kettle that sat on a rock near the fire. As she prepared herself a cup of tea, she said, "It's not me. It's Everon."

"Perhaps," said Aria as she handed Cherrí a plate filled with scrambled eggs and acorn bread, "but he is doing it through *you*."

"Why would he?" said Cherrí. "I'm no one special. *All* of my people honored him, not just me."

Aria's voice was gentle as she slowly said, "Yes, and all of your people are dead. Perhaps he was angered and has decided to use you to exact his vengeance."

"What, like a paladin? That's ridiculous."

"Is it?" Aria said as she drew Cherrí's attention back to the fire. It had curled around itself to take the form of a serpent. It hissed, then broke apart into flames as if it had never been.

Cherrí blindly reached for another piece of acorn bread on her plate and was disappointed to find that she had already consumed every morsel of her breakfast. She set the plate down and said, "Starting a cooking fire isn't exactly a recipe for vengeance."

"Maybe not, but I intend to find out what you can do."

"*I'm* not doing it. I can't control it."

"You don't know that. You didn't know you had the ability until last night."

"Everon isn't a vengeful spirit," Cherrí said. "His power isn't to be used as a weapon."

"I'd say that's for *him* to decide. If you're a paladin, then you're the vessel for his power. He's still in charge. That's the difference between a paladin and a magus."

"How do you know so much about paladins?" said Cherrí. "I've never heard of one existing outside the stories."

Aria grinned. It wasn't the rueful mirth of a lost soul. It was a cheerful smile. "I've always liked the stories. My grandmother told me one every night while my mother was helping the other elders. Of course, the warriors were my favorites, but the paladins always inspired hope—hope that a greater power was watching over us and would lend us power in our time of need."

"But you said you never believed in a greater power."

"That is true, but I had never met a paladin and hadn't had such great need of hope."

Cherrí's anger suddenly boiled to the surface seemingly out of nowhere. "This is not *my* time of need, and I have nothing left to hope *for* except the destruction of my enemies. *My* time of need was when my babes were sick and dying; when Runi and the rest of my clan were being slaughtered; when I wandered alone and desperate."

"I understand," said Aria. "Trust me, I do. I lost everyone, too. But the Fire Serpent Clan was dedicated to Everon, and he has chosen *you* to be his vessel. Your purpose is no longer about *your* time of need. It's about his."

Cherrí abruptly stood, her blood simmering beneath her fevered skin. She dropped the sheepskin that was wrapped around her shoulders and stormed from the tent. A layer of ice coated the ground and hung from branches in long, glistening icicles. Fresher dry snow danced across the ice on swirling drafts, and the crackling of boughs breaking under the added weight echoed through the woods.

A cold breeze crawled across her fevered skin, and Cherrí shivered. In the brief moment she had been observing the deserted campsite, the bottoms of her feet and toes had already gone numb. She had made a mistake. It was too cold outside for a temper tantrum. She growled, threw back the tent flap, and stomped back into the tent.

"That was fast," said Aria with a smirk.

"The temperature dropped. I need my coat and boots."

"They're still damp." With a merciless grin, she said, "You'll just have to put up with me."

Cherrí's retort hung silently on her lips as she paused to listen. A bird called out in the forest. A second later, another replied from the opposite side of the camp. Aria grabbed the broken spear as she leapt to her feet. Cherrí grabbed her still-soggy boots and shoved her bare feet into them. Without bothering to tie them, she stumbled from the tent. She glanced around for anything she could use as a weapon and spied a hunting knife beside a toppled drying rack a dozen feet away. After sprinting across the short expanse, she grabbed the knife and then ducked down between a small cart and a half-collapsed tent. Aria crouched behind a small bush beside their tent as she surveyed the forest near where the first call had sounded, so Cherrí peered around the tent to seek the location of the second. She had just set the knife down to free her hands for the task of tying her shoes when she was suddenly jerked from the ground.

Cherrí screamed as something sharp dug into her shoulder and then screamed again when a firm, scaly hand wrapped around her throat. At least, she tried to, but the sound was clipped as the assailant's grip tightened. A gurgling hiss rushed past her ear, and had she not been struggling to breathe, she might have been sick from the creature's fetid breath. Cherrí clawed at the fingers wrapped around her neck. One of her boots fell off as she kicked wildly. Her ears had barely registered a muted whistle followed by a *thunk* before the creature wailed and released her. She was gripping ice-coated detritus and gasping for breath as the creature surged past her, its attention captured by something in the trees. She noticed the lyksvight had an arrow protruding from its shoulder. A surge of renewed hope rushed through her that someone had come to their rescue. They weren't alone.

Her vision cleared, and the sounds of the wild registered with her mind once again. She realized there was more than one of the horrid creatures. In fact, a swarm of them were emerging from the western edge of the wood. Her savior was still hidden, but it quickly became apparent that there were many more nestled in the trees.

Motion to her right caught her attention. Another of the creatures was rushing at her from where Aria had been, and a surge of anxiety struck her as she realized she had lost track of her friend. The lyksvight released a terrible gurgling growl. Its pasty, grey skin hung from its bones like fat sloughing off of a roasting carcass, and saliva dripped from its deformed lips. She stumbled over her lost boot as she lunged for the knife on the ground. Her fingers brushed the deer antler handle just as a clawed hand grabbed her ankle. A second set of claws dug into the back of her thigh, and she screamed as the creature dragged her toward it.

Cherrí twisted as she slid over the ground, the rough ice cracking and breaking off to form a sharp gravel that scraped her back. The putrid monster lunged down at her, and Cherrí closed her eyes and threw her hands up in a useless effort to protect herself. Suddenly, her hands were wrapped in a tingling warmth that quickly suffused the rest of her body. The next thing she knew, the creature atop her was enveloped in blistering flames. It shrieked and stumbled backward as its saggy flesh sizzled and popped.

Shocked by the sudden development, Cherrí scrambled back to grab the knife, kicked off her other boot, then started running toward the tree line. Her shoulder, calf, and thigh screamed with every motion of her body, but the rush of energy she felt from the sudden battle kept her moving.

When she reached the underbrush, she saw that whoever had saved her was also under attack. Three humans were struggling against four lyksvight. Cherrí paused, unexpectedly entrenched in a battle against her own nerves over the prospect of jumping into the fray. In that brief moment, one of the lyksvight sliced a man's throat open. The spray of warm blood slapped her in the face, waking her from her fear-filled stupor. Cherrí hurried forward and stabbed the lyksvight in the back with her hunting knife. Its back arched as she held her grip firmly and pulled the knife free. Flames erupted from the wound, and the creature's skin began to split and crackle, revealing a fiery glow beneath it. The lyksvight abruptly exploded, flaming shards of flesh, bone, and bubbling blood flying in every direction. The three other lyksvight, having forgotten their original prey, turned toward her. One was immediately impaled by a short spear through his back, but the other two rushed at her.

With two opponents closing in on her, Cherrí dearly wished she had a shield. One of the lyksvights' former prey sliced the larger creature across the back with the blade of a short sword. The creature barely registered the attack as it reached for Cherrí. The second creature grabbed at her from the left, and Cherrí raised her arm to protect herself while stabbing at the first. A glowing disk of fire ignited between her and the second creature, which caused the first to pause. Cherrí stared at the disk in awe for a brief second, then hardened her resolve and smashed it into the lyksvight's face. Acrid black smoke escaped between its leathery fingers as it gripped its face, and Cherrí used the momentum of surprise to attack the larger creature. As she did so, the swordsman nearly took the second's head clean off its shoulders.

The larger lyksvight avoided the glowing inferno that was Cherrí's shield but failed to dodge the slash of her knife. As the wound across its chest sizzled, Cherrí struck again and again. She finally buried the knife up to its hilt in the creature's abdomen, then ripped it upward, spilling its burning entrails over the ground. Fire consumed the lyksvight, turning it to a charred heap in a matter of seconds.

Cherrí turned to find the next foe. After several heaving breaths, she realized both the forest and encampment had quieted. She blinked away tears she hadn't realized were falling from her eyes and noticed that others, *humans*, were gathering around her. Nearly a dozen strangers surrounded her, but there was only one person that truly concerned her. Finally, she spied her. Aria's blood-spattered face appeared haggard as the woman limped toward her. She was supporting an injured stranger despite her own wounds. She helped the young man to the ground and propped him against a tree before walking over to stand in front of Cherrí. Her gaze was assessing as she studied Cherrí.

"This is a good look on you," she said.

"What? Beaten and bloody?"

Aria shook her head. She limped a few feet toward the swordsman and held out her hand. "Aria," she said.

He cautiously handed Aria the sword and said, "Hamman."

She nodded. "Nice to meet you, Hamman." She wiped blood from the sword using her own tunic as she walked back over to Cherrí and held up the sword. Cherrí gazed at her reflection. She had never seen anything of the like. There she was, bloody and disheveled, covered in bits of gore, yet she did not recognize herself. The image was one of the most magnificent sights she had ever seen. Her entire form was surrounded by an aura of fire, a corona of sunlight. Her shield of flame and glowing knife looked like holy relics from the Godsland. She had the appearance of a warrior of the gods.

"Paladin indeed," said Aria.

Cherrí stared at the stunning image as it began to subside. The shield shrank until it was no more, and it seemed as if her radiant aura was absorbed by her skin. Soon enough, she could see *herself* again in the reflection. She looked at Aria in wonder, then turned her attention toward the others. No one spoke. They all seemed to be waiting for her.

Without knowing what else to say, she muttered, "I'm Cherrí."

Aria turned to stand next to her and announced, "Cherrí is the Paladin of Everon."

Cherrí didn't like the questioning stares. Some appeared skeptical while others, more disturbingly, looked upon her as if she, herself, was a god.

"Paladins aren't real," said a man to her right. He was stout with a thick, bushy beard. He wore a floppy grey cap and carried a longbow ideal for hunting on the vast emptiness of the plateau.

"You saw her power," said Aria.

"Aye, I did. Why a mage needs to pretend to be a paladin is a mystery to me."

"I'm not a mage," said Cherrí. "No one in my bloodline has been a mage."

"That you know of," said the man.

Cherrí exclaimed, "No, I just got this power after my clan was slaughtered!"

"What does it matter? She saved your life," said a hearty-looking woman carrying a spear. She appeared to be in her forties and looked to have had a rough life like many of those belonging to the migratory clans.

"Only after I saved hers," grumped the older man.

"You were the archer who saved me?" said Cherrí. "Thank you. I thought for sure I was dead when that horrid lyksvight grabbed me."

"Lyksvight?" said the woman.

Aria said, "That's what the grey creatures are called. They're usually accompanied by a Berruvian magus, but it seems these were on their own."

Cherrí looked at Aria. "How many were there? How did you defeat them?"

"Maybe fifteen. Your light distracted them. You lit up, and they turned to attack you. We were able to pick them off from behind. We were lucky these people came along, though. I doubt we would have lasted long on our own, even with your power."

"How did you find us?" said Cherrí.

"We weren't looking for you," said the old man. "We were tracking *them*. They came through the forest along the mountains from the north. They must have smelled your campfire."

"Huh. I didn't think of that," said Aria. "I should have."

"We were both exhausted. Neither of us were thinking straight," said Cherrí.

A sudden gust tousled the ice-crusted leaves, and a violent shiver rocked Cherrí to her core. Her teeth chattered as she said, "I n-need t-to g-g-g-get inside."

Aria's eyes widened as she appeared to see Cherrí for the first time. "What were you thinking? You should be frozen by now."

"I g-guess it w-was the b-b-battle," said Cherrí.

The woman barked a short laugh. "More likely the fire you were swimming in."

Aria wrapped her arm around Cherrí and guided her back toward their tent. The rest of the clan followed except for a few who stayed behind to act as lookouts. The tent seemed much smaller with seven of the clan members, Aria, and Cherrí occupying it. The fire was still burning smoothly even though the logs had long ago burned to ash. Aria placed a fresh log in it anyway. At Cherrí's questioning look, she said, "Probably uses less of your energy this way."

"I don't feel anything," said Cherrí.

Aria shrugged. "It doesn't hurt to try."

"What's this about paladins?" said the older man.

"Quiet, Broden," said the woman. "Have some manners." The lines on her face deepened as she smiled at Aria and Cherrí. "My name's Hennis. That's Broden. We've been sharing the burden of leadership over the Yellowtail Clan since our leader was killed."

"More like squabbling over it," muttered a young man of about fifteen as he tossed his shaggy brown hair from his eyes. He sat cross-legged near the opening of the tent.

"The sullen boy over there is Pongin, my son."

"It's just Pong," said the boy.

"You'll get to know the others in time." She turned to Aria. "I didn't catch your name."

"I'm Aria of the Great Oryx Clan."

The woman nodded. "That explains your battle prowess. And you said your name is Cherrí?"

"Yes, of the Fire Serpent Clan."

"Ah, there you have it," she said with an elbow to Broden's ribs. "If anyone were to become a paladin of Everon, it would be a Fire Serpent."

Broden merely grunted, and Cherrí said, "My clan is dead. I'm the last. Aria's as well. We had joined a gathering of members from other clans who had been attacked. They, too, were killed yesterday."

"You couldn't save them with your power?" said Broden doubtfully.

"I didn't know I had it," said Cherrí. "I mean, something happened after my clan was killed, but I thought it was just a dream. Now, I'm not so sure."

"Tell us about these—what did you call them—lyksvight? How do you know what they are, and where did they come from? What do they want?"

"We don't know all the answers," said Aria, "but we'll tell you what we know."

# CHAPTER 14

CHERRÍ WIPED HER BLADE ON THE BLOOD-CRUSTED CLOTH SHE'D BEEN using to clean it after each battle. The white blood was thicker than normal human blood and bore an acrid smell, hinting that it would likely damage the steel quickly if left to dry on the blade. It was the second time that day she had found occasion to use the knife. The first was that morning shortly after dawn. They had arrived at the trading post that marked the entrance to the Desding Pass. The pass would take them to the upper plateau that was Mouvilan. Upon reaching the trading post, though, they found that it had been already overrun by a small band of lyksvight. Her new clan members were becoming more adept at fighting the creatures with each encounter. They had endured four battles already between the time they left the encampment and when they had arrived at the trading post. After the short battle, she had turned to find Aria. Her friend was busy ignoring Pong as he bragged about how many lyksvight he had killed. Cherrí was sure it was no more than one and was equally certain the boy claimed at least three.

"What do you think?" said Hennis.

"There are fewer lyksvight up here," said Cherrí. "Maybe they haven't yet made it here, or maybe they don't like the altitude."

"The cold doesn't seem to bother them."

"No, but they're not very agile. Perhaps they have a difficult time scaling the mountain. At least the trading post seems to be intact."

"Over here!" hollered another man.

Cherrí didn't know his real name. Everyone called him Skinny. And he was. She and Hennis joined Skinny at the entrance to the East Ridge Trading Post's root cellar. A man and woman stared up at them. The woman was holding a little girl while the man trained an arrow on them.

"Now you don't go shooting us," said Hennis. "We killed the lyksvight. You can come on out now."

The trading post owners glanced at each other, then hurried up the wooden steps to the snow-draped surface. The man settled a pair of broken spectacles on the bridge of his nose and peered back at the trading post. "It looks okay. Did they get in through the back?"

"Doesn't appear so," said Skinny, "but did you have a horse?"

"Two, actually," said the man.

"Not anymore," replied Skinny.

"Oh no! Not Pollen and Honeysuckle. They were such sweet mares, both of them."

"Well, this one survived!" hollered Broden as he led a honey-colored palomino toward them. She had several deep gouges on her hindquarter and was obviously disturbed.

"That's Pollen," said the woman. "At least we can ride away from here. What if more of those things come?"

"You'll probably not be any safer out there. At least here you have supplies and walls," said Cherrí.

"We could come with you," said the woman.

"I'm sorry, but we can't take you with us. We're moving fast and will be avoiding cities and towns until we get to Chelis."

"But surely there's safety in the cities."

"We're not going to risk it," said Cherrí. "We have a mission."

"Come," said the man. "We can thaw ourselves inside and have something warm to eat while we talk."

Cherrí glanced at Hennis, then relented. "All right. But we can't stay long. We must get moving so we can reach the end of the Desding Pass before nightfall."

"Fair enough. You wouldn't want to get stuck in the pass if there's an attack."

That was exactly what had happened, though. It had started to snow and sleet around midday, and the fresh layer of snow and ice had made the trek treacherous at best. Expanding ice fractured stone that would have taken many workers months to chisel away, and the sharp boulders and loose talus had formed a hazardous labyrinth for them to navigate. On more than one occasion, Cherrí had slid into a hole that she had, at first, thought herself unable to escape. The feeling of entrapment had nearly overwhelmed her, but the presence of Aria and the others had kept her from losing her mind.

Skinny was the only clan member who had ever been through the pass. He claimed they were still not two-thirds of the way through when night fell. They had taken refuge among the larger boulders. Using their coats and skins, they covered the cracks and openings between the rocks and started a fire inside their little den. They would not have survived the frigid night without it. Their efforts had not been enough to hide them from the magi, though.

The enemy had come down the pass from the western entrance right at dusk. A magus and another that looked young enough to be an apprentice were accompanied by a band of about twenty lyksvight. The lyksvight didn't seem to care about the sleet and cold, but the magi had created a magical shield over their heads that partially wrapped around them to block the elements. It was the metallic patter of frozen droplets against the shield that had alerted Cherrí's new clan to the enemy's presence.

Cherrí had nearly fallen asleep when their sentry hissed for everyone to be quiet. They listened, and as they did so, it became apparent they were not alone. Soon after they heard the drumming, the scent of fetid corpses suffused the air. It was followed by the terrifying hoots and growls that only the lyksvight could produce.

"We're surrounded," whispered Aria.

Broden moved to push one of the sealskin coats aside and paused. He said, "Douse the fire."

"What's the point?" said Aria. "They already know we're here."

Broden looked to Hennis. She, in turn, looked to Cherrí. Cherrí's gaze dropped to the soothing yellow light that was evidence of the great spirit's favor. "No," she said. "Everon will protect us with his light and warmth."

"Like he's protected all the people who have fallen prey to these monsters?" said Broden.

"You don't know what happened to the sentries. Let us remove the barriers against Everon's light and allow his power to shine upon our enemies."

"What?" he exclaimed. "You want us to expose ourselves?"

Cherrí had felt confident in Everon's powers in that moment, but she still questioned her ability to wield them. If she had done nothing, though, they would likely have died. It was only then that she resolved to become the paladin Aria thought her to be.

"What protection are a few coats and furs against these monsters?" she retorted before getting to her feet with her staff in one hand. She had gripped the fur-lined cloak that had been laid across the boulders to create their roof. Her prayer to Everon for protection and strength felt muted in the stifling makeshift tent yet seemed to resonate in her core.

"Please, Everon, Great Spirit, protect us with your light and grant unto me the power to slay your enemies who seek to extinguish your flame."

The others scrambled to collect their weapons as she whipped the cloak away. The other furs and coats dropped to the icy snow, and the lyksvight released a unified howl.

"Get back!" shouted one of the sentries to another. The man was too slow to move, though, and he was the first to fall.

Cherrí's grip tightened on her staff as her heart pounded. Her confidence faltered, but Everon's power did not. Just as she became certain she had made a mistake, flame erupted from her hand to encapsulate the tip of her staff. The flamed licked the air as if it had a mind of its own. She stepped away from those who were huddled around her and swung the staff in a circle. Fire streaked from it in great arcs as the staff sliced the air. It settled into an expanding ring between her clan and the enemy without injuring her companions.

Among the snarls and squeals of the lyksvight, who continued to test the barrier even after having been burned several times, Cherrí could hear the low drone of chanting. A flash of light to her right was quickly followed by another to her left. Something powerful struck the fire barrier, causing it to waver. The chanting continued, and mage-born attack after attack threatened to collapse the protective ward. Cherrí wasn't sure what to do, having never faced an actual magus, much less two.

The ring of fire was suddenly struck with a surge of liquified snow, and a small opening allowed for one or two lyksvight to press through. Aria met the first lyksvight, slamming it in the face with the blunt end of her spear, then slashing and stabbing it. As she wrestled the creature, another fell upon Broden, and two more went after the others.

Cherrí prayed for guidance and found herself swirling the tip of the staff in small circles in front of her. A flaming whirlwind began to form above the staff. It grew, streaming into the air like a fire tornado. Then, she cast the tornado toward the opening. It plowed through the lyksvight crowding the opening, then continued to wreak havoc among the others. Although the lyksvight screeched from the flames, they did not seem to acknowledge when they had been set aflame, and they continued to press against the fiery barrier until their limbs charred and fell away. Eventually, those who were not overcome by the flame were dispatched by Cherrí's companions. The tainted scent of burning hair and bone mixed with that of charred meat was enough to make her stomach flip.

Just as Cherrí thought she would vomit, a flying boulder the size of a goat struck her. She had managed to turn so that only her left side took the brunt; but, still, it forcefully knocked her to the ground. The boulder tumbled down the slope behind her, and she slid after it. Her descent was abruptly arrested when she collided with another large boulder. Cherrí did her best to ignore the pain as she got to her feet. She had lost her staff, but her knife was still sheathed at her waist.

Cherrí drew the knife, and at the same time, the flaming shield manifested on her left forearm. Although her arm would not respond, and she couldn't wield the shield effectively, she was glad it was there to protect her injured side. She breathed heavily as she pressed through the pain of climbing back up the talus slope toward the battle. Just as she reached the scene, a spattering of debris pummeled Aria, causing her to stumble into Broden, who was fending off two lyksvight. One of the creatures slashed Broden across the chest with its sharp claws, and Hennis screamed. The beefy woman barreled toward the younger magus who had cast the attack. The young man scrambled to release a blazing ball of light toward Hennis, and just as he succeeded, Cherrí threw her knife toward him. She had no idea why she did so. It was not designed to be a throwing knife, and Cherrí had never learned to throw knives anyway. Still, it surged forward with flaming tongues spiraling from it until it buried itself in the young magus's chest. Hennis followed up with an attack of her own until there was no doubt the foreigner was dead.

Cherrí's shield was abruptly struck by a powerful jolt. Her left side screamed in pain as she crashed into the boulder beside her. She pushed away from the rock that had prevented her from falling down the slope again and scrambled toward the other magus. Another bright red javelin of power surged toward her, which she managed to knock away with her flaming shield. As she got closer to the magus, he lobbed another, then another. She ducked the first, and the second glanced off her shield, not without causing another burst of searing pain. The agony she felt was nothing beside the rage that was growing at her core.

The magus created a swirling ball of flame. Cherrí clenched her fist, and before he could cast it, the fire winked out. When she was nearly upon the magus, she picked up a rock. With another prayer muttered to Everon, the rock became a roiling ball of lava. The lava grew hotter until the gaseous flames burned vivid blue. The magus turned to run, and Cherrí lashed out with her shield. It sliced through both his legs, taking them off just above the knee. From his crumpled form emanated an anguished wail so pitiful it might have garnered sympathy from the soulless lyksvight, but not from Cherrí. She leaned over the fallen magus and smashed the lava ball into the back of his head. It seared straight through the cranium and into the ground, leaving behind only a bulbous ring of burbling flesh.

Cherrí felt an abrupt emptiness. A frigid wind blew across her sweaty skin, nearly stealing her breath. Her vision began to clear of the bright spots that had briefly blinded her, and she realized she was bent over a corpse panting in the pitch-black night. The terrible aromas of fetid corpse, burnt flesh and bone, and white and red blood finally overcame her, and she vomited all over the cadaver. She quickly turned away and stumbled back toward the center of the battle.

It was over. She could hear her companions calling to each other in the dark. Some moaned in pain, while others implored them to be still. Somewhere, someone said her name. Another asked if anyone had a fire stick.

"Cherrí!"

Again, she heard her name. She swallowed again as bile threatened to invade her sinuses. It was all she could do to keep it down, and the burning pain of her injuries was only making it worse. "Here," she croaked, but she could barely hear her own voice.

"Cherrí! Where are you?" the voice called again. This time she recognized it as Aria's.

Cherrí cleared her throat and said a little more loudly, "I'm here. I'm okay—more or less."

"Oh, Cherrí, I'm so glad you're okay," said Aria as she grabbed for Cherrí in the dark. Aria's fingers were freezing as they wrapped around Cherrí's hot, moist hands.

"I'm a little injured, but not too badly. I think my arm is dislocated. How about you?"

"Some cuts and scrapes. My wrist hurts. I don't think it's broken, though—maybe just sprained. When all the fires went out at once, I was worried you'd been killed."

Cherrí blinked into the dark. Her vision had temporarily abandoned her, so she hadn't seen what had happened. "Can someone start a fire?" she said. "I don't think I have anything left right now."

"Skinny's on it. I'm sure he'll have one going in no time. Hennis and the others are putting the shelter back together."

"Already? How long has it been?"

"Only a few minutes, but no one is wearing their coats, and we're all freezing, so that's our priority."

"Fair enough, but we shouldn't camp here."

"We don't really have a choice. It's pitch-black down here in the pass, and you know what the terrain is like. To try to move even a few yards could be disastrous. Besides, the firepit is primed here, and we can't wait."

So it was that Cherrí and her companions spent the rest of the night among the corpses of their enemies. Once inside their den, Hennis threw some fragrant weeds onto the smoky fire, which helped to make the smells somewhat bearable. When morning came, Cherrí wasn't really surprised that scavengers hadn't touched the bodies of the fallen lyksvight. Nothing seemed to want to be near those things. Aria had helped pop her dislocated shoulder back into place before they lay down to rest, and Cherrí had begrudgingly placed a packet of icy snow on it. Although the swelling was down, her shoulder and the rest of her body ached as though she had been buried in an avalanche.

She had collected her staff and her knife and there she stood cleaning the blade as she stared at the slaughter. They had lost three of their own. To Hennis's relief, Broden had not been one of them. The wounds across his chest were deep and would likely fester without treatment, but he was alive.

"We should go," said Cherrí.

"I'm not sure he can make it," said Hennis.

Cherrí looked at Broden and remembered all the fallen clansmen she had lost. "He'll either make it or he won't. We can't stay here. We're all injured, so we'll be moving slowly. We need to make it out of the pass, hopefully with a few hours to spare. I doubt those will be the last of the Berru to try to use it."

Hennis pursed her lips but didn't argue. She had to know Cherrí was right. They divided up Broden's supplies so that he wouldn't have to carry them and set off toward the west. It was still a very long way until they reached Chelis.

# CHAPTER 15

AASLO SLID THE BOOK HE WAS SKIMMING BACK ONTO THE SHELF AND grabbed a scroll that had been stuffed between it and the next tome. He was certain he was getting close. Each book on the shelf had contained a little information about using spells to travel, and a few had mentioned the evergates. Teza was at the other end of the shelf working her way toward him, and Ijen was across the room sifting through books containing information about runes.

The chamber was full of shelves, trunks, baskets, and racks each containing books, scrolls, tapestries, and story crystals. The bookcases created an odd labyrinth of passages, and although they had been in the magi's library for nearly two hours, Aaslo still had not seen its entirety. False flame torches that appeared as fire but were constructed of spells that didn't burn lit the recesses, gracing the room with a warm, golden glow. Tables with parchment and various writing utensils were scattered throughout the chamber, and a small drinking fountain stood by the entrance.

Aaslo unrolled the scroll and frowned. The script was strange but legible. It was a letter from one magus to another regarding the aftermath of a battle. Aaslo skipped to the bottom to see who had written the note.

His voice echoed through the room as he said, "Have you heard of a Sorcerer Wythmor? It sounds familiar."

"Um, I don't think so," said Teza.

"Did you say *Wythmor*?" said Ijen as he crossed the room.

"Yes, was he important?"

Ijen glanced at Teza with disapproval, then said, "He was an ancient, one of the original magi." Looking back to Teza, he said, "You should know that."

Teza threw up her hands. "Please, I can't be expected to remember *everything*. He lived like . . . thousands of years ago or something. And there were so many of them."

"Sixteen. There were sixteen. You couldn't remember sixteen names?"

She shrugged. "I had better things to do."

Ijen shook his head and looked at Aaslo. "What do you have?"

"It's a letter written by Wythmor about a battle."

"Oh? That must have been during the Power War. Who was the recipient?"

"I think it says *Enchantress Tryst*."

"Oh, Tryst! I know that name," said Teza. "She was the one who disappeared after the war. No one knows what happened to her. Most assume she was killed, but her body was never found."

Ijen looked at her again. "Wythmor went on to father one of the great bloodlines with hundreds of descendants; yet you remember Tryst, who vanished, never to be heard from again."

"She was an *enchantress*," said Teza. "Besides, we made up stories about what really happened to her. In one of them, a massive golem of her own making fell in love with her and scooped her up to—"

"You are unbelievable," said Aaslo.

*"Why did you interrupt her? I want to hear the story."*

Teza grinned at him. "Thank you."

"Does the scroll say anything of use to us?" said Ijen.

*"Everything is of use, just not necessarily at this moment."*

"That's not helpful," Aaslo muttered. Then to Ijen, he said, "Maybe. Wythmor mentions that he was in Lyzen, which I believe was present-day Lodenon. Apparently, he had a meeting with Etrieli the following day in Monsque. He says he's nearly perfected distant travel."

"Really? That's interesting," said Ijen. "I thought that kind of travel had been developed long before the Power War. I also didn't realize Wythmor was the one to do it."

"Evidently, he wasn't. He says that Saft and Arlouelle won't be able to keep the secret to themselves any longer."

"That makes more sense," said Ijen. "Saft was a leader in magical advancement, and Arlouelle was known for taking risks."

"So, this is about building the evergates?"

"No, no. Those were built many generations after the Power War. I believe I mentioned the ancients could travel great distances without the gates."

Aaslo placed the scroll back between the books. "Useless," he muttered.

*"Is it?"*

He released a heavy sigh. "What about *that* was helpful?"

"I suppose it's not," said Ijen as he walked back to his stack of tomes.

*"Maybe you can find out how they traveled."*

"That doesn't help us destroy the evergates," Aaslo said as he grabbed the next book on the shelf.

*"You can be so dense."*

When Aaslo was finished scanning the book, he went on to the next, and then the next, and the next.

"Ow!" Teza shouted when her head struck a shelf. She had bent to retrieve a small pamphlet that had fallen out of another book. While rubbing her head, she said, "I think I found something."

Aaslo placed the book he was skimming back on the shelf and walked over to her. "What is it?"

"It looks like an instruction manual. And it has a drawing of an evergate on the front." She flipped through it as Aaslo looked over her shoulder. "Nope. Never mind. It's just instructions for how to use one, which we already know."

"Wait," said Aaslo as he stopped a page from turning. "What is that?"

"It's a diagram of the runes around the gate. Remember? You saw them in Yarding."

*"Yeah, remember, Aaslo the Great?"*

"I didn't get a good look." Aaslo glanced at Ijen who appeared to be pondering the books without actually picking up any of them. "Ijen?" The prophet didn't seem to hear him. "Ijen!" Again, Ijen stood tapping his lip as his unfocused gaze rested on the book spines. Aaslo strode over to the prophet and patted him on the shoulder. Ijen turned, but he seemed dazed.

"I think he's caught up in a prophecy," said Teza. "This is why people make fun of prophets for being absentminded. Get it? Because their minds are absent—since they're seeing—"

"I get it."

*"Of course you do. You're an expert in mindless tasks."*

"Forestry is *not* a mindless task," he grumped. Then to Teza, "How long does it last?"

"I don't know. I make it a policy to know as little as possible about prophets."

*"That's how I felt about the forest."*

"I don't understand willful ignorance," said Aaslo. "What does it hurt to know something?"

*"Says the man who complained about Grams's lessons."*

"I wasn't complaining. I was just saying that if I had to learn your stuff, you needed to learn mine."

"You want me to learn to be a forester?" said Teza.

"What? No. I want to know about these runes—and the others."

"Which others?"

"All of them."

Teza's eyes widened. "There are thousands of runes—*tens* of thousands. You'll never know *all* of them. People spend their entire lives studying them."

"Why are there so many?"

It was Ijen who answered, as though he'd been engaged in the conversation all along. "Runes aren't carved in stone—I mean, they *are*, but their meanings aren't, metaphorically speaking. Each rune is a map for a spell. It doesn't really matter how it looks. I could use one rune to draw water from a well, while you could use the same rune to burn down a house. What the rune actually *does* is specific to the runesmith who created it."

"If that's true, how can you learn any of them?"

"Some runes have been standardized so people can recognize them. Those who follow the standard use the same runes for the same purposes."

Teza smirked. "We get in big trouble for making a rune do something it shouldn't, even if it's just a prank."

"I can see there's a story there, but I'm not sure I want to know it," said Aaslo.

Teza winked at him. "You will."

*"She's weird."*

"Indeed." Aaslo took the pamphlet from Teza and showed it to Ijen. He pointed to the diagram of the evergate. "I want to know what these runes mean."

"These, here, contain the travel spell, this one connects your power to the spell—so you don't get lost in the paths—and these are all destination runes. Different combinations will send you to different evergates."

"What happens if you choose a combination that doesn't go anywhere?"

"That's a problem and one reason fledglings aren't allowed to use the gates until their fifth year. You may end up at a random gate or you could be lost in the pathways *or* you could be pulled in many directions at once."

*"That sounds like fun."*

"You'd be torn apart?" said Aaslo.

"It's possible."

"What if you connect to them all at the same time?"

Ijen tapped the book he kept tucked into his tunic. "I cannot say."

"You can't because you don't know or can't because you won't?"

"Both."

Aaslo narrowed his eyes at the prophet. Every time something came up that was relevant to his prophecy, the man bottled up.

*"That means you're on to something."*

"Yes, but is it good or bad?"

"That depends on your perspective," said Ijen.

"I'm asking from *my* perspective."

"Yours is the most difficult perspective of all. Your ability to raise the dead is truly terrible and disturbing, and I wholly disapprove, but it's also been helpful to your cause."

*"My* cause? Don't you mean *our* cause?"

"Of course."

Teza jumped between them and turned to face Aaslo with her finger raised. "You see? He can't be trusted."

Aaslo didn't know what connecting his power to all the runes would do, but based on the prophet's reaction, he knew he had done so in at least one branch of the prophecy. If he had, he must have had a reason for doing so. Then again, if *this* was the branch, then he had only done so *because* it was in the prophecy, thereby creating a paradox. He abruptly realized why Ijen *couldn't* say what would happen. Aaslo had to make the decision on his own *without* foreknowledge of the outcome.

"Let's do it," he said.

"Do what?" replied Teza.

"We'll go into the evergate and connect to all the runes."

"But we could die!"

*"That's my boy! Here you come, and you're bringing your friends with you."*

Aaslo looked to Ijen to gauge his reaction; but, as usual, his face was blank. Did it appear a little pale? Aaslo pointed to the diagram. "You said combinations of runes would send you to different places, but you only had me connect to this one rune back in Yarding."

Ijen cleared his throat. "Yes, this one will always bring you back here no matter where you are."

"So, this is like a central evergate? It's the main one?"

"Yes."

"Good, then we'll do it here. If we can destroy the central evergate, maybe it will destroy all the others."

Teza appeared skeptical. "I don't think it works that way."

"It doesn't matter how it works," Aaslo said with a huff of frustration. "We don't have time to go gallivanting across all of Aldrea destroying each and every evergate. We need to somehow destroy them all at once."

*"Now who's believing in fairy tales?"*

Teza thrust her hands onto her hips and scowled. "What happened to all that forester wisdom? Just because you want to be able to do that doesn't mean it will work."

*"Hear, hear!"*

"I'm not an idiot," said Aaslo. "I know it's a long shot, but we need to do something quickly. Even if it only destroys this one evergate, we can at least keep the citadel out of enemy hands. Destroying this one may not destroy the others, but if it does, all the better."

"We don't even know if your foolhardy plan will work. We may succeed only in destroying *ourselves.*"

"If we don't do something, we'll be destroying ourselves anyway. It'll just take longer."

Teza crossed her arms. "This is stupid."

*"Agreed. I think she's smarter than you, Aaslo."*

"Your opinion is noted," growled Aaslo. "You don't have to participate. Stay here with Ijen. Live out your days in the comfort of the citadel."

"Now you're being even stupider. What is it you always say? Brothers in all things?"

*"Hey, that's my thing!"*

"You're not my brother."

"Well, I'm *something,* and I'm coming with you."

They both turned toward Ijen. The prophet didn't look happy, which wasn't unusual. He merely shrugged and looked away with apathy. Aaslo wondered, not for the first time, what madness must go on inside the mind of the prophet. The man had seen countless paths and the horrors that went with each of them. He wondered how such a person could stay sane.

"So, uh, when are we doing this?" said Teza.

"There's no time like the present."

*"I knew you were in a hurry to see me again."*

Aaslo's stomach soured. "We should do it before I change my mind."

With a quaver in her voice, Teza said, "Right, I'll just get my stuff and meet you at the evergate." Then she headed toward the platform that would elevate her to the room above.

Aaslo's stomach continued to churn with anxiety as thoughts of what might happen to them flooded his mind.

*"Getting cold feet already?"*

"Not as cold as yours," Aaslo muttered.

*"Ha! That's funny. Because I'm dead, right?"*

A pang of guilt struck Aaslo for the errant comment. There had been a time when he could jest with Mathias, but since his brother's death, he felt only loss where there should have been laughter.

"I'd like to grab a few things while we're here," said Ijen, "since there's no telling if we'll be able to return." He waved to the collected works of the magi throughout time and said, "This place has numerous magical artifacts in addition to all of this."

Aaslo could see how, as one of possibly the only two remaining Endricsian magi in Aldrea, the loss would be painful for the prophet. The books were Ijen's trees, and Aaslo was taking him from them.

"I'm sorry, Ijen," he said.

The prophet turned to him with a fathomless gaze that seemed both present and *not*. He said, "I have always known that you would eventually take everything from me. That is why I never bothered to accrue anything of worth." Then, Ijen stepped farther into the stacks and lost himself in the tomes.

Aaslo was alone with his thoughts.

*"I'm here!"*

No, never alone, but somehow Ijen's words had cut him to the bone. If what Ijen said was true, why would he stay and subject himself to the torture? Aaslo felt guilt for something he couldn't have prevented. Then, he wondered if there *was* a way to prevent it, and he just hadn't chosen that path. Was the prophet destined to resent him for his choices when only Ijen could clearly see the alternatives? *Did* Ijen resent him? Would such resentment cause the prophet to eventually turn on him? Was Ijen already the enemy? There were too many questions without answers, and it made Aaslo uneasy.

*"Surely you have some sage forester wisdom for this."*

"Forester wisdoms are meant for the *forest*. These are people, and you know how I feel about people."

*"Yet you work so hard to save them."*

"Not just them. Besides, I admit they should exist. I just don't need to exist *with* them all the time."

*"Except me, of course. I'm always with you."*

Aaslo's hand brushed the sack that hung from his belt. He wasn't sure if it was a blessing or a curse. He hated the implication of hearing Mathias's voice, yet he dreaded the day it ceased.

Aaslo glanced at the rune books Ijen had been perusing when he had lost focus. One stood out to him, as it seemed to have been misplaced.

The spine read *Encyclopedia of the Fae and Other Magical Beings.* Aaslo was surprised at the thickness of the book. He was astounded there were so many magical creatures in Aldrea and that the magi seemed to know so much about them. He grabbed the heavy tome and then activated the spell to call the platform that would carry him into the upper room.

*"Another weight to bear."*

Aaslo grunted his agreement and said, "Come."

Greylan stepped from the shadowed corner where he had been standing sentry to join Aaslo on the platform. Aaslo briefly wondered if the undead guard had thoughts or if he was merely an empty vessel. Did Greylan also resent him? Did he blame Aaslo for his death? Just as Aaslo thought to ask, they arrived in the student library. He put his questions aside and returned to his room to collect his belongings. Afterward, he went to the courtyard, where Rostus waited with the horses. The living horses were restless, but the undead horses looked exactly as they had when they died. It was as if they were frozen in time.

As Aaslo approached Dolt, the ornery horse turned to face the other direction and swatted him in the face with his tail. Aaslo growled and rounded the beast. As soon as he reached the horse's head, Dolt turned around again, lifted his tail, and defecated on Aaslo's boots.

Mathias's laughter resonated around Aaslo's skull.

"Look, you miserable horse. Stop this now." He stepped around Dolt once again. This time, Dolt laid his ears back and rolled up his lips to expose his teeth. He turned around a third time and kicked Aaslo squarely in the chest.

Aaslo was thrust onto his back, unable to breathe. As he struggled for air, his vision began to darken. The last pinpoint of light disappeared, and then Aaslo was standing in a garden. It was a bright, beautiful day, the perfect temperature. Greens were deeper than he had ever imagined green could be, and reds, blues, and yellows popped with an unnatural, luminous brilliance.

"What are you doing here?" said a melodic, albeit *upset*, voice from behind him.

Aaslo turned around to find the most stunning creature he had ever seen looking at him with displeasure. She had bloodred hair streaked with golden highlights that shimmered like fire, a sultry figure, skin the color of black walnut, and a powerful glow that demanded worship. It was her eyes that captivated him, though. They were the color of amber interlaced with flecks of emerald.

"Who are you?" he said.

She took three strides toward him, closing the distance more quickly than he would have thought possible. It was at that point that he realized she was a giant. She towered over him such that his head barely reached her chest—a lovely, yet uncomfortable, view. She stared down at him, not with anger but curiosity.

"I'm Aaslo," he said. "Forester of Goldenwood."

She tilted her head. "What is a forester of Goldenwood? Are you an intelligent species? No, never mind that. You obviously are. Is your species magical?"

"Foresters aren't a species. We're human. Some humans possess magic."

The giant woman tapped her lip as her gaze turned upward toward the deep blue sky. "Hmm, *human.* Human, human, human. It sounds familiar, but there are just so many. It's strange that Arayallen didn't make you symmetrical."

"What?" Aaslo followed her gaze to his dragon side. "Oh, no, that happened more recently. An unfortunate accident—sort of."

"What world are you from?"

Aaslo surveyed the garden once again and realized he couldn't identify a single plant. "I'm from Aldrea," he mumbled in dismay. "Where am I?"

"You don't know? How odd. You are in Celestria."

The name tickled his memory, then his gaze shot toward the giant woman. "The realm of the gods?"

She smiled, and it was as if the whole garden brightened. "How did you get here?"

"I don't know," he said. "Who are you? Are you a god?"

"My, you're direct. I am Enani. Are you not in awe?"

Aaslo frowned. Something didn't feel right. With a start, he reached for the sack at his waist and realized Mathias was gone. He was also missing his pack and weapons. "The gods have been less than friendly," he growled. "Where are my things, and why am I here?"

She tilted her head. "I don't know why you're here. You were supposed to tell me."

"Well, I didn't do this," he said.

"I did," said another woman—no, *god*—who seemed to have just appeared on the garden path beside them.

"Arayallen, what is this all about?" said Enani. She spoke gently and without a hint of the frustration that Aaslo felt. "You know you are not supposed to bring soul bearers here."

"Hmph. If Axus can do it, I can."

Enani nodded. "I heard about that. Still, he didn't bring the creature *here,* only its essence." She pointed toward Aaslo. "This is completely different."

"This," the golden-haired goddess said, "is the same creature."

Enani looked at him as if he were a strange bug to be studied. "What is so special about this one?"

The one named Arayallen sighed. "Nothing."

"Why did you bring him here, Arayallen?"

"I need a favor. You are the Goddess of Realms. I want you to help him travel the paths."

"You want me to bless him? *Him,* specifically?"

"No," said Arayallen. "He's already blessed. Did you not notice?"

Enani shrugged. "I wasn't paying that much attention. If he's already blessed, then what do you want of me?"

"I want you to teach him."

"Ha! You want *me* to teach this . . . this . . . *human* to walk the paths? What makes you think I'll waste my time on such a menial endeavor, and why do you care?"

"I care because Axus cares. You know Axus is intent on destroying all my hard work on that world. It's not fair."

"Existence isn't fair, Arayallen."

"Axus is up to something, Enani—something more devious and significant than the fate of this one world," she said with a wave toward Aaslo. "I don't know what it is, but if I can disrupt his plans, it'll buy me time to find out."

"And *this*"—Enani looked at Aaslo—"one creature can do that? I thought you said he wasn't special."

"I have it on good authority that he is willing to *try* and has already succeeded once."

"According to whom?"

With nonchalance, Arayallen said, "A reaper."

Enani laughed. It was a full-throated, genuine laugh. "A *reaper* is an *authority*?"

"She's Trostili's reaper. He and Axus have been using her to further Axus's cause."

"The cause you want to disrupt. Does Trostili know?"

"No, and he's not going to. This is important, Enani."

Enani sighed. "Fine." Then she smacked Aaslo in the forehead.

Aaslo awoke with a start. He was lying on the ground in the citadel courtyard with several human and equine corpses hovering over him. He rubbed his chest, uncertain as to why he was in so much pain. Then he remembered Dolt kicking him.

"Dolt!" he shouted as he pulled himself from the ground with more than a few pained grunts. "You've gone too far this time, you horrid beast."

Dolt trotted up to him and nickered as he nuzzled Aaslo's neck.

"Stop it. Is this your attempt at an apology?"

The horse bobbed his head, then nudged Aaslo's hand with his muzzle.

*"Hey, Aaslo, you can talk to animals!"*

"Anyone can talk to an animal."

*"Yes, but yours understands you."*

"He doesn't understand me. If he did, he wouldn't have kicked me. He's just an impetuous idiot."

*"Well, at least you can talk to the dead."*

Aaslo glanced toward Greylan and Rostus. "I guess there's that," he said. "We may be doing a lot more talking after I attempt to destroy this evergate."

Aaslo rubbed his chest as he led the odd group of horses and undead toward the chamber where he was most likely going to meet his own death. He saw no one, which he figured was probably a good sign at that point. Then he wondered if he would be capable of seeing reapers besides Myropa if they were present.

After a few minutes of walking, he realized it wasn't just his chest that hurt. His head was beginning to throb as well. He reached up to rub his forehead and found a sensitive lump. At first, he thought he must have struck his head when Dolt kicked him, but the lump was on his forehead and he had fallen onto his back. Had the cantankerous creature also managed to kick him in the head?

Ijen and Teza were both awaiting him at the evergate.

"It took you long enough," said Teza. "How can you possibly need so much time to pack when you travel so light?"

*"I'm heavier than she thinks."*

Aaslo had to agree, but he disregarded the comment and addressed her instead. "What are you talking about? It's been no more than ten minutes."

"Ten minutes? More like half an hour. I was about to go looking for you."

Aaslo rubbed his temples, careful not to claw out his eye *or* touch the painful bump.

Teza stalked up to him. "How did you get that?" she said as she poked the lump.

"Ow!" he shouted, smacking away her hand. "Dolt kicked me."

Her eyes widened. "In the head? You're lucky to be alive."

"No, in the chest. I awoke on the ground. I'm not sure how I got the lump on my forehead."

She reached out and pressed his chest.

"Will you stop that? It hurts."

"Stop being a whiny baby and let me heal you."

"I'm not whining."

*"You really are."*

"You're not helping," he said to Mathias, then to Teza, "and *you* have a terrible bedside manner."

"So you've said," she replied as her power suffused the aches in his chest and head. "And I *am* helping, so be thankful."

Aaslo heard the rustle of pages and looked over to find Ijen frantically flipping through his book. "What is it?" he said.

"No, no, no," Ijen mumbled. "A kick to the chest and hit to the head."

"Ijen, what is it?" Aaslo repeated.

"Hit to the head," the prophet muttered as he scanned a page, then flipped to another.

Teza stopped her ministrations and turned her ire on the prophet. "Hey! Tell us why you're so upset."

Ijen abruptly glanced up at them and snapped the book shut. "What? I'm not upset," he said defensively.

"You are," said Aaslo.

"No."

Teza grabbed the book from the prophet's grip and jumped away. Without warning, Ijen lashed out with a concussive spell that knocked her from her feet and sent the book flying into the wall before it struck the floor. The prophet scurried across the small room to reclaim his treasure.

"Don't *ever* touch the book," he said, looking down at her. "And don't forget that I am more powerful and experienced than you as well, *Fledgling*."

Teza scowled up at him. "I'm a Healer Mage now."

"A poorly trained one," Ijen said with a haughty sniff.

"Stop, you two," said Aaslo. "We don't have time for this."

*"But you had time for a nap?"*

"It wasn't a nap. I was unconscious," said Aaslo.

"You were missing," said Greylan.

They all turned toward the undead guard. "What?" they said in unison.

Greylan didn't respond, and after a moment of silence, Aaslo looked back to Ijen. "Why were you upset?"

"It's nothing. I just remembered witnessing a path in which your chest and head were injured. I can't seem to find it now."

"But you remember it being upsetting?"

"Yes."

Aaslo released a heavy sigh. "It always is with this prophecy. Let's get to this."

After Aaslo laid the living horses to rest and temporarily collected their souls, he turned toward the evergate. The runes, so clearly carved into the stone, were still largely a mystery to him; but, somehow, he felt as if they were speaking. It sounded like a warning or perhaps a plea. What he was about to do felt wrong. He was going to do it anyway.

*"Obstinate."*

"Determined," Aaslo muttered as he once again opened himself to his newfound powers. He found the power he needed to activate the evergate and attached it to the first rune as Teza had instructed the first time. He felt small fingers wrap around his clawed, scaly dragon hand, and he looked over to see Teza staring at him pensively. She nodded, and he turned back to the evergate.

He reached for the power again. The angry, violent power of the beast leapt forward. On a whim, Aaslo snagged it rather than push it aside as he always had. It purred with pleasure. It felt as if something inside him were rolling around and flapping with glee. He couldn't help but grin. The expression felt awkward on his face.

*"That's not determined. That's disturbing."*

He latched the beast's power onto the other runes, then looked back at Ijen. The prophet gave nothing away, as usual, so Aaslo activated the spell.

# CHAPTER 16

PITHOR STOOD BEFORE THE EVERGATE ADMIRING ITS IRIDESCENT BEAUTY. Similar methods of travel had been created in Berru, but their portals were called *realm doors* and weren't nearly as refined. He turned back to examine the forward troops. There were too few. Pithor felt little confidence in his campaign at that moment. A mere three dozen magi were hardly an army, and without the evergate keys, his strategy was severely limited. This would be a pitiful excuse for an invasion. If only they could wait for the main army to arrive by sea and for the magi to resolve the keys. It would be a glorious war, a tale recalled throughout the ages—*if* anybody survived to tell it. No one would, so he and those faithful in service to the gods would be forgotten, at least in *this* world. He would no doubt become kin to the gods in the Afterlife as had been promised.

The magi standing in rank and file before him began to shift, and he frowned. They were trained to be better than that. They should not be moving. Then he saw the source of the disturbance.

"Sedi."

The woman needlessly shoved a few of the younger magi out of the way and sidled up to him with a grin. "Hello, Your High and Mightiness."

Pithor swallowed his ire and said, "You have news? Good, I hope."

Sedi shrugged. "Good, bad, it's all the same to me."

"But it isn't to Axus," he snapped. "What is it?"

Sedi looked curiously at the evergate before turning back to him with a smirk. "Haven't figured it out yet, have you?"

"We have some of the keys."

"But not all. Your plan won't work without them *all*."

"I realize that," he said through gritted teeth. "Plans change. We must be willing to compromise."

"Huh. I didn't know you knew that word. Well, you'd best be moving quickly, then, because that forester is about to do something drastic."

Pithor's anger finally escaped. "He's not dead? You incompetent fool!"

His legs abruptly buckled, and his knees struck the floor with a crack. The muscles in his back seized, and his entire torso began to arch backward. Sedi stepped forward to look down at him. Her typically dismissive demeanor had been replaced with fiery indignation.

"Listen carefully, puny little bug. I could crush you under my boot if I wanted. You are *nothing*. The fact that your zealous dedication to Axus led him to *use* you is the only reason I put up with your pathetic, swollen ego. *I* am neither incompetent nor a fool, and you'd best remember that."

Just when he thought his spine would surely break, she released her hold on his body. He fell forward to catch himself on the cold stones and inhaled the many breaths he had missed during his brief yet infinite torment. Out of the corner of his eye, he spied his troops staring at him. This was unacceptable. Sedi had made him appear weak in front of them. He would certainly be reporting the incident to Axus. Eventually, he *would* make an example of her. For now, he stood and met her challenging gaze. He saw in it laughter, which infuriated him all the more.

"You think to play games, Sedi? Axus will not be pleased by your behavior."

Her attitude shifted to the carefree sadist that she was. "I'm counting on it. Axus can do nothing to me without giving me what I want."

"What does that mean?"

"It's nothing that concerns you."

"Axus—"

He and Sedi both abruptly jumped back as the evergate began to emit a loud wail. The shimmering, translucent opening started to waver and stir, and the color shifted from soothing blue waves to tumultuous reds and oranges. Then each of the runes began to crack one by one. When the last rune broke, the noise stopped, and everything calmed. Pithor reached out to touch the turbulent red-and-orange portal.

Sedi tilted her head and looked at the gate curiously. "Well, that's interesting."

"What is this? What's happened?"

She chuckled. "I told you to hurry, but you wanted to stand around stroking your ego."

He turned to her and growled, "Tell me now!"

"This?" She shook her head. "I don't know what *this* is. I was trying to tell you that the forester and his friends were working on a way to destroy the evergates. *All* of them. It looks like he succeeded in doing *something*, although it's not exactly destroyed. Should we go in and see what happens? This'll be fun."

Pithor rubbed his face with his hands and then pointed to one of the young magi Sedi had shoved. "You, come here."

The young man scurried forward looking like a mouse caught under the cat's paw. "Y-yes, Your Mighty Light. How may I serve you?"

Pithor pointed to the broken evergate. "Go in there. Use the gate to go to the fourth gate in Helod. Then return immediately and report what happened."

The magus, a lanky redheaded man with buckteeth, looked at the gate and swallowed. "You want me to go in *there*?"

"Yes, we need to know what's happened to it. We can't very well be sending troops through if it's going to tear them apart or send them to the bottom of the ocean." Pithor saw the terror on the young man's face and was disgusted. "You serve Axus, do you not?"

"Yes, of course!"

"Then you will not be upset to give your life to advance his cause. No servant of the God of Death should fear dying."

"Oh, no, Your Grace. It's not dying I fear. It's the *manner* of death."

Pithor looked back at the angry portal and supposed the young man's concerns were not unfounded. He abruptly reached out and backhanded the magus, sending him sprawling on the ground. He waited as the magus rose and settled in front of him, this time holding his jaw as tears stung his eyes.

"You should be grateful when death chooses to take you, no matter the method."

"Of course, you're right," the young man mumbled. Then he turned and stepped through the evergate without further pause.

Neither Pithor's nor Sedi's gaze left the evergate as they waited. Sedi said, "For once, I agree with you."

Pithor's muscles tensed. Anything but hostility from Sedi was suspect. "About what?"

"Any death is better than no death."

He was, again, reminded of *why* she'd chosen to serve Axus. Unlike himself and the rest of the Berruvians, Sedi was not a true believer. Her service to the god was merely a means to an end.

After thirty minutes, the young magus still had not returned. Pithor sent another into the evergate to inspect the chamber. Upon exiting, she reported that nothing appeared to be amiss.

"Well," said Sedi. "At least the chamber wasn't filled with the bloody gore of an exploded magus. Perhaps the gate is only working one way now." She waggled her fingers toward the waiting magi. "Go on now. Send them through. Axus can't be kept waiting." Then the woman vanished.

Pithor exhaled. His relief over her departure frustrated him. She should not hold so much power. *He* was the Deliverer of Grace. *He* should hold the power, not that contemptable woman who held no official position yet involved herself whenever and wherever she desired.

He looked at the magi, then back to the evergate. He couldn't send them through without knowing where they would go or if they would survive.

Margus tromped up to him. His heavy boots sounded like war drums booming with every step. "Are you all right?" he asked.

Pithor crossed his arms behind his back and turned to face the general. "The keys are useless now."

"What do you mean?"

"The gates are broken. We don't know where they go, with or without the keys."

"Are you sure?" said Margus.

"I'm no longer sure of anything except that we must continue to serve Axus and that the prophecy will see us through." As he said them, the words rang true in his heart. The Lightbane was dead, and *he* was destined to win. No matter the setbacks, they *would* prevail. "Flood the gates," he said with confidence.

Margus raised an eyebrow. "You just said the keys are worthless."

"It's no matter. Send them through as planned. We will prevail."

AASLO LAID ON HIS BACK HOLDING HIS STOMACH WHILE IT CALMED. HE had hoped his second trip through the evergate would be less unsettling. It wasn't, but he was glad to be alive. He opened his eyes to see Teza looking down at him.

"Why are you on the floor?"

"I felt dizzy. I figured it was better to lie down than to collapse and risk striking my head."

"That's very sensible of you," she said. "But you can't stay down there all day. You have horses to revive."

He took a deep breath. "Right. There's no telling how the second time will affect them."

Aaslo returned the souls to the horses, and they seemed none the worse for wear.

"That's just wrong," said Teza as she frowned at the living horses that had been dead the previous moment.

"It's better than those," said Aaslo, pointing to the *undead* horses.

"I can't argue that, but I don't think anyone should be able to go about stealing souls. What if you decide to take *my* soul? Could you do it? Just suck it right out of my body?"

"Of course not," Aaslo replied a little too quickly.

*"Liar."*

She gave him a dubious look.

He said, "At least, I don't think so. Maybe. I don't know, but I wouldn't."

"May we leave this chamber?" said Ijen, who seemed suddenly anxious.

"Is there a problem?" said Teza.

"Only that it's a bit crowded in here with the horses and corpses."

Aaslo turned to the portal opening. It looked the same as the one they had entered in the citadel, forcing him to wonder if his magical efforts had caused any effect. After chasing Dolt around the small chamber for a few minutes, he was finally able to get hold of the ornery beast. He pulled his axe from Dolt's saddle and took the reins in his free hand. The horse tugged against him, but the dragon arm was strong. Dolt laid his ears back and gnashed his teeth at Aaslo.

"What is your problem?" Aaslo blurted.

Teza said, "Maybe he's angry with you for killing him—*again.*"

"I doubt he remembers it," said Aaslo. "Besides, the other horses are fine."

"Yes, but Dolt's always been a little *special,*" she replied.

*"That's an understatement. It's just like you to try to save the world with a defective horse."*

"I should have asked the marquess for a trade," Aaslo mumbled. Then he turned back to the gate. "Okay, let's go."

He and his companions piled through the evergate to find themselves standing on a rocky, deserted plain. The wind whipped through his clothes as if they were made of sheer linen, and it felt like the icy hand of death were wrapping around him.

"By the gods, it's cold!" said Teza as she struggled to wrap her cloak around her. "Where are we?"

"Tyellí?" said Aaslo.

"This isn't Tyellí," she snapped as if it weren't obvious. "You did it wrong."

While they were surveying the nearly barren wasteland, Ijen was staring back at the evergate. "I don't think our displacement is a result of user error, but rather due to Aaslo's very intentional destruction of the evergate at the citadel."

"What are you talking about?" Teza said as she turned. "What, for the sake of the Afterlife, is *that*?" she blurted.

The evergate was housed in an ancient temple made of sharp black rock. The stone on the majority of the temple was rough, but parts had been smoothed and carved in bas-relief. The gate had turned a vicious, chaotic chorus of reds and oranges, and each stone was cracked through the rune carved upon it.

*"Congratulations, Aaslo. You broke the evergate."*

"Obviously, I failed to destroy it," said Aaslo.

"True," said Ijen, "yet it did not take us to where we intended. You must have destroyed the keys."

Aaslo glanced across the vacant plain as snow flurries riding a frigid wind slapped his face. "So, the evergates are still standing, but the spells take you to the wrong places?"

"It's hard to say for sure. Some of them may be destroyed. Others may no longer lead to another gate in Aldrea."

Aaslo unrolled his jacket, which had been tied to his pack. It was a good jacket but not nearly warm enough for the frigid wind. "Fantastic," he muttered. "Where are we, then?"

*"Somewhere cold."*

"I'm not an idiot," Aaslo snapped.

Ijen looked at him crossly. "I never said you were. I don't know where we are."

*"No, Aaslo, think of the map."*

"The map? Right, the map." Aaslo pulled the map tube from Dolt's saddle. He knew the horse was miserable, too, since Dolt didn't rouse to stomp or snap at him when he approached. Dolt and Ijen's and Teza's horses had clumped together for warmth, but the corpse horses stood with their corpse riders as if completely unfazed by their surroundings.

Teza's teeth chattered as she said, "P-perhaps it w-would be best if we moved inside while we f-figure out what to do."

"I agree," said Ijen. "You'll lose your map to the wind. We need to find an entrance to the temple *besides* the evergate."

Aaslo sent Teza and Ijen to one side of the small structure while he searched the other. When they met in the rear, they realized there was no entrance.

"Can't we just go back into the evergate chamber?" said Aaslo.

"That would be unadvisable," said Ijen. "The evergate is compromised. It may be dangerous."

"More dangerous than freezing to death?" grumped Aaslo.

"We should go there," said Teza.

Aaslo followed her gaze to the distant mountains. "Why?"

"Maybe we can find a cave or something. We need to find shelter before nightfall."

Aaslo looked back at the evergate, then to the mountains. "We have shelter here for sure, but it *may* lead to a horrible, untimely death. We have no surety of shelter out there, and we may freeze to death while seeking it."

"That about sums it up," said Ijen.

*"This is getting good. What will they decide, and what will be their fates?"*

"What would *you* choose?" muttered Aaslo.

He didn't think he'd spoken loud enough for the others to hear, but Ijen pulled his cloak tighter and said, "I'd rather make the decision when my brain is thawed. Maybe it wouldn't be so bad to just pop into the gate for a few minutes. If we don't activate it, it shouldn't do anything."

*"Shouldn't, he said."*

Teza turned so the wind was to her back and said, "I'd rather not be torn to bits as each of my body parts is sent to a different path. I say we go to the mountains."

"I want to know what the chosen one would do," said Aaslo.

They both stared at him, and he thought he saw no small amount of pity in their eyes. That was the moment he realized they did think he'd lost his mind, yet they were willing to follow him anyway.

*"It doesn't matter what I'd choose. You knew what you wanted as soon as you saw the mountains. You're just taking forever to make a decision as usual."*

"It's best to consider all your options before making an important decision."

*"With you, every decision must be important. I look forward to you joining me when you freeze to death while trying to make this decision."*

Aaslo secured the map tube to Dolt's saddle, took his reins, and started walking toward the mountains. "Every decision *is* important," he said. "Our choices define our lives. They make us who we are. And I've made a lot of decisions since . . ."

*"Since what?"*

"Nothing."

*"Since I died? Say it, Aaslo. I died."*

"Did you? You're still here. These were supposed to be *your* decisions. *I'm* stuck making *your* decisions. Forgive me for trying to think it through. I'm just a forester."

"I think you're more than a forester," said Teza.

Aaslo had been so caught up in his thoughts that he hadn't realized she was walking next to him. Then he noticed the crunching of snow where Ijen walked on his other side.

"There's no need to be anything more than a forester," Aaslo said. "When this quest is over, I'll either be dead, or I'll return to being a forester."

"I'm not saying there's anything wrong with being a forester. It's just that you're more than that now."

Aaslo flexed his dragon hand and ran a claw down the scales on his neck. "Perhaps I'm less."

"You think that's a disability? You're *better* now. You have built-in armor, fire protection, greater strength, claws that cut like knives, and you can see in the dark! And those are only the obvious changes."

Aaslo knew she was right about the last part. There was more. He could feel it inside him, scratching at the surface, wound tightly and ready to spring as soon as it found a weakness.

The wind whipped across his face, snagging his hood. Aaslo pulled the strings tighter but couldn't manage to tie them with his clawed hand. The thing that had changed him had made many things difficult. Just getting dressed without shredding his clothes was a task, and most of his apparel now had more than a few punctures. Teza refused to help with the mending. "I'm not a seamstress or servant, and I'll not have you start thinking of me as such," she had said rather adamantly. When he pointed out that he hadn't asked for her help, she simply said she knew he'd been thinking it—which he *hadn't*. It was Mathias who had suggested it. Aaslo had told him the idea was absurd, and Teza had confirmed he was right in no uncertain terms. He still couldn't fathom why she'd gotten angry with *him*. It wasn't *his* idea.

"What's that?" said Teza, snatching Aaslo back to the present.

He looked up and squinted into the flurry-filled wind. It was a familiar shape in an unfamiliar land. Aaslo picked up his pace and nearly walked off the edge of a crevasse. He stopped just in time to avoid an embarrassing plunge, and then Dolt happened. The horse collided with him from behind, and Aaslo went tumbling down a sharp embankment. Luckily, the drop was less than a dozen feet, and his thrashing against the rocks slowed his descent so that he came to an easy, if painful, stop.

"Aaslo! Are you okay?" yelled Teza.

He looked up to see her, Ijen, and Dolt leaning over the edge to stare at him.

"I'm fine," he grumbled.

His hands were scraped, and his pants had a new tear that would leave an impressive scar to go with the rest. He fumbled at his waist and realized his bag had ripped and lay flaccid at his side. His heart leapt as his gaze jumped around the rocks. Then everything stilled. His breath left him, and the world drifted away. Mathias lay a mere four feet from him in the bottom of the dry creek bed, and it wasn't just his head. Mathias's whole body lay there, one ankle resting on a raised knee, his hands clasped behind his head, and his lips parted in a broad smile as he gazed up at the blue sky. A shadow fell across Mathias's face, and Aaslo looked up to see the swaying trees with their glittering gold and green leaves fluttering to the soft, moss-covered ground.

"Wouldn't it be great to be able to fly?" said Mathias.

Aaslo swallowed hard. He had heard the question before, long ago, in a place just like this. What had he said then? He whispered, "Why would I want to?"

Mathias waved a hand in the air and said, "To see the world—the whole of it—all at once."

Aaslo said the next line in the conversation, but it lacked the strength of the first time he had said it. "Why would I need to see the whole world at once when I can only exist in one place?"

Mathias rolled onto his side and propped himself up on an elbow. "It's not about where you *are*, Aaslo. It's about where you could be, where you *will* be, if you can just break out of your shell."

"I'm not in a shell," Aaslo mumbled. Mathias looked perfect. It was the same face Aaslo carried in his bag day and night, but his eyes shined with light, and his smile carried warmth. Mathias didn't seem to notice the tears that stung Aaslo's eyes.

"You *are* in a shell. It's made of wood and leaves. Come on, Aaslo. Why be satisfied with one little piece when you could have it all?"

Aaslo knew what he was supposed to say next. He was supposed to dismiss the notion of travel, condemn greed, and grouse that no place was better than where he was. If he could go back to that place, in that moment, he might have said it again. He might have done all he could to prevent Mathias from ever leaving the forest. But it wasn't real. He knew it wasn't real. Mathias was dead, and he was sitting at the bottom of a rocky chasm in a frigid, foreign land.

So instead, Aaslo said, "I'll go with you. I'll go wherever you need to go."

"Really?" said Mathias. "Are you being serious?"

"Yes. I'll go to a plain or a swamp or a frozen wasteland. I'll visit the capital and sneak into the palace and meet the king and queen. We'll get in sword fights and defeat bandits and discover magic." Tears rolled down Aaslo's cheeks. "We'll go on a quest to save the world."

Mathias smiled at him in a way he never had in life. He was pleased but not with himself. He was happy for Aaslo, yet somehow equal parts proud and sad. "Thank you, Aaslo. Brothers in all things."

Then he was gone. The forest was gone. The golden rays of sun were gone. All that remained were rocks dusted in snow, a gloomy, grey sky, and a severed head. Aaslo wiped the frozen tears from his cheeks and gathered what was left of Mathias back into his bag. As he stuffed the golden locks into the sack, he noticed something moving in the rocks. At first it blended perfectly—a brown-and-white lump among the other brown-and-white lumps. He forced his eyes to focus; and suddenly, with a stomach-churning leap, his vision jumped forward to reveal Dolt standing among the snow-shrouded boulders. The horse was staring straight at him, and his only movement was the wind rustling his mane and tail.

Rocks began to tumble around Aaslo, and Teza came sliding down the slope. When she reached the bottom, she grabbed Aaslo's shoulders and jerked him around to look at her.

"Aaslo, are you okay? Aaslo, say something!"

He looked at her and frowned. "I'm fine. There's no need to get all worked up."

Teza's demeanor abruptly shifted as she shoved her hands onto her hips. "Well, why didn't you say anything? You'd have saved me the trouble of climbing down a cliff and scuffing my hands."

"I said I was fine the first time you asked," he grumped.

"Right, but what about the other thirty times? I thought maybe you'd passed out—or *bled* out."

Aaslo looked down at the spot where Mathias had lain. "Perhaps I did pass out. I saw . . . something."

Teza grabbed his head while muttering under her breath. It felt as if water were rushing back and forth between Aaslo's ears, and just as he thought he was becoming too dizzy to stand, Teza stepped back.

She crossed her arms and frowned at him. "Your head's fine. At least, there are no injuries. I can't speak to your mental state."

"*I can. He's completely nuts.*"

"I'm not—"

"Not what?" she said. "Not crazy? Are you sure?"

Aaslo glanced down at the rocks again and then up at the sky. There were no trees anywhere, and the sky was naught but a gloomy expanse of greys. He shook his head, then pointed to a rock fall farther down the chasm. "We can climb up there. It'll be easier. If Dolt can get down here, then we can go up there."

"Dolt? What's he got to do with this?"

"He's right over there," Aaslo said, pointing to where the horse had been standing. Dolt was no longer there, though.

Teza tugged his sleeve and said, "You mean that Dolt?"

He followed her gaze up the cliff to reveal Dolt and Ijen still staring down at him from atop it. Wind whipped at the horse's mane and Ijen's hood until both became tangled.

"I think I'd rather stay down here," muttered Teza. "At least we're out of the wind."

Aaslo began picking his way over the rocks as he said, "I swear that confounding horse was down here a minute ago. You have a point about the wind, but the horses are up there, and I want to see that giant tree that was across this ravine."

"The tree's gone," said Teza as she trod over the scree beside him.

"Gone? What do you mean it's gone? How can a tree just be gone?"

"I don't know. It disappeared as soon as you fell down here."

"I didn't *fall* down here. Dolt pushed me."

"I know you have issues with your horse, but he's a horse. He's not homicidal. He bumped into you. He didn't *push* you."

"So says you."

"That's ridiculous."

*"It's pretty bad when even your horse wants you dead."*

"I see a tree that doesn't exist, then Dolt pushes me into a chasm, and next thing I know I'm seeing Mathias in a forest and Dolt is somehow both in the chasm and atop it at the same time."

Teza didn't reply, but Aaslo felt her gaze on him more than once. He knew she was quickly losing whatever confidence she had left in his sanity and regretted telling her what he had seen; but the experience and all the feelings it invoked were too much to keep inside. The past few months without Mathias, without Pa and Grams, without the forest and Goldenwood and Reyla, had been worse than anything he could have imagined. The strength he had been holding onto out of sheer necessity was beginning to crumble.

Aaslo swallowed the sadness, anger, and self-pity that had been pooling in his chest as he climbed the last few feet to the top of the cliff. As soon as he reached the top, his hood was whipped from his head, and the frigid wind bit his nose and ears. Ijen reached down to give him a hand, then Aaslo immediately turned to seek the tree. Teza was right. The looming monstrosity they had seen in the distance was gone.

"I've read of mirages—images people see of things that aren't really there. The books say they occur in the desert where it's hot. I've never heard of any occurring on a frozen, rocky plain."

"I don't think it was a mirage," said Ijen.

"What was it?" said Aaslo.

"I don't know. Well, I *do*. I've seen it. But I don't know what it is right now."

Aaslo turned to the prophet. "What have you seen?"

"I can't say."

Teza abruptly growled and kicked a rock over the chasm. Then she turned on Ijen. "You are *worse* than useless, Ijen *Mascede*! You're doing this on purpose."

Ijen looked both hurt and surprised. "Of course I am. I'm a prophet. It's my job."

"Why are you even here?" she shouted.

"I tell you what I can—more than I should, really. I like to think I've helped in other ways."

"You have," said Aaslo. "Actually, your help has been invaluable. What can you tell us *now*?"

Ijen had no gloves, so his hands were tucked into his sleeves. Even so, he tapped the bulge under his tunic where Aaslo knew he kept the book of prophecy—the book of *Aaslo's* life. "I, um, well, we're already going this way, so I suppose I can tell you we need to go there." The prophet untucked one hand and pointed into the distance toward the mountains.

Teza growled, "When we asked you earlier, you said you didn't know where we should go."

"I *didn't* know at the time. Then the horse pushed Aaslo into the chasm, and now I know we need to go there." He pointed again toward the mountains.

Aaslo grabbed Dolt's reins and stomped past Teza. "I *told* you he pushed me."

The group piled on as many layers of clothing as they had, and it still wasn't sufficient to cut the cold. Luckily, the wind shifted so that it was striking their backs rather than blasting them in their faces. It was possibly the most miserable trek Aaslo had ever endured.

"Trees would fix this," he muttered.

*"Trees aren't the solution to everything."*

"They are for wind."

*"But there is nowhere for the enemy to hide out here."*

Aaslo paused at the edge of another fissure, then sought a path to navigate around it. "An entire army could be down in these crevasses. We wouldn't see them before they dragged us in."

*"It's too bad there aren't any magi around to surround you with wards that could block the wind* and *the lyksvight."*

Aaslo groaned at his own incompetence. He turned to Ijen. "Can you surround us with some kind of shields to protect us from the wind and attack?"

Ijen's voice was muffled when he spoke. His hands were wrapped in pieces of unidentified cloth, and he was holding his hood closed over his face except for a small slit through which to see. "I could if we stayed very close together, but it wouldn't last more than an hour. I'd be too drained to help in a fight."

"What if you and Teza did the spell together?"

"Don't even think about it," groused Teza. "It's all I can do to keep my fingers and nose from falling off."

"You're using magic to keep yourself warm?"

"Of course. I'm not a masochist."

He looked back at Ijen. "Are you doing that, too?"

"Indeed."

"How?"

"By the time you learned, we'd all freeze to death."

Sardonic laughter echoed through the chamber of Aaslo's mind. It wasn't Mathias. "Stop it, Ina. If I die, your power goes with me." He didn't know if that was true. According to Ijen, his power was borrowed, which implied Ina would get it back when he and all his potential descendants passed. The thought nearly elicited a chuckle. He would have no descendants. He was destined to die like the rest of life.

Ina wasn't going to help him, so he inwardly turned to a second source. The beast. Dragons had fire—at least, his did. He wondered if the dragon part of him possessed a way to generate, or at least retain, heat.

The beast was pacing, as usual. The monster, never quiet, was seemingly ready to jump at the first sign of weakness. It purred with pleasure as Aaslo approached. He tentatively reached out, and it abruptly chomped down on his will. Aaslo recoiled, but it was too late. The beast was ready to roar. Aaslo's skin tingled and stung as the heat reached it from the inside, and wisps of steam rolled off it like those of a lake on a frigid winter morning. His muscles began to loosen, and he started to shiver. After a few minutes, the shivering subsided, and Aaslo felt warm and relaxed. Then Dolt headbutted him.

Aaslo stumbled to one side but managed to right himself before falling into the slush. "What was that for?" he exclaimed.

The skin across Dolt's entire body trembled, and Aaslo noticed that tiny icicles had formed on the horse's muzzle. He wondered if he could warm Dolt and the other living horses without setting them on fire. He was both surprised and impressed that he had been able to generate the heat to warm himself, but somehow transferring that effect to another creature—or several other creatures—seemed insurmountable.

He raised his gaze to the horizon and wondered exactly how far the mountains were from their present location. It was hard to determine distance on the dreary expanse. Dolt nudged him again, and this time he was unable to arrest his fall. Weighed down by his pack, he struck the ground hard. Luckily, his work glove prevented his human hand from being shredded on the rock shards, and he barely felt the impact with the dragon arm. His knee, on the other hand, was another story. He hadn't considered wearing kneepads to trudge across an empty expanse.

"Are you okay?" said Teza.

"I'm fine. Just a scrape."

"You're bleeding. It's on your pants. Let me help."

"It's nothing. Save your energy for warming yourself. We have no idea how long we'll be out here."

"Two hours," said Ijen.

"What? How do you know?" said Teza.

"Because that's how long it took us in the story."

Aaslo looked up at him crossly as he checked to make sure his knee injury wasn't going to cause him to bleed out. "That's awfully specific. Why are you suddenly so forthcoming?"

Ijen peered at Aaslo from beneath his hood. "It won't change anything for you to know that. It always takes two hours."

"What's this?" said Teza as she knelt beside Aaslo. He looked over to see her staring down at something in a small crevasse. She abruptly leapt backward with a shout. "Ah! It's a body."

"A dead body?" said Aaslo. "Human?"

"By the gods, that's awful," said Teza. "I think it's frozen solid."

Aaslo rolled over to peer down at the body. It was snagged on some rocks beside a pool of water. The darker power within him jumped at the chance to overcome the dragon. Before he knew it, he had latched onto the corpse with a tentacle of power. A second tentacle, then a third and a fourth latched onto others that he could not see. Eventually, there were fourteen such tentacles. His inner beast snapped at the dark power, and Ina's laughter punctuated Aaslo's struggles.

"Aaslo! Aaslo, can you hear me?"

He wanted to say, "Of course I can hear you," but his jaw was locked by his efforts to take back control. The dark power tugged on the tendrils, which seemed to become tangled on the dragon's claws. As the dragon struggled for freedom, the tendrils grew tighter. The dragon reared backward, then took flight, and the tendrils were dragged with him. The first tendril *popped*. It felt as if a high-tension line suddenly came free, and a soul was sucked into him. The other souls quickly followed, but they all seemed trapped.

The dragon, eager for his freedom, released a stream of fire so intense that it escaped Aaslo's core to inundate the crevasse. It raged for several minutes, and Aaslo could hear Teza screaming somewhere, seemingly far away. The tendrils loosened and sloughed away from the dragon, and then all of the powers settled. Aaslo was left panting on his hands and knees in the slush. Teza placed a hand on his shoulder, then recoiled.

"Ow! You're burning up. What *was* that, Aaslo?"

*"Tell her. Tell her how you lost control. Tell her you're not alone in that tangle of weeds you call a mind."*

"Tangle of weeds? Since when do you think in terms of plants?" Aaslo grumbled, but Mathias was silent.

"What are you talking about?" said Teza. "I've never seen anything like that. I can't believe it. You nearly melted the rocks."

Aaslo looked to where she pointed in the crevasse. The small pool had vaporized, and all that was left was scorched rocks and over a dozen bodies in remarkably good condition. The cadavers began moving, at first slowly, then with more conviction. Their milky gazes surveyed their surroundings, and they seemed to take note of each other. One woman even appeared to smile.

As the undead crawled up the side of the crevasse, Teza said, "What's going on? Who are they, and how did you do that? Ugh! So many questions." She paused and stared at him in alarm. "They're yours, right? You're in control?"

Aaslo took stock of the powers inside him that seemed satisfied to have expressed themselves so thoroughly. "Yes, they won't hurt you."

"Why did you do that?" she snapped as the first to reach them stopped a little too close for her.

"I didn't mean to," said Aaslo. "I mean, maybe I did. I remember looking down at that one and thinking that I should raise him. We need an army, Teza. We need more people on our side."

"So, you have to pick the dead ones?" she squawked.

"It makes more sense than trying to convince the living. Think about it. They're already dead. Who better to send into battle?"

"I guess," she said doubtfully. "But how did you know about the others?"

"I didn't. At least, I don't think I did."

*"Make up your mind. You sound like a complete nutjob."*

"Sometimes it feels like the power is a part of me—an extension of my abilities. Other times, it feels like it's another entity entirely."

"I get that. I feel that way, too, sometimes. Can you at least warn me next time? It's a bit terrifying to suddenly experience scorching flames everywhere followed by walking cadavers."

"Sorry about that. The bodies were frozen stiff. I guess I had to thaw them."

Aaslo looked to the smiling woman standing as close to Teza as she would allow. "Who are you?"

He thought, at first, that she wasn't going to answer. Then her mouth contorted awkwardly, and she said, "We are of the clans."

"The clans . . . the Cartisian clans," he reasoned. "What happened to you?"

"The lyksvight came. We chose the river. We did not survive."

"Yeah, that's obvious," Teza muttered. "Where are the rest of your people?"

The woman's milky gaze remained on Aaslo, and she didn't answer. Aaslo sighed and repeated the question. She said, "They are eaten."

A shiver passed through him, and Aaslo finally pushed to his feet. Dolt immediately stepped forward and tried to headbutt him again. Aaslo leapt away before the horse made contact. "What's wrong with you?"

"I believe he's cold," said Ijen. "He wants you to warm him."

"You saw that in your prophecy?"

"No, it's just a bit obvious."

Aaslo waved to the newly animated corpses. "Look at this," he said. "I've got fourteen more undead to deal with, and my horse is throwing a tantrum."

"You!"

Aaslo spun, searching for the source of the unfamiliar voice. At first, he thought it one of the newly raised, but it had come from the other direction. He squinted into the searing wind and noticed a man storming toward him, only the man appeared completely out of place in the frigid wasteland. He wore a short white overcoat that stopped at the waist and snug, white slacks. A gold sash crossed his waist, and his shiny white shoes had raised heels and lacy white frills across the instep. The dress, as well as the short, slicked-back black hair and thin mustache, were indicative of another time altogether, one at least a hundred years in the past. The man's face appeared flushed but not from the cold. He was irate.

"What do you think you're doing? Those were mine! You can't just go around stealing souls. What am I supposed to do now?"

*"A thief you are, Aaslo. Told you so."*

"Who *are* you?" Aaslo said.

"Who—who am I? Who are *you*? How did you do that? Why can you see me?"

*"Because he's lost his mind. He can see and hear all kinds of things that aren't there."*

Aaslo glanced at the undead, then back to the anachronistic man. "You're a reaper."

The man's eyes bulged, then he scowled. "What do you know of reapers? What's going on here? Tell me now."

That did it for Aaslo. He was tired of people—and horses—ordering him around, particularly when he was already miserable. "Listen here, Reaper. You're in no position to be issuing orders. I have a right to be here. I'm alive. *You* are just visiting, and visitors don't get to boss around the residents."

"Aaslo, who are you talking to?" said Teza.

"That's what I'd like to know," said Myra, who was suddenly standing beside Teza without her knowledge.

Aaslo threw up his arms. "Does *everybody* have to show up *now*? You couldn't all wait until we were tucked in nice and warm by a fire?" He looked at Teza and hooked a thumb over his shoulder. "I'm talking to an impertinent reaper who I can only assume was supposed to take the souls of these dead people."

"Hey," said Myra. "Who are you calling impertinent?"

"Not *you*. Him," he said, pointing to the unwelcome guest. Teza, Ijen, and Myra all stared blankly in the direction he pointed. "Oh, for the sake of all that grows and blooms," he growled.

*"Language, Aaslo. There are ladies present."*

"Can you not see him?" he said to Myra.

"See who?"

"The other reaper."

If Myra was surprised to hear another reaper was present, she didn't show it. "No, I can't see other reapers."

"Are you saying there's another reaper here?" said the man in white.

"Yes, but both of you can leave. I've already claimed these souls."

The man began shouting into the air as if to some unseen audience. "I was doing my job! You didn't need to send another. It's not my fault! This man-lizard stole the souls from me." He turned back to Aaslo. "You can't do that!"

"I already did. There's no point in watering a dead tree."

"Axus will hear about this!" shouted the white-clad reaper before he abruptly disappeared.

Aaslo turned to Myra. "He's gone. You may go, too. These are mine."

Myra shook her head. "That's not why I'm here. I came to update you about the marquess and the others. I don't know where they're going. The marquess won't tell me because he doesn't trust me. I found them going northeast. I don't think the marquess is well, though. He's been having terrible migraines."

"And we're about to freeze to death like these corpses," said Aaslo. "If he's still having problems once we've figured out how to rejoin them, Teza can take a look at him. Until then, he'll just have to deal with it."

"Who's having problems?" said Teza. "Is someone hurt? Is it Mory?"

Aaslo plucked an icicle off Dolt's bridle and concluded that the horse might not be acting difficult for the sake of being difficult. He said, "We need to find shelter *now*. Thank you, Myra, for your assistance, but we need to be going."

Myra smiled and ducked her head, then disappeared, and Aaslo and his companions, now fourteen stronger, headed toward the mountains.

# CHAPTER 17

MORY PEERED THROUGH THE TINY SPACES BETWEEN THE THICK BRANCHES of the tree. He had never seen such a tree before reaching the eastern edge of the Uyanian plain. Its branches were spaced close together like a bush, but the tree was taller than he by three or four times. The leaves were sharp, thin, spiny things that scraped his arms when he brushed against them but nicely hid him from view.

"You done yet, boy?" said a gruff voice. "Yer back end is gonna fall off if you stay like that for much longer."

"I'll stay like this forever if it means not going into those ruins." Mory knew Bear was right, though. He wiped himself with some of the broader leaves that dotted the ground, pulled up his pants, then stepped from his hiding place. His stomach soured as the looming towers entered his field of view.

"You've never struck me as a coward," said Bear.

"I'm no coward. I've just been close to death enough for one lifetime."

"Yeah, well, from what you've said, this is a different lifetime for you."

Mory paused to think about that. Bear was right. He was on his second life, and he hadn't died in that life yet. Still. "What if it's different for me in there? You know I can see things others can't. What if it's too much?"

"Seems to me it's better to see the enemy than not," said Bear.

"I think that depends on whether or not the enemy can see *you*," said Mory. "What if we're no realer to them than they are to us? Except for *me*."

"Bah, it's prob'ly just a bunch of grifters who done come up with this plan to keep folks from finding their hideout. Ghosts aren't real."

"*I* was a ghost for a little while."

"Hmm, prob'ly just a bad dream. Anyhow, we got to get going. It's time."

Tohl Gueron wasn't what Mory had expected. He had thought to find a gloomy relic of a forgotten era with crumbling walls, toppled towers, and carrion birds roosting in the rafters beneath every broken roof. Instead, he found it to be a welcoming sight of well-preserved buildings, mostly two stories or less, each colorfully painted in varying hues of blue and green. Most of the roofs were sturdily made of grey terracotta tiles, but a few that had been composed of wooden shingles had collapsed. The enchanted community fountains that graced the common areas still gushed, although a thick layer of algae had coated the statues and bowls. All of this, Mory could see from outside the gates that were open but still securely attached to the walls that enclosed the city.

He followed Bear to where the marquess stood discussing the structures with the engineers. Daniga and Peck weren't present. They were supposed to be off with the other scouts searching for signs of life—or unlife—and a way into the city. Mory was to be the go-between if someone needed to get a message to the others.

"Anythin'?" said Bear.

"No. It appears truly abandoned." The marquess pointed toward the sky. "Even the birds don't fly past the walls."

Mory could see a few kites flying lazy circles over the surrounding forest. One flew toward the city but turned back long before reaching it. "Maybe there's nothing for them to eat in there. No point in wasting the energy to fly over it."

"True," said the marquess. "It doesn't appear as ominous as the stories make it out to be, and that worries me."

"The stories have been exaggerated," said Bear. "An abandoned city don't make for a great story if it don't have a bit of mystery."

Mory jumped when Peck unexpectedly stepped into his personal space from behind a shrub. Peck snickered and elbowed Mory in the ribs. Then he turned to the marquess. "There's no other way in or out—at least, not for our numbers. There are no major breaks in the walls, which are at least fifteen feet tall, and the forest is cleared back by thirty yards all around."

A sudden, resounding crack broke the relative silence. It was quickly followed by a concussive wave that shook their insides. Between the tallest of the three towers and the temple spire opened a massive tear in the sky. Within the jagged rip was a purple-black darkness dotted with tiny specks of light. Mory was slapped in the face by a chill wind emanating from the direction of the tear that was churning with unrestrained power crackling at its edges. The tear began to twist in on itself, and just as quickly and loudly as it began, it ended.

The goose bumps that prickled Mory's flesh subsided, and the marquess said, "Report."

"I've got nothing," mumbled Peck, his gaze still seized by the now-empty sky.

The marquess turned to stare at Peck. Mory could see the man was wrestling with his own fear. He didn't know how he knew it, but he did.

"I'll go, Peck. I'll find Daniga."

A loud "No" rushed past Peck's pale lips, and he swallowed hard. "I'll go. You stay here. Stay away from . . . from that . . . um, there." Peck was still mumbling when he walked away, his voice eventually becoming too faint for Mory to hear.

The marquess rubbed his temples, and Mory felt for the man who had been enduring daily migraines since they left Ruriton. The marquess said, "I don't suppose that reaper friend of yours is here."

"No," Mory said just as he caught a movement at the edge of his vision. He turned to see a woman walking toward them. She wore a plain brown frock with a white apron and simple white bonnet. Her walk was casual, and she smiled at them and waved—as if there hadn't been a terrifying rip in reality above her just moments prior.

Bear's gruff voice carried to everyone in their immediate vicinity as he ordered them to be on guard. Archers nocked arrows, and swordsmen drew swords. The intensity of their preparations against the lone woman would have been laughable to anyone just arriving.

The woman stopped about thirty yards short of them and waved again as she smiled sweetly. With a tilt of her hand, she beckoned them to come to her. Then she turned and began walking back toward the now-open gate. When she was halfway there, she turned back and beckoned to them again before disappearing into the city.

Mory looked to the marquess. He feared whatever the man decided. To stay out in the open left them vulnerable to attack, not just from the Berru and lyksvight, but from their own countrymen as well. Like them, desperate people driven from their homes by attacks, fear, or hunger had begun banding together for survival. Just as the lyksvight preyed on Uyanians, Uyanians preyed on each other. The worst of the attacks had come when they were traveling a few days east of Tyellí. They had already been set upon twice when they were attacked by the marauders calling themselves the Silver Brigade. Most of their attackers were former king's soldiers and mercenaries. They were organized and brutal, and although the marquess's guards were well trained and loyal, they were no match for the force that assailed them. The marquess had shown his worth when, with his quick wit, he stayed the hand of death.

Mory glanced toward the swordsmen and archers at his back. Nearly two-thirds of them wore silver shoulder cords, but only Bear wore gold. Mory turned back to the marquess, who chewed his lip as he considered their predicament.

"The Silver Brigade—outside Tyellí—how did you know?"

The marquess turned to him with a frown. "What?"

"How did you know their leader would accept your challenge?"

The marquess glanced at the city gate, then turned back to Mory as though he was glad for the delay. "The leader, Hegress, was a good man—at least, before all this he was."

"You knew him before?"

"I did. Fairly well, actually. We attended university together. I hadn't seen him since he gained his officer's commission with the King's Army. I remember being surprised. He was always more of a follower than a leader. He had wanted to be an engineer. The army had been his father's idea."

"So, you figured he was looking for a leader?"

"No, not just any leader. It had to be someone he respected—an alpha."

"And he respects you?"

The marquess looked over his shoulder to where Hegress was organizing what little cavalry and artillery they possessed. "I believe he does. We would not be here if he didn't."

"You think they would have killed us?"

He shook his head. "Me, at least. Perhaps not you. I doubt he has fallen far enough to destroy an entire town's worth of innocent civilians. Besides, they're worth more to him alive right now."

"How's that?"

"Bodies," the marquess said flatly. "The more people, the greater chance of survival. More to feed, but more to steal as well. I doubt he ever had designs on becoming a king or some such, though. No, he was thinking only of short-term survival."

Mory looked to the city, and his stomach sank. "What are *you* thinking?"

The marquess sighed heavily, obviously having had the same thought. "We go in."

Twenty minutes. Twenty minutes, exactly. That's how long it took Peck to return. It was the second-most agonizing twenty minutes of Mory's life. The first, of course, had been when he was dead, and the healer had momentarily given up on him. Mory slipped the time crystal back into his pocket. The small device had been not so much a gift as a requirement by the marquess. Since Mory was the official link between them and Aaslo, he, apparently, needed to know at what time things occurred. He had also learned to write his numbers so that he could record the times of his interactions with the reaper, if not the conversations themselves. Mory had protested vehemently when the marquess had threatened to assign him an assistant to do just that. He hated the idea of someone following him around all the time, so he had taken to practicing the memory exercises Peck had taught him with gusto.

"Daniga says it's clear to go in," reported Peck.

"Clear?" said the marquess. "How can it be clear? A strange woman came out that gate right there. We all saw her."

Peck glanced at the open gate, then turned back to the marquess and shrugged. "I don't know what to say. None of the scouts saw anyone in or around the city."

"I saw her," said Mory as he tapped the little leaf sewn onto his tunic.

Peck rolled his eyes. "Fine. *One* scout, apparently, saw a woman, which you already know about."

The marquess looked as if he would berate Peck for his insolence but instead sighed roughly and rubbed his temples again. "It is decided. We shall enter the city." He turned to Bear. "We had best do it now so that we will have plenty of time to make preparations before dark."

Peck plucked a golden blade of grass from his velvet coat as he said, "What about . . . you know . . . that *thing* . . . in the sky?"

"We shall deal with that if and when it happens again. Until then, it is better to be securely within the walls than out here where anyone and any*thing* might attack."

"All right, boss," said Peck with an inscrutable glance toward Mory. "I'll let Daniga know we're going in. Mory, I need to talk to you alone a minute."

As Bear and the marquess joined Hegress, presumably to discuss strategies for taking up residence in a city that may or may not be inhabited by people who may or may not be dead, Mory joined Peck in the shade of a tree.

"I get it now," said Peck.

"Get what?"

"Why Aaslo's always talking about walking in the shade. It's hot out here. I don't remember it ever being this hot in the city."

"I don't think it was. To be fair, though, you *are* wearing a coat."

Peck tugged on his lapels and flashed a brief grin. "And I look *good* in it." His grin fell, and he said, "Listen, Mory. Something's really weird about this city. I don't feel right about taking you in there."

"Weirder than the walking dead and grey monsters?" Mory said, his voice rising with his irritation. "Weirder than a man-dragon? Weirder than a reaper?"

Peck's face scrunched as he looked at the city. "I don't know. I just don't want you to get hurt. I couldn't handle it if I lost you again."

"Next time I die, I'll just refuse to go with them."

"Next time, you may not have a choice. You got lucky with Myra. She sounds nice, but I doubt the other reapers will care."

"What about *you*? What am I supposed to do if *you* die?"

Peck gave him a practiced, self-assured smile but stopped short of his usual braggartly placations. "You'll stay with the marquess until you can join Aaslo again. He'll take care of you."

"You don't know that," Mory snapped. "You don't know *him*."

"I know enough to realize he's our best chance at survival. He's not *here*, though. None of the magi are. There's something weird in that city—something magical or cursed—and no one's here with the power to deal with it. You should find a place to hide."

"Hide? *Alone!* No. I don't want to be alone, Peck. There's no point in living if I'm alone."

Peck laid his hands on Mory's shoulders. "Just until we know the city's safe."

Mory brushed Peck's hands away and straightened his back. For the first time, he realized his head was even with Peck's, which made more sense than his earlier thought that his pants had shrunk. "I'm not running away. I'm a man, whether or not you admit it."

"Don't be so eager to grow up," said Peck.

"I've been learning to fight, and I have an ability that no one else has. The marquess needs me. Aaslo needs me. *You* need me, Peck."

"Don't you think I know that? Yes, I *need* you. That's why I'm telling you to do this."

Mory pointed to the city. "I'm going in there, same as you."

He could see the moment Peck realized he had lost. It was strange talking to Peck like that. It was even stranger that Peck backed down. A few months before, he would have given Mory a good walloping for the disrespect.

"All right," said Peck. "But we go in together. You stay right beside me the entire time, got it?"

"Fine," said Mory, still fuming. He didn't know why he was so angry. In the past, he had appreciated Peck's protection. At times, it had been the only thing of value that he possessed. Things had changed since Tyellí, though. *He* had changed.

Mory didn't protest when they entered the city together. He was glad Peck was there, mostly because he could protect Peck when he was close; and Peck needed protecting. Sometimes he got full of himself and took on too much, and sometimes he thought he was a much better fighter than he really was. Mory knew he wasn't the greatest fighter either, but so long as they had each other's backs, they had a chance of survival.

Peck and Mory walked beside the marquess as they entered the city, surrounded by the combined forces of the marquess's guards and the Silver Brigade. Pikemen with kite shields and mounted cavalry flanked them, but Bear and Hegress had insisted it was too dangerous for the marquess to ride into the city where he could be singled out by archers that may be in the taller buildings. As they marched down the central boulevard, they saw no one—at least, no people.

"Did you see that?" said Peck with an elbow to Mory's arm.

Mory rubbed the sore spot. "Yeah, I saw it. What was it?"

"I don't know. Never seen anything like it."

"What did you see?" said the marquess.

"It was about the size of a cat, and it was furry, but it weren't no cat. It had bright purple fur with pink spots."

"Hmm, that sounds a bit more normal than this insect that has latched onto my finger. I *think* it's an insect."

Mory looked over to see that the marquess appeared quite pale, and a strange creature was indeed wrapped around his finger. It was eight-legged like a spider, yet fuzzy and winged like a bee—and it was bright red. It had two large fangs and was poised to bite. Peck suddenly lunged at the marquess, knocking Mory out of the way. His sleeve-knife flicked out to stab the insect through the thorax. When he pulled the knife away with the creature impaled, he saw that its fangs had collided with the blade.

"Thank you," said the marquess, his color returning. "That might have been bad. You're quick with that knife."

Mory wished Teza were there. If she could give Aaslo a dragon arm, she could surely cure the marquess's headaches—and perhaps any other ailments they acquired from the strange creatures they had been seeing about the city. None had been larger than a dog, although, as the marquess's insect demonstrated, size had little to do with danger.

They had not quite reached the city center when they came upon a boxy, two-story building surrounded by a cobbled patio that was lined with columns. The overlarge double doors stood open at ground level. Through the opening was darkness.

The procession stopped; and, with a flick of the marquess's fingers, Peck and Mory slinked past the forward troops to join Daniga. While the other scouts were fanning out within a two-block radius, it was up to the three of them to keep the main body of migrants safe. Daniga entered first. When she did not immediately reappear, Peck followed. After a moment, his arm snaked out to flick his fingers for Mory. Upon entering, Mory was immediately struck with awe. Inside the building was not the perpetual darkness that had concerned him. In the center of the dirt floor of the large arena was a thin, silver ring of light surrounded by glowing runes. A jagged pillar of frozen lightning rose from the center of the ring to the domed roof. At one end of the arena was a dark, descending maw that swallowed three sets of mining tracks. The tracks continued around the arena in a crisscrossing maze, and several housed long-forgotten carts frozen in place by rust.

Mory could feel the presence of *something* hidden in the dark recesses. His heightened sense of awareness was further justified by a jumble of faint clangs and drawn-out, metallic groans. Daniga had paused about ten paces into the building, and Peck had ducked behind a cart that sat empty just inside the opening.

A loud pang, like a toppling metallic structure, echoed through the building, and Daniga began backing toward the doors. Before she had taken three steps, a hidcous creature shot out from the shadows and surged toward her. Its undulating movements made it difficult to track and even harder to identify, although Mory was pretty sure nothing like it could possibly exist anywhere else in Uyan. It looked to be made of hundreds of segments and associated pairs of legs and was at least twenty feet long. Its black body was covered in sparse, white hairs, and it had six bloodred eyes clustered above a narrow beak-like, toothy mouth. While the majority of the body hugged the ground and reached not halfway up Daniga's shin, the front five segments rose into the air to meet her height.

Daniga released an arrow at the creature as she backpedaled, but the arrow might as well have been a child's toy. It bounced off the hard carapace with no effect as the creature closed the distance. Daniga dodged as the beast lunged at her, but its pointed beak scored a deep gash in her thigh. Peck ran toward the downed scout, and Mory made to shout back toward the marquess's party for help. When he turned, however, he found that the opening was gone and in its place was naught but a wall covered in dozens of miniature versions of the centipede-like creature— miniature in that they were *only* about his size. They didn't immediately attack, but they were intently watching the battle with the larger creature.

Mory sprinted to join Peck and Daniga in their fight while running through a checklist in his mind. He paused long enough to draw his short sword. His grip was firm but flexible, his shoulders were loose, his weight centered, and his breathing deep and steady. Even so, he struggled to still his shaking muscles as the sour fire of anxiety inundated them. The creature reared back after a second attempt to impale Daniga, and Peck hurried to pull her to her feet before it struck again. When it looked like the centipede might strike before they had recovered, Mory rushed forward. His blade struck the creature's back just below the raised segments. Although his sword glanced off the hard exoskeleton, he did succeed in gaining the centipede's attention.

It turned on him and released a chirruping squawk like that of an oversized raptor. Its head danced back and forth just before it attempted a strike. Mory ducked below the lunging torso and struck at the forwardmost set of legs, which he was surprised to find were easily separated from its body. It squawked and snapped at him, and, as he emerged from a roll, he amputated three more of the creature's legs. Mory's heart leapt as an arrow shot past his head to sink into the space between segments on the centipede's torso. When he focused back on his own situation, he was horrified to find the beast had coiled around him. He was surrounded by spiny legs and hard, hairy plates. It began to tighten the coil, reducing the space by half in seconds. It reared back to strike at him again, and then Mory saw Peck clinging to the monster's head. Peck stood on one of the segments and pushed himself upward, then he thrust his dagger into the centipede's eye. It slammed its face into the ground, and Peck tumbled into the dark.

Another arrow stuck between two of the creature's segments, and it began to list, forcing it to release Mory from his imprisonment. It was during the centipede's uncoiling that Mory noticed its final segment was rooted into the ground. As it struggled to right itself, he observed that this final segment was without the hard shell of the exoskeleton. The wet and fleshy wormlike terminus gave the monster the leverage it needed to keep its forward segments elevated and nearly inaccessible. Mory raised his sword and slashed at the exposed muscle, easily separating it from the rest of the body. With this, the beast began to thrash across the arena floor like the severed tail of a lizard. It fell into the illuminated disk on the ground. When its head struck the stagnant energy bolt at its center, it was split in two with one side vanishing completely. The scent of scorched chitin stung Mory's nose, and the crackle of popping exoskeleton echoed in his ears long after its source had settled.

Suddenly, five of the Silver Brigade entered the arena, passing straight through the wall. The structure wavered, and the smaller centipede-like creatures scattered back into the dark recesses of the arena. Another four soldiers passed through the wall behind them unimpeded. Mory caught sight of Peck stumbling into the light. He appeared bruised but not seriously injured. Daniga had dropped to the ground and was attempting to stem the flow of blood from her wounded thigh. A couple of the soldiers moved to help her. As the energy of battle waned, Mory felt the sudden need to run. He headed straight for the wall and later considered himself lucky that he'd passed through it without experiencing a messy and painful collision.

When Mory emerged into the daylight, it was to find himself surrounded by soldiers, a number of whom aimed weapons at him. The marquess pushed forward and said, "Well? What happened? Where are the others?"

Mory took several deep breaths and swallowed the panic that had taken hold. Then he said, "We were attacked by a nasty creature. It's dead now, but there are plenty more hiding inside. Daniga is injured. You need to send in the soldiers—"

"I do, do I?"

"But tell them not to touch the lightning."

"The lightning? If there is lightning in there, I doubt any of the men would want to touch it. Go!"

As the soldiers filed into the building, Mory took the opportunity to finish catching his breath. "I hate this place," he muttered.

AN HOUR LATER, THE BUILDING HAD BEEN CLEANSED OF THE CENTIPEDE infestation as well as the nests of other odd creatures that may or may not have been a threat. Guard stations were erected at the entrance to the building as well as around the opening to the mine shaft, and all camp-sites were positioned well away from the glowing runes in the center of the arena. Mory watched from where he sat leaning against a crate on the ground as one of the field medics stitched Daniga's leg. He hoped she wouldn't succumb to infection.

The marquess approached and sat down on a folding stool beside Peck. Mory looked up at him sideways as he hunched over to rest his elbows on his knees. The nobleman rested his chin on one palm and grinned as his gaze fell unseeing on the bloody sight. Peck seemed to notice the marquess's odd behavior as well.

"Are you drunk?" he said.

"It's medic-ci-cinal," said the marquess, his speech slurred.

"I think you passed *medicinal* a few pints ago," said Peck.

The marquess's lopsided grin fell. "Perhaps I overdid it a little, but my head doesn't hurt."

"I don't mean any disrespect, but it seems like a bad time to lose sense."

"Seems like a bad time to have your brain explode, too," the marquess muttered before he burst into a fit of giggles.

"He's not drunk exactly," said the medic, who was seeing to Daniga's injury. "It's blauchney, an alchemical potion used to reduce pain. He was meant to take a swig, but he downed the bottle. His head will start to clear in a few hours. It's unfortunate, though. With the magi gone, the stuff's in short supply, and there's no one to produce more."

"What is it?" snapped Daniga as one of the scouts approached.

"I'm sorry, ma'am, but we have a problem. Lyksvight have been spotted near the gate. They're trickling into the area now, but their numbers are rising. It looks like it's going to be a swarm."

"Great," she muttered. "Let Bear and Hegress know."

"I heard," said Bear as he joined them. The big man squatted and began drawing in the dirt. "The lyksvight haven't entered the city yet. They seem to be gathering, waiting. Here's the city wall. We've swept the city here, here, here, and here. These areas are still unexplored. We can close the gate, but we risk trapping ourselves in here with who knows what. Then again, there won't be any escape with a horde of lyksvight out there."

"Why they are here?" slurred the marquess. "They're coming from . . . uh . . . where?"

"We don't know where they're coming from, but they seem to be captivated by the rip in the sky."

"But the rip's gone," said Peck.

"It's back," said Bear. "In fact, it's directly over this building."

"Here?"

Another scout appeared from the same direction as the first. "It's gone again," she said before scurrying away.

"So, it's a recurring phemonenum—phememanon—phenomenenon," said the marquess. "Well, that's okay, then. The city's still standing, so it can't be so bad."

"I'm not sure that's the conclusion we should be drawing," said Peck.

"I'm not drawing," said the marquess. He pointed to Bear, who was still crouched. "He's drawing."

Peck groaned and buried his face in his hand. Then he said, "Where's Hegress?"

"At the gate," said Bear as he pulled his gaze from the marquess, who seemed to be intently listening to a shovel that was leaning against a makeshift weapons rack.

"No, I told you the mead's not ready yet," said the marquess, still intent on the shovel.

"I guess that means you're in charge," said Peck.

Bear shook his head. "I've gotta direct my men. Can't do that sitting around a command post."

"Isn't that what a *command* post is for?"

"I'm more of a hands-on leader."

"Then who's in charge?" said Mory.

Bear pointed to Daniga, who had just lost consciousness. "She's next in line. Don't think she'll be giving any orders for a while. Don't worry. Most of the decisions'll be made in the thick of it. You'll do as good as anyone with the rest."

"Me?" shouted Peck.

Bear shrugged. "It's either you or my second, but he's needed at the perimeter. I figure if they get this far, we're prob'ly done fer anyway."

Peck tugged his lapels and smoothed the velvet over his arms. "I, ah, I'd love to help, but I think my talents would be better applied elsewhere— like on a rooftop somewhere overlooking the battle."

Mory said, "Are you scared, Peck?"

"Who, me? Nah, I'm the smoothest thief in Tyellí. I can't afford to be scared."

"We're not in Tyellí, and you're not a thief."

"Once a thief, always a thief," muttered the medic with a disapproving glance.

Mory took no offense. Before meeting Aaslo, he and Peck had always said the same. For them, it was a matter of pride. He looked at Bear. "What makes you think he's qualified to lead a battle?"

The marquess abruptly stumbled into Mory's personal space. He wavered back and forth, then abruptly sobered. He placed a hand on Mory's shoulder and said, "The streets of Tyellí are hard on the worst of criminals. Our man Peck here—only a child, himself—not only survived but retained his sense of humor, a sense of honor, and his soul—all the while raising a small boy." The marquess's gaze was sharp for the briefest moment before his pupils again became unfocused, and he fell into a fit of giggles.

"There you have it," said Bear. "The marquess has confidence in him. So should you."

"Never trust the confidence of a man hopped up on blauchney," said the medic as he stood. He bowed to the marquess, saluted Bear, and left to assist others.

Peck grabbed Mory by the arm. "I need to speak with you a second." He dragged Mory out of earshot of the marquess, who had engaged in an intense discussion with the still-unconscious Daniga. "I can't do this, Mory. I've never been in charge of anything in my life."

"What about me? You've always taken care of me."

"That's different. We have to find a way to stall an attack."

"How are we going to do that?"

"I don't know. We need to think of something. Maybe your reaper has an idea."

"She's not *my* reaper, and she's not here."

"Let me know as soon as she reappears. In the meanwhile, I'm going to see if I can find a distraction."

"How do I find you?"

Peck glanced over his shoulder to make sure no one was looking, then he held out his hand. Two small, clear, olive-sized crystals lay in his palm. "I took these off Hegress and that big oaf he calls a second."

"What are they?"

"I think they're some kind of communication crystals."

"How do they work?"

Peck held one out for Mory. "Here, hold this. Hegress rubbed it like this and—see? When I rubbed this one, yours started glowing."

The glow subsided as Mory rubbed his thumb across the smooth crystal face. He rubbed it again, and Peck's crystal began to glow. "Hey, that's great. I wish we'd had these back in Tyellí."

"Eventually, maybe we can work out a system of communication with them. For now, if it starts glowing, I'll know you need me. We can meet back here."

"All right. It's too bad it doesn't shake or something. I won't notice it glowing in my pocket."

"I thought of that, too," he said as he pulled two tiny segments of chain mail from his pocket. "I lifted this from the smith's supplies." He wrapped a piece of chain mail around one of the crystals, making sure to leave the top face of the crystal uncovered, and tied to it a short length of braided leather cord. He then wrapped the cord around Mory's wrist. He repeated the process with his own crystal. "This way, we can see them when they glow, but Hegress and Oaf won't realize we have them. If someone *does* ask about them, say Aaslo gave them to us."

"What if they think Aaslo stole them?"

"They won't. They haven't even met Aaslo, and I only took them an hour ago."

For the first time, Mory felt a little bad for taking something that wasn't his. He supposed that, in the past, his empty stomach had overridden the feeling. He said, "It's not really stealing if we're all on the same side, right? It's more like . . . redistribution of supplies."

Peck grinned and slapped him on the back. "Now you're getting it. Besides, Hegress and Oaf probably stole them off some of the Silver Brigade's victims anyway."

"This means we're splitting up?"

"I'm going to explore the city."

"But you're supposed to be in charge."

"Look, they don't want to say it, but if those lyksvight do come in a swarm, we're all done for. This is a strange city built during a time of great magic. There's got to be something here that can help. Remember the woman at the gate? What happened to her? There might be more people here who can help."

"Then I'm coming with you. No, don't argue with me. It's you and me, Peck, and I don't want to get left behind if something happens to you out there."

"You'd rather die with me?"

"You know I would."

"Well, all right, then. If we get separated, we'll meet back here. Tap the crystal to let me know you're safe."

"Okay. Where are we going first?"

"I'm curious about those towers. Magi are always keeping important things in towers."

"They are?"

"Well, that's what the stories say."

Peck and Mory walked out of the building pretending they were on official business so as not to attract attention. The nearest tower was two streets over and a hundred yards to the south. As they walked, Mory couldn't shake the feeling they were being stalked. Every so often, he would glance into a dark doorway or window and find eyes staring back at him. Most of the creatures were small and seemingly too scared to leave their hideaways. When he and Peck were only a few feet from the entrance to the tower, however, they met their first challenge—a winged boar-like beast that looked far too fat to fly hovered in the air about ten feet off the ground. Its tusks were short and unthreatening, but the sharp claws that protruded from its front lionlike paws would have no problem ripping into their abdomens.

Mory and Peck froze, and just when Mory thought the creature would pounce on them, it growled and soared over their heads. The next thing they heard was a ripping sound and the slathering gurgles of a lyksvight. Mory looked back to see that the winged boar was instead attacking a small group of the Berruvian fiends that were following them.

"Run," said Peck as he tugged on Mory's tunic. They ran toward the tower and through the open doorway. The dusty wooden planks beneath their feet groaned and cracked, and before they knew what was happening, they were falling. Mory collided with something that buckled under the force, then he kept falling. While he was sure it had been an eternity, the fall could only have taken seconds. The hard stone floor and debris from above arrested his fall. He coughed, struggling to take a breath, as the dust in the air above him settled. He could see that they had fallen at least thirty feet, plenty far enough to kill a man.

"Peck," he sputtered as he tried to sit upright. "Peck, are you okay?" Mory shook his arms and legs to make sure they worked. He had a few cuts and ample pains that were sure to become bruises. He heard a groan from somewhere to his right. He felt along the hard ground, seeking Peck in the lightless subterranean hole. He wished he had Aaslo's ability to see in the dark but admitted to himself that the blessing wouldn't be worth the curse that accompanied it. Then it occurred to him that he had a light source *and* a way to find Peck.

Mory tapped the crystal tied to his wrist and saw a responding glow two paces away. He scrambled over the chunks of broken wood to find Peck unconscious and bleeding from several deep gashes. He pulled a splinter the size of his finger from a wound at Peck's shoulder. Peck shouted as he abruptly regained consciousness.

"Ow! What did you do?" said Peck.

Mory handed him the bloody splinter and pressed his palm against the puncture wound. He said, "Do you have anything we can use as a bandage?"

Peck pulled a wad of cloth from his pocket and handed it to Mory. "It's not very clean, but it'll have to do."

Mory felt the fine material rife with embroidery. "What is it?" he said as he wrapped it around Peck's shoulder.

"It's one of the marquess's flags. I took it in case I needed to signal them or prove my identity."

"You mean you stole it. That was a good idea. I should have thought of it."

Mory helped Peck to his feet. He tapped the communication crystal again, eliciting another soft glow from its sister, and studied their circumstances. They were in a room that appeared to be much larger than the tower above, although they could not see the far recesses with their meager light. The floor was natural, uncut stone, as were the walls. A partially collapsed staircase ascended to the level from which they fell, and Mory wondered if it was strong enough to hold their weight. Beside the staircase was a sconce holding a metal, hand-length baton atop which a glass sphere was mounted. Mory tapped the sphere, which started to glow. As he stared at it, the glow grew brighter until it filled the space around them for at least twenty feet.

"This is great. Look, Peck," he said as he swung the small scepter in front of him.

"Yeah, don't break it."

Mory rolled his eyes. "I wasn't planning to. What now?"

With a groan, Peck said, "Let's go this way."

Mory followed Peck past the staircase and found a second light scepter. With both scepters lit, they could see most of the room in which they were possibly trapped. It appeared to be a storage room of a sort, or perhaps a museum. Mory had only been in a museum once because Peck had contemplated stealing something. Fortunately, Peck had come to his senses and hadn't done anything to attract the attentions of the magi that guarded it.

Everywhere they looked were amphorae, some on pedestals, others on shelves and tables, and still more piled on the floor. Each was plugged with a stopper secured by a metal clamp. Mory brushed the dust from one and found that it was beautifully decorated with colorful enamel and gold inlays, some of which appeared to be a script unlike anything Mory had seen.

"What are these?" he said.

"I don't know. Wine? Oil?"

He picked up a smaller one and shook it. "I don't hear any liquid inside."

"Maybe it's leaked out or evaporated."

Peck took the small vessel, released the clamp, and unstopped it. Then he upended the amphora, pouring out a pale, soft powder. He took a pinch, sniffed it, then placed a small amount on his tongue.

"What do you think?" said Mory.

"I don't know. Whatever it was, it's no good anymore. It stinks. It must have been worth something, though. The price for the amphorae alone could have kept us fed indefinitely."

"I guess they're not worth much now, though."

"No. Too bad it wasn't wine."

They walked among the amphorae, randomly checking anything useful. Upon opening one, Peck released a flood of small red insects. Peck dropped the amphora, which remained unbroken, and the insects fell from its mouth like a red waterfall onto the floor. They scattered to the far reaches of the room and disappeared into the cracks in the stone.

Mory scratched his neck, then his side, sure the little bugs were crawling all over him. "Are they on me? Peck, tell me they're not on me."

"They're not on you. It's in your head."

Mory shivered, scratched a few more spots, then wandered far from the infestation. "Peck! Hey, Peck, come here," he called.

"Whoa," said Peck upon seeing what had excited Mory. "I've never seen an amphora so huge. It nearly reaches the ceiling."

"Look at all the gold," said Mory. "We're rich."

"Only if it contains food."

Mory scanned the length of the vessel as Peck ran his fingers over the embellishments. "How are we gonna reach the top to find out?" said Mory.

"I don't think we can. I haven't seen a ladder down here. What do you suppose this is?" Peck pressed his palm against a fist-sized carnelian cabochon that adorned the vessel. It composed what looked to be the thorax of a winged insect-like being. With a click, the cabochon came free from the amphora. The cabochon was secured in a gold setting with a small loop hidden on the back.

"What is it?" Mory said as he reached for it. "Ow!" he exclaimed, releasing it back into Peck's hands. A trickle of blood oozed from a tiny puncture wound in Mory's palm. "It poked me. Careful, there's something sharp."

Peck turned it up in time to witness a small needle receding into the base of the setting. He said, "I hope it wasn't poisoned."

Mory's head felt dizzy with dread as he looked at Peck. "Am I going to die again? Please, Peck. Don't let me die."

"You're not going to die," said Peck. "Stop worrying so much. Besides, the reaper is your friend."

"Maybe, but she's not the only reaper."

Peck handed the cabochon to Mory, who took it with greater care. "Here, I think it's a pendant or maybe even an amulet. I'll see if there are more." As Peck rounded the amphora, running his hands over its surface, Mory examined the creamy red-orange carnelian. Only months ago, he would have been elated by the find. As it was, the extraordinary piece was practically worthless.

"I think I found another," said Peck.

Mory suddenly felt as though he were moving.

"Watch out!" shouted Peck.

Mory glanced up in alarm to find that he wasn't moving. The amphora was falling, and it was about to crush him. He leapt out of the way, crashing into a stack of amphorae and barely missing another untimely end. The massive amphora burst, releasing a thunderous roar, and thick, black smoke rushed from the shattered vessel up through the broken floor above them.

With a groan, Mory pushed to his feet again. By the way he felt, he figured he'd have bruises nearly covering his body. Peck scrambled over the debris as he rushed to Mory's side.

"Are you okay? I'm so sorry, Mory. That could have killed you."

Mory rubbed his sore ribs. "I'm not sure it didn't."

"Don't joke like that. You've been dead one time too many."

"What was that?" Just as he said it, a piercing cry like shrieking metal echoed down on them from above.

"I, ah, think we may have released something." Peck glanced around at all the amphorae. His eyes widened, and he hurried over to where he had dropped the smaller vessel. He picked it up and brought it into the light. "Look," he said, "each of these amphorae looks to have the image of a creature on it. This one looks like a red bug. I think these amphorae are filled with creatures—probably creatures from the rift. And I think we just released one—a really big one."

"You mean things are *alive* inside these?"

Peck shrugged. "Maybe some of them. Others must have died and turned to dust. Maybe some even contain mummies."

"Mummies? Of *people*?"

"Probably not, but who knows?"

"Let's get out of here, Peck. I don't like it. Besides, you're supposed to be in charge at the command center. Bear and Daniga will be furious with us for being gone so long."

"If we *can* leave," Peck muttered as he picked up his own light scepter and headed back toward the stairs.

"Don't talk like that. I don't want to die down here."

# CHAPTER 18

PECK AND MORY MANAGED TO REACH THE GROUND LEVEL WITH ONLY A few minor issues. The stairs had held their weight, and the missing section with which Mory had collided on the way down was not large enough to prevent their passage. Their entire adventure had taken less than an hour, yet Mory couldn't help but feel it had been a terrible waste of time. They had gone to the tower looking for a way to ward off, or at least delay, the inevitable Berruvian attack, and they had come away with nothing more than cuts and bruises.

As they walked back toward the command center, their gazes roved the streets for enemies. Mory pulled the cabochon from his pocket and held it out for Peck. "Here, you take it. It's worthless."

Peck looked at it and shook his head. "No, I think you should have it." He winked and said, "You bled for it, after all." Mory rubbed his injured palm. It was red and irritated, but the wound didn't look to be festering. "Here, I have some leather cord left. Put it through the loop on the back, and you can wear it around your neck."

"Why would I want to do that? It's huge. It'll look ridiculous."

"Maybe it's magical. You can hold on to it until we see the magi again."

"Do you think we ever will?"

"I really don't know, but if I know Aaslo—and I think I do, at least a little—he'll come back for us if he can."

"Yeah, he's good that way." Mory looked up at the sky and said, "Is something burning?"

Peck looked, too. Above them was gathering a thick, black smoke not unlike the one that escaped the excessively large amphora. As they watched, the smoke coalesced into a creature unlike anything they had ever seen. It had the head, thorax, abdomen, and wings of a wasp, the tail of a serpent, and the face of an opossum, complete with razor-sharp teeth, all wrapped in a shiny blue-black carapace.

The creature hovered in the air above them as it took form. It seemed to be looking for something. Peck and Mory didn't move. Its attention was captured by a couple of lyksvight that came around the corner chasing a doglike animal. Before either of them caught their prey, the wasp-thing swooped down on them. It emitted a black smoke from its fang-filled mouth as it attacked, and the lyksvight began contorting and dissolving before their eyes. Peck and Mory took advantage of the distraction and escaped while the wasp-thing tore into the lyksvight and dog-thing alike.

When they were a few streets away, they paused to catch their breaths. "That was the most terrifying thing I've ever seen," said Mory. "It was worse than the lyksvight and undead combined."

"Too right," said Peck. "Let's hope we lost it."

Then they heard a faint hum, the buzz of massive insect wings. As they ran toward the command center, the hum grew louder. They were still a street away from their goal when Mory tugged Peck to a stop.

"Wait," he said. "I think it's following us. We can't take it to the others. It'll kill everyone."

"If we don't get help, it'll kill *us*."

"Maybe it'll follow us to the Berru. They move in a frenzy, and there are a lot of them. We could kill two birds with one stone."

"That's not a bad idea, assuming we can make it there before it catches us *and* assuming the Berru don't kill us when we get there."

"I think we have to try. It's kind of our fault it's here."

"We didn't do it on purpose."

Mory stared at Peck with determination, and he could see the conflict brewing behind Peck's troubled gaze. The wasp-thing emerged over a building on the other side of the street, and their time to decide was up. Peck grabbed Mory's sleeve and began running east toward the front gate. They ducked into doorways and tumbled through open windows in an effort to slow the wasp-thing's pursuit. Still, it followed. Mory gripped a hitching post as he hurdled over it, and a sharp pain reminded him of the small injury to his hand. They were within sight of the front gate when Mory pulled Peck around a corner and stopped.

"Peck," he said through deep gasps. He pointed to the puncture on his palm. "I think it's following *me*. You should go back to the command center. I'll take it to the Berru."

"Are you crazy? I already thought of that. How can you think that I would abandon you?"

"Please, Peck. I don't want anything to happen to you."

"I lost you once, Mory. I'll not lose you again. I can't go through that twice."

"Even if the Berru distract it, it'll probably still come after me. You need to go."

"We just need to change its target. We'll sneak over there, use the amulet to prick someone else—someone important—then we'll escape back to the command center."

"Really, that simple?" Mory said facetiously. He pointed toward the iron gate that blocked the entrance. Many of the marquess's men, including the Silver Brigade, lined the walls and crouched behind a hastily erected blockade inside the gate. "Look out there," he said. "There are probably hundreds of lyksvight and magi and even some seculars gathered already. How do you expect for us to get past all of them *twice* without being seen?"

Peck stared at the forces they could see through the gate with a look of consternation. Then he said, "We won't. You said there are seculars with them. They've been forcing people from the towns and villages to join them. We'll pretend we're with them."

"How will we get back *out*?"

Peck grinned and placed a hand on Mory's shoulder. "We're world-class thieves, Mory. It'll be no problem."

The buzz of the wasp-thing grew to a deafening din, and Mory knew they were out of time. He nodded his assent, and Peck and he began running toward an unmanned side of the wall that was overgrown with a reddish-purple vine. Mory dearly hoped it didn't have thorns and wasn't poisonous, but he didn't like their chances. It seemed like everything that came through the tear in the sky wanted to kill them. Neither would have stopped them, though. They were determined and, truthfully, had little choice. Mory was concerned about Peck's shoulder injury, but he didn't complain once as they ascended. Peck had always been a tough one, though, when it came to pain. He never wanted to worry Mory.

Once they had made it to the top of the wall, they realized there was no way to get down to the other side, at least not in a controlled manner. Peck began pulling at the large vine that *did* have thorns—very large, painful thorns. Mory's hands were already slick with blood when he began helping Peck. Together, they pulled up lengths of vines that could, hopefully, get them to the ground without breaking their legs. After securing them to the wall, he and Peck climbed down. For once, things worked in their favor, and he was fairly sure they would be able to reach the vines for the return trip.

The two ducked behind the overgrowth as they crossed what had long ago been a clearing. The enemy ranks consisted of poorly organized chaos, and no one seemed to be watching for people coming *from* the ancient city. The hazy-eyed lyksvight ambled restlessly in circles. Some gnashed their teeth at the Uyanian recruits, and even the toughest mercenaries were obviously terrified. Mory peered through the branches of a bush as Peck quickly padded toward a clump of overgrown wild grass. When Mory turned to follow, his back pressed against something—*someone.* He nearly screamed in fright, and his heart jumped into his throat. After falling onto his rear, he turned and looked up into the lyksvight's distorted, grotesque features. The monster stared down at him through milky-white eyes, but it didn't move.

Mory swallowed a whimper and bit his tongue to keep from crying out as the thing leaned down to sniff him. The smoky haze in its eyes shifted as it stared at him from only a few inches' distance. The putrid stink of decay on its breath was strong enough to cause his stomach to turn, and Mory had to swallow again. Then the lyksvight straightened and shuffled in the opposite direction Peck had gone. Mory glanced over to see Peck staring at him from the grass, his pallid face stretched in an expression of dread. Mory took a few steadying breaths, then darted across the expanse to join his companion. Peck immediately pulled him into an embrace and didn't release him for a long time.

"Okay," Mory whispered, "you can let go now."

Peck only gripped him tighter. When Peck finally released him, he turned quickly, probably hoping Mory wouldn't catch sight of the tears that wet his lashes. They crept up on a group of captive Uyanians whose obvious terror seemed to have drained them of their souls. Some sat on the ground rocking back and forth, others anxiously shuffled about, and still more appeared as if frozen in place, yet all of them stared vacantly.

Mory crouched on the ground next to a middle-aged woman who gripped a butcher's knife with white knuckles. He leaned toward her and whispered, "Where did the magus in charge go?"

She turned her head, but her wide eyes seemed to stare straight through him. "I can't let go," she said.

Mory's brow furled, and he said, "What?"

She raised the knife so that the point was nearly touching his nose. "I can't let go," she said again. Then she dropped her hand and resumed staring into the distance. Mory and Peck shared a look, neither needing words to express their thoughts regarding the woman's mental state. Peck nodded toward a man who stood slightly apart from the others. He rolled several long pieces of grass between his fingers and appeared contemplative. They shifted toward him slowly so as not to draw attention.

"It's fourteen to one," the man said without prompting.

Mory looked around to see to whom the man was speaking and decided it must have been *them*. Peck said, "What is?"

The man placed one of the blades of grass between his lips and held it there. Then he went back to fiddling with the others as he stared toward the city. Mory could see the wasp-creature circling the city and getting ever closer to them. "The chances of a lyksvight killing you in a fight. I figured it out. If you're an average man bearing a knife or sword, that is. It's because they keep fighting even when they're dying. They don't care if they die. Who knows? Maybe they're already dead. I heard there's a half-man, half-monster thing going around raising the dead. Could be his fault. Yeah, I figure it's fourteen to one."

"I think your numbers are off," said Peck. "We've fought them a lot, and we're still alive."

The man still didn't look at them. He only shrugged and said, "I guess you're not average men."

"I like to think so," said Peck. "But I need to know something. Where's the guy in charge? The head magus?"

The man chewed the blade of grass for a moment, then said, "It's about seventeen to one for a woman. Of course, she'd have better odds if she learned to fight—maybe better than a man. They're smaller, you see. And more agile. Maybe twelve to one. Unless she's pregnant."

Peck shook his head and motioned for Mory to follow him to another group. The screaming rip of metal wrenched the air, and Mory's instinct was to run away as fast as he could. Peck gripped his wrist and caught his eye. He gave him the same steadying look that he'd given him every time they were about to hit a difficult target. Mory swallowed and nodded, then they moved slowly with purpose. When they were within five feet of the second group, a man overtook them from behind.

"Hey, swine, where do you think you're going?"

Peck and Mory turned to find a Berruvian magus frowning down at them. He was a willowy man with long, black hair and sharpened teeth. He pointed at Mory with a talon-like, black-lacquered nail. "What are you?" he growled.

Mory opened his mouth to answer, but nothing came to mind.

"He's just a kid," said Peck, tugging Mory behind him. "We're looking for the boss man. Where can we find him?"

"What is this boss man?" said the magus, still eyeing Mory.

"You know, the head magus. The high wizard or whatever."

The magus's sharp gaze snapped to Peck, and he leaned forward. "Why do you seek the incendia?"

"Uh, we found something we thought he might like to have. It looks important." Peck turned to Mory and tugged the amulet over his head rather forcefully. He practically threw it at the magus, who caught it by instinct. The man hissed and raised his hand to expose a fresh trickle of blood. Then he studied the cabochon carefully. His attention returned to Peck. "Where did you find this?"

Peck hooked his thumbs behind his lapels as he always did before he wove a tale and said, "We were sitting over there, you know, with the others. There in the grass. I was, ah, just digging around with a stick, thinking, you know? And there it was, buried in the dirt. I thought maybe if we give it to the boss—ah, the incendia—we could get a reward."

The man pursed his lips and narrowed his eyes at Peck, making it obvious he didn't completely believe Peck's story. "This is very clean for having been buried."

Peck grinned. "Well, I had to clean it up for the boss now, didn't I? We can't be giving the incendia a ball of filth."

The hairs on Mory's neck began to stand on end, and he glanced back toward the city. The wasp-monster had turned and was heading in their direction. The hum of its insect-like wings grew louder. The magus turned to see what had captured Mory's attention. When he turned back to them, his expression had soured. "Sit," he said. Peck and Mory both dropped to the ground without hesitation. "Await your orders. If you move, the lyksvight will eat you." The man moved away quickly into the crowd of Berruvian invaders.

Mory leaned over to whisper into Peck's ear. "Do you think it worked? Did it prick him?"

"I think so," said Peck.

"I thought we wanted it to prick the head magus."

"Maybe if that one gives it to him, it will. Either way, you're free. Let's go. I don't want to be here when that wasp-thing arrives."

Their escape was not as smooth as they'd hoped, though. Before they could distance themselves from the lyksvight, the wasp-monster began its attack. It swept down upon the crowd, gleefully releasing its acrid smoke. The lethargic gathering quickly became a swarm of activity. Peck and Mory didn't run straight for the city, though. Having seen what the smoke could do to someone, they were careful to stay upwind from the wasp-monster. The monster's carapace seemed invulnerable to magical and non-magical attacks alike; but, it seemed, as the magi's attentions were turned toward the wasp-monster, they began to lose their hold over the lyksvight. As the terror continued its assault on anything that moved, the Berruvians and lyksvight began to scatter, the bulk of them moving toward the city as a disorganized flood.

Peck and Mory were momentarily swept up in that flood, but they deftly maneuvered through the throng toward the side of the city where they'd made their escape. As they neared the hanging vines, they encountered a couple of lyksvight on the fringes that were apparently far enough removed from the danger to be less concerned about escape and more about their hunger. Both of them went after Peck, ignoring Mory until he came to Peck's rescue. One grabbed Peck from behind while the other attacked from the front. Mory came up behind it and plunged his knife into the fiend's neck. Then he smashed the other in the face with a rock while Peck attempted to squirm out of their grasps. Once he was free, Peck's knives came out quick as a whip. He stabbed the first in the back with six quick thrusts in succession. Then he pivoted to plunge his knife into the other's eye socket. Both monsters crumpled to the ground. Without waiting a beat, Peck grabbed Mory's sleeve and tugged him toward the vines.

"Wow, Peck. That's the fastest I've ever seen you," said Mory.

"I think that's the closest I've come to visiting the Afterlife." He cupped his hands in front of him with crossed fingers and said, "Here, I'll give you a boost. Hurry."

"What about you?"

"I can jump higher than you. Now get up there."

Mory scaled the wall with Peck on his heels. By the time they reached the top, lyksvight were encroaching on their escape route. They quickly reeled the vines up onto the wall, leaving the frustrated lyksvight chomping their teeth below.

"What now?" said Mory as he watched the wasp-monster picking off lyksvight like a bird to beetles. "Didn't we make things worse? They're invading the city."

"No, look," said Peck, pointing into the city on the other side of the wall. "The stream of lyksvight is thin. Our guards are picking off most of them that make it into the city through the breaks in the walls. Those that do make it through are scattering. No one is there to direct them into an organized assault."

"Then we helped?"

Peck looked back over his shoulder at the wasp-monster. "For a while, at least."

"I'm supposed to convince you to go to Chelis," said Myra. Aaslo craned his neck so that he could see her sitting atop a large boulder.

"Chelis?" he said.

"What about Chelis?" said Ijen as he appeared to unconsciously reach for the book in his tunic. As usual, Aaslo couldn't tell if Ijen's suspicion was a good omen or bad.

"What's in Chelis?" said Aaslo.

"Um, *hello*. It's the capital of Mouvilan," said Teza as she dropped a pack at his feet. Aaslo reached for it, but she stepped on the strap and said, "Careful, it could be booby-trapped."

"You're the one stomping on it," he said. "And I do know basic geography."

*"You're welcome for the education."*

"Why should I be thanking *you*?" he muttered. "I was the one who made the effort to join your lessons."

*"But you never would have had the opportunity had I not been there."*

"Had you not been there, I'd be relaxing in the shade of a rowan tree."

*"Ha! Without me, you wouldn't even know the word* relax."

"You're right. Every frivolous piece of knowledge I have is your fault."

"Stop it, Aaslo," Teza barked. "I'm standing right here. Talk to *me*."

"Maybe he *is* talking to you," said Ijen.

"What? That doesn't even make sense," she said.

Ijen tapped the book and nodded. "Many things don't make sense, and yet they continue to be true."

Teza sighed, then plopped down next to Aaslo. She reached for the pack. "I'll go through it. I can't believe whoever killed these things left this behind."

"Maybe they didn't see it," said Aaslo.

"Who are you talking to, anyway? Mathias or Myra?"

"Both."

"What does she want?"

"I don't know yet. You interrupted us."

"Well, *excuse* me. I thought you might be interested in *this*," she said as she pulled from the pack a hollow glass sphere the size of her fist.

"What is that?"

"I don't know."

*"That was anticlimactic. She found a paperweight."*

"That pack belonged to a Berruvian magus," said Aaslo. "I doubt it's a paperweight."

Ijen said, "Not to mention that a sphere would make for a terrible paperweight."

*"Touché."*

"That's it," said Teza as she tossed the pack aside. "There's nothing else of interest in here."

Aaslo looked up at Myra. "Do you know what it is?"

She tilted her head and said, "I think it's a map sphere. I see nothing in it, but I've watched the Berru use them."

Aaslo shook the sphere to no effect. "How does it work?"

She shrugged, then returned to the earlier conversation. "You're sup-posed to find a smith named something like Bordeshi or Bondeski."

"Why?"

"It's not clear. Something about acquiring armor. It could be a trap."

"Did Axus send this message?"

"No, Trostili."

"But Trostili is working with Axus."

"Yes," she drawled, "but he has his own agenda. It's equally possible he's trying to help you."

"You're saying my enemy, the God of War, wants me to go to Chelis to get some armor, and it might be good or bad."

"That's the gist of it," said Myra.

Teza said, "I can't believe I need to say this aloud, but that sounds like a terrible idea."

*"Go for it, Aaslo. Armor sent by the God of War? Totally worth it."*

"You think I should go?"

"No," barked Teza. "I just said it was a bad idea."

Aaslo scowled at Teza, then looked to Ijen. "What say you, Prophet?"

Ijen shrugged. "Is armor a priority?"

"Well, we *are* at war," said Aaslo.

"Yes, but is it a war in which special armor will help?"

"How should I know? You're the one who's seen it."

"I can't tell you whether or not you should get the armor. We're doomed either way, although I must admit one damnation is better than the other."

"Well, which one?" snapped Teza.

Ijen pursed his lips as he usually did when making it clear that he wasn't going to talk.

"It doesn't matter," said Aaslo as he rolled the sphere around in his gloved hand. "We don't need to decide now. I just want to get somewhere warm."

"I wonder if we can make it out of this ravine before dark," said Teza. "Clearing these fallen boulders for the horses is tiring. It'd be nice if they had wings."

"The boulders or the horses?" said Ijen.

Teza tapped her lip. "We could try that."

"What?"

She tapped the scales on his left arm. "Giving them wings."

"No," Aaslo said flatly. "We are not messing with the horses."

"Says the man who regularly steals their souls."

"That's different. Come on. Let's get moving." Aaslo secured the glass sphere in his pack, which was strapped to Dolt's saddle, then began pick-ing his way around the boulders, trying to find a route the horses could follow. He sent his undead minions ahead to clear rubble where they could. They did so without complaint and never seemed to tire. The guilt he felt each time he caught himself considering the benefits of having an army of the dead sent him running back to his beloved forest; and each time he mentally visited that forest, Mathias was waiting there with laughter in his eyes. The painful loss elicited another round of guilt, and the process began anew.

The trek through the pass was made in silence as they reserved their energy for the effort. During one unfortunate fall, a member of Aaslo's undead unit broke a leg. The man tried to press forward in spite of the injury, and the break only worsened. Teza stepped up to heal the break without a hint of discomfort and reproached the man for his carelessness all the while. Oddly enough, the sightless man apologized.

"You're okay with this?" said Aaslo.

"Okay with what?"

"Treating the dead."

"Actually, I'm good with the dead. I think I may prefer them over the living." She must have seen the horror on Aaslo's face. She quickly said, "No, I don't mean that. I only meant that it's easier to treat them because they don't whine and fuss."

"In other words, you can treat them like dung."

"Is that what you think of me?"

"I'm only saying you occasionally come off too strong."

*"That's an understatement. Still, you'd best not piss off your only healer."*

"Why would she be angry? She's aware of her crusty temperament."

Teza crossed her arms. "Now I'm crusty?"

"Only when it comes to treating people."

"Like you're any better."

*"She's got you there."*

"You're right. We're a lot alike," said Aaslo, "but I think you knew that already."

Teza dropped her vexed façade and grinned at him. "Since the first time I met you—even if you did get me fired. I'm a good judge of character." She pointed ahead to where the sky had darkened with an early twilight thanks to the heavy cloud cover. "Look, there's a light. If it's the end of the pass, it could be another trading post."

They trudged another half hour and finally exited the pass. They didn't find another trading post, and the light didn't seem to be getting any closer. In fact, it appeared to be retreating.

"I think it's moving," said Ijen.

"People. We need to decide whether to intercept or avoid them," said Aaslo. "On the one hand, we need information. On the other, it might be the enemy, and I'd like to avoid stirring up trouble."

*"Wimp."*

"At least until we've had time to rest," Aaslo grumped.

"I think we should find out if they have any food."

"We brought our own food."

"I know," she said, "but theirs might be better."

Aaslo looked at her sideways. "You want to steal their food?"

"Did I say *steal?*"

He shook his head at her. "We'll hang back and follow them for a while. Once they stop, we'll move closer to see if they're friends or enemies."

*"You've become so sensible in your independence."*

"What are you talking about? I'm a grown man. I've been independent for a decade."

*"Not from me."*

"Huh. Still, *you're* haunting me."

*"Boo!"*

Aaslo found himself grinning at Mathias's laughter. He could almost feel his friend rolling around in his mind. He patted the sack at his waist and was briefly comforted by Mathias's presence. His stomach soured.

"I think I'm losing my mind," he muttered.

"I'm pretty sure you lost that a long time ago," said Teza.

Aaslo glanced at Ijen, who was nodding his agreement. "Yet you follow me anyway."

The prophet shrugged. "You don't need to be sane to be a hero."

"You think I'm a hero?"

Ijen tilted his head. His face had nearly disappeared in the darkness of the hood. "I think you try, and that has to be worth something—even if it is for naught."

Teza said, "The light went out. What do we do now?"

Aaslo looked toward where they had last seen the light. It had indeed been extinguished, which was particularly odd since it had only gotten darker. They continued following the deeply rutted dirt road that led from the pass, scanning the darkness as they traveled. Just as Aaslo began to think they had made a mistake in not stopping earlier, his concern was confirmed. His vision flashed from the black of night to red just in time to see a cluster of glowing figures hidden beyond the road.

An arrow struck one of the undead horses in the neck. The horse didn't react, and they might not even have noticed if not for Dolt, who yanked the arrow from the other horse's neck with his teeth and abruptly charged into the darkness from which the arrow came. Aaslo could hear many shouts and the nerve-racking wail of a horse in distress. By the time he realized they'd walked right into an ambush, the enemy was already upon them.

A thin stream of fire spewed across the road. In Aaslo's mind, it invoked a vision of a scorched hero toppling from his horse into a pack of white-blooded monsters. This wasn't the battle in which his brother had fallen, however, and present company was in trouble. An arrow glanced off the scales on Aaslo's neck. The lucky miss woke him from the nightmare of his memories. Another fire blast followed, but Aaslo raised his dragon arm to shield his face. He turned so the inferno struck the scales along his side and rushed into the bushes that had hidden their enemies.

Something didn't set right with him as he confronted the first attacker. In the midst of the battle, he couldn't form a coherent thought of what was bothering him, but it continued to tickle the back of his mind as he slew the archer. As the man fell dead at his feet, Aaslo's power reached out to him. Corporeal existence after death was offered—and rejected. Unlike the others, the archer did not rise to fight beside him. Aaslo didn't have time to think about it as his assailant was quickly replaced by another. Behind him, he could hear shouts and blasts as fireballs, wards, and magical javelins collided. The clash of Greylan's and Rostus's swords with those of the enemy reverberated through the night. Aaslo wished he had his axe, but it was still strapped to Dolt's back. Instead, he drew Mathias's sword—for all the good it had done him—and met the next attacker.

The feeling of unease, of something *not right*, squirmed in his mind again. Just as his sword impaled the man's chest, Aaslo realized what had been bothering him. It was in his vision—the glowing figures—they *glowed*.

"They're alive," he said aloud.

"You won't be for long," said another attacker. This one was a woman. She was petite, and although he couldn't see her features in the dark, her power was mesmerizing. In one hand, she held a rune-studded shield of golden light. In the other was a driftwood staff that blazed with an unnatural fire that licked the air like a snake.

"Wait!" Aaslo said as she released her first attack. A flaming serpent struck him on his scaly torso. Although he was relatively uninjured from the fire, his tunic was set alight. He quickly tore the ruined cloth from his body and raised his sword. "Stop!" he said to no avail.

*"Aaslo, didn't you pay attention to anything Cromley taught us? Never stop to talk during a battle."*

"Fiend!" the woman yelled. "I'll send you back through the demon gates from which you came. Your hideous monsters will no longer feast on my clansmen." She lashed at him with her staff, and he deflected the attack with his blade. On the second clash with her flaming weapon, she stepped into him. Her shield abruptly disappeared, and a fiery knife was thrust toward his side. Aaslo twisted to avoid the worst of it, but the heated blade scored his flesh, cauterizing the wound as quickly as it formed.

Aaslo pushed her away with a clawed hand and shouted again, "Stop it! I'm not your enemy!"

*"You look like enemies to me."*

The woman snarled at him. "He who walks with the dead is the enemy of the living."

"No! I'm not one of them. I'm not with the Berru. I'm from Uyan."

She lunged at him with her flaming knife and tried to knock his sword from his hands with her staff. Upon failing, she stepped back to ready another attack. "Then you are a traitor. Your monsters are evidence of your pact with death."

"No," said Aaslo, taking a step back to put more space between them. "Death is my enemy." He waved toward the mayhem and said, "These are my *undead* soldiers. I stole them from Death so that they may fight *against* him."

"You expect me to believe that? *You* are a monster. I don't know what kind of creature you are, but I'll make sure you don't live through the night."

*"You seem determined to find every bloodthirsty woman in Aldrea."*

The woman bounded toward him. Having realized they were truly on the same side, Aaslo had decided to save these people if he could. He blocked her attack, but as their weapons clashed, flames licked his scales. He looked into the woman's eyes. In them, he saw unfathomable anger—hatred.

"Listen to me," he said. "I don't want to hurt you, but you and your people will die if you persist. You cannot defeat me."

*"Arrogant much?"*

Her eyes flashed with a golden light. "I am the Paladin of Everon. With his grace, I will prevail."

Beyond the stories, Aaslo had never heard of a paladin. He didn't know who Everon was or what kind of power she wielded, but from what he had already seen, he was pretty sure he could best her.

"I can see that you have power, but you are up against *three* magi; and as you can see, I am changed. We're on the same side. Let us join forces against our common enemy."

"Aaslo!"

His heart leapt at the distress he heard in Teza's voice. Reining in his dragon strength so as not to seriously hurt her, he shoved the woman a good five yards. Then he turned to see that Teza was trapped against an outcrop with five attackers hammering at her wavering ward. Aaslo could tell that she was quickly losing energy. He looked back to see that the woman had already recovered and was closing on him.

It felt as though something inside him capsized. A thrill of potential sent shivers through his muscles, and it was as if time slowed. *"You want me,"* whispered a feminine voice.

"Ina?"

The voice turned dark. *"Beg."*

"We had a deal. You lent me your power, but you may not have my will."

*"One day . . ."* she sang. Then the power snapped, and Aaslo could tell it was once again at his call. He sheathed his sword and thrust his hand toward the woman who was nearly upon him. She squealed as she was abruptly snared by sharp brambles that wrapped her in a cocoon like an iron maiden. The brambles dragged her kicking and screaming into the thicket.

Aaslo turned back toward Teza, who looked ready to pass out. He snagged the brambles near the outcrop and sent them shooting toward Teza's attackers. Before he could complete the process, he was struck in the back by a blast of fire. The flesh along the right side of his body sizzled, and an inhuman growl escaped him as he turned to see the paladin readying another ball of flame. The beast inside him reared to release its wrath.

Through gritted teeth, Aaslo growled, "I had hoped to spare you."

"*I am not the threat. You are.*"

Aaslo slapped her fireball away and stepped toward her. He abruptly felt like he was shrinking, becoming overshadowed by something monstrous. "You want to play with fire, little paladin?" He felt a pleasurable purr as the deep, gravelly voice reverberated through his chest. "I will show you *fire.*"

HE BLINKED. IT FELT AS THOUGH HE WERE JUST AWAKENING FROM A LONG sleep, but he was already standing. The scent of scorched . . . *everything* reached his nose. He looked around the clearing lit with a number of small fires burning haphazardly and untamed. The brush and junipers that had dotted the roadside had been reduced to cinders, the rocks were ashen and scorched, and the people—they were scattered about like discarded lumps of fleshy coal. Some groaned and whimpered, while others remained silent. Teza and Ijen appeared unharmed, although shocked. They had been protected by their magical wards, as had the horses, save for Dolt, who was still missing. The undead were charred but moving. The only other person who seemed to have escaped relatively unblemished was the paladin. She lay unconscious within an outline of scorched earth. Although it seemed the flames that had consumed everything else had done little to harm her, the blast that must have accompanied them had apparently caused her to strike her head.

Aaslo hurried over to help Teza. Her hands were damp and clammy as she gripped his arms with shaking fingers. Her face was pasty and dotted with droplets of sweat. "Are you okay?" he said.

"I, um, I'll be okay. It was a long day, and I've overdone it."

He wasn't convinced but took her word for it anyway. "What happened here?"

"You don't remember?"

"You exploded," said Ijen. The prophet walked over to join them. He, too, appeared pallid but not as worn as Teza.

"I did what?"

"*You heard him, Aaslo.* You *happened.*"

"I've never seen anything like it," said Teza. "It was like the air around you suddenly heated. It wavered and distorted. Then *BAM!* Fire everywhere."

"The blast knocked me from my feet," said Ijen.

Aaslo glanced around at the other people who were beginning to stir. Their injuries didn't look quite so terrible once the ash had fallen from their tattered clothes and skin, although they all appeared dazed. When Aaslo turned around, he noticed the paladin had found her feet and was leaning heavily on her staff. She limped toward him but stopped a few yards away.

"What are you?" she said.

"I don't know," said Aaslo. "I used to be human."

"Don't be so dramatic," said Teza. "You're still human—just, with some minor improvements."

"Minor?" said the paladin. "He just incinerated everything for a good twenty yards."

"Not everything," said Ijen, pointing to the people who were beginning to recover their wits and their feet.

"I see," said the paladin.

One woman, who seemed to push past her discomfort more quickly, hurried over to the paladin. She placed a hand on the paladin's shoulder and said, "Cherrí, what did you do? You could have killed us all."

"It wasn't me," she said. "He did it."

The second woman turned to face Aaslo. She leaned into the paladin and said, "What is it?"

He could only imagine how he looked, his visage marred by inhuman features enhanced by shadows and flame. If he were in their shoes, he would have assumed the power-wielding dragon-man with monstrous arm and torso, an eerie reptilian eye, and an assemblage of undead men and horses was the enemy.

Teza stomped forward to stand between Aaslo and the women. She wavered a bit, but so did they. She held a finger in the air and said, "*He* is a human—a forester—and a magus. *He* is leading the fight against Death, and *he* chose to let you live."

The paladin said, "If you truly are not our enemy, then you'll let us go."

"We're not stopping you," said Aaslo.

Teza added, "Remember, *you* attacked *us*."

"*Don't let them go, Aaslo. It'll come back to bite you.*"

The two women backed toward their comrades, who had mostly recovered. Many were injured, and one lay dead. None looked to be able to carry the dead man, but a quick exchange between the paladin and an older man and woman had her setting the body alight. It continued to burn as the attackers retreated. The scent of burning hair and bone caused Aaslo's stomach to tighten.

"Come on," he said. "Let's get away from here. The fire and smells will surely attract any lyksvight in the area."

"You want to follow?" said Ijen as he moved to join them.

"No, we'll give them some space. Where's Dolt? I haven't seen him since we were attacked."

Teza and Ijen peered into the dark, but both seemed too tired to light the night.

Aaslo stood with his back to the blazing pockets of fire and focused his night vision. Few animals remained in the vicinity. A good fifty yards from the road, he spied a large, glowing red blob that was slightly horse-shaped.

He was glad to see that Dolt had survived the encounter, even if he was hiding out in the dark alone.

"I think Dolt went that way. We'll be safer away from the road."

Ijen said, "So we're following the lead of a horse now?"

Mathias's laughter bubbled over. *"Better than Aaslo's."*

Aaslo looked at him sideways. "If only there was a way we could know which choices were right."

"That is the problem with people who do not understand prophecy," said Ijen. "There are no right or wrong choices. There are only desirable or undesirable outcomes."

"Perhaps, but choices are required to achieve those outcomes."

"But *you* are not the only one making choices. For example, this little roadside skirmish we just endured that left only one dead could have gone very differently. In fact, it was a pivot point."

"A pivot point?"

"An event from which major branches of prophecy extend."

"Are you telling me that a major event just happened, and you didn't bother to warn us?"

"I'm telling you now."

"But it's already over!"

"Is it?"

"Do you think she's really a paladin?" said Teza.

"I don't know," said Aaslo. "Does it matter? She's either a paladin or a magus. Either way, she has power. We could use someone like her."

Teza turned to Ijen. "What do you have to say about this, Prophet?"

"I suppose it's a necessary evil," he said, although he looked wholly unhappy about it.

While the paladin's forces seemed fairly drained, he wasn't sure Ijen and Teza had the energy to fight them off should they choose to attack again. He glanced toward where Greylan and Rostus were gathering the group of undead he had acquired on the plateau. Although they were a bit scorched, none seemed much worse than they had been before the battle.

Aaslo glanced back to Dolt, then called to Greylan. "We're leaving the road for a bit. It'll be difficult in the dark, but I'd like to get at least a mile from the road. Get everyone moving."

*"Careful, Aaslo, you're starting to sound like a leader."*

"I just say what needs to be done. They don't have to follow my orders if they don't want to."

*"I kind of think that they do—the dead, at least."*

Without waiting for acknowledgment, Aaslo trotted off to collect Dolt. He found the horse grazing on the small tufts of long grass. Aaslo's saddle and pack were still secured to Dolt's back, and nothing seemed out of place. He moved to grab the reins, but Dolt shied away. Although the horse continued munching, he could see that Dolt was focused on him by the movement of his ears and tail.

"Dolt, hold still. Listen, you ugly beast. We have to get back to the others. They're worn out and need our protection."

Dolt lifted his head and looked at Aaslo. Then he turned back to the grass. The horse didn't move away when Aaslo reached for the reins, and Aaslo was finally able to retrieve him. Aaslo was patting the horse's neck when he noticed a subtle glow moving toward him.

"An odd-looking horse for an odd-looking man," said a deep voice.

A man unshuttered his lantern as he stepped from behind Dolt.

Aaslo's vision seemed to stutter, shifting back and forth between normal and night vision. It felt as though his brain unraveled; and suddenly, he was seeing both at the same time.

"Who are you?" he said as he pulled his axe from Dolt's saddle.

The man laughed. It was a boisterous, joyful laugh. "I'm just a lone traveler. I saw all the commotion over there and decided to sit it out. I found this horse and thought I'd keep him company until things settled."

A slight breeze blew across Aaslo's exposed torso, and he remembered his unconcealed state. "Are you not put off by my appearance?"

"I suppose it is a little odd, but many things are odd these days."

"I can't argue that. Are you not afraid out here alone?"

"Fear is a rich man's game. I, for one, have nothing to lose."

"Except, perhaps, your life."

"Are you threatening me?"

"Of course not. I have no reason to harm you."

"Ah, a traditionalist, I see. Many have given up on reason."

"What's your name, stranger?"

"Sorry about that. I seem to have forgotten my manners. My name is Ord."

"Ord? I've never heard such a name."

"It's an old name for an old man. And you are?"

"Aaslo, Forester of Goldenwood."

"A forester, eh? You're a long way from home, Uyanian."

"I'm surprised you know what a forester is."

"I get around. Would you mind terribly if I joined you? Even a loner like myself needs company every once in a while."

Aaslo considered the request carefully. He could understand where the man was coming from. It was dark, and the world had been inundated with man-eating monsters. What concerned him, though, was the man's utter *lack* of concern over joining a group like *his* after watching a power-injected battle.

*"He's definitely not trustworthy, but he seems so nice."*

Aaslo tested his grip on his axe and said, "How much of my party did you see?"

"Enough to know that not all of them are breathing."

"And you're okay with that?"

"Well, it's not ideal, but beggars can't be choosers."

"You could've asked the other group."

"Yes, but they lost. Yours seems the stronger bet."

*"Nope. There's something wrong with this guy."*

"I agree."

"Great! You won't regret it."

Aaslo groaned. He hadn't meant to agree to anything. Once again, his dead or imaginary friend had gotten in the way of real life.

Aaslo led Dolt and Ord in the direction his group had gone. After a while, they saw a light. The light grew to a glow, and Aaslo realized they were seeing the window of an old farmhouse. When they arrived, they found that the dead were standing sentry around the house and a lean-to that looked ready to collapse. The horses, alive and dead, had been secured in the pen around the lean-to, and one of the undead women was pumping water from the well into a rusted trough. Aaslo removed his pack and saddle from Dolt and handed him off to another of the undead for a brushing and feeding before turning toward the farmhouse. As he went about his duties, he surreptitiously watched Ord. The man seemed completely unfazed by the dead, which only served to raise Aaslo's suspicions. Was the man comfortable because he was used to the lyksvight?

"Come with me. I'll introduce you to the others," he said.

"Sounds great. I'm looking forward to having a roof over my head. I think it'll rain tonight."

Aaslo glanced at the clear night sky. The moon was nearly full, and the stars shone with their typical brilliance. "How can you tell?"

"The ring around the moon," said Ord. "You see? When that is present, it's going to rain within a day or two."

"I've never heard of that. Then again, I'm not used to seeing much of the sky."

"No, I should think not. Tell me. Why is a forester so far from his forest?"

"I'm sure you've noticed that we're under attack."

"Yes, I'm aware of that. Those people seem to want to kill *everything.*"

"They do, and my friends and I are trying to stop them."

"Sounds like a heavy burden."

"How so?"

"Well, they have magi and monsters."

"*We* have magi and monsters."

"True, but they have greater numbers."

"*We* have greater need."

"Need and desire. Both can be great if wielded by one of strength."

Aaslo paused to knock on the door. He looked at Ord and said, "You think I'm not strong enough to wield the power I have?"

Ord grinned. "You will be." He then raised a canteen to his mouth and took a long draw. He held the canteen out to Aaslo and said, "Cheers."

Aaslo's first instinct was to refuse the drink, but then he felt the sudden urge to take it. The liquid had the musky sweetness of mead, although quite strong.

Ord lifted the canteen again and said, "To strength." He handed it back to Aaslo, who, again, felt inclined to drink.

The door swung open, and Ijen was standing there with a protective ward wrapped tightly around him. "Ah, I'm glad you made it. I wasn't sure you would."

"What do you mean?" said Aaslo. "Was there a path in which I didn't?"

"Several, actually. In one, you were lost in a labyrinth, which I still don't understand."

"An actual labyrinth? Where?"

"I don't know," Ijen said absently as he retreated from the doorway.

"This is Ord," Aaslo said.

Teza looked at him quizzically. "Who's Ord?"

Aaslo turned to find that Ord was gone. "I—he was right here. I was just talking to him." He licked his lips and could still taste the faint sweetness of the liquid.

"That's it. To the bed with you," said Teza. "We're all exhausted, but you're the only one picking up new imaginary friends."

Aaslo looked around the small room. It held only one bed large enough for a single person. Ijen had set his pack and a bedroll on the floor near the fire, and Teza started positioning hers between them in the only space left. "I don't care about food right now. I just want sleep," she said.

Aaslo's stomach grumbled, but his head began to feel light. He stumbled toward the bed, then he was falling. He had strange dreams that night. He was walking along a cold, windy beach. Frigid water splashed over his boots. He looked down to find that the water was red. Turning his gaze to the horizon, he saw that *all* the water was red. The sky was red. The lifeless, rocky expanse behind him was red. Something moved in the distance. He squinted, and suddenly the figure was in front of him. The paladin approached. She was wearing a white tunic-style dress and no shoes or coat to protect her from the cold wind. She stopped about a pace away and said, "Here, you'll need this going forward." Then, she handed him a severed arm. He looked at it and knew it was his own.

The woman disappeared. In her place stood the man, Ord, grinning and looking entirely too pleased with himself. A loud crack sounded above them. Aaslo's gaze shot toward the sky, where far, far above soared six dragons. They swooped in lazy circles like raptors searching for their prey. He looked back to Ord with alarm.

"We have to get away. They'll kill us."

Ord said, "Yours is the strength to live, but you lack the strength to die."

"Aaslo? How did you get here?"

Aaslo looked over his shoulder, and suddenly the scene was different. He was standing by a pond surrounded by the most magnificent redwoods he had ever seen. Myra was staring at him with wide eyes, and she looked *solid*. The reaper's gaze shifted to Ord, and her expression of mild surprise turned to shock.

"You!" she said. "What's going on? How did he get here?"

Ord strode over to Myra, took her hand, and pressed his lips to her fingers. "Beautiful lady, I seek to do your bidding." Then he continued past her to enter a stone temple of sorts.

Aaslo looked at Myra. "Where am I?"

WHEN HE AWOKE, AASLO STRUGGLED TO OPEN HIS EYES. HIS HEAD FELT thick and his mind groggy. The sweet taste of the drink Ord had given him lingered on his tongue. He squinted, then raised a clawed hand to block the warm sunlight that was streaming through the window directly into his eyes.

"Finally," drawled Teza. "I thought you were going to sleep the whole day away."

"What time is it?" Aaslo said as he righted himself with a groan for his achy joints.

"It's past midday already. We tried to wake you, but you were *out*."

*"No one's so lazy as a forester with no forest."*

"I'm not being lazy," Aaslo snapped. "I think Ord drugged me."

"Who's Ord?" said Teza.

"He's the man I met last night. I told you about him."

"Right, your imaginary friend. I don't think anyone drugged you. I checked for things like that when you wouldn't wake."

"I had the strangest dreams."

"Was I in them?"

"No. It was the paladin and Ord and Myra—"

"I see."

Aaslo paused and looked up at her, half expecting to realize he was still dreaming. "Do you *want* me to dream about you?"

*"You might want to check her for a head injury."*

Her face flushed. "That's—that's not what I meant."

"Teza, do you—"

Teza abruptly grabbed the pack he had dropped when he fell into the bed the night before and thrust it into his hands. "It's super late. If we're going to get any traveling done today, we need to leave."

Aaslo's stomach protested another delay. "I need to eat first," he said. He glanced around the single room that held the bed, a small table, a couple of chairs, and the hearth. He spied a pot hanging beside the hearth. In a flash, he was spooning the warm sustenance into a bowl. He had consumed it all before he had even tasted it.

"Whoa, slow down," said Teza. "You'll make yourself sick."

"I feel like I haven't eaten in a year."

"I get it. We had a long, hard day yesterday, and the frozen food we brought from the citadel wasn't very appetizing."

"Where's Ijen?"

"He's out there with your corpse corps."

"Corpse corps?"

"Yeah, he said something about a major shift in the paths, then darted out the door."

Aaslo inhaled another bowl of whatever they had cooked (he hadn't slowed down to check), smothered the fire, grabbed his pack, made sure his weapons and sack were secure, and stomped out the door with Teza on his heels.

"What's he doing?" Aaslo said as they approached the gathering of undead.

Ijen was deep in his thoughts as he paced around the yard flipping through the pages of his book and making notes.

"What's happening?" said Aaslo.

Ijen muttered something to himself, scribbled in his book, then continued his pacing as if he hadn't heard Aaslo.

"Ijen!" Aaslo shouted. "Is there something we need to know?"

The prophet stopped and looked at them. "Ah, no, not really." Then he went back to his pacing.

"You seem a bit disturbed," said Aaslo.

*"You would know all about that."*

"Will you stop that?" Aaslo hissed.

Ijen paused. "Oh, sorry. I didn't realize I was bothering you. It's easier for me to think this way."

Teza said, "If you're going to suddenly lose it, you could at least tell us what the problem is."

"Lose what? Never mind. It's not a big deal. Well, it *is*, but not as far as you're concerned. We seem to have jumped to an entirely different line of the prophecy."

"Does this one have a better outcome?"

"No, death still prevails. It's just—I didn't expect to ever be on this line because I could never see what caused it. I still don't know. Nonetheless, here we are."

"How do you know?"

"You slept too long."

"So, I sleep late and suddenly we're on a completely different path? You make it sound like *I'm* in charge of this destiny."

Ijen looked at Aaslo as if he were daft. "You *are*. We all are. Each of us makes choices that change the course of our lives."

"But *your* choices can change *my* life."

"Yes and no. You live in *this* reality because it is the one *you* control. In another reality, we were on a different path because of a choice *I* made or one Teza made."

"But you live in this reality, too."

"Yes, but only by choice. I could choose to leave, to go off on my own. I could have joined the other magi. I would no longer be aware of *your* reality because I wouldn't be here. We are both aware of *this* reality because we are currently making choices that affect each other."

*"He's making less sense than you make when you're talking about soil composition."*

Aaslo sighed. "Okay, does any of this change what we need to do next?"

"What are we doing next?" said Ijen.

Aaslo threw up his hands. "I don't know! I was hoping you could provide some guidance."

"I chose to become a part of *your* reality, Aaslo. It's your decision to make."

"Fine. Then we'll go to Chelis and see if we can round up an army."

"How do you plan to do that?" said Teza.

"We'll go to the parliament and ask for one."

"You think we can get an audience with the Mouvilanian parliament?"

"We're probably the last magi on Aldrea that aren't trying to kill everyone. I think they'll see us."

# CHAPTER 19

Myropa extinguished the thread that connected her to the young man as his soul filled the small orb. She glanced back in the direction of Aaslo and his companions—they weren't far—then followed the paladin. The encounter between the two the previous night had been unexpected. She hadn't anticipated finding Aaslo in Mouvilan, and the fact that the two groups had been fighting seemed to be more than a coincidence. Even more concerning was seeing Aaslo in Celestria, albeit briefly, and in the company of Disevy. The God of Strength had agreed to help Aaslo for her—a mere reaper—but he was also the leader of the pantheon whose members had declared war on Aldrea. Myropa worried over what Disevy had been up to.

The paladin's group had hurried down the road as quickly as they dared in the dark. The lack of light hadn't bothered Myropa. She could see the bright threads of life that twisted through the living, plants and animals alike. After about an hour, they had stopped to rest. A couple of the clansmen threw together a pile of twigs and started a fire while the others refilled their waterskins in a small creek that ran beside the road. Once they were all gathered around the meager light source, Myropa had surveyed their faces and found only fatigue, sadness, and anger. They were the typical sentiments she observed around someone's deathbed. What concerned her was the target of those feelings.

"He can't get away with this," said the woman named Hennis. "He killed my boy."

An older man said, "What would you have us do? You want us to go up against three magi? We can't even kill their soldiers because they're already dead."

"Broden, you're a coward."

"Don't call me a coward. I'm being reasonable."

"That's enough," said Aria. "We cannot turn on each other."

"What does she plan to do about them?" said Hennis. "We can't just ignore what they did."

Aria said, "Pong died as a result of his wounds incurred during battle. It is an honorable death."

"It's wrong," said Hennis. "That monster and his walking dead need to be destroyed. What are you going to do, *Paladin*?"

Myropa wandered over to where the paladin sat on a boulder a few paces from the road. She looked into Cherrí's eyes, and, in them, she saw the pain of loss, anger, and resentment, and—worse yet—self-loathing. Cherrí blinked away her tears and stood. She walked back to the group slowly and looked down at the boy's empty shell.

"I'm sorry, Hennis. This is my fault. I allowed my hatred of death to cloud my judgment. We should have waited and attacked after we knew more about them."

Broden said, "If we had waited, they would have attacked *us*, and we'd all be dead."

Before Cherrí could respond, Aria snapped, "Horse dung. If they wanted us dead, they could have killed us. We were defeated, yet they let us go. How do you explain that? You all pressured Cherrí. You know how she feels about those monsters. *You* said we should attack them before they attacked us. *I* said we should find a more advantageous location and do some reconnaissance."

Hennis's fresh pain saturated her voice and would have brought tears to Myropa's eyes if she'd had any. "Are you saying it's *my* fault that my son is dead?"

"No, I'm saying people die in battle. You must recognize you could be making the ultimate sacrifice *every* time you choose to engage. We attacked them, and we lost."

"Of course, a Great Oryx would be so indifferent about death."

"I'm not without feeling," said Aria, seemingly surprised that Hennis would say such a thing. "As the greatest warrior clan, we learned to *never* overestimate our position in battle. And don't think that I'm indifferent about Pong's death."

"Maybe that dragon-man can steal Pong back from death," said Skinny.

Myropa saw the others all staring at him, horrified by the suggestion, and wondered if it would ever be possible for them to accept Aaslo as an ally.

"Don't you dare say that," growled Hennis. "I would never wish for my Pong to become one of those monstrous lyksvight."

"I don't think they were lyksvight," said Aria. "They didn't look or act like the others. For one, they weren't trying to eat us."

"I don't care what they are," said Hennis. "They're unnatural. My Pong will be waiting for me in the Afterlife. I expect it won't be a long wait."

"Let's hope it's long enough to punish that monster who's responsible," said Broden.

Hennis nodded vigorously, and Myropa was alarmed by the turn of events. Aaslo didn't need another enemy. Pithor, Sedi, the gods, and a damning prophecy were enough. Aaslo needed recruits. He needed friends. Myropa dearly wished she could communicate with the Cartisians, to let them know he wasn't the monster they thought he was; but she knew *wishing* never accomplished anything. She looked down at the newly inhabited sphere hanging from her belt. A terrible idea came to her—one that she could not possibly implement. It would be wrong, and she would surely fail. Axus would be angered when he discovered she had tried. In the off chance she succeeded, though, she'd very well be making enemies of the Fates themselves.

Although Cherrí agreed with Broden about exacting vengeance on Pong's killer, something about the circumstances didn't settle well with her. The dragon-man could have killed them all, yet he let them go without pursuit. He had insisted he wasn't the enemy. Her past experiences with the Berru had taught her that they *never* offered mercy and certainly not an alliance. Likewise, the dragon-man's accent was unlike that of the few Berru she had heard. Even if he was from Uyan, as he had said, that didn't mean he wasn't her enemy. The very fact that he was allied with the dead proved that.

"What do you want to do?" said Aria, breaking Cherrí out of her morbid thoughts.

"I don't think they'll attack us tonight. We'll set a watch, of course, but we'll rest and move quickly tomorrow. Skinny said the town of Foresight is less than a day from here."

"That's right," said Skinny. "It's the first large town in Mouvilan out of the Desding Pass. My clan of rearing used to travel there twice a year to trade. Sealskins go for nearly twice what they do in Jule, and grain and wool are cheap there."

"That's good," said Aria. "We need fresh supplies."

"Let's hope the Berru haven't made it there yet," said Cherrí. "I'm worried they may have already overrun it since they made it to the pass."

"They could have gotten to the pass through the evergate," said Skinny.

Cherrí's heart pounded hard in her chest. "There's an evergate near here?"

"Sure," said Skinny. "The nearest one is a few days to the southwest. At least, that's what I was told. I've never seen it myself. There used to be a lot of travelers between the evergate and Foresight." He rubbed the back of his neck and shifted uncomfortably. "It's actually been worrying me a little that we haven't seen more people."

"Why didn't you say anything?" said Broden.

"I was a kid. I thought maybe I remembered it wrong."

Cherrí gripped her staff, finding comfort in its silky smoothness and the power it channeled. She said, "There could be an entire Berruvian army approaching from the south. What if they've already taken the north, too? We could be trapped between them."

"Stop it," said Aria. "It does no good to panic. We plan for what we know and remain vigilant for what might be."

"You're right," said Cherrí, thinking about Pong's lifeless body. "I'm sorry. I don't know how to fight this enemy. They're all so strong. The Berru have magi and hordes of lyksvight, and the dragon-man seems invulnerable to fire."

"We need only fight one battle at a time," said Aria. "Once we get to Chelis, we'll have the Mouvilanian army beside us."

From just beyond the fire's reach, she heard the painful lament of a mother mourning her child. Cherrí's gaze fell onto the small fire as she remembered her own losses. The emptiness at her core was filled with the warmth of Everon and the ever-growing spark of something else—unadulterated rage. It was within that rage that she slept through the remaining night, and it had only grown when she awoke at dawn.

As Broden and Aria negotiated their entrance to the city, Cherrí's gaze caressed the walls made of wood, stone, and mortar. She surveyed the guard towers and noted the placement of buildings, stalls, stables, and guard posts.

"What do you think?" said Aria. "It's kind of exciting. I've never been to a city outside Cartis."

Although she had committed their passage through the city to memory, Cherrí realized she had seen nothing of the people and culture. She looked up at the sign that hung over the door on a copper hook. It had a picture of a fork beside a quarter moon, under which was an illegible script.

"What is this place?" she said.

"It's an inn. They only have room for half of us. The others are going to stay over there." Aria pointed to another establishment whose sign held the same images but different script.

"How do you know all that? We just got here," said Cherrí.

"Your mind has been completely absent all day. We've been standing here for over half an hour while they asked around."

"I—I don't remember that," said Cherrí. "I was thinking about the city's defenses. They seem to be on alert, but it doesn't look like they've been attacked."

"*Yet.* The innkeeper said they've heard reports of raids from the south. It's not clear how many. I'm hoping it was just the group we killed in the pass."

"Don't anticipate being so lucky. Nothing, these days, is easy."

"You're right. The world has gone mad."

"It's strange to see so many people in one place," said Cherrí as a girl ran past them carrying a basket laden with fresh linens. "It seems like it's been forever since every moment became about survival."

"These people haven't been touched by the loss we have. Hopefully, the Mouvilanian army will put a quick end to the monsters and their masters."

Skinny called to them, and Cherrí and Aria followed him into the inn. The interior had been painted white and the tables a sunny yellow. Each of them had a small vase containing a single daisy. Paintings of flowers decorated the walls, and soft rugs woven from thick braids of wool covered the floor.

"I've never seen such a place," said Cherrí.

Aria smiled. "It's so cheerful."

"More than it has a right to be," muttered Cherrí. The room was in direct conflict with her state of mind and completely incongruent with her state of life. She followed Aria to an open doorway on the back wall, through a short passage, then through another open door. The room was just as bright as the first except that everything was white and pink. Two narrow beds were pressed against the far wall, and a small table by the door held a large, hammered copper basin. Cherrí peered into the basin and then looked up at the woman who carried linens into the room.

"How does it hold water? It has holes in it."

The woman set the linens on one of the beds and looked at her. "What?" she said, blinking in confusion. A look of understanding came over her, and she smiled. "I'm sorry. My Aldrean is a bit rusty. I only recently moved here, and there are far more foreigners here than in my village. Here, let me show you." The woman tapped a rounded bump on the back of the basin, and water began pouring from the upper hole. "This allows the water to run into the basin. If you want it warmer, tap this side of the knob. The water runs into the drain unless you plug it with this." She handed Cherrí a cork plug, tapped her lip thoughtfully, and said, "I can't remember the name for that." Then, she went back to dressing the beds.

Cherrí watched the water run from one hole into the other. "How do you make it stop?"

"Just tap the knob on the other side," said the woman.

"That's amazing," said Aria. "I would love to have one of these in my tent."

"Oh, you couldn't have that in a tent," said the woman. "It requires, um, *plumbing*—that's the system of copper pipes that carry the water to and from the basin. They run all over the city in the tunnels beneath the streets. Some of them used to work without the plumbing, but most of those have stopped functioning since the magi left. There's been a mad rush to fix them all. It's a good business to be in right now. My son is a plumber's apprentice. I've barely seen him of late. Do you have children?"

The question struck Cherrí like an arrow to the chest. She swallowed hard and blinked away an errant tear but could not bring herself to answer the question. The woman didn't wait for an answer, though. She continued rattling on as if she needed to impart every bit of her knowledge on them before she left the room. Cherrí was no longer interested in listening. She set her pack down and began washing her face in the basin, scrubbing her skin with the hand towel hard enough to turn her flesh red. As soon as the woman left, she stripped to wash the rest of her.

"Are you okay?" said Aria.

"I'm fine," she snapped. She took a deep breath and corrected herself. "No, I'm not fine, but I'm as well as I can be right now. I'm glad to be clean. It's been a long time since I had the luxury."

"The innkeeper said there is a bathing room down the hall."

"Really? I've never seen so much copper."

"It's a mining town. It's mostly copper and tin, but Skinny said they occasionally strike a gold vein."

"I guess they can afford to waste it on this *plumbing*, then. Maybe I'll make use of that later. For now, I want to sleep."

Cherrí snuggled under the blankets of the nearest bed and was quickly enveloped in the deep embrace of a dreamless sleep. When she awoke, however, her first thought was that she was having a nightmare. It was dark, and firelight flickered through the window near her bed. She looked through the glass pane and saw men and women rushing through the street with torches and glowstones to light their frantic passage. A squad of patrolmen charged past the inn, and Cherrí's door burst open.

"Good, you're awake," said Aria. "We need to get to the nearest command post as quickly as possible."

"What's wrong? Is the city under attack? Is it the Berru?"

"I don't know. I heard someone shouting about a group of walking dead being spotted outside the city."

Cherrí fell back onto her pillow and pulled the blankets up to her chin. "Let the city guard deal with them. It's not our problem right now."

"What if it's the dragon-man?"

"So what if it is?"

"They need to know what they're up against. He could wreak havoc on the city. Remember what happened to Pong."

"I thought you said that was our fault."

"It was our fault for prematurely attacking, but that monster still killed him."

Cherrí cringed and drew her knees up to her chest. Pong's loss had been hard on them all. He had been a light in the encroaching darkness, but her desire to remain in the warm bed outweighed her obligation toward the Mouvilanians. "Go, then. Tell the city guard what you know. Then get some sleep."

"This is *your* responsibility, Cherrí. You must go."

"Why *me*?"

"*You* are the paladin. You were chosen by a great spirit to lead this fight."

A small flame ignited in Cherrí's chest, and the thread of sleep that had been tying her to the bed was incinerated. All the anger she had been feeling on their ride into town was fueled. She thew off the blankets, exposing her bare skin to the cool night air, but she wasn't cold.

"Here," said Aria, handing her a package wrapped in burlap. "Hennis brought this for you earlier while you slept."

Cherrí untied the twine that secured the package. Inside, she found a fresh wool tunic that would reach to her knees and a pair of heavy but loose pants that cinched at the ankles. "They're white," she said. She had never owned white clothing. It was impractical for the harsh environments endured by the migratory Fire Serpent Clan.

"Perfect," said Aria. "The paladins in the stories usually wear white."

"Why?"

Aria's brow scrunched. "I don't know. They just do."

Cherrí quickly dressed, donning her leather knife belt and sheepskin boots as well. She felt odd in the white clothes and quite uncomfortable with the prospect of standing out in a crowd.

"Don't forget your staff."

"Why would I need it? We're in the city."

Aria handed her the driftwood staff and said, "Because now you look the part."

"Why do I need to look the part? We're just telling them what we know."

"Do you think if *I* go down there and talk about an invading force from another continent or a half-dragon, half-man monster, they're going to listen to me? Do you think they'd listen to Hennis or Broden? No, we'd all sound crazy. *You* are a paladin. You wield the power of Everon. They'll listen to you."

"They won't even know who Everon is."

"Trust me. You start throwing fire around, and they'll listen to you."

Cherrí, Aria, Broden, and a young clanswoman named Mayla rushed through the throng of people between them and the command post near the front gate. Most of those people were hurrying in the other direction, dragging their sleepy children or small livestock with them. Aria grabbed the arm of a man pushing a cart stacked with crates of chickens and said, "What's going on? Where are you all going?"

"They're evacuating the southern district. We're told to go to the temples. They said not to bring your animals, but how could I leave them?" The man quickly turned away, and they pressed on to the command post.

When they arrived, they saw city guard units receiving orders and rushing about their business. One such unit surrounded them, preventing them from reaching the command post.

"What is this?" said Broden. "We need to see the commander immediately."

The unit commander said, "We don't have time to deal with you right now. You need to go back to where you came from."

"This is important," said Aria. "We have information that could be useful."

"Information about what?"

"We heard that walking dead have been spotted outside the gate. We've encountered them before."

"Very well, one of you may go. The rest need to stay here. It's a madhouse in there."

Aria tugged Cherrí forward and pushed her toward the man.

"I, uh, I'll go," said Cherrí.

The patrolman led Cherrí to a squat building that contained an armory, a jail, and a large room filled with people. In the center of the room was a long table with a scale model of the city complete with walls and stalls and little human figures to represent patrol positions.

A uniformed brunette woman with multiple medals dangling from her breast leaned over the table. Cherrí didn't know what she was saying since the woman was speaking the Mouvilanian tongue of Akyelek, but she was alarmed by the numbers and locations of enemy figures on the model.

The unit leader stopped beside the table and saluted the commander. He rattled something off in Akyelek, and all eyes turned toward Cherrí. The crowd parted to permit her, and the woman barked, "If you have information, give it over now. We don't have time to dither."

"I have much information," said Cherrí. "It will be faster if you tell me what's happening so I can give you that which is relevant."

The woman hissed. "We don't have time for this. Fine. The city appears to be under attack from two sides. On the east is a couple of dozen of what appear to be mostly dead people led by a monster that looks like a lizard-man. The larger force is to the southwest where there are possibly hundreds of grey, humanoid monsters and what appear to be about half a dozen magi."

The woman, along with everyone else in the room, looked expectantly at Cherrí. Cherrí said, "The grey monsters are called lyksvight. They are mindless creatures intent on killing everything. Sometimes, they eat the dead. Other times, the magi stop them so they can use the corpses to create new lyksvight. The magi are from a continent to the south called Berru. You cannot negotiate with them. They want nothing less than our deaths."

"And the lizard-man?"

"Leave him to me. He claims to be from Uyan, yet he walks with the dead. We encountered him and his people yesterday, during which one of ours was killed. He must answer for that death. I will face him."

"You? Alone?"

Cherrí raised her chin and spoke with a confidence she didn't feel but the importance of which Aria had impressed upon her. "I am Cherrí of the Fire Serpent Clan. I am the Paladin of Everon. My companions and I will face the dragon-man and his undead so that you may concentrate your forces against the Berru."

A bearded man, presumably the commander's second, said, "Paladins are myths from children's stories. You should arrest this foreigner. She seeks to divert our attention from the true threat and leave our flank open to attack. She is obviously working with the enemy."

Cherrí's blood rushed, and she suddenly felt as if the shackles were already on her. Her anger toward the enemy bubbled over at the thought of being accused of aiding them. "I am *not* with the Berru," she said. She slammed her staff into the ground, causing the pieces on the model to rattle. Flames ignited along the staff's length and traveled upward to create a small glowing sphere at the tip. The people nearest her shifted away, pressing the others against the walls. "I *am* the Paladin of Everon. We fight, not in the name of justice, but for vengeance against the Berru and all who aid them. He is powerful, but if this dragon-man is worthy of his wrath, Everon will incinerate him."

The commander looked to her second. "Report to the southern gate. You will lead the defense against these *Berru*. Markus will lead the fourth, eighth, and fifteenth units *with* the paladin at the eastern gate."

The unit leader who had led Cherrí to the command center saluted, then turned toward Cherrí. He looked apprehensively at the fiery staff. She extinguished the flames, and his anxiety seemed to ease.

Cherrí followed Markus back to her group and relayed the message while he rounded up the other units. She looked to Mayla and said, "Gather the others, and meet us back at the eastern gate."

"Yes, Paladin."

As Mayla ran away, Cherrí marveled at her newfound authority. Although her new companions had often deferred to her over the past two weeks, they had treated her more as a respected equal than a leader. It seemed that as people granted her power, the more others were willing to do so.

"What did you do?" said Aria.

Cherrí blinked at her. "What?"

"How did you get them to listen? That soldier looked scared. What did you do?"

"I didn't do anything, really. I just created a bit of fire, and they caved."

"They're desperate," said Broden. "I think they know more than it seems. Surely, they've had reports of attacks from other towns."

"Perhaps," said Aria, "or maybe the threat of a horde of undead monsters is enough to scare them into compliance."

"It doesn't matter," said Cherrí. "They're willing to listen, so now we must follow through. We are to defend the eastern gate against the dragon-man and his ilk."

"How do you expect us to do that? He nearly incinerated us the last time we encountered him, and don't forget the other magi with him."

"I have a plan," said Cherrí.

"I DON'T LIKE IT," SAID TEZA.

"They're willing to talk," said Aaslo. "We shouldn't spoil the opportunity for peace with suspicion."

*"I can't think of anything more suspicious than you."*

"Why do you say that?"

*"Look at yourself. Who wouldn't suspect you of . . . everything?"*

Teza raised a finger. "For one, she was trying to kill us just *yesterday.* Two, they've locked us out of the city, and there are guards on the walls with weapons pointed at *us.*"

"They're just being cautious," said Aaslo. "It's easier to prevent pests from infesting the forest than it is to rid the wood of pests already in residence."

"We are not pests!" said Teza.

*"Well . . ."*

"Stop it," said Aaslo. "Look, we'll parlay. We'll see if we can come to an agreement, and we'll help them defend the city against that lyksvight horde on the other side."

Teza crossed her arms. "And if they reject our help? Will we move on and leave them to their fates?"

Ijen said, "Technically, this is destiny, not fate."

"What do you mean?" said Teza.

Ijen crossed his arms over his chest and absentmindedly tapped the book tucked into his tunic. Finally, he said, "This event occurs in all of Aaslo's paths. It's what we call a point of convergence."

Aaslo said, "I thought you said what happened *yesterday* was the important event."

*"Why do you even listen to this guy?"*

"Wouldn't you?" said Aaslo.

*"I might, but I'm not you. Or am I?"*

"Wouldn't I what?" said Ijen. "Never mind that. Yesterday's event was a pivot point, but it is also what we call a *focus* point. It has a significant impact on what happens as a result of the convergence."

Aaslo pinched the bridge of his nose and sighed. "Please explain."

"Imagine the paths are light and the convergence is a lens. When the paths emerge, they will be refracted in different directions. The focus point determines the refraction index—ah, the degree and angle of refraction."

"Considering yesterday's outcome, do you know which way this is going?"

"Yes and no, but I can't say because it would change the outcome."

"Then I don't see how any of this makes a difference to us," said Aaslo.

"It doesn't, I suppose. Only to me."

"Does that mean you're satisfied with the current outcome?" said Teza. "You don't *want* to change it?"

Ijen appeared lost as he stared at Teza. It was as though he had never considered the option of *changing* the outcome. "It's not my place to change anything."

Teza tilted her head, and her curls brushed her shoulder. "You know what your problem is, Prophet? You just observe life. You don't actually *live*. What is the point in that?"

"Someone must bear witness."

"Why?"

"Because without a witness to our accomplishments and follies, what is the point in living?"

"I do things for my own sake." She nodded toward Aaslo. "He apparently does them for others'. Neither of us is doing them so you can watch."

"He comes," said Greylan's hollow voice.

The undead guard had walked up to stand beside Aaslo without him noticing, so it was a bit of a shock when he spoke. Aaslo looked over his shoulder to see the messenger approaching from the eastern gate.

"They'll want an answer," Aaslo said. "I'm going to accept."

Teza dropped her stubborn demeanor and took Aaslo's hand. "I know you want to help them, and you think doing this will earn their acceptance, but you are too trusting."

*"About as trusting as a pit viper and, apparently, as trustworthy. Honestly, I didn't know you had it in you, Aaslo."*

Aaslo wasn't sure how to tell Teza that *trust* wasn't the issue. In fact, the only thing he did trust about the paladin was that she would kill him the first chance she got. He wasn't meeting with her as a sign of trust. He was banking on an attack. If he told Teza he was intentionally walking alone into an ambush, she would insist on coming with him; but he couldn't do what was needed *and* protect her.

The messenger stopped a good fifteen paces short of their group. His hands shook as he stared at the undead. Mathias laughed. When the man turned his gaze to Aaslo and released a squeak, Aaslo internally cringed. Something inside him growled, and although he knew why the man was there, he felt the urge to make the man talk.

"What?" he snapped. Ijen and Teza both glanced at him, but he ignored their inquiring gazes.

"Th-the p p-paladin requestssss your a-answer, ah, sir, ah, m-magus?"

The beast inside him flapped its wings, and Aaslo could tell it was feeling feisty. He said, "What makes you think I'm a magus?"

"Ah, well, ah, y-you have *them*," the man said, eyeing the undead.

*"Give the guy a break. Just answer him."*

"Give him a break or break him?" Aaslo muttered, and the beast snorted. To his prey, he said, "Do magi typically travel with corpses?"

Sweat beaded on the man's brow as he stared wide-eyed at Aaslo. "I w-wouldn't know, sir."

The man hadn't yet turned tail and run, so the beast abruptly lost interest. Aaslo sighed as the cool shade of his own thoughts slid back over his mind. "Tell the paladin that I accept her invitation."

Although he tried to ease the man's fright, the gentle timbre of his voice only stirred the man's trepidation. The messenger squeaked again, turned and walked faster than would be considered proper. The beast inside Aaslo reared at the man's rapid retreat and chomped its jaws with a bark. The messenger, nearly thirty paces away, cried out, and broke into a sprint. The dragon flapped its wings and lashed its tail against the ground as it took flight.

"No!" Aaslo growled.

The beast turned and snapped at him, but Aaslo didn't back down. In his mind, a forest grew, and Aaslo snagged the creature in the viny tendrils of a massive wisteria. The limbs wrapped around the beast, arresting his flight and forcing it toward the ground. Aaslo pulled himself from his internal struggle to find Ijen and Teza staring at him.

"What was that?" said Teza. "Why were you so mean to him? I thought we were trying to convince them we're allies."

"I didn't mean to."

"When did it start?" said Ijen with a knowing look.

"When did *what* start?"

"The battle between you and your powers?"

Aaslo ran clawed fingers through his hair, a move so natural now that he didn't have to remind himself to be careful of his claws. "I don't know. I guess ever since I got them. The others have been growing stronger."

*"It's getting crowded in here."*

"Others?" said Teza.

"Can we talk about this later? Right now, I need to meet with the paladin."

Teza placed a hand on his shoulder. "Aaslo, this is important. We need to know what's going on with you *before* something else happens." Her rich brown eyes, filled with concern, made him think of the oak he had planted for Reyla. In that moment, he realized that Reyla had been far from his thoughts since he met Teza; and he wondered if, perhaps, Reyla had not truly been the woman for whom he had planted the tree. A seed of the ash tree under which they stood was caught in one of Teza's curls. He pulled it from her hair and gently placed it in his pocket before answering.

"There are warring powers inside me. Each seems to have a personality, wants, and desires of its own. Sometimes *I* am not in control, but I'm trying."

"This is my fault," said Teza.

*"She's right."*

"I gave you the dragon arm. I knew it was wrong. We were warned to never, *ever*, cross species—no, *forbidden*! I'm so sorry, Aaslo."

Aaslo took her hand from his shoulder with his human one and held it. "No, you did what you thought was best at the time." He looked down at his claws and clenched his scaly fist. "Although I'm loath to admit it, I'm glad you did. To live without an arm would have been far worse. My tasks would have been immeasurably more difficult."

"But you would have done them," she said as she wiped moisture from her eyes.

"Of course, but trust me when I say this is better. I only require more time to adjust. I'm sure I'll be fine."

Ijen took a step toward them. "Although I applaud your attempt to assuage Teza's fears, you are most certainly *not* fine. Most magi struggle to overcome *one* power. *You* seem to have several, and they are particularly strong. I will tell you now that there are many, many lines of the prophecy in which you do not overcome these powers. If this happens, you will lose your humanity. Now, if you are going to meet with the paladin, you'd best be going. The Berru will be attacking soon."

Teza dropped Aaslo's hand and turned on Ijen. "What makes you a sudden font of information?"

Ijen merely looked at her, then raised an eyebrow at Aaslo. "Now?"

*"Listen to the prophet. If he's suddenly willing to talk, it must be important."*

As Aaslo mounted Dolt and turned him toward the eastern gate, he muttered, "Or he's just bored."

*"There's nothing more dangerous than a bored prophet."*

"How so?"

*"Think of the havoc they could wreak. It wouldn't even matter if what they're saying is the truth."*

"Use their fears against them."

*"Now you're thinking like a dragon."*

"I don't want to be a dragon," he said as he pulled his hood over his head.

*"It's better than being dead."*

"You seem to be doing just fine."

Aaslo pulled Dolt to a stop just before the drawbridge that led to the open gate on the eastern side of the city. The moat was an empty pit of dirt and rocks mixed with an overgrowth of bushes and brambles. It might not drown an enemy, but it would at least slow one down. Dolt lurched as he made to cross the bridge, and Aaslo pulled back on the reins again. The horse stomped his foot and bobbed his head, then stepped forward anyway. Aaslo decided it would put him in an embarrassing light if the guardsmen and paladin saw him struggling with his own horse, so he gave up on fighting the stubborn beast. Dolt's hooves clattered as they crossed the thick planks, then settled again in the dirt of the road on the other side. Aaslo had to duck to pass through the gate while mounted. Once on the other side, he found himself on an empty road with shuttered shops and homes on either side. Most of the buildings were constructed of clay bricks and wooden beams, but a few had stone façades. If the windows held glass, he could not see it, and everything was natural and devoid of paint or embellishment. Aaslo felt the hairs on the back of his neck stand on end, and suddenly the gate behind him slammed shut. Although Aaslo felt a sense of entrapment, Dolt continued walking without concern.

Aaslo leaned forward and whispered into Dolt's ear, "Listen, you stubborn, ugly mule. When I die, you'll be lucky if they don't turn you into hog slop."

Dolt abruptly stopped, and Aaslo nearly tumbled from his back as the horse sat back on his haunches like a dog. Luckily, Aaslo was able to free his feet from the stirrups in time to dismount, albeit awkwardly, with a few choice words. He pulled his axe free from where it was secured to the saddle and rested it on his shoulder as he lifted his gaze to survey the street.

The paladin stepped from the dark chasm of an open doorway. "Well, that's different," she said. Guards and clansmen appeared in doorways and alleys and on balconies, and Aaslo was suddenly surrounded. The paladin perused his hooded form and said, "Why do you bother to hide yourself? I have already seen you. What manner of monstrous creature are you, anyway?"

"I'm not a monster. I'm a man—only a man."

*"Liar."*

Aaslo looked at those besieging him and saw in their expressions only hatred, anger, and disgust. He said, "I am Aaslo, Forester of Goldenwood, and I am the leader of the Uyanian resistance. Not long ago, I was mortally injured. A desperate healer cut the arm from a dragon and attached it to me. I'm no more a monster than any of you."

*"Again with the lies."*

"That's a sad story," said the paladin, "but hardly the all of it. Dragons are not real; and although you may have been a man once, you are surely a beast now."

*"She knows you better than you thought."*

Aaslo didn't feel the snarl of the beast but rather heard the tinkling bells in Ina's giggle. Dolt abruptly stood. "Dolt, come back here!" Aaslo shouted as the horse strolled over to the paladin.

She watched the horse warily as he made to nuzzle her hair. "Control this ugly creature!" she said. Dolt then continued down the road into the city. A few guards looked like they might try to stop the horse, but ultimately chose to keep their weapons trained on Aaslo.

"He has a mind of his own," said Aaslo. He dismissed the wayward horse and turned to the subject at hand. "I am here, alone, surrounded by your clansmen and the city guard. I place myself at your mercy, Paladin. What say you? Can we be friends?" As he posed the question, Aaslo couldn't help the beastly grin that turned up his lips, and he knew that even he wouldn't trust him.

"I do not believe you to be so helpless," said the paladin, seemingly echoing his thoughts. "We are not helpless either."

The people who had surrounded him abruptly withdrew, and Aaslo knew something was about to happen. The paladin lifted her staff and slammed the butt into the ground. He heard several blasts, and the ground shook harder with each one. For a split second, he felt weightless; then he was falling. He collided with hard stone just as another blast rocked the world around him. In the dark, his vision flashed red just in time for him to see a mountain of debris crashing down on him.

Aaslo's eyelids fluttered as he tried to clear the grit from his eyes. They were too dry to produce tears, though. A moment later, the pain struck him. It was beyond excruciating and encapsulated his entire body. He couldn't move his head. Something heavy was atop him, pressing his face into the stone. In fact, he couldn't move even a finger. Every piece of him was being crushed under the weight of an entire building. A building. The paladin had dropped a building on him.

He now understood the source of the blasts. Foresight was first and foremost, a mining town, and where there was mining, there were blast tubes. At least, there were until the stocks ran out on account of the magi leaving. They must have been desperate to waste any on trying to kill *him*. He had hoped that allowing the Cartisians to leave the previous night without further incident would have convinced them that he wasn't their enemy.

*"Now I know you've gone mad. You always told me that hope was for*

*those who were too incapable or unwilling to make things happen on their own."*

Aaslo licked his dry lips and worked his jaw. He took as much air into his lungs as he could with the weight of a two-story building atop him, then pushed with all his muscles against that weight. There was not even the slightest movement. He was good and truly buried alive—again.

*"At least this building isn't on fire."*

Mathias was right in that, he supposed, but when he had been buried under the marquess's estate, he had been able to move.

*"You're focusing on the problems, not the solutions. Sometimes I think you're denser than this building you're under."*

"I must be since it hasn't crushed me yet," Aaslo muttered. His voice was stifled in the confined space and muffled from the rock that pressed against each side of his head. Still, the sound of his own voice gave him comfort that he was still alive. "Okay, solutions, not problems, then. What resources do I have? My body is completely immobilized, but my mind is relatively clear. I also have power, but for the life of me, I don't know how to use it to get out of this mess."

*"It* is *for the life of you. Tap, tap, Aaslo. The time crystal is turning. You're going to run out of air."*

Aaslo's heart leapt. He hadn't thought about running out of air. After surviving the fall *and* being crushed by a building, he might suffocate alone in the dark.

*"You're not alone. We're here."*

The maniacal laughter that followed was unlike Mathias. He might have hazed Aaslo a bit in fun, but he was never cruel. Aaslo searched inside himself for the source of the voice. It wasn't Ina's taunting snicker or the dragon's beastly snarl. This was different. It was dark and insidious. It was pleasure and peace and promise and eminently enticing. He couldn't resist its call. As he reached for it, he began to feel sluggish, like he was swimming through mud, and it was getting thicker. Eventually, the mud became too thick for his mind to move. His body was trapped. His mind was trapped. He simply existed in stasis for minutes. Years? He didn't know. Nothing moved, not even time.

The first movement across his mind was a whisper.

*"Not alone."*

He tried to capture the words, but they slipped away too quickly, and he couldn't follow them.

*"You're not alone."*

It was stronger that time, and he knew the words. Were they his, or did they belong to someone else? Then there was the tiniest scratching, and he wasn't sure if it was coming from within his mind or without. The scratching began to grow in strength. It became clawing, then gouging. He screamed, and this time he knew he had made the sound aloud, but there was no more air to inhale. His next scream was empty. His abdomen and chest were imploding. Dark power lashed out of him in every direction, seeking the dead as another of his internal powers called to the living. There were hundreds, possibly thousands, of answers. Aaslo could feel the earth deep within the rocks and soil all the way to the surface, and things were moving. The load above him began to shift; but, still, he couldn't take a breath. Every beat of his heart was agonizing as the time crystal in his mind began to turn again.

"I'm here, Aaslo." Myra's voice sounded far, far away. "I can't get you. You're stuck. It won't budge."

He wanted to respond, to tell her . . . something, anything.

"Aaslo, just let go. It's okay. You don't have to keep fighting."

But he wasn't fighting her. He was trying to break free with all that he had, and it didn't matter if he escaped his imprisonment or went with her so long as he got *out*.

"Aaslo, please, just let me take you. You don't have to suffer."

He felt something slither over his skin. Something else tickled his neck. Tiny, sharp claws dug into his pant leg. Then *things* were all over him. They were moving everywhere, and the rocks and soil were moving. The noise became deafening, and he could no longer hear Myra's voice. His body was moving—at first, slowly, then more quickly, upward. The beast inside him roared and pushed with all its might against its confines. He wasn't sure if it was trying to break him out of the ground or if it was breaking out of *him*. He pushed with the strength of a thousand unclaimed breaths, and the debris above him erupted in a fountain of deadly meteors.

Aaslo's clawed hand breached the surface first, and he pulled himself from the liquified building wreckage with desperation. Searing pain shot through him as his lungs expanded for the first time in what felt like an eternity. Then he was struck in the head.

A terrified man fell in front of him, having tripped over Aaslo during his escape. Two lyksvight jumped on top of the man and began tearing him apart in a flurry of growls and screams. As Aaslo wrenched the rest of his body from the rubble, he realized the city had fallen into chaos. Panicked people who climbed the debris pile in their rush toward the collapsed city gate were easily overtaken by the grey-skinned monsters. The clash of weapons and *slurch* of impacted bodies was punctuated by the wail of horses and crash of buildings and stalls. The air was filled with pungent smoke, and something *else* moved among the rubble. Aaslo looked around him to find hundreds of small creatures. Rats, mice, voles, beetles, snakes, dogs, cats, and all manner of city dwellers—alive and dead—clawed, slithered, and squirmed through the ground as they worked to clear the rubble of Aaslo's impromptu mausoleum.

An emaciated dog—Aaslo wasn't sure if he was alive or dead—barked and growled as he yanked something from the ground. Aaslo shifted his weight as he awkwardly reached for the sack. His fingers felt numb as he fumbled with tying it to his belt. Then he achingly bent to retrieve the axe that had been laid at his feet. Satisfied that he was put together again, he thought to get the creatures' attention, and they all looked at him as one. He set them to another task—destroy the lyksvight.

Aaslo took his first step and nearly collapsed. He looked down to find that his right knee was dislocated. The pain of it was nothing when compared with the agony of his recent burial. He chuckled, then laughed outright.

"Aaslo!" said Myra, who was suddenly standing beside him. "Why are you laughing? Are you okay?"

He smirked. "I was just thinking of the irony. I expend my power raising the dead from their graves while I am buried alive."

"You struck your head and were deprived of air. This isn't the time to laugh."

"Of course I struck my head. I struck my *everything.* And I'm alive. It seems a laugh-worthy moment."

*"It isn't fair. I get knocked off a horse, burned, shot, and stabbed, and I die. Meanwhile, you have an entire building dropped on you—twice—and live to tell of it."*

"Yeah, well, life isn't fair. And, trust me, a few minutes ago, I would have gladly thanked the gods for my death."

Myra said, "About that—"

"I'm sorry, Myra, but I don't have time to chat. I have no idea how long I was down there, but it's apparent the city has been overrun." He bent over and grasped his knee with both hands. Using his dragon strength, he wrenched his knee back into place. He shook his leg, then stumbled down the debris pile toward the gate. He needed to find Teza and Ijen.

"Wait, Aaslo!" Myra said as she began drifting beside him. "This is important."

"Where's that blasted horse?" Aaslo muttered. He slid down a partially preserved wall that was somehow leaning against a portion of the building's roof and buried his axe in the back of a lyksvight that was trying to claw the face off a city guard. When the guardsman saw Aaslo, he screamed, shoved the dead monster off of him, and scrambled over the remainder of the debris toward the gate. Unfortunately, he didn't get much farther before another lyksvight jumped on him. The man was dead before Aaslo could reach him, but his axe splattered the assailing creature's brains over the rubble anyway.

Aaslo was about to turn away when a tether of bright light shot from the man into a well-kempt elderly woman—no, a reaper—who suddenly appeared over him. An idea struck him. Aaslo grabbed the tether, and the end that had previously connected the reaper to the dead man snapped toward Aaslo like lightning bending to strike a tree.

"He's mine," Aaslo growled.

"What? What are you doing?" said the elderly reaper. "How did you do that?"

The dark power that had teased Aaslo mercilessly under the earth heeded his call. It snaked down the tether and into the dead guard. Deep inside him, Aaslo heard the whisper of promises and a question asked. The man replied.

The dead guard, whose throat had been ripped open, began to move, awkwardly at first. Once he was on his feet, he stared at Aaslo with a hazy white gaze.

"Stop!" said the elderly woman. "Give him back. I need to take him to the Sea."

"He may go when I let him," said Aaslo. "Until then, he has agreed to serve me."

Myra moved in front of Aaslo. "Are you talking to another reaper? Can they see me?"

Aaslo glanced between the two but found no recognition in the elderly reaper's gaze. "I don't think so," he said.

"You don't think what?" said the elderly reaper.

"You can't see the other reaper, can you?"

The old woman crossed her arms and lifted her chin. "I'm the only one. Never seen another."

"You honestly think you're the only reaper in the world?" said Aaslo. He waved a hand at the carnage around them. "How many of these have you taken? What about the rest?"

The woman looked uncertain, then her jaw firmed. "I suppose they just don't go to the Sea. Not my problem."

"You're right," said Aaslo. "These are coming with me."

Aaslo released the stranglehold that had been keeping the dark power at bay. Black tendrils snaked from him in all directions, each finding a mark, each whispering, beckoning. The souls of those who answered streamed into Aaslo, and he felt stronger. Some of the bodies were already devoid of their souls. Those that still had limbs rose as well, but they did not whisper back. He knew that these would not stay active for long, for they were using *his* power to animate.

Turning from the gate, Aaslo walked deeper into the city. As he neared the southern gate from which the lyksvight had invaded, the number of dead rose quickly, but those whose souls remained dwindled in number. He realized the lyksvight must have been attacking for hours to have already toppled the gate and decimated so much of the city. Ahead of him, a ball of light streaked into the sky and burst in a shower of smaller lights that fell back to the ground and exploded.

Aaslo picked up his pace, running toward the source of the spell, expecting that he would find either his companions or the enemy magi. He came upon a market, in the center of which was an auction block. On one side of the block were five Berruvian magi. They were lobbing wicked spells toward the other side of the auction block, where someone was taking cover behind a pile of collapsed columns that had likely surrounded a grand public fountain.

The second party sent a spell that seemed unusual to the relatively inexperienced forester. It looked like two spells wrapped around each other. A ball of purple energy encapsulated five sizzling arrows. The ball neared the enemy magi and evaporated with a bang. The arrows were propelled with lightning speed toward the enemy magi. Two of the magi dodged or blocked the shots, but three were struck—one in the thigh, one in the shoulder, and one straight through the eye. The latter magus fell over dead while the two injured ducked behind the auction block. Meanwhile, the unscathed magi continued their magical onslaught of the city's defenders.

A third of Aaslo's collected undead army broke away to guard the defenders' flanks, and he threw the rest at the offending magi. Dozens of lyksvight refocused their attentions on Aaslo's undead soldiers to protect their magi. Aaslo pulled his hood over his head and ducked behind his soldiers, hoping to close the distance to the magi before he was detected. He had only cleared half the distance when one began targeting him. A ball of flame caught his coat alight, and he was forced to abandon it. Now exposed, his presence caught the attention of the others. They turned so that they were able to cast their spells in both directions.

Aaslo closed his clawed fingers around the neck of a rotund lyksvight female, holding it before him as a shield while he continued his advance. A sizzling whip of green flame separated the lower half of her body from the top, and Aaslo was forced to toss the remainder aside. Mathias's maniacal cackle stole his attention with its uncharacteristic destruction-fueled joy. Then he realized it wasn't Mathias that was laughing but *he*.

"*Don't blame me for* your *madness.*"

He didn't have time for the alarm the realization caused, because he was within six paces of the magi, and it finally struck him that he hadn't made a plan. Something beastly had set him on a warpath, and he had only been along for the ride.

An explosion rocked the city, followed by several smaller blasts. Somewhere not far away, on the other side of the Berruvian magi, someone was setting off blast tubes, and the bursts were getting closer. Mathias began chanting one of the poems Magdelay had taught them. Aaslo didn't know what the spell would do; but since it was at the forefront of his mind, he joined his fallen brother in the song. He dropped to avoid a spray of hurtled debris, regained his feet, and smacked a lyksvight in the face with the butt of his axe. He chopped through the shoulder of a second before taking the head off the first. Then he was on fire again. He tore the tattered, burning remnants of his shirt from his torso and lobbed it into the face of the nearest magus. The young man screamed as he scrambled to remove the small inferno, but he never got the chance to retaliate. Aaslo's axe was buried so deeply in the man's chest, he had to abandon it to avoid the next magus's attack.

He still had seen no effect from the spell, and he had just decided he had failed in casting it when the ground shook with the detonation of another blast tube. Only, the ground didn't stop shaking. In a good two-thirds of the square, the earth began to slosh and flow like liquid, including the area beneath his own feet and those of the enemy magi.

"*Time to leave!*" sang Mathias.

"I just got here," Aaslo growled.

A massive crack punctuated the uproar, and Aaslo looked up to see the bell fall from the bell tower. In fact, the entire spire was leaning precariously over the square. The bell slammed into the ground, crushing two of the Berruvian magi as it sank into the liquified earth.

*"Looks like you'll be buried again."*

Mathias was right. The tower was going to fall, and he was directly in its path. Aaslo didn't think his mind would survive another burial, even if his body did. He ran toward one side of the base of the bell tower, hoping to make it to the other side before it crushed him. He passed a third magus who had already begun to sink into the softened ground. The woman, buried up to her thighs, reached out to him for help, but he had no time to put her out of her misery. Aaslo dove the last few feet and just managed to avoid another crushing experience.

He lay still, curled into a ball and covering his head, as the dust and debris settled over the square. The ground slowly stilled and became solid again, and Aaslo dug himself out of the shallow mound of rubble that covered him. His skin was wet with sweat and blood, both red and white, and the wounds that afflicted his exposed flesh stung; but he thought himself to be otherwise unharmed.

All was still in the heart of the square that was now buried under the remains of the bell tower. He could see movement down some of the side streets—likely lyksvight looking for another meal; but there were no signs of the Berruvian magi.

Aaslo clambered across the debris to the location of his greatest priority in that moment. He heaved chunks of stone and wood aside with the might of a dragon—

*"Ha ha! You—a dragon? A lizard, maybe, or a gecko."*

—Or, at least, the *arm* of a dragon. His fingers closed around his query, and Aaslo pulled his axe from the wreckage of the bell tower. Then he stumbled down the slope toward the makeshift barricade, behind which, he hoped, his companions were hidden.

He stopped, weary and haggard, a few feet from the barricade. With naught but his axe resting on his shoulder, an unused sword at his hip, and a head in a bag, he said, "Who goes there?"

Ijen stepped from his hiding place. "Good of you to finally join us again."

A few city guardsmen peered over the barricade, but it appeared they hadn't yet worked up the courage to face him.

*"Stop looking so scary, Aaslo. You'll never make friends that way."*

Aaslo couldn't imagine how he must have looked to the frightened men. What truly disturbed him, though, was the typical unruffled appearance of Ijen and his nonchalance toward the battle they had all just endured.

"What's going on?" said Aaslo. "Where's Teza?"

Ijen shrugged. "I don't know. We came into the city after the first explosion to find that the paladin had dropped a building on you. Then, the Berru attacked, and chaos ensued. We were separated."

Aaslo couldn't help the growl that escaped as he said, "Did you know I was going to be buried alive?"

Ijen shifted the book in his tunic and lifted his chin as though to say he didn't care for Aaslo's attitude. "I knew you would be buried, and I knew you would survive. Whether or not you were alive remains to be seen."

"What is that supposed to mean? I *am* alive."

"Of course."

Aaslo tapped his own chest. "And I'm *human*."

Ijen tipped his head. "More or less."

"Well, I'm not a lyksvight, and I'm not one of these wandering dead."

"This is true."

Aaslo kicked a stone with frustration, and it struck the barricade, causing the men behind it to yell in fright. "Let's just get on with this. The city is still overrun. Where was the last place you saw Teza?"

"At the sight of your burial."

"Okay. Have you seen Dolt?"

Ijen pulled his book from his tunic and stood poised with his pen ready to write. "No. Was he buried, too?"

"He ran away before the paladin set off those damned blast tubes."

Ijen tapped his lips with his pen. "Hmm, he ran *before* the blast. Interesting. I wonder if he knew it was coming."

"Now you think my *horse* is a prophet?"

"Of course not, but you have to admit he is a bit odd."

Another blast shook the ground, and Ijen tucked his book away. Aaslo said, "It sounded like that one was only a few streets away. Let's go find out who's setting them off."

"My money's on the paladin."

"I'd never bet against a prophet."

"Oh? It seems you've been betting against us since the start of this endeavor."

Aaslo didn't reply. Ijen was right. He *was* betting against the prophets—and the gods. As they trod through the remnants of the city, he felt more and more that his fight was in vain. He longed for the peace and bliss he found within the fresh air of the forest and wondered if his time wouldn't be better spent enjoying what life he had left.

He paused, and Ijen stopped beside him. Aaslo inhaled deeply, bringing the dust and scents of blasting powder, fire, and blood into his lungs. The acrid air caused his stomach to burn, the intensity of which spread to his limbs. Before he knew it, he was reaching out, calling to the victims of Axus's assault. The Berru may have been the attackers, but they rested in the palm of the God of Death. Aaslo intended to steal back from them what he could.

Waves of dark power, fanned by the wings of the dragon, rolled out of him into the surrounding buildings and alleys as he walked toward the source of the explosions. Few were able to answer, but those who did crawled from their death sites to amble in his wake. He had collected nearly two dozen undead by the time he found what remained of the resistance. He stopped before a hastily built barricade of broken carts, barrels, stands, and stone and allowed his power to snake down alleys and through windows and doors. "Paladin, is that you?"

Teza's head popped up over the barricade. "Aaslo?"

Her eyes widened, and she clawed her way over the barricade before hurrying over to embrace him. He hissed through the stinging of his wounds and held her with little of the mental effort it usually took from him.

"I can't believe you're alive." Tears traced rivulets through the dirt on her face. "The paladin said she buried you under a building."

"I did," said the paladin as she, too, scrambled over the barricade.

Anger burned in his chest hotter than the fires that had scorched him, but he didn't have the energy or desire to fight her if it wasn't required. "It wasn't the first building that's been dropped on me," he grumbled. Then he turned to Teza. "What's going on here? If you thought she had killed me, why are you with her?"

Teza blinked away tears and said, "The enemy of my enemy . . ."

"I see," he said, pulling her arms from around him.

"Aaslo, it all happened so fast. I didn't even have time to think about what had happened to you before we were fighting for our lives. I wanted to kill her—I did—but I also needed her to stay alive."

"I understand," he said coldly, and he did; but something inside him was incensed over finding the two women together. It was as though his life and his death were conspiring against him.

Aaslo didn't need to look toward the figures that were closing in on them to know that they were his undead subjects come to serve his cause. The paladin anxiously backed toward her barricade but found the effort futile as her people, having been approached from behind, came clambering over it to join her.

"What's this?" she said with alarm.

"These are my soldiers come to fight in this war against death."

Greylan approached with a bedraggled, ugly horse in tow. Aaslo looked at his menacing horse and said, "You and I need to have a talk later."

*"Disembodied voices of the dead, dragons, and fae aren't enough? Now you must start talking to horses, too?"*

"Dolt's *special*," said Aaslo.

"That's for sure," said Teza, crossing her arms and looking at the horse with disapproval. "Where's he been all this time? I thought he was buried with you."

"He has a knack for survival."

"Much like his owner," said the paladin. "Tell me, dragon-man, are you dead or alive?"

"I'm alive, obviously. Why does everyone keep questioning that?"

"*You never know these days.*"

"*I* know," Aaslo snapped. "I'm *not* a monster. I'm just a man, a simple forester."

"Far from it," said Ijen. "Perhaps the paladin would like to try to kill you again to test it."

Aaslo scowled at him. "Whose side are you on?" Ijen shrugged, and Aaslo turned to the paladin. "Shall we call a truce—at least until we get this city under control?"

"The city is lost," said the paladin. "This was to be our last stand. We were to hold the magi off while survivors escaped through the north gate."

Aaslo looked at Teza in dismay. "You were going to waste your life on *this* city? How would that further our cause?"

"I thought you were dead!" Teza shouted. "I thought there wasn't a cause left."

Aaslo gripped her shoulders and stared into her eyes. "*I* am not the cause. No matter what happens to me, you keep fighting. Do you understand?"

Tears dripped from her lashes as she said, "I'll fight to the very end, Aaslo, but you're all that's left of hope." She wrapped her arms around him again, and this time she didn't let go. He marveled at how she didn't flinch or pull away. By the look on the paladin's face, she was considering the same.

The paladin pulled her gaze from Teza to meet his own. He said, "How long was I buried?"

She pursed her lips, then said, "The better part of the day. I don't see how you could possibly have survived."

Aaslo waved a clawed hand toward the destruction that surrounded them and said, "All of *this* might have been avoided if you'd accepted my help instead of attacking me. We'd best salvage what we can. The lyksvight are on their own now. They'll be searching out meals indiscriminately. The survivors will need protection."

The paladin glanced at the dead magi, then to her clansmen and clanswomen. They still looked at him anxiously, but none argued against him. It was apparent they were willing to accept the paladin's decision.

"You could easily kill us all now if you wanted, could you not?"

"I wouldn't do that," grumped Aaslo.

"But you *could.*"

He clamped down on the tiny growl that escaped him and said, "I welcome you to stand in the shade with me. Let the river refresh our souls and wash away the sand that chafes us."

The paladin looked to her closest companion. The woman nodded as she tightened her grip on the shaft of a broken spear. It was an odd gesture that Aaslo took to mean she approved but with caution.

"Very well," said the paladin. "A truce—for now."

Peeling Teza away from him, he said, "We will gather survivors as we make our way to the north gate." He turned to Ijen. "Where are your horses?"

Ijen abruptly cast a spell that produced the tiny image of a horse in the air above his palm. "They are currently where we left them under the ash tree. As you know, my horse is bespelled. I will command him through our connection to lead the others to the north."

"I didn't know you could do that," said Aaslo. "Can we do that with the others?"

"It is possible with the right connection, although I'm not sure about *your* horse."

Aaslo's muscles twitched when he spied Myra suddenly standing beside Ijen as if she'd been there all along. She said, "Aaslo, there are still many souls to be collected here, but they will not be for long."

At first, he was confused, then he realized what she was telling him. He hung his head and clenched his fists.

Teza said, "Are you okay?"

He knew he should accept things the way they were. Wishing did no one any good. He hated what he had become, though, and mourned the loss of his humanity.

*"You were never really human, were you, Forester?"*

"Very funny," he growled. Then to Teza, he said, "No, I'm not okay. There's something I must do as we go, something that will upset the people we strive to protect."

Teza firmed her jaw, and the stubborn light in her eyes returned. "Better they're upset than dead. What do you need? I'll help."

"This is not something with which you can help."

Aaslo focused inward. He shoved the beast out of the way and ignored Ina as he wrangled the dark power that pooled in his core. It didn't take much to get the power moving. It was pleased to be released. This time, though, he needed it to be focused, concentrated, and intentional. Tendrils of power snaked out of him in every direction. They crossed the square, wound down alleys and over buildings. Each connection felt like a thump to the chest, and every soul captured felt like cool refreshment and fire in one.

"Come," he said, and he wasn't sure if he was speaking to his companions or the dead. Aaslo took Dolt's reins, and as he walked, the broken and departed rose to join him. The paladin and her followers were at first alarmed, but when the dead did not attack, they cautiously followed as well. The going wasn't without risk, though. The numbers of lyksvight grew as they left the square and headed north. The living and undead fought the Berruvian monsters, but Aaslo's numbers grew. The living fell only to rise again, and it happened so quickly that the survivors didn't have time to recognize the loss.

By the time they reached the north gate, Aaslo had amassed an army of nearly seventy undead. Combined with the living, he had over a hundred fighters. He hoped it was because most had escaped but worried that more of the living still occupied the city in hiding, not just from the lyksvight, but from his undead minions as well.

He was heartened to find that the north gate was still standing until the paladin spoke.

"We must bar the gate closed behind us," she said.

"People may still be alive in there," said Aaslo. "If we close it, they'll be trapped."

She looked at the gate, and he could see the struggle in her eyes. She turned back to him and said, "It's a chance we must take. The lyksvight will follow us if we don't."

*"The forester becomes the executioner."*

"No," he said. "I'll not be responsible for their deaths. What if it were *you* who was left in that city and had no way to flee? The lyksvight will follow us anyway through the other gates. The dead will protect the living from the rear."

The paladin looked at the undead in disgust. "On your oath, they will do as you command? Do you swear they will not hurt the refugees?"

"As surely as leaves fall in the autumn." The beast inside him uncurled, and he added, "Either way, you no longer have a choice."

*"I see you haven't lost your charm."*

The paladin stepped back, her expression a mixture of fear and resentment. "I will go ahead and warn the survivors of your coming so they don't attack."

"Be sure that they don't," Aaslo growled. Disturbed by the threat in his voice, he swallowed the dragon's fire and said more calmly, "I desire only to help. No more should die unnecessarily."

The paladin nodded, then she and her companions jogged ahead to find the survivors.

"Do you think they'll betray us?" said Teza.

"No," said Aaslo. "They'd have to be on our side to betray us."

# CHAPTER 20

THE UNDEAD ARMY WAS ENTRENCHED TO THE SOUTH AND ON THE OPPO-site side of the road from the survivors' camp that night. Although the paladin presumably had spoken in their favor to the refugees, many had panicked at the sight of the undead and run. Some were eventually brought back to the group, but others were either lost or killed by stray lyksvight. In all, there were nearly a hundred *living* survivors. Aaslo understood their abhorrence for the undead. If he hadn't been the one to raise them, he would have felt the same. Although they still disturbed him, his connection to them allowed him to sense their true intentions, and they were only concerned with protection and vengeance.

Teza and Ijen settled down to sleep near the single campfire among the mass of undead, and Aaslo crossed the road to access the small creek that trickled beside the road toward the south. The night was dark—although not beyond Aaslo's senses—the stars and moon were hidden behind the clouds, and a chill wind blew in from the south. Lightning danced on the horizon, and Aaslo feared they were in for an uncomfortable night.

Aaslo crouched beside the water and began washing the dirt, sweat, and blood from his exposed torso. He glanced up to see a feminine figure slinking toward him from the other side of the creek.

The paladin approached with a glowing fireball hovering over one hand.

"What do you want?" he said as he splashed water over his face.

"I was just keeping an eye on you. I don't trust you."

Aaslo grunted. "That's funny because I trust you."

*"What? Have you lost your mind completely?"*

"You do? But you don't know me."

"I do. I trust that you'll attack us again if you think we're a threat, but I also trust that you'd rather be fighting the Berru."

She pursed her lips, then nodded. "This is true. I've spoken with the others. They are willing to accept the truce for now—on one condition. A few of our people are injured. You said you have a healer. We require her services."

Aaslo rubbed his scruffy jaw and considered growing out a beard to save the effort of shaving. "You may call me *Aaslo* or *Forester.* I prefer not to be called *dragon-man.*"

"Very well. I am Cherrí. She's Aria," she said with a nod toward another figure standing a dozen paces away in the dark.

"The healer's name is Teza, and she may choose to help if she wishes. She's an excellent mage, though, so you'd best not test her."

*"Again with the lies."*

"It's not a lie. She's greatly improved since she started using her pow-ers again."

"I see," said the paladin. "She does not heed your will, then?"

"They follow me of their own free will."

"Even the dead?"

"Especially the dead. My power does not work on those unwilling to serve."

"You mean to say that *all* those people *agreed* to rise from their graves and serve you?"

"Yes, that's what I'm saying. They are here because they *want* to be here." Aaslo stood and wiped his damp skin with a dry—although ques-tionably clean—cloth.

"What happened to you?"

"I told you already. I was injured. Teza saved my life; this was the result."

"This is what gave you the power to raise the dead?"

"No, that was something else—something I don't entirely understand."

"How are your wanderers unlike those of the Berru?"

"Wanderers?"

"That is what we are calling your walking dead. Because, you know"—she flicked her fingers at one—"they *wander.*"

"For one, mine don't eat people." He ran his fingers across his scruffy jaw and was glad to find no scales had grown over his face—*yet.* "Actu-ally, I don't think they eat *anything.*" He pondered whether or not he should tell her that he claimed their souls.

*"Go on, Aaslo. I'm sure she'll love the idea of a dragon-man stealing people's souls."*

Deciding against it, he said, "We're going to Chelis in hopes that the Mouvilanian army is organizing against the Berru."

*"Good one. It's always beneficial to start an alliance off with a lie."*

Aaslo told himself he wasn't lying to her, exactly. The Mouvilanian army was *one* of his reasons for going to Chelis, but the woman was far from a trustworthy ally. Telling her everything would be irresponsible.

*"Whatever helps you sleep at night."*

"You know as well as I do that nothing helps me sleep," Aaslo grumped as he pulled his pack from behind Dolt's saddle.

"Fair enough," said the paladin. "I suppose there isn't much sleep to be had since the Berru invaded. We, too, are going to Chelis. It would be safer for us to all travel together."

Aaslo riffled through the pack until he found his least-smelly tunic. He was frustrated to find that it was actually his *last* shirt. A small growl escaped his throat as he slipped it over his head. "Safer for *you,* maybe, but a large group will invite attack. *We* would be better going incognito."

The paladin's fiery light flickered angrily, and her voice was just as heated when she spoke. "The Berru want everyone dead. If your goal is truly to fight them, then protecting people should be your priority. *You* said the survivors need protection. Help me protect them."

"You think I'm being coldhearted? It's only practical. If I am to truly help these people, then I must find a way to defeat the Berru. I can't do that with a bunch of helpless villagers in tow."

"If all the helpless die, there won't be anything left for which to fight."

Aaslo was truly torn. He needed to get to Chelis as quickly as possible, but the people of Foresight were terrified, injured, and without supplies or weapons. His internal struggle only proved to him one thing—he wasn't prepared to make these kinds of decisions. This was Mathias's job. He could hear the echo of his father's voice. *Don't waste your thoughts on fallen trees. You can do nothing for them, and those that stand need tending.*

It was un-forester-like to dwell on things that could not be changed. He had taken up the chosen one's mantle, and he would have to decide whether he should sacrifice what was left of a city's worth of people. He searched for Mathias's voice. "What would you do?" he said.

The paladin replied, "*My* people had no one to protect them when the Berru came. I will not leave these people to be slaughtered like mine."

"I have much to think about," he said. "I will have an answer for you in the dawn."

"Very well. I pray to Everon that your blood is warmer than your visage."

When Aaslo finally lay down to sleep that night, he was surrounded by the sleepless dead. They wandered in the dark, their hazy gazes searching for the slightest disruption. The constant ebb and flow of animated corpses across the roadway was enough to make anyone's skin crawl, but Aaslo tried to find comfort in their presence. After all, if *he* couldn't achieve a state of balance with the dead, then no one could.

*Need* pervaded his thoughts—the *need* to help the survivors of Foresight, the *need* to get to Chelis, the *need* to get back to Uyan, the *need* to build an army, and the *need* to keep his friends alive. He was fitful even before he fell into slumber, and the redundancy of his nightmares did nothing to diminish the anguish he felt every time Mathias—or anyone else, for that matter—lost his head. He almost felt a sense of relief when the head that was removed was his own. His dream that night, however, was the most disturbing he had endured since that fateful night in the forest when Mathias had fallen.

Aaslo rode astride Dolt toward the blue door. Nothing seemed amiss, at first, then he realized the door wasn't a door. It was a tree—an ancient, gnarled tree that stretched so far into the sky he couldn't see the top. He was relieved. It had been a long time since he had relaxed beneath the boughs of such a majestic being. His gaze traced the path of one such branch. He furrowed his brow as his gaze continued. Dolt stopped, and Aaslo turned in his saddle. His heart jumped when he realized he couldn't turn far enough to see the end. He jerked around to the other side and saw that the boughs on the left side of the tree also stretched beyond the limits of sight. Actually, they didn't stretch into infinity. They curved. They completely ringed him and Dolt, and the space between them and the trunk was getting smaller. The branches were closing on them.

He kicked Dolt into a run, and again there was a blue door—this time built into the side of the trunk. Amid the snapping and crackling of branches cinching tighter, all other sound was drowned. The ground began to shift, and craggy roots erupted through the soil, all threatening to ensnare Dolt's legs. Aaslo wanted to shout at the horse to stop, lest he break a leg, but stopping would mean certain death. Aaslo nearly laughed at the irony. He had been born to the trees, and he had lived for the trees; he figured it was only fitting that he should die by them. It wasn't even the first time he had been threatened by a tree.

When they reached the door, Aaslo swiftly dismounted and lunged at it. His hands roved the wooden planks, but there was no latch or handle. His fingers gouged the blue paint, and flecks dappled his skin. He hammered against it with his fist, then reached for his axe. Dolt screeched in a completely un-horselike manner, and before Aaslo could bring his axe down on the door even once, he and his horse were snared. He couldn't move but for his breathing, and it was too quick. He took large, heaving breaths, and his head began to spin. He closed his eyes and clamped his mouth shut. He struggled greatly to steady his breathing as he drew long breaths through his nose. When he opened his eyes again, the branches had relaxed enough to allow some movement. He wrenched his arms loose, then his feet. When he turned to do the same for Dolt, he found the horse lazily munching on leaves, where he stood completely unhindered. Dolt looked at him and snorted, then went back to his snack.

"You're even a pain in my dreams," Aaslo said. That's when it struck him that he was, in fact, dreaming. It was a dream—only a dream. If all of it were in his mind, why was his mind attacking him?

Aaslo caught sight of something hanging from one of the branches. It was a sack—a familiar sack. He reached for the bag at his waist, and it was still securely attached.

*"I'm here. You can't get away from me that easily."*

Relieved, he looked back to the sack in the tree and found hundreds of such sacks dangling from the branches along one limb like leaves. He pulled his attention from the distressing image, and it landed on a tangle of branches that were, thankfully, sackless. There was something strange about the branch, though. Miniscule people were piling into an angry, red evergate. Reaching forward with a clawed finger, he poked at one of the people, but his claw passed straight through the scene to no effect.

A loud snap caught Aaslo's attention, and he looked back to find Dolt angrily wrestling a branch that was covered in miniature lyksvight attacking what looked to be a farming community. Aaslo quickly turned his gaze to another branch—to an image of strange, swimming creatures engaging in something that could have easily been either battle or sport.

*"Oh! Let's play. I'll be the side with yellow fins. You can be green."*

"This isn't the time for lighthearted banter," Aaslo grumbled. Everywhere Aaslo looked, he saw new images, some familiar, others completely alien to him.

"What strange dream is this?" he whispered.

"Oh, you're not dreaming," answered a woman.

Aaslo jerked back as he spun to find her. When he did, he saw that she was absolutely stunning—and familiar.

*"Dibs!"*

Mathias's joyful laughter was in direct conflict with the alarm Aaslo felt. He was utterly confused. If he had ever met this woman, he would certainly remember it; yet he knew her, and he didn't remember.

"You're Enani," he said, knowing it to be true and uncertain how.

"Yes," she said. "I'm surprised you remember."

"I don't," he replied, and she laughed as though she understood. He said, "We've met before?"

"Yes, in my garden. Well, one of them. I have thousands. There are probably thousands I've forgotten. The years do go on."

"I . . . I don't remember who you are."

"It is no matter. The real question is, who are *you?*"

*"I think the real question is, who am I. Greetings, I'm the chosen one extraordinaire."*

"Shut up," Aaslo hissed. Then to the woman, "I'm Aaslo, Fore—"

She raised a hand. "Yes, yes, I know all that, but that's not really who you are anymore, is it? No, you've become something else."

*"Something ludicrous."*

"I don't often see Arayallen toying with an already formed being. It is curious."

Aaslo knew the name but couldn't place it. That wasn't what held his attention, though. "You said I'm not dreaming."

"Yes," she drawled. "I said that."

"Then what is this? This can't be a real place."

*"Like I'm not a real voice!"*

She tilted her head thoughtfully. "It is, and it isn't. This is a place in the paths where realities meet. It doesn't exist, exactly. It's like a metaphor that you can visit." She tapped her lip and looked at him curiously. "Well, *you* can't. You don't have the power, so you couldn't have come here on your own. Something else had to have brought you here."

"One of the gods?"

"No, no. There are few of us who know how to access this place and none who would spend their time or energy on *you.*"

*"It just occurred to me that these gods don't respect you."*

"You think they would have helped *you?*"

Enani laughed. "I don't need their help. The paths are mine. I created them. *I* am what connects every world, every realm, every *thing.*"

Dolt abruptly wandered over to the woman, who towered over the horse head and shoulders. He tilted his head up and sneezed directly into her face. He shook his mane; and, with a lash of his tail for good measure, he meandered into the thicket.

"Don't get lost, you big dolt!" Aaslo shouted after him. "I'm sorry about that. He's a beastly creature."

"Yes," she said absently as her gaze followed the horse, "I see." She snapped back to attention and said, "No matter." With a few dainty steps over the roots, she was standing in front of him, and she had shrunken to his height. "We must get on with this. I don't have all day to spend separated from my own body."

"What do you mean? You're not really here?"

"Neither of us are. This is a memory of an event you are only now experiencing."

"I don't understand. You're saying that I'm remembering something that hasn't even happened yet."

"You do understand. Good. Now, on to the important bits. I agreed to teach you this, but I didn't agree to spend all day. You are here to learn to walk the paths."

"The paths? Wait, you agreed? With whom?"

"Yes, the paths between realms." She waved her hand at the branches and said, "You have created an apt metaphor here. Each limb is a major path, and the smaller branches are, well, smaller paths. This is a map, and you are here."

For the first time, Aaslo saw a small glowing sphere hovering over him. She pointed elsewhere. "There is your body."

Aaslo pushed through a tangle of branches to see their encampment laid out before him. The dead wandered aimlessly whilst the living slept, including *him*.

"To get to your body, you would walk through that door and follow the correct path."

"The door won't open."

"Don't interrupt. You'll have to figure it out. The knowledge is inside you. You've been granted this gift by someone who shouldn't have been in your realm."

"You're speaking of Ina?"

"Yes, what you call the fae—strange and frustrating creatures. They scatter throughout the paths, taking up residence wherever they want like vermin. They've gotten a bit out of control. . . . Never mind. I digress."

"So, I go through the door and follow the path to my destination. It's that simple."

"It's not simple, really. I anticipate you'll struggle with it quite a bit, but once you get the hang of it, you'll be traveling in no time. I mean that literally, of course. Most of the paths exist outside of time. That means time will not pass in your realm while you are traveling. This is both a boon and a drawback. The *paths* exist outside of time. *You* do not. Creatures have wandered the paths for years before returning to their realms, only to find that they are far older than their contemporaries."

"Is there a way to use the paths to move through time?"

"Yes, but you do not possess the knowledge or power to do so." She grinned and with a wink said, "*That* prerogative belongs only to me. Well, I think I've said everything that needs to be said. Oh, yes. Beware the paths. They are extremely dangerous. You may easily become lost, and once so, you will not easily be found. The paths do not always go where you think they go, and all manner of creatures have become lost—many of them quite dangerous in their own right. They're lost, frightened, and often *hungry*."

Aaslo blinked. The woman had disappeared before his eyes. He searched out Dolt. The horse had wandered into a cluster of branches in which teeny, winged people lived. Aaslo stared in amazement at the fly-ing people for a moment, then grabbed Dolt's reins just as the horse failed to nab one of the people. If occurred to Aaslo that he had removed Dolt's tack before turning in that night. Nothing about the dream-not-dream was making sense.

Dolt didn't wait for Aaslo's lead. The horse dragged Aaslo toward the door, stopped, and looked back at Aaslo as if to say, *Hurry up, I've been waiting all day.*

The blue door seemed familiar to Aaslo. It occurred to him that it was the same color as the door to the inn in Yarding. It was of simple construction, and just large enough to permit Dolt's entry. The paint was scored where his claws had raked across it in his panic. Aaslo's hands wandered over the planks, this time more deftly, as he searched for some way to open it. He could feel no divots, latches, or secret pressure plates. He pushed it, then threw his weight into it, but it didn't budge.

Aaslo sighed. He was tired, and his sleep-that-wasn't-sleep wasn't helping. His head drooped forward so that his forehead rested against the door. Enani had said the answer was already inside him, but he could think of nothing that might force it open. He considered wedging it open with one of the branches, but he wasn't sure what effect breaking one off might have. He figured there had to be a better way. After all, it was a door. It was intended to open.

Aaslo felt hot breath on the back of his neck, and his flesh prickled with goose bumps as Dolt's whiskers tickled his skin. A glob of slime slithered down his neck.

"Hey! Stop that!" he shouted as he squirmed to reach the mucus that was making its way down his spine. "Ugh, that's disgusting—and *rude*."

*"Ha ha! I never thought to hear you complaining about poor man-ners."*

"Why's that? I have manners."

*"You have manne*risms. *Forester mannerisms. Sometimes they inter-sect with manners."*

"I learned the same manners as you."

*"But I actually use them. You don't even know how to approach a strange door."*

Aaslo struck is forehead with his palm. "I'm an idiot."

*"Agreed."*

Turning back to the door, Aaslo raised his fist and rapped against it with his knuckles. He heard a click as though it were unlocking, but it didn't open. The knowledge was supposed to be inside him—knowledge from Ina. The fae were not human, though. Would they even carry their knowledge the same way? What had Ina given to him? Power. Knowledge was power.

Aaslo searched inside himself for the power lent to him by the finicky fae creature. It was wrapped around his core; and for once, it didn't unfurl at his call. In fact, it was stubbornly refusing. He pulled at it, but it held tight. Aaslo was becoming frustrated, frustrated with the door, with the goddess, with the fae, and with the power that refused to answer to him. He wrapped his claws around the power and yanked. *Mine!* he growled in his mind. It snapped free but thrashed all the way. When it finally settled, it felt sluggish, as though the power were pouting.

He raised his hand again, and this time, he filled his fist with power as he sought the perfect spot on the door. Then he pounded against the obstruction in a way that only a forester could. The ring of the gong echoed through the branches as the door swung open. On the other side of the door was an illuminated mist. The mist wafted around, and Aaslo could see a path, then another and another. Through the shifting mist, he saw hundreds, even thousands of paths. Aaslo wondered how he could possibly find the one that would take him back to his body. In the distance, he saw a spark of light that surely had to be his destination. The light became obscured by the mist, and he was again at a loss. Dolt didn't appear to have the same problem. The exasperating beast began plodding through the mist seemingly without concern. Aaslo hurried after him.

"Stop! You can't just go wandering through the paths. There's no telling where we'll end up!"

*"Well, it looks like I'll be seeing you soon."*

# CHAPTER 21

AASLO AWOKE TO THE ECHO OF MATHIAS'S LAUGHTER, AND IN THAT moment, he forgot that his brother was dead. His mind began to clear, and his eyes stung with tears as he rejoined reality. He reached for the sack beside him and clutched it securely against his chest.

"That's disturbing," said Teza. "I get why you carry that around with you—sort of—but to cuddle with it is just messed up."

Aaslo dropped the sack and sat up. "I'm not cuddling it," he grumped. "Where are we? What time is it?"

Teza clicked her tongue at him. "We're in the same place we were last night—a few hours north of Foresight. It'll be dawn soon."

"I'm surprised you're already awake."

"I was surprised you weren't. Your *soldiers* have been getting restless. It's making the rest of us anxious."

Aaslo rubbed his eyes, then noticed flecks of blue paint stuck to his talons. He swallowed his bile and looked around the hastily erected camp. It was little more than a few bedrolls arranged around a campfire. On the other side of the road was much more activity. The people of Foresight seemed to be readying themselves for a move. Ijen crossed back to their side looking dourer than usual. Several paces behind him, the paladin and her companion, Aria, followed. Ijen sat down beside Aaslo, then stared at the smoldering remnants of the fire that Teza had used to boil water for tea and egg dumplings. Teza looked curiously at the prophet as she handed Aaslo his breakfast.

"What's got your knickers in a twist?" she said.

"I don't wear knickers," Ijen said defensively.

"You know what I mean. What's wrong?"

"Nothing. And . . . something."

After checking them for snakes and spiders, Aaslo pulled on his boots. He said, "Is this one of those times you want to tell us something you shouldn't, or are you going to tell us something you don't want to say?"

"We need to be moving—like, an hour ago."

"Why is that?" said Cherrí as she took a seat beside Teza on the other side of the campfire.

Aaslo's heart struck like a drum. "What is it? Are we about to be attacked?"

"We are. I can tell you this now because it's too late to do anything about it. It'll be a large force, and we won't survive."

"What do you mean *we won't survive*?" shouted Teza. "You couldn't have told us this an hour ago?"

"No. If I had, things might have changed."

"That's the point!" she screamed as she bent and began stuffing her things into her bag. She tossed the near-boiling water from the pot and chucked the burning hunk of iron at Aaslo. "We have to go. Now! Why are you still sitting there? Let's go!"

"What is he talking about?" said Cherrí. "Is this true?"

His heart racing, Aaslo simply looked at Ijen. The prophet looked like he had just swallowed a bug, but he didn't have the countenance of a man who knew he was about to die.

"What's going on, Ijen? You know something more. How do we get out of this?"

Ijen shook his head. "I don't see how we can."

"But we must," said Aaslo.

"Why?"

"Because we haven't saved the world yet."

The prophet looked at him as though he were mad. "I've told you since we met—the world is doomed. Death follows you, Aaslo."

Aaslo stood and opened his arms to take in the extended area covered in wanderers. "Yes, Ijen, the dead *literally* follow me."

Ijen nodded. "You understand now."

"*You* don't understand. That's not a bad thing. These people would have died were I here or not. This way, they can rise again to fight for us."

"Even so, it will not be enough this time. Those who attacked Foresight were just the forward troops. More follow in their wake, and they are nearly upon us."

Cherrí stood and looked past Aaslo to her people. "They cannot die. I've lost everyone I hoped to protect. I need them to live."

Aria turned to her. "What does it matter if we are dead, too? We should tell them what's happening and run. Some of us may escape."

"We can't abandon them," said Cherrí.

"*We* must survive to fight another day. We will find more people."

"No," said Aaslo. "The paladin is right. I won't abandon these people. I think I know a way."

Ijen abruptly stood and pulled his book from his tunic but did not open it. Instead, he gripped it before him as though it could somehow ward off whatever Aaslo was about to say.

"I had a dream last night, except I don't think it was a dream. If I'm right, I may be able to get us out of this."

Aria said, "You're going to entrust our lives to a dream?"

"It wasn't exactly a dream. It doesn't matter. Just give me a little time to figure it out."

The blare of a horn suddenly rang in the distance. It was followed by the uproarious cry of hundreds of lyksvight. Aaslo spotted several bright lights that streamed into the air before dropping toward their camp. Within seconds, things began exploding around them.

Cherrí said, "You're out of time. If you can do something, best do it now."

She and Aria then turned and ran back to their people on the other side of the road. In the few seconds since the alarm, their camp had become an ant storm of activity. On Aaslo's side of the road, the wanderers simply stood staring in the direction of the enemy to the south. Aaslo quickly stuffed the remainder of his belongings into his pack, then sought out Dolt. The horse was antagonizing one of the undead horses, but the lifeless beast ignored Dolt's taunts. Aaslo grabbed his saddle and began preparing Dolt for their escape while Teza and Ijen did the same with their own mounts. The living horses startled with each explosion, but the placid energy of the dead kept them from a full panic.

Aaslo had to think quickly. If the dream wasn't a dream in truth, then he could access the paths on his own *without* the assistance of an evergate. He searched around him high and low for the blue door. He searched with his eyes wide open, then closed them and searched again. He growled in frustration and yelled, "Where's the damned door?"

*"Since when do foresters care for doors?"*

"What?" he shouted. "I don't care for doors, just *this* door!"

*"I never saw a forest path with a door."*

"This isn't a forest path. It's a . . ."

Aaslo's thoughts came to an abrupt halt. In his dream-that-wasn't-a-dream, the paths *were* forest paths. Enani had said *he* had created the metaphor. *He* was a forester, and foresters didn't need doors. All he had to do was open . . . open what?

The screech of things dying snapped Aaslo out of his contemplations. The forward lyksvight were beginning to clash with his army of wanderers.

Teza screamed, "Aaslo, wake up! They're attacking! We must run!"

Aaslo wasn't sure which power he needed most in that minute, so he grabbed all three. The fae power, the dragon, and death had no time to fight among themselves as he stuffed them all into his need to access the paths. In his mind, a gong rang so clearly he wasn't sure it hadn't been audible to everyone else. The sky before him was ripped open in a jagged assault on reality. A wicked wind rushed over them from within the tear. Dolt knickered then trotted through the tear before Aaslo could grab him.

"Teza," he shouted, "get through the rift! It's like an evergate but without the gate. Wait for me on the other side."

Teza's face blanched as she looked at the sky rift. "You want me to go in *there*? Alone? Where does it go?"

"Everywhere!" Aaslo shouted over the din of the wind and slavering lyksvight.

"I can't!" she screamed.

"Why not?"

"Someone has to get the others. I'll go. You maintain the rift and keep the lyksvight from going through."

She was off and running before Aaslo could respond. He could hear her yelling for people to run toward the rift, and despite their terror—or perhaps because of it—they listened.

"I'd best go in ahead of them," said Ijen, who was suddenly standing next to Aaslo, looking as calm as ever. "Someone will need to keep them from wandering off and becoming lost forever." Then, without a care, he stepped through the rift with his horse in tow. The first of the refugees near the rift took one look at the advancing lyksvight and leapt into the rift. He was quickly followed by a flood of others.

Aaslo turned back to see the wanderers fighting off the lyksvight as though the world depended on it—only, it wasn't *their* world anymore. It was strange to see the stoic cadavers fight with such ferocity.

"Mama?"

The voice was small and immediately set Aaslo's heart to a gallop. A girl child of no more than ten had stopped in her tracks just before the rift. She was looking out over the battle scene. Again, she screamed, "Mama!" this time more forcefully. She began running toward the attacking creatures.

Aaslo searched the scene and finally found the source of the girl's horror. A woman turned wanderer was wielding a broken broom handle against a lyksvight. She jabbed it in the solar plexus, then smacked it in the face. It turned back and hissed at her, and she shoved the jagged end of the stick into its mouth and through its skull. She pulled the stick free and struck another lyksvight that was attacking a second wanderer across the back. The little girl reached the woman and tugged on her loose tunic. The woman's hazy white gaze fell on the young girl. She handed the stick to the girl, then stooped to pick her up before running toward the rift. She paused in front of Aaslo as if searching for an answer.

He said, "Go."

Then the wandering woman rushed through the evergate with her daughter.

It was only in that moment that Aaslo realized how aware the wanderers were. They were dead, but they were still people; and they were people who had something for which to fight. Aaslo glanced back to see that only a third of the Foresight survivors had made it into the rift. Some had run away and didn't look to be returning. Many were anxiously awaiting their turn to fit through the small opening, while a few appeared too fearful to step through. Aaslo feared their protective force would fall apart before everyone had escaped.

*"What are you going to do, General, sir?"*

Their forces had spread too far apart. They were too thin, and the lyksvight were pushing nearer to the escapees.

"They need to fall back," Aaslo said.

As soon as the words left his lips, the wanderers began to move as one in a wave toward the rift. They still fought the enemy, but every extra step brought them closer together. A streak of blue lightning struck the farthest wanderers from him, and he knew the Berruvian magi were nearly upon them. At that point, it would be too late. The wanderers would be almost useless against the magi, and he wouldn't be able to hold them off by himself.

Aaslo glanced over his shoulder to see that a little over a dozen survivors—those who were still near enough to save—remained on his side of the rift, and most of them were city guards or Cartisian warriors. Several were already clashing with stray lyksvight that had gotten past the wanderers.

*"Watch your back."*

Aaslo turned in time to catch a descending mace before it struck him in the head. He wrenched the lyksvight's arm forward, smashed its face into his knee, then scored his claws down the creature's back. A howl burst forth, and he wasn't sure if it belonged to the creature or if it was his own. The creature slid to the ground, its upper limbs still flailing while its lower half had been stilled by a severed spine. Aaslo backed toward the rift as the remaining refugees filed through. He slashed another lyksvight through the gut with his axe and backed up again. He was the last to enter the rift, and just as he did so, he looked up to see a furious magus staring at him from atop his perch on a black-eyed monster. Aaslo had never before seen such a creature and doubted it came from his own realm.

A gong echoed through the paths as the rift sealed, but Aaslo seemed to be the only person who heard it. The others were all clutching each other as they stood in the mist. Paths, shimmering with a metallic glow, stretched into the distance in every direction, but between them towered fresh evergreens and aspens. Aaslo took a long draught of fresh, moist mountain air, which went far in alleviating the tension he had been feeling only seconds before in the midst of a battle. With the closing of the rift, the others appeared relieved; but upon seeing *him*, they cringed in fear. It occurred to him that this was the closest most of them had been to him, and his monstrous side was clearly visible since he had run out of shirts.

Cherrí stepped forward and tapped her pale driftwood staff against the ground. Then she raised her voice to hush the crowd. "This is Aaslo, a forester of Uyan. He has brought us to this sanctuary. He will do you no harm." If the paladin doubted her own words, her calm demeanor revealed nothing of it.

One man called out to her. "What about *them*?" he said with a wave toward the wanderers who had made it through the rift and were huddled in a small cluster at the rear of the group. "Are they really dead? Are they going to eat us?"

Cherrí looked at Aaslo for several drawn-out seconds, then said, "It is true that they are dead, but they are his. He will not allow them to hurt you."

"What is this place?" said a woman with a shaky voice. "Where are we?"

The crowd followed the paladin's gaze to him. Aaslo began walking toward the front of the group and spoke loudly enough for everyone to hear. "We are nowhere, yet. These are the paths between places. When we leave this place, we will be somewhere else, hopefully far from where we were."

The same woman said, "It's peaceful here. Can't we just stay here until it's over?"

"No," said Aaslo. She jumped, and he realized he had spoken too harshly. He softened his voice and said, "Time does not pass in our world while we are here. No matter how long we spend here, when we return, it will be to the same fate as when we left. That's why it's important that we take the right path out of here. Take hold of your loved ones and stay with me. Anyone who wanders away will be lost for good."

Once Aaslo reached the front of the group, he looked out over the paths. He couldn't believe that he'd managed even to get there, but his greatest feat was yet to come. Somehow, he had to get them *out*. He glanced at each of the nearest and largest paths, thirteen in all. Dozens, possibly hundreds of smaller paths ran between them and each branched into numerous others.

"This is phenomenal, isn't it?" said Ijen, who was abruptly standing beside him. "It's like prophecy drawn out for us."

"Except these paths do not lead to future or past events. They go to different places, and they are all *now*."

"How do you know?"

"The Goddess of Realms told me."

Ijen's typical indifference was replaced with shock, and Aaslo felt some satisfaction in it. "You didn't know?"

"It has always been unclear how we get to the next events. I have never seen this place in my visions."

"It's not a place," Aaslo said, "not exactly. It's the space between places. We can't stay here for long. It isn't safe. According to the goddess, we're not the only beings to occupy it."

"Then let's get going," said Teza as she sidled up to him. "Where will you take us? Please tell me it's somewhere with good food and hot baths."

Aaslo looked back to the paths as a sudden panic shot through his nerves. He had no idea where he was going.

*"I'm proud of you, Aaslo. I thought I'd never see the day when you leapt without looking."*

"You didn't see it," Aaslo grumbled as he shifted the bag at his waist. He then realized what he had said, and a pang of regret swept over him.

"See what?" said Teza.

"Uh, Dolt. Where is he?"

"There," she said, pointing down one of the paths. She had already started walking down the path as she said, "How did you get him to go where you wanted?"

"Wait, I—" Aaslo stopped as his gaze met Dolt's. The horse appeared to be issuing a challenge. Aaslo looked to the path beyond Dolt and inhaled to calm himself. He tried to feel where the path might go. The thought occurred to him that the path went somewhere he had never been. Then it occurred to him that it went somewhere he wanted to go. Before Aaslo could further explore the phenomenon, Dolt turned and continued ambling down the path.

*"Don't do it."*

"Do what?" he grumbled.

*"You're going to let your horse decide, aren't you?"*

"Do you have a better idea?" Mathias was silent, so Aaslo said, "Neither do I." So, he followed Dolt, and the others followed him. All the while, he prayed to the Goddess of Realms that he was going the right way.

# CHAPTER 22

AASLO HAD THE SENSE THAT SOMETHING WAS CRAWLING UP HIS NECK. HE slapped at it, expecting to swat away a bug, but encountered nothing. He took a deep breath and pressed on, but after only a few seconds, he felt it again.

"What *is* that?" he muttered.

*"Your good looks waving goodbye?"*

"You admit I had good looks?"

"I think you still do," said Teza.

Aaslo started to say more to Mathias, then realized what Teza had said. "Really? You don't think I'm a monster?"

She pulled him to a stop next to her as the crowd continued forward. She looked at him thoughtfully. Her finger caressed the skin of his face, then passed over the scales on his neck. *"This* isn't bad-looking. It makes you look dangerous. It's kind of sexy."

Mathias started laughing, and Aaslo shoved him away. He wondered if he was blushing. Not since Reyla had he seen a woman look at him that way.

She said, "You have the most stunning emerald-green eyes."

"Eyes? Both of them?" he said.

"Yes, this one human, this one dragon—both beautiful. It's like looking deep into the forest. I probably shouldn't say this, but I feel a little thrill every time you look at me."

*"I believe that's called the fight-or-flight response."*

A small growl escaped him, and Teza's presumptive expression caused his face to heat. "I'm not a predator," he muttered.

Teza replied with a wink, "I'm not so sure about that."

Aaslo felt the crawling sensation on the back of his neck again, and he spun to see what had caused it. Something dark quickly slithered back into the fog.

"What is it?" said Teza.

"I don't know. Something is following us. I think it's best we get out of here before it decides we look like a tasty meal."

Aaslo jogged past the wanderers and refugees that had passed them. Upon catching up with Dolt and Ijen, he said, "Are we near to leaving yet?"

Ijen gave him an incredulous look. *"You're* the one leading us. You tell me."

Deciding it best not to tell Ijen that they were actually following an insane horse, Aaslo turned to survey the way ahead. The path split and then split again, and at varying distances down each lane, he saw blue doors.

*"The doors are back. Are you feeling indecisive?"*

"We have to get out somehow," Aaslo muttered.

*"Perhaps you should get out the same way you got in."*

"Fine," said Aaslo. "You're right, okay? The problem is that I'm not exactly sure *how* we got in. I was under a lot of pressure, and it sort of just happened."

Ijen said, "That is not reassuring."

"No, it's not," said Teza, who had apparently joined them. This time she was scowling at Aaslo. He much preferred the adoring look she'd been giving him earlier.

*"She's a dynamic individual, Aaslo. She's not here just for your pleasure. You must appreciate her for all her sides."*

"I know that," Aaslo snapped. "What kind of man do you think I am?"

"A bit crazy, maybe, but I'd always thought you were steady. Are you saying you don't know where we're going?"

Dolt had stopped at a split in the path and nearly knocked Aaslo over as he turned down one to the right.

"Not at all," said Aaslo. "I know exactly where we're going."

*"You just don't know how to get there."*

Aaslo set his jaw and said, "We're going the right way."

"You seem sure of that," said Teza. "I'm just not sure I believe you."

Dolt snorted and came to a halt. In front of the horse was a blue door. Aaslo walked up to the door, glanced back at Teza and Ijen, and said, "We're going through here." Then he knocked.

The door didn't simply unlatch or swing silently ajar. It didn't burst open and suck them through. No. Aaslo heard the clang of a gong, and then he and everyone who had accompanied him into the paths of the between space were standing on an artificially cultivated lawn. The sun blazed in the bright blue sky that held only a few fluffy white clouds. To one side were neat rows of fruit trees; to the other was a cobbled driveway that continued through an iron gate accented with scrollwork and gold gilding. The polished white stone of the wall sparkled in the sunlight, and a plethora of songbirds filled the air with their joyful chirps.

Aaslo followed the driveway with his gaze in the other direction and discovered, to his amazement, that they were standing in front of a unique building he knew from drawings in Magdelay's books. It possessed multiple domes stacked atop each other like a pyramid of soap bubbles but missing the pinnacle. Towers extruded from the apexes of the upper three domes; and hovering in the air between the three was the final piece, a proper pyramid that emitted a soft, silver glow. As his gaze rested on the sight, Aaslo couldn't help but wonder how much time would pass before the pinnacle fell, thanks to the exodus of the magi.

Cherrí stepped up beside Aaslo. "What is this place?"

"It's the Vilusten in Chelis."

"This is the Mouvilanian parliament?"

"Yes," he said, "but it looks to be abandoned."

"*Very observant. What gave it away? The overgrown weeds or the shuttered windows? Perhaps it was the rubble and building-sized boulder that are blocking the entrance or maybe all the decaying corpses in the driveway.*"

"We're too late," said Aaslo. "Death has already been here."

Cherrí said, "Is no place left unscathed? Is no place safe?"

Teza spoke from where she was hunched over a corpse. "This looks fresh. In this weather, I'd say he can't be more than three days dead."

"Then we'd best be on the lookout for lyksvight," said Cherrí.

"No," said Aria as she pushed past the stunned crowd. "The corpses are undisturbed. If lyksvight were about, they'd have been eaten."

"She's right," said Aaslo. He looked to Ijen. "Who did this?"

"I suppose there's no harm in telling you that it was Pithor's army of magi—or, at least, a small contingent of them."

Aaslo looked toward the gate that stood open. "Where are they now?"

"I couldn't say," said Ijen.

Aaslo knew better than to ask again if it was that he *couldn't* or *wouldn't*. Instead, he said, "Is the Vilusten empty? Is it safe for the refugees?"

Ijen shrugged and turned his dispassionate gaze to the corpse at his feet. He and Aaslo watched as a beetle crawled out of an empty eye socket that had been pecked clean. Then the prophet said, "Does he still have a soul?"

It took Aaslo a moment to process the question. He hadn't considered checking since the reapers were usually present at the time of death. It occurred to Aaslo that, if the reapers were prepared to take their souls as they died, *someone* had to know before the death happened. As if summoned by the thought, he noticed Myra was suddenly present and effortlessly floating over to stand beside Ijen.

She said, "Their souls have already been released to the Sea."

Aaslo said, "Do you know when someone is going to die?"

"No," she replied, "I am not a prophet."

Ijen said, "I know only if the potential to die in a moment lies upon the path a person has taken."

Aaslo waved at the corpse, then turned away. "These have already been taken."

"It's too bad," said Teza as she stood from examining another corpse. "This one was a magus. We could have used him."

"How do you know?" said Aaslo.

"His ring. Not all magi wear them, but only magi can own one. He was one of ours, I'd say. I doubt the Berru adhere to the tradition."

Aaslo heard an odd clacking sound and turned to find Myra mindlessly toying with the strings of orbs hanging from her belt. Some were empty, but others were brightly illuminated. Another disturbing thought occurred to him. Those little orbs that she so casually tapped were people's *souls*, the essences of their beings, all that truly constituted a life.

His attention rose to her face, and she was staring back at him with consternation.

"Must you do that?" he said.

She abruptly dropped the orbs such that they clattered and stilled on their strings. "Sorry. I was thinking. I wonder—"

Teza said, "Aaslo, are you listening?"

Aaslo realized Teza had been talking to him, but he hadn't heard her. He didn't answer, though, considering his silence was proof enough, as he waited for Myra to finish her thought. She didn't, though, and instead went back to fiddling with the orbs. He said, "What were you wondering?"

"I wasn't wondering anything," said Teza. "Wait a minute. You're not talking to me, are you? Who is it now?"

*"Oo, oo, it's me! Tell her it's me. I want to tell you things. One time, while you were out trolling for saplings—"*

"Stop it. I can listen to you later," Aaslo grumped.

"Well, that's rude," said Teza.

"What were you wondering?" Aaslo prompted once again.

"Who is he talking to?" said Cherrí.

"Shhhh," hissed Teza. "Just let him speak."

"I think I've had a terrible idea," said Myra. "What if you had loose souls that hadn't been delivered to the Sea? Could you sort of *reattach* them—but to a different body—and raise it as one of your wanderers?"

Aaslo blinked at her, then looked to the empty vessel at his feet. "I . . . don't know. Maybe. Why would I want to do that?"

Myra twirled one of the strings around her finger and unwound it again. "Well, you could increase your army."

"But where would I get such souls?"

She worried her lip, then meekly said, "A reaper could give them to you."

"You would do that?"

"I might—if it would help."

"Wouldn't you be betraying your position? Wouldn't you be betraying the gods you serve?"

"Maybe not," she said. "The gods don't own the souls; and, technically, I work for the Fates. They decide what happens to the souls."

"They would allow this?"

"I don't know. I suppose we could try."

"What will happen to you if you're wrong?"

"I don't know that either."

"No, it's not worth it, then."

She looked at him with surprise, and a faint smile caressed her lips. "You're concerned for me?"

"Of course," he said. "I won't risk your—existence—for an experiment."

He felt a sharp tug on his arm.

"What is it?" said Teza.

"Nothing," said Aaslo. "Myra is here. We're not doing it, so it doesn't matter."

"All right. What *are* we doing, then?"

The paladin said, "Who's Myra?"

"Never mind that. We may discuss it later. For now, we need to scout the Vilusten and get these people inside. Pithor's magi could be anywhere."

Myropa watched pensively as Aaslo's wanderers and the paladin's people searched the Vilusten. In the two decades she had been a reaper, she had visited the parliament four times—once for a heart attack, once for a suicide, and twice for assassinations. It had always been a lively place with pages, scribes, secretaries, and politicians running about at all times of day and night working to ensure that their causes were furthered. This time was different. The once-bustling center of Mouvilanian government had been relegated to a mausoleum, and the number of dead were far more than the few hundred who had previously occupied the building. It was determined that at least some of the Chelisian people had to have taken refuge there during the attack and that they had also died there. The bodies were, for the most part, whole—which meant the carnage had been wrought by *humans*.

Years of soul gathering had left her heart cold and empty, but Myropa still recognized evil when she saw it. What Pithor was doing in the name of Axus was wrong. The people of Chelis, like those across Aldrea, should have been allowed to live out their lives as the Fates had designed. Axus's meddling had unhitched that horse, though. She fumbled with the spheres hanging from her belt as she thought, then stopped herself. Aaslo had thought her insensitive and disrespectful for doing so, but he didn't know the full extent of what she had been thinking. It wasn't something she approached lightly. In fact, she risked distancing herself from her one supporter, if not outright betraying him. If someone was dedicated to her, though, did that mean she was automatically supposed to be dedicated to him? She had a cause of her own—one she had managed to pursue in spite of her duties toward the Fates and gods.

She spied Teza walking toward her from the other end of a corridor and waited. She had expected the girl to show up sooner or later. After all, where there was Aaslo, there was Teza. She suspected Teza's interest in Aaslo was more than professional or platonic; and why wouldn't it be? Aaslo had been a competent, respectable, handsome young man before the war; and since its onset, he had acquired enigmatic and potent power. Teza couldn't hold his somewhat less-than-human appearance against him, since she was the one who'd caused it. It only made sense the healer should favor him. Although Teza's brash impulsiveness had initially put off Myropa, the girl had proven herself to be a loyal friend and useful companion to Aaslo. All that kept Myropa from approving of the union was that, during her intermittent visits, she had seen no sign that Aaslo returned Teza's favor—and *also* that Myropa had only just found him and wasn't ready to let him go.

"Well?" said Aaslo.

"It seems safe enough," replied Teza. "There are a lot of dead people but no Berru. It's a shame you can't turn them into wanderers."

"What makes you say that?" Aaslo said, somewhat defensively.

"It would increase our numbers. If the Berruvian magi return, we could use the help."

Aaslo frowned, then looked over to Myropa. She held up the dangling collection of souls, and he turned away again. "What did you do with the magus?"

"We put his body in the chantry for now. We didn't find any other magi. He, alone, must have stayed behind to keep the Vilusten functioning properly. There are many enchantments that require a magus here."

"What if—what if we *could* raise him?" Aaslo said. "Would he retain his power?"

"Um, I suppose. The power is genetic. As long as he remembers how to use it, it should work."

"So, we'd need the soul of a magus."

"Uh, *yeah,* his soul *is* the soul of a magus."

"But we don't have *his* soul," said Aaslo.

Teza's eyes widened, and she grinned broadly. "Are you thinking of putting someone else's soul in his body?"

Aaslo glanced at Myropa and said, "It was just a thought."

Teza raised her hands defensively and said, "Hey, I get it. If it would work, I'd be all for it. I didn't want to say anything, but I'm really worried that those magi will be back. Why are we still here? Can't you open the paths again so we can go somewhere else?"

Myropa had wanted to talk with Aaslo about his use of the paths. She had so many questions, but time had not allowed for her to speak with him yet; and there was another subject that had yet to be broached. It was important, but she supposed it could wait.

Aaslo looked back to Myropa. "Do you have any magi?"

She held up the orbs and considered each of them. She didn't have any magi, but she did have—she looked at Aaslo—but was it time, she wondered. "I, uh, not as such, but I have something you could *try.*"

"What is it?"

"Well," she held up a brilliant green orb, "this one."

"Who was it?"

Myropa pursed her lips. "I can't say."

"You want me to put an unknown entity into the body of a magus and raise him from the dead? I'm not sure I trust you that much."

Myropa's frozen heart cracked as it sank. She knew he had no reason to trust her and many not to; but she had hoped her desire to help him being greater than her duty to the Fates would have meant something to him. She swallowed the pain and said, "I understand. I can't say because—well, I don't know. I didn't collect this one. It was given to me for safekeeping. It's pertinent that Axus doesn't know I have it. I think it's important."

"Given to you by whom?"

Myropa's lips turned down as she mulled over her conflicting feelings. She was strongly attracted to Disevy. He made her feel alive again, and what's more, he had shown her why she should *want* to live. He had helped her find some small value in herself, and he seemed to truly care for her. Her feelings toward Aaslo were greater than those she had for Disevy, though. She *needed* him to accept her. Was she betraying Disevy by giving the soul to Aaslo? Probably. Was she going to do it anyway? Yes, she was.

"Please, Aaslo. It was given to me by one of the gods—one who wants to help you . . . or, at least, he wants to help *me*. He will probably hate me for giving it to you, though. If you turn me down now and he finds out I offered, you may not get another chance."

"If he wants to help me, why would he be angry with you for giving it to me?"

Myropa closed the distance between them and said, "I know it doesn't make sense, but please believe that *I* am trying to help *you*."

After a moment's thought, Aaslo said, "I do believe you, Myra. I'm asking myself what Mathias would do—as the chosen one. He refuses to answer."

She pressed her hand against his face and thought she could *almost* feel him. "Mathias isn't here, Aaslo. Ask yourself what *you* would do."

"We don't know what the gods will do to you if they find out about this. As a forester, I would err on the side of caution. It's not worth the risk. Even we foresters have been known to take chances at times, but not with the lives of *others*."

Myropa shook her head. "I don't have a life, Aaslo. I'm already dead."

"But you exist."

"It's a tormented existence. Every day and night, I take people from their loved ones, from their dreams and aspirations; and I am never allowed any for myself."

"You've been helping us, which means you maintain free will."

"Sometimes, but I'm still beholden to the gods. I don't know whose soul this is or if he or she will be sympathetic to your cause, but I know it's important. You have control over your undead. Would it not be better for you to control this soul than for Axus to get ahold of it?"

"I'm not sure using this mystery soul is the most responsible choice, but I do see your point. The wanderers serve me because they *agree* to serve me in exchange for a chance to walk again. Perhaps this soul will not accept, and we will be no better or *worse* than we are now."

Teza placed her hand on his arm and said, "Wait a minute. Are you talking about using someone else's soul in this magus—someone you don't know?"

Aaslo turned to her and said, "Take me to the chantry."

Sedi followed her prey down the main corridor of the Vilusten. It was bright enough that she could be confident they wouldn't see her. With the light wrapped around her as it was, she was rendered invisible to their eyes. Aaslo might have figured out how to look past her camouflage if he knew she was following him. Fortunately for her, he was oblivious to what he couldn't see in the light. She had noticed that he had another sight, though—one he had acquired from the beast with which the inept healer had bound him. Sedi had toyed with making such chimeras in the past, but with her miniscule healing ability, they had never been viable. This one was the best she had seen, and not just because she found his unique form appealing. Aaslo was still merging with the dragon, acquiring its strength and senses, and perhaps even some of its power. He was intriguing, and that alone was enough to keep her from killing him quickly.

She smirked as her gaze traveled over the healer apprentice who had never finished her training and never would. She was no more than a child—an infant, really; but she had a natural talent for the obscene, if not true skill. It occurred to her that she could use such talent, but then she realized she'd never have the chance. They were going to die. Everyone was going to die. Even she. She smiled at the thought.

As they entered the chantry, a solemn, under-furnished space with a few benches, an altar, and twelve unlit sconces, Sedi mulled over the one-way conversation between Aaslo and the reaper. It seemed he was going to try an experiment with souls. For so long, nothing that had happened in the world had been new to Sedi. For the first thousand years, Sedi had been thrilled to explore everything the world had to offer. Then she realized that history repeated itself over and over. Everything had happened before, and it would happen again. Nothing was new. Until now. For the first time in hundreds of years, Sedi was filled with excitement and wonder, and it was all because of Aaslo.

As Aaslo and Teza approached the altar upon which the dead magus rested, Sedi stepped onto a bench, sat on the seat back, and rested her elbows on her knees. Watching Aaslo raise the dead was fun, but watching him put a random spirit into the body of a decaying magus was going to be thrilling—maybe, if it worked. One particular detail that had caught her attention was that, for some reason, the gods would become angry over this, which made it all the more enticing.

While she waited for something to happen, she pondered how Aaslo had ended up at the Vilusten. Had he gone through the broken evergate? After the Citadel of Magi, she had lost track of him. The evergate had not taken him to Tyellí as intended. She had checked. Thanks to Pithor's summons, she had arrived in Chelis a few days prior to participate in the wanton destruction. She hadn't expected to find Aaslo again so soon, but there he was in the middle of things again. He was too late to stop the destruction of the Mouvilanian parliament, and Pithor would be pleased to destroy the forester himself.

Sedi frowned as it occurred to her that she didn't want Pithor to kill Aaslo. She had begun to feel a kinship with Aldrea's newest magus. She felt that when he died, it should be by *her* hand. She let the feeling slip away. After all, what difference did it make who killed him? They were all going to die anyway.

She heard a snap, and snakes of black power erupted from Aaslo's body. Some slithered down his arms and through the air toward the magus's corpse, while others converged on a point in the air to one side of the altar. Sedi leaned forward and squinted at the spot. No matter how hard she tried, she could not see what was creating the convergence, which she assumed was the reaper—the reaper that was, apparently, a double agent.

As she stared at the point of convergence, it began to emit a green glow—a light shining through black veins. The light traveled up the veins toward Aaslo, then disappeared into him. She waited a second, then another, and another. Aaslo clenched his hands, and his muscles across his chest and back rippled as they tensed. Black veins traveled over his skin and under his scales; then they receded, and a small green thread slid down the black tendril toward the corpse. The thread recoiled, then pressed forward over and again until it finally slid into the magus's body. The magus's eyelids fluttered, then opened. Through the white haze of his eyeballs roiled a fiery green light. The mouth opened. An inhuman wail was released, it felt like, into every realm at once. Utter terror filled the room followed by anguish, torment, and agony. It screeched with a hundred thousand voices, each one of which spoke of unmentionable suffering.

The pain-filled bellow struck Sedi with the force of a hurricane, knocking her from her perch with a thud. She peeled her teary eyes open as she clamped her hands over her ears. Across the floor, she could see that Teza had also succumbed to the sorrowful keen, having crumpled to the floor at Aaslo's feet. Sedi couldn't concentrate on maintaining her invisibility, so she crawled on her elbows and knees to the end of the bench. She peeked from behind it to see Aaslo standing erect, his back bent slightly backward, and his arms cast wide. A stream of brilliantly glowing green smoke wafted toward his eyes, which filled with the green fire. His mouth was open wide, and Sedi could no longer tell if the screams were emanating from the corpse or Aaslo. The black tendrils that laced Aaslo's skin squirmed angrily and thickened. The keening abruptly stopped, and the snake of light disappeared.

Sedi shook as she took deep breaths to regain her composure. Her ears continued to ring long after the sounds had stopped. Teza, having been closer to the source, took longer to recover. Aaslo, however, merely stared at the lifeless body of the magus as he took great heaving breaths. The dead magus raised an arm, then placed it on the altar and pushed himself to a seated position. Within his hazy white eyes, his irises continued to blaze with fiery green light.

"What are you?" Aaslo huffed between breaths.

The magus looked at him and opened its mouth. It emitted a series of clicks followed by a short chirrup and another, subtler, screech. Teza had regained her feet, although she stood doubled over with her head held between her hands. She looked up at Aaslo and said, "What, in this gods-forsaken land, was that?"

Aaslo cleared his throat and said, "It's not human. I don't know what it is, but it's terrible, probably the most terrible thing to ever exist. I can *feel* it."

After another heavy breath, Teza said, "Well, will it follow you?"

"It must. I am what is keeping it tethered to that body."

"Is it going to be able to use the magus's power like we'd hoped?"

"I don't know yet. I do know that it's powerful and it doesn't belong here."

"Then what do we do? Are you going to get rid of it? Release it or whatever?"

"No. We'll watch and see."

She waved her fingers at the magus and said, "What are we calling it? It's like a spirit or shade except housed in a body."

"I don't care. *Shade* is good enough for me."

"Is it dangerous?"

"Yes."

Teza finally stood straight and said, "I don't know if that's good or bad."

Abrupt shouting reached them from the corridor. A cacophony of crashes and explosions followed. Sedi grinned. Pithor had returned, and things were about to get interesting.

AASLO RAN FROM THE CHANTRY WITH TEZA AND THE NEWLY RISEN SHADE toward the second-level balcony. He ducked behind the balustrade and peered down onto the lawn. The echo of the shade's awakening still resonated in his skull, and he couldn't hear much of the commotion. Beyond the meager wall that surrounded the Vilusten was an army so massive he couldn't see its end. At the fore were beasts found only in nightmares. Five were smaller than a man but larger than a dog. They had sharp claws and fangs from which dripped a frothy mucus. Their forms were slight, as though their leathery, black skin was stretched directly over the bones. Three of the monsters were comparable to the largest of horses, except they bore fangs within overlarge, round heads held aloft by unusually long necks. The greatest of the creatures was nearly the size of Aaslo's home. The beast had short, bulbous legs, a bulky body covered in mottled brown fur, and a long head shaped much like that of a rat.

On the largest creature's back was a framed platform that held two Berruvian magi and a man in gold-embellished, beige, leather armor over a long white tunic and pants. Gold clasps at his shoulders secured a white, waist-length cape lined with smooth, brown fur. Over his head was a gold helmet crested with spiky brown fur, and he held an unsheathed sword that appeared to emit a light of its own. Aaslo thought that if anyone had the look of the world's savior, it was this man.

*"I would have looked better."*

"I'm sure you would have," Aaslo muttered.

*"You should look better. If you want to save the world, you need to look the part."*

"I'm not trying to win a battle of fashion. I need to kill monsters and magi. What do I care for appearance?"

"It's not about fashion," said a strange yet somehow familiar voice. Aaslo spun to find a woman standing behind them. She leaned casually against the doorframe with one hand on her hip. Her smile was both inviting and lethal. The woman's dark hair hung loosely over one shoulder past her waist, where her scarlet tunic stopped, and her tight breeches left her shins exposed down to her short, sensible boots. Aaslo immediately felt as though he were in the sights of a predator, and his own beast was thrilled for the looming fight.

"You," he said as his hand went to his sword hilt. "You're the one who's been trying to kill me."

The woman rolled her eyes. "Don't bother. You can't kill me, especially not with that piddly chunk of metal. You're more than welcome to try, but it would be a waste of time and energy."

"Who are you?"

"I am Sedi Tryst, and I will *eventually* be your death."

"Eventually?"

Teza gripped his hand and said, "Did you say Tryst? As in the ancient? Are you a direct descendant?"

Sedi's gaze left Teza to rest on Aaslo. "No, I *am* the ancient."

"That's impossible!" said Teza. "You'd be thousands of years old."

"I am painfully aware of the amount of time that has passed. I'm not here to speak with you, *Apprentice*. Let the adults talk."

"Hey, I—"

Aaslo pushed Teza behind him. He didn't like the way Sedi was eyeing her like she was sizing her up for a meal. "You are one of the ancients?" he said. "One of the first magi?"

"That's what I said."

"What do you want? Why are you here?"

She tapped her tip and grinned. "Those are similar questions with different answers. I am here to kill you. I *want* to talk to you."

A crash broke the air as another section of the wall fell. The echo of the shade's wail had finally subsided from Aaslo's eardrums, and he could hear the cacophony of the nearing army. "Can't you see that we are under attack? I don't have time to talk."

Sedi waved her hand in the air. "Pithor won't attack right away. He's more methodical than that. He'll want to find out how many people are here, how many are magi, how many are these undead of yours—oh, he doesn't know about them yet. He'll be so intrigued." She frowned. "Not really. He hates surprises. I almost wish I would be there when he discovers your abominations. No, I don't, actually. He's insufferably boring. It's always, *Kill this, kill that, blah, blah, blah.* He never comes up with anything original." She winked at Aaslo. "Not like you."

Teza pushed Aaslo out of the way as she stepped up again. "Can't you see? She's trying to distract you. She's keeping your attention here when you should be organizing our defense."

Sedi laughed. "Defense? Have you *looked* at that army? You can't hope to prevail. You have less than two hundred people, half of whom are already dead, and a quarter of whom are simple peasants."

Aaslo spied Ijen approaching through the empty foyer that led to the balcony. Oddly, the space had no furnishings or décor but enough windows to provide lighting. The prophet stopped at the threshold, sparing only a glance for Sedi. "Ah, I see you've arrived," he said. His casual stance and unconcern worried Aaslo.

Sedi raised an eyebrow and greeted him, her tone only slightly suspicious. "Prophet."

Teza gripped Aaslo's arm again and whispered, "You see? We shouldn't have trusted him."

*"She's right, you know. I never liked the way he carries around that book all the time like it's sooo important."*

"What are you talking about?" said Ijen. "I've done nothing."

Teza said, "You don't seem too concerned about *her* . . . or the army down there."

*"The only thing he's ever shown concern for is that book!"*

"Truly?" he said. "How do you know I'm not concerned? What you're really asking is if I'm surprised, and I'm not. I'm a prophet, remember?"

"You saw this coming?" she said.

"That's why I'm here," he said with a hint of exasperation. "But you are right. I have little concern. Nothing *I* do will change the outcome. In about half an hour, none of us will be here."

Sedi chuckled. "Prophets have always amused me. Aen became so annoying after he started having his *episodes,* as he called them. It took them forever to figure out what truly was happening."

Ijen said, "You know Aen Ledrian, the first prophet?"

"Of course. We all knew each other. How do you think we got our powers in the first place?"

Teza said, "You borrowed them from—"

"Yes, yes, we *borrowed* them from the fae, but we were with the fae for a reason."

Aaslo felt the mounting tension of the army at his back. He drew the sword at his hip and pointed it at Sedi. "As interesting as I'm sure this is to you all, it's hardly important right now. Either stand aside and let us get to this battle or you and I will have it out now."

Sedi grinned. "I told you. You can't kill me with that, but I look forward to you trying." She held out a hand to indicate he could pass but said, "I came here to inform you that I will be attempting to kill you throughout this battle. I do hope you bring something interesting to our encounters." Before Aaslo could respond, she was gone.

"Great," Aaslo muttered.

*"It was nice of her to give you a heads-up."*

"She's toying with me. I have no doubt that she'll kill me when she gets bored."

*"If we all acted like that, I'd have killed you long before we became friends."*

Aaslo stormed into the foyer. "I probably would have killed *myself*," he said as he headed down the corridor to the main room where they had left the refugees. On one wall was a public fountain, and on its opposite were the entrances to the water closets and baths. It had, apparently, been custom for visitors to the parliament to bathe before addressing the counselors. He no longer had time to take advantage of the facilities, though. The battle for survival had caught up to him *again*. Aaslo couldn't help but feel as though they'd somehow already lost. The enemy was always one step ahead. His only victory had been in damaging the evergates, and that hadn't seemed to help their cause.

"What are we doing?" said Teza as she jogged beside him.

"You heard Ijen. None of us will be here in half an hour. That means we're either dead or gone from here. If it's to be between the two, I'd prefer the latter."

*"I don't know, Aaslo. You should consider the benefits of death. You no longer require medical care, and when someone accuses you of being brainless, you can assume they mean it literally."*

"I'm not brainless, for the thousandth time. I just have different priorities from yours."

"I don't think you're brainless," said Teza. "Senseless, maybe, but not brainless. And my priority right now is to not die. You're saying yours is different?"

"No, that's why we're rounding up all these people. I'll open another pathway, and we'll get out of here."

"So, we're going to keep running?" said Teza. She pointed in the direction of the army. "That's Pithor out there. He's *here, now.* If we kill him, this can all be over."

"How do you propose we do that?"

"We can set a trap or—"

Teza was suddenly flying across the room. She landed with a splash in the fountain, and Aaslo quickly joined her. As he landed, he struck his head on the foot of the statue of the water spirit. His blood poured from his skull to turn the water pink, but no one reached in to help him. Instead, refugees screamed and ran in every direction. One man pulled Teza to her feet and helped her to vacate the fountain. Aaslo stood, wet and dazed, trying to focus on the empty air where he and Teza had previously been standing. The ringing in his ears was accompanied by harmonic laughter.

"Sedi," he growled as he stepped over the lip of the fountain.

Teza began forming a spell before Aaslo had gathered his wits. A horizontal blade of light whipped through the air. It split around an invisible barrier, then slammed into the far wall. Dust and debris were strewn everywhere, and, as the dust wafted through the air, he began to see the slight shape of a person.

"Look!" said Teza. "She's there. Aaslo, the light. It split around her. Light can't touch her."

"Okay?" he grumbled as he pressed his hand to the back of his head. He could feel the split in his scalp, but the bone was still hard, so he didn't think he had crushed it.

"That means she's using light to make herself invisible. But *you* don't need light to see, do you?"

Aaslo stared at the blood on his hand. He was unable to put his thoughts together in a coherent order. He looked up and blinked at her, trying to force the two images into one. Teza smacked his hand away and grabbed his head. He felt the tingling sensation of healing suffuse his body, then he was flying across the room again to the sound of more laughter. His body swiped a pillar and spun, causing him to strike the wall face-first. Although his head was no longer reeling, his face pulsed with hot, throbbing pain. Blood poured from his nose over his lips to fill his mouth. He spat a glob of bloody phlegm onto the floor, then pushed to his feet. His vision swam with red, and he reached up to find that his forehead was also bleeding. As blood filled his eyes, his vision began to shift back and forth between human and dragon sight. Each time it flashed red, he could see the bright yellow-orange glow of a person standing in front of him—a person who was otherwise invisible.

He tried to ignore his aching face as he pushed his vision into the dragon sight. He ducked just in time to avoid a kick to the head, and he slammed his dragon arm into her back. Sedi stumbled forward but caught herself. She immediately turned and cast a netlike web of light at him that stunned his vision and forced him back several paces. Aaslo didn't have time to think of poems and spells. He lashed out with raw power. Dark tendrils shot toward the ancient magus. She dodged, but one managed to snag her ankle. He yanked it, causing her to trip; but she severed the attachment with the swipe of a blade. The blade wasn't metal, though. It was made of light, and it seemed to have no limit to its reach.

Aaslo spied Teza a few feet away. She was unconscious, but he thought he saw her breathing. Sedi came at him with her luminous blade. She slashed and swiped as he dodged and rolled. He ducked behind a pillar, and the light burned through it as if it were butter. At that distance, he was at a severe disadvantage. On his next roll, he closed the distance and drew his sword, wishing dearly that his axe were on hand. The sword glinted in the light of Sedi's blade, although he avoided contact. If her light could cut through stone, it would surely destroy the sword.

Aaslo's blade thrust forward, stabbing at her, but she stepped back with the grace of a dancer and the laughter of a lush. The scales on the left side of his torso sizzled as Sedi's light blade swept across them. He was glad to have little feeling on that side and knew his human side wouldn't be so lucky. Aaslo instinctually raised his sword to block the light as it descended toward his right arm. His heart leapt as he realized what he had done, but it was too late. The light struck the blade and scattered in every direction like sunlight through a prism. Hundreds of tiny rainbows were cast throughout the room. Sedi's laughter abruptly stopped, and Aaslo took advantage of her shock. He pressed her, bearing down on her with a flurry of strikes and lunges. As he did so, she guarded herself with the light; and each time they clashed, Mathias's blade scattered that light in a dizzying array of colors.

"Interesting," Sedi said, and she abruptly vanished. Aaslo ran forward and, upon reaching her previous location, found himself somewhere else entirely. He was inside a corridor lined with crystals that sparkled with dispersions of light that originated from a river of luminescence filling the canal at his feet. The bare walls of the corridor were interrupted only by hanging vines and ferns. Farther down the corridor, Aaslo saw Sedi running away from him. She looked over her shoulder and appeared surprised to see him.

She turned and said, "You are so fascinating. No one has followed me here in a very, very long time."

"Where are we?" he said as he attempted to close the distance.

"You don't know? You've been here before, have you not?"

"I've never—"

"They look different, of course. These are *mine.*"

It dawned on him that he had, in fact been there. Recently. "These are the paths."

"Indeed. I didn't expect you to be capable of following me."

"You were running away?"

She laughed again, and it occurred to him that if she hadn't been his mortal enemy, he might have thought the sound pleasing. "I need not run from *you.* I was merely repositioning myself."

Aaslo took a few steps closer and casually wiped the blood from his face. He knew he looked like a true monster—deformed and scaly and covered in blood—and he hoped she found it to be at least a little intimidating.

As if she had read his mind, she said, "You are resilient, I give you that; but I doubt you're as resilient as I am. I told you. You can't kill me with your silly sword."

"You didn't think it would scatter your light either, but it did."

Sedi spread her arms wide and smiled. It appeared to be a genuine smile, almost inviting. She said, "Go ahead and try. Kill me."

"*She's taunting you.*"

Aaslo studied her warm eyes. "No, I think it's a plea," he muttered. "You want to die."

"I've been alive far longer than any human should be," she said. "Countless times, I've watched my loved ones die."

"You are trying to use me to commit suicide?"

With a mirthless laugh, she said, "If only. I cannot die."

"Then why do you serve Axus? Why help him kill *everyone* if you are afraid to lose those you care about?"

"My days of caring are long past. People inevitably die, and I am left alone. He has promised me death in exchange for my service."

"So, you would help destroy all of humanity just so you may die?"

"What do I care for humanity once I am dead?"

*"I've asked myself that question so many times."*

"You were not always like this. The histories say the ancients went searching for the power to end a devastating war. You are like this now because you cared."

She took several steps nearer him. "You could never understand," she said. "You kill me, or I kill you."

Aaslo took a step back. "I will not be used like this. If you wish to die, you should find another way."

"I will only keep coming for you. I'll come for your friends. I'll come for your family. Do you think that healer will survive losing *her* head? Perhaps the thieves will enjoy hanging from the walls of Tohl Gueron. Yes, I know where they are, *and* I know the danger they're facing. Do you?"

"What do you know?"

*"A lot more than you."*

She winked at him, then stepped through a rift in the wall that seemed to have opened on its own. Aaslo rushed after her, but the rift was already gone. He ran his hands across the wall, searching for a door or a latch, knowing it was absurd. Sedi hadn't needed a door. She could come and go from the paths instantaneously. If he were going to keep up with her, he would need to learn to do the same. The goddess Enani had told him the knowledge was inside him. He had opened a rift once. He should be able to do it again.

Aaslo closed his eyes and dug into his memory. How had he done it before? What had been different? They had been under attack, and his need had overwhelmed his sense. Perhaps that's all it was. He had a need, and he knew what he wanted to happen. Perhaps it didn't matter what he did. With his need firmly in his mind, he pushed against the wall. Nothing happened. He released an inhuman growl and slammed his clawed fist against the wall. Still nothing.

A flicker of light caught his attention. He anxiously turned expecting to find Sedi behind him and saw only the luminous river and crystals.

*"How about a swim?"*

It occurred to him that he could jump into the light and let the river take him where it would.

*"Or it may burn you to a crisp."*

Aaslo turned again to kick the wall in frustration; and the next thing he knew, he was falling. When he caught himself, he was no longer in the paths but standing over Ijen who knelt beside Teza's limp body. He quickly surveyed his surroundings, first with human sight, then with that of the dragon. Satisfied that, at least in that moment, Sedi wasn't about to stab him, Aaslo knelt to check that Teza was still breathing. He shook her as he called her name.

"Get some water," said Ijen.

Aaslo retrieved a ladle of water from the damaged fountain and carefully handed it to Ijen. The prophet took the ladle and unceremoniously dumped the water on Teza's face. She startled awake with a quick intake of breath. She struggled to sit, but her eyes appeared unfocused. Aaslo grabbed her shoulders.

"It's okay," he said. "It's me, Aaslo—and Ijen. You're okay."

Teza stopped struggling and looked up at him. After a few steadying breaths, she appeared more aware. "Aaslo? What happened? Why am I wet? Was I drowning?"

"No," Aaslo said with a pointed look at Ijen. "You have him to thank for that."

Her face flushed a little as she said, "I guess it's better than a slap." The sounds of boots striking the stone and jangling weapons were getting louder. "Help me up," said Teza.

Aaslo effortlessly lifted her to her feet and was surprised by the ease.

"Wow," said Teza as she steadied herself. "You've always been strong, but I think you've gotten stronger."

*"I'm your true strength. Without me, you'd still be planting seeds."*

"And happier for it," Aaslo muttered.

The paladin and her entourage filed into the room in a hurry. "What's happened here?" said Cherrí. "Are the Berru already inside?"

"I don't think so," said Aaslo. "It was just one. I don't think she's a threat to you for now. She's after me—sometimes. I think I can get us out of here the way we came in, but I'm still figuring out how. You may need to hold back Pithor's forces while I work on it."

"He has a great many magi, plus those creatures. What would you have us do?"

*"She is a paladin, isn't she? Put her to work."*

"How much fire can you make?"

"I don't know. I haven't tested it, but the power of Everon is great."

Aaslo nodded. "Very well. We will move our people into the back rooms and wait until the Berru breach the Vilusten. Once they're inside, you, Teza, and Ijen will set the building ablaze."

"With us inside?" said Teza. "Are you crazy?"

"With any luck, I'll have the rift open again, and we can escape without incident."

"Luck? You're depending on *luck*? If you don't get your rift open, we'll all roast to death."

"If you have a better idea, I'm all ears."

"Well, I don't know, but almost anything is better than burning to death."

"How about being eaten alive?"

"*I* like the idea," said Aria. "Cherrí will protect us from the flame."

"And if you're wrong?" said Teza.

"Then at least they won't be able to turn us into lyksvight."

Aaslo took Teza's hand. "Please, Teza. I need your help with this. We don't have much time."

Teza looked to Ijen. "What do you have to say about this?"

"I like very few of his ideas."

"Fine. I'll do it. But if I'm charred to a crisp, you'd better not turn me into a wanderer."

Aaslo raised his hand. "I promise. Now let's get everyone to the rear of the building."

# CHAPTER 23

SEDI WATCHED AS HER RIVAL CONVINCED HIS OWN PEOPLE TO SET themselves on fire—or, at least, the building they couldn't escape. His brazenness astounded her. She had been curious as to how he planned to confront Pithor's forces. In one regard, she was disappointed that he planned to run. In another, she was intrigued. He was betting all their lives on his ability to take them into the paths. Walking the paths was not easy. It had taken her hundreds of years to become proficient, and taking others through them was still a task—mostly because guests tended to wander away. Aaslo, though, had not only already opened a rift but had successfully navigated his way to his intended destination. He had even managed to follow her into her own paths. She wondered how long it had taken him to escape them. He didn't look any older than when he had entered, so it couldn't have been terribly long.

She took one last look at Aaslo and his mismatched coterie, then stepped into her paths once again. She took a few moments to check her reflection on the face of a massive crystal. She liked to show up to all her meetings with Pithor appearing unruffled and composed. She could see how it unnerved him. She considered changing into something more militaristic, then decided her present attire exuded more confidence through its sheer inappropriateness.

When she exited the paths, she was standing on the platform aback the taurini. It was an ugly beast, and slow, but vicious and nearly impossible to stop once it was moving. The magus nearest her jumped upon her appearance and nearly fell from the platform. Pithor, too, was startled, but he was more successful in hiding his shock.

"What are you doing here, Sedi?" he said, his voice still slightly choked.

"Oh, just checking in. I thought I'd see how things were going."

"Have you done it yet?"

"Done what?" she said innocently.

Pithor growled. "Don't test me, Sedi. You have orders from Axus to kill that forester."

She turned her palms toward the sky and shrugged. "Can I help it if he's so resilient?"

"Stop playing games and get it done."

"But this next part is going to be interesting. I'd rather like to see how it plays out."

"Do you think we are all here for your entertainment?"

She pondered the question for a brief moment, then said, "No, I think we're here for the gods' entertainment. I just happen to be more godlike than you."

"*You* are not a god, Sedi. Don't forget that."

"How do you know I'm not a god? I'm immortal after all."

"The gods' power is far greater than your own. They *create*. They make people and plants and animals and entire worlds. They bring things to life."

She tapped her lip and hummed for effect. "Axus doesn't do any of those things."

"He creates *death*."

"Does he? I'm not so sure anymore."

"Never mind this. What is happening with the forester?" He pointed to the Vilusten. "What are those people up to in there?"

"They aren't up to much of anything. They came here to see the parliament, and the parliament is dead. What more is there for them to do?"

"You know what I mean. What are they planning to do about *us*?"

Sedi grinned. "I couldn't say. Eavesdropping is rude."

Pithor dipped his head and pinched the bridge of his nose. "Ah, Sedi. You may have Axus fooled, but you don't fool me."

"I'm not trying to fool anyone. I've been very clear about my motivations. Axus knows that. The empress knows it. And, whether you like it or not, *you* know it."

He looked at her, and had she been anyone else, she might have mistaken his expression for one of compassion. "Believe me," he said, "if I *could* kill you, I would."

She smiled sweetly and said, "Sadly, you'll never have the chance." Then she was all business. "Now, Aaslo and his pets are trapped inside the building. Just"—she walked her fingers through the air—"send your little army in, and we'll be done with him."

"That's it? I just go in and kill him? This man who has been a thorn in Axus's side for weeks, who has eluded you at every turn, is just there for the picking?"

She spread her hands. "Yep, that's it."

Pithor turned his gaze to the Vilusten and narrowed his eyes. "Why don't I believe you?" he muttered. He looked over his shoulder and said to the magi, "Send in the lyksvight and Alterworlders."

The magi nodded, then waved their hands through the air. The army lurched forward as one, the vights and their larger cousins—the fang-toothed, long-necked rublisks—taking the lead. The vights were nasty little creatures that Sedi likened to demonic vermin. The rublisks, however, were almost majestic in a horrifying way. She had been disappointed when she discovered they couldn't be ridden because they tended to turn and eat their riders. She had been eaten before—albeit by a much larger creature—and she did not relish experiencing it again.

Sedi left Pithor's side and stepped out of the paths at the center of Pithor's army, where the less-than-dedicated new recruits were kept. A man sat hunched atop a wagon bench, his eyes empty and his face long as he stared unseeing at the rear ends of the horses.

"Hello, Bordecci."

His gaze rose to hers, and he gifted her half a smile before going back to moping.

"Bordecci, I said, 'Hello.'"

"Yeah, right, I heard ya. What do ya want?"

"You know what I want. Are you ready to start talking?"

"Bah, I can't tell ya what I don't know. Pithor's got me working on other stuff now."

"What does he have you doing?"

"Swords," he said, with a thumb toward the pile in the back of the wagon. "It's always swords. Swords are easy. They're just slabs of metal that're sharp and pointy. A smith's true measure is in armor."

"How close did you get to finishing?"

"Nearly done. Just needs a few tweaks after the fitting. Armor's got to protect a person, ya know? It's got to stop all the sharp and pointy things. The blunt ones, too. Men like Pithor, though, they only care about sharp and pointy."

Sedi smirked. "Could have something to do with the whole *kill everyone* goal."

Bordecci tucked his chin to his chest and lowered his eyes. Sedi knew he was trying to appear meek, or at least tame, but since his capture nearly a week prior, the smith had been plenty vocal with his opinions about Pithor's goals. He wasn't fooling anyone.

"Look, I know you think the world's worth saving, but we passed that path long ago. If you show me how it works, I might be able to make what life you have left a little more comfortable."

Bordecci shifted, causing the chain that was shackling his feet to the wagon to clink. He tried to stretch his legs, but the chain would only stretch so far. He sighed and hunched forward again. He said, "You wear a purdy smile, but your heart is dark and cold as ice. If hope is pointless and the living be damned no matter what, you ain't got a need of my help."

"True, but wouldn't it be interesting to at least see your work put to use?"

He raised a finger and said, "See here. That armor's to be used for protection—protection of the wearer and protection of the people, not for killin' them."

Sedi crossed her arms and rested her chin on her fist as an idea formed. She laughed, at first, then realized it wasn't so terrible. In fact, it was rather amusing; and it would annoy Pithor, which was always a pro. "What if I did as you asked? What if I turn your armor over to someone who would use it *against* Pithor?"

"I'd say you'd be lying."

"No, no. I'm serious. I am, let's say, *acquainted* with a leader—possibly *the* leader—of the Endricsian resistance. If I give your armor to him, will you tell me how it works?"

With a disdainful scowl, he said, "Why would you do that?"

"To make things interesting, of course." She waved toward the encampment and said, "All these skirmishes and battles become ever so boring after a while. It's the same thing over and over again. Wouldn't you rather have some excitement? I know I would."

"Excitement? Five days ago, I was working in my smithy by day and having dinner with my wife and kids at night. Today, my smithy's overrun with monsters, I'm chained to a wagon, my boy's been conscripted, and I ain't seen my wife and daughter since those same monsters took 'em away screaming. I'd be happy with things going back to normal and boring."

"Yes, well, I would normally say not to worry about the family. You could always have another, but that's just not the case. There won't be time. That's all in the past, now, though. You have to look toward the future."

"What future? You just want to kill everyone."

"Yes, but what kind of death would you prefer? I can make it happen. Just tell me about the armor."

"I tell ya what. You find this savior, and I'll tell *him* how it works."

Sedi tapped her lips and said, "Very well. That can be arranged."

Then she stepped back into her paths, leaving the old man gawping in her wake. As she walked, she pondered her plan. It was devious, but that didn't bother her. Nothing she did would change the outcome of the war. Somehow, she needed to get Bordecci and Aaslo together, and then she could see the armor in action. She wondered how she would get Aaslo to go with her. After all, there wasn't a lot of trust between them. Plus, he was about to roast himself and his followers in a burning building. She figured there was about a fifty-fifty chance of him being able to open the paths again. It would be disappointing and anticlimactic if he ended up killing himself. She thought perhaps she could taunt him into chasing her, thus killing two birds with one stone. She could get him to the smith and keep him from sharing the fate of his companions.

When she stepped out of the paths, it was into the sheer chaos of battle amid a raging inferno in the upper corridor of the Vilusten. She could see through a partially collapsed wall into the adjacent room that was filled with Aaslo's refugees. At the far end was the man himself. He was surrounded by anxious and terrified faces that begged for him to save them. It was obvious from his focused yet frustrated attempts to open a rift that she likely wouldn't be able to get him to follow her on his own.

A spread of orange and red stars suddenly whizzed by her from behind. One struck her squarely in the back of the head. Had she been anyone else, it would have caused her head to explode; but, as it was, she felt the same discomfort she had the thousands of times she had endured them. They were, after all, her invention. She looked to see who had projected them and found a young Berruvian sorceress preparing to cast another round. She couldn't blame the girl for striking her, considering she was presently invisible, but the sorceress could definitely work on her aim. None of the first volley had struck a target.

The Endricsians answered with a spiral of yellow light that passed her from the other direction. It picked up loose debris as it twisted, flinging it toward the Berruvians with godlike force. The sorceress was pummeled, some of the debris striking with such force that it passed straight through her body. Sedi grinned. That had been another of her spells—one she had never taught the Berruvians. The fact that it had been cast by the incompetent mage that followed Aaslo around like a lovesick puppy should have earned the girl some respect, but it didn't. Sedi snapped her fingers as another idea came to her.

She deftly stepped over and around bodies and pieces of wreckage, some of which were un-differentiable, and stopped beside Teza. She watched the young woman cast spell after spell—spells a healer shouldn't have been casting. Teza wasn't really a healer, though. She had never taken the oaths—had never even finished her education. Sedi figured the prophet must have been training Teza in the advanced combat skills she was using because there was no way the Council of Magi would have allowed an apprentice to practice them. The council bred weak magi with even weaker spells, something Sedi had ensured never would happen in Berru. It was one of the many reasons *her* progeny had retained power greater than that of the Endricsians.

Sedi took a deep breath, prepared herself for a round of pitiful protests, then reached out and grabbed a fistful of Teza's hair. The screams and flailing had been expected, but the biting was a surprise. Despite her throbbing arm, Sedi maintained her grip on the dark locks. "You're coming with me," she bit out as Teza smashed a ball of light into her chest.

"Let go!" said Teza as she swiped the air with her nails, just missing Sedi's face.

"No, and stop struggling. You'll only hurt yourself."

Sedi was surprised when Teza tackled her, causing them both to fall painfully onto the rubble that was once part of an elegant depiction of the city's greatest leaders in bas-relief. Teza sat up and straddled Sedi as she tried desperately to subdue her. Sedi, however, had the advantage of hundreds of years of training. She set her feet and thrust her hips, causing Teza to launch over her. As Sedi turned and grabbed at the girl, Teza screamed.

"Aaslo! Aaslo, she's back!"

Sedi saw Aaslo turn and look at them with one human eye and one belonging to a mythical predator. He turned toward them, and Sedi grabbed Teza by the tunic.

"Thank you," she said as she opened an unnecessarily large rift. After casting a spell to increase her strength, she thrust Teza into the paths. Once Aaslo was within spitting distance, Sedi followed. She didn't care if the girl got lost in the paths. She needed only for Aaslo to pursue her, hopefully before the rift closed and time stopped on Aldrea. Otherwise, she'd be forced to open another so that time could continue.

She found Teza sprawled on the floor of the temple path half hanging over the ledge that dropped into the river of light. "Oops," she said as she reached down and used her increased strength to pull Teza to her feet. "You're lucky you didn't fall in there. It wasn't my intention to vaporize you."

"As if you would care," snapped Teza.

"No, you're right. I don't. Once Aaslo comes through that rift, your usefulness ends."

"Is that what this is? I'm bait?"

Sedi didn't answer and instead studied the rift, as if doing so would make Aaslo appear. "What's taking him so long?" she growled.

"He won't come," said Teza. "A lot of people need his help. He's not going to abandon them."

"You'd best hope he does. Without him, you're just extra baggage."

"You're forgetting one thing. I don't need Aaslo to save me."

As she said the last, Teza cast a spell that was intended to propel Sedi at least fifty feet. Had Sedi been anyone else, it would likely have killed her since she would have impacted the wall with considerable force after only about twelve feet. Sedi, however, recognized the spell before it was cast and made preparations of her own. With her feet anchored to the floor and a shield ward to reduce the spell's impact, Sedi was virtually unaffected by the fledgling's spell.

She laughed. Teza looked at her hands in confusion over the spell's failure. Sedi said, "I've been spell-slinging for longer than most of the surviving histories. I can overcome anything you throw at me, and you should be glad of it. If you had been successful, I would be dead right now, and that rift would have closed, leaving you in here *for-e-ver.*"

Teza stubbornly lifted her chin. "Aaslo would eventually get me out."

"Darling, you'd be dead long before he found you—*if* he ever found you." Sedi huffed and said, "Don't wander off," then turned back to the rift and stepped through. She perused the chaos of the Vilusten battle. It was one that would surely have been recorded in the histories if anyone was left to record them. There was so much carnage that Sedi could no longer tell the living from the undead. Blood, entrails, and burnt masses were draped over nearly every piece of rubble, yet people continued to fight. The encroaching fire in the corridors heated the air to stifling. Without a care for the consequences, Sedi blasted a hole in the window-less back wall. She knew Aaslo had chosen the room to prevent the lyksvight from flanking them, but she thought it a poor choice considering he had not been able to open a new portal to the paths. The instant the wall burst open, hot air rushed past Sedi, and a massive, roiling ball of flame swept through the room. Those who had time to duck behind barriers screamed as the backdraft consumed the world. An instant later, the inferno had passed, and the unlucky ones cried in agony as they burned.

Sedi frowned as she realized that most of those who burned were the Berruvian magi and lyksvight since the defenders were mostly entrenched behind fallen rubble. Her actions had done more harm than good, but at least she could breathe again as fresh air infiltrated the room, subsequently stoking the fires. It was no matter. This battle would be just one of many that would ultimately end in *everyone's* death.

She finally spied Aaslo hunkered down behind a fallen chunk of the upper floor with a group of Foresightian refugees that included two men, a woman, and three children. His gaze met hers, and he shouted, "Where is she? Bring her back!"

Sedi brushed her frazzled hair behind her and said, "If you want her, come and get her."

One of the men shouted, and the woman screamed. Aaslo looked over the barricade as Sedi turned to see the rublisk thundering down the corridor toward them.

"Ijen!" he shouted. "Shield, now!"

The prophet was across the large room, guarding the horses and most of the other Foresightians, a few of whom were forced to defend themselves as lyksvight began climbing over the balcony and filtering into the hall through the hole in the wall. Sedi took a brief moment to appreciate how her impromptu actions had significantly affected the course of the battle, but her attention was quickly drawn back to the rift. The opening was beginning to waver as the portal spell started to fail. She could, of course, open another, but even she could not do so with enough accuracy to find Teza again.

"Aaslo," she growled. "It's now or never! Choose: Teza or these strangers who are destined to die anyway."

Aaslo lifted his axe and prepared to confront the rublisk that hammered against the prophet's meager shield. Without looking, he called back to her, "I won't abandon these people."

Sedi's disappointment soured her stomach against the previously alluring scent of roasted meat. *People,* she thought. *That smell is people.* The fact that she hadn't been bothered by it earlier might have been disturbing to her a millennium ago, but such details rarely concerned her anymore. Frustrated, Sedi stepped back through the rift as it sizzled out, and she sighed. She could open another, but she begrudgingly accepted that Teza was right. Aaslo wasn't going to come for her.

"So much for your boyfriend," she muttered.

"He's not my boyfriend," said Teza, a little hastily. "H-he could be, but he's not. I mean, we haven't kissed or anything . . ."

Sedi scowled at the girl. "I don't care. You'll have to do. Follow me or die here. It's your choice."

"What is your problem?" said Teza as she hurried after Sedi.

"I don't have a problem."

"Why are you after Aaslo? Why do you hate me?"

"I don't hate you. I don't have any feelings about *you.* You're boring, insignificant. The only interesting thing about you is your association with Aaslo." Sedi stopped and turned to the girl as she opened another rift. She grinned and shoved Teza through the opening. "That's about to change."

Aaslo saw the rift close from the corner of his eye during mid-swing. His axe cleaved the lyksvight's head in two, causing white blood and grey matter to splatter everywhere. The other lyksvight were not deterred, however, as they continued the onslaught. The fire that had swept the room had given them a brief reprieve, but the monstrous creature slamming into Ijen's wavering shield demanded the prophet's full attention. Lyksvight were now attacking from the front *and* rear, and Aaslo began to worry that his group would be cut off from Ijen's. A magus cast a barrier spell at the backs of Aaslo's front and center soldiers preventing them from retreating farther into the room. He knew that if he didn't do something to stop it, they would quickly become overwhelmed. He didn't have time to consider what had happened to Teza, he didn't have time to create a well-considered plan, and he certainly didn't have time to figure out how to open another rift. *Time*, he thought. He needed more time.

He sifted through the warring powers that occupied his being. He figured one of them must have an idea of how to stop or at least slow events.

Aaslo shivered in response to a chilling, deeply inviting whisper.

Mathias echoed the sentiment. *"I have time."*

"Obviously," Aaslo grumbled as he kicked a lyksvight in the stomach, then charged an older Berruvian magus. "And you have nothing better to do than annoy me."

*"You could join me. It's much more relaxing here. No chopping of anything or anyone."*

A blast of lightning knocked him from his feet, and he nearly landed on his axe. He slipped on the spilled entrails of an absent corpse as he recovered his feet. Once he righted himself, he raised his axe and charged the magus again. The old man was either too shocked or too slow to cast another spell before Aaslo was upon him.

"I. Like. Chopping. Things," he said as he wrenched the axe downward through the man's skull.

*"But, Aaslo, look around. You see them, don't you?"*

Aaslo knew to whom Mathias was referring. Reapers. They popped in and out of the battle as people fell. Aaslo had successfully snagged the souls of most of his fallen, but the Berru largely refused to join him. Still, a few disgruntled magi accepted his offer of another chance to walk the world in return for their service.

"What about them?"

*"You could go with them. Just give in, and the next thing you know, you'll be soaking your soul on the shores of a peaceful sea."*

"I thought you were on my side." Just then, the monstrous creature the size of a horse burst through Ijen's ward. It charged directly at the horses that were gathered in a sedating cloud of magic in the corner of the room. It crashed through Ijen's hastily crafted shields, and just as its fangs descended upon Dolt, a large, craggy rift opened between them.

The monster stumbled into the rift, and the portal snapped shut behind it leaving Dolt unaware and unharmed.

"You figured it out!" said Ijen with a heavy dose of relief.

"Not exactly," said Aaslo, skidding to a stop in front of him. "It just happened."

"Yes, but you can do it again."

"Are you being supportive or prophetic?"

"Both. Hurry, though. I'm nearly spent, and our numbers are dwindling—of the *living*, at least."

Aaslo released a shrill whistle, the sign to fall back to the corner where the horses were blessedly still bespelled. His group from the other side of the room made a run for it as the remaining Cartisians and Foresightian soldiers closed around them. Aaslo's undead created the final fleshy shield.

"I'm too drained to cast the shield on my own," said Ijen. "Teza was supposed to help."

"I can do it," said Aaslo.

"Are you sure?"

"Yes, I know the spell from Magdelay's teachings."

Ijen nodded, and together they cast a shield spell large enough and thick enough to encompass everyone in their party. One of the vicious, black, dog-sized creatures was trapped on their side, though, and it began tearing into the undead with abandon. It seemed to relish the slaughter. Aaslo hefted his axe, took a step toward it, and came up short as Myra suddenly appeared near the thing. She pressed her hands together as she said something that was drowned out by the reverberating screeches, snarls, and screams that filled the hall. The reaper opened her hands, and a light suddenly burst from between them toward the creature. It shrieked and writhed as the light wrapped around it and pulled it into a thin shard in reality.

*"I didn't know she could do that. Did you know she could do that?"*

"What was that?" Aaslo said. He blinked, and Myra was suddenly standing in front of him.

She said, "You need to leave. Now. Pithor is coming. You cannot face him now. He's too strong."

"I haven't been able to open the rift yet. What was that thing?"

"It's called a *vight*. That is the creature that fills the bodies of the lyksvight. They usually can't cross fully into this world, so they need bodies to inhabit. Axus must have spent a great amount of power bringing these creatures here from the Alterworld."

"Alterworld? What about the other creature that was here? The larger one?"

"Pithor rides a taurini. They're nearly indestructible. The others with the long necks are called *rublisks*. They all come from the Alterworld. In their *between* state, I have power over them. I wasn't sure it would work on one that's fully crossed over. That's not important now, though. You need to escape."

Aaslo nodded and rubbed his eyes. Most of the smoke was venting through the collapsed ceiling into the third floor; but, still, it stung his eyes and nose. "How do you do it?" he said.

"Do what?"

"How do you move distances in an instant?"

"I don't know, exactly. I suppose I *feel* where I want to be then sort of step to it."

Although Myra's technique sounded very different from what he had done, he considered that the underlying premise might be the same. Each time he had opened a rift, it had been because he'd *needed* it. His powers had somehow become unified in their intent. He needed to consciously re-create the effect. He tried to imagine a rift opening in front of him, but all he could see in his mind's eye was the blue door. He supposed it didn't matter how the portal looked, so he then imagined that he, Ina, the dragon, and the dark power all wanted to go through the door. To his surprise, the blue door opened.

"You've done it," said Myra, and Aaslo felt a chill slide over his arm where she touched him.

"Thank you," he said.

*"Good job, Aaslo. I couldn't have done it better myself."*

"*You* couldn't have done it at all," Aaslo grumbled. He turned to Ijen. "Get everyone through the door. Keep them together."

"You are not coming with us," stated Ijen.

"Not yet. I have to find the paladin and Aria. We can't leave them behind."

"I have seen two lines of prophecy here. In one, we are all lost to the ether. In the other, we are returned to Aldrea. I would rather not visit the first, so how do we bring about the latter?"

Aaslo glanced at the blue door, then looked toward Dolt. The supposedly bespelled horse was staring at him through the cloudy haze of magic. He didn't want to tell these people to entrust their lives to an idiot horse, but Dolt had somehow led them straight to the Vilusten. Dolt snorted, and Aaslo turned back to Ijen. "Follow the damned horse."

The prophet's eyebrows rose toward the ceiling. "I'm not sure I heard you right."

"You heard me. Dolt knows where to go. I don't know how, but the menace knows the paths."

Ijen started to reach for his book, then jerked as the shield ward wavered under the enemy's assault.

Aaslo muttered, "I don't know why you bother if we're all going to die anyway. No one will be around to read it."

*"Perhaps the dead can read. Have you asked them?"*

Aaslo hadn't considered the prospect. He hadn't explored much of what his undead minions could do, but he made a mental note to do just that if he ever had a chance to sit down and breathe. Aaslo's cough brought his attention back to the matter at hand. An uncharacteristically agitated Ijen led a tranquil Dolt over to Aaslo as the refugees filed through the door.

"Are you sure we can trust our lives to this horse?"

"I trust him only slightly more than a lyksvight," said Aaslo as he pulled Mathias's sword from Dolt's saddle. He abruptly wondered once again if Dolt could understand him when the horse sneezed directly into his face.

*"Huh, I don't think I've ever seen a horse sneeze."*

"You still haven't," muttered Aaslo. "You're dead."

"Excuse me?" said Ijen.

*"You sound more certain of that. Why do you keep me around?"*

Aaslo patted the sack hanging from his waist. "Dead or not, you're here, and I need you."

Ijen said, "I appreciate the sentiment, but I have to lead these people wherever it is your crazy horse decides to take us."

Although his words were light, his tone was anything but. Aaslo knew the prophet would hold this against him, but Cherrí and Aria had placed enough trust in him to go off on their own to wreak havoc on the Vilusten and therefore the Berru. It would be terribly wrong to leave them behind, and he couldn't leave the portal open for the lyksvight in the event the shield ward fell.

As soon as everyone was through, Aaslo slammed the door shut. He knew that if they had found their way, they would already be at their destination. If not, then they were lost. Such were the machinations of time. He again wished he had a way to communicate across distances. It was another item on his list of things to consider when he wasn't being bombarded by monsters. It was *not* this time.

Without Ijen there to hold his portion of the shield, it abruptly fell. Without thinking, Aaslo opened another portal, grabbed Myra, and pulled her through with him. As it closed behind them, Myra grabbed Aaslo's wrist, preventing him from letting go of her.

"You're touching me," she said. "How?"

Aaslo shook his head. "I don't know. I wasn't thinking." His gaze rose to the illuminated paths shrouded in fog beneath a quiet forest canopy. He abruptly realized he had no idea which way to go. He was without his *un*trusted steed. Then it occurred to him that he hadn't told Dolt where to go either.

Myra shivered. "I don't know if I can be here," she said. "I feel *odd.*"

"I didn't intend to go far," he said. "I only wanted to get out of the hall without being torn to bits. Do you know where the paladin is?"

"No, and I don't know where *we* are."

Aaslo looked at the multitude of paths. He knew where they were. He just didn't know how to get to where he wanted to go. He had seen the far end of the Vilusten through the hole in the wall, and it had already been ablaze. If the paladin had made it there, she might have gotten out of the building. He imagined the exit on the western wing and searched for any difference in the paths. One of the paths seemed to glow brighter than the others, and he could see a light flickering in the distance.

He pointed. "I think it's there."

*"You have to know, Aaslo. There's no room for thinking here. Ah, never mind. You don't have that problem."*

Aaslo ignored Mathias's taunting laughter to focus on the path that was slightly brighter.

"It seems miles away," said Myra. "The distance to the end of the Vilusten couldn't have been more than a hundred yards as the crow flies."

"I think that doesn't matter here. If I understood Enani correctly, we're between worlds. Time and distance don't matter here."

"Enani? You spoke with *Enani*? You saw her?"

"Yes, twice, actually. The first time was in a garden. Arayallen wanted her to show me how to use the paths. I had forgotten that time until the second time when we were in a sort of nexus in the paths. It was as if I was looking at a living map of all of them at once."

*"Look at you, cavorting with the gods."*

"We were hardly *cavorting*," Aaslo grumbled.

"So Arayallen and Enani are *helping* you?"

"I'm not sure," said Aaslo as he started down the path. "They definitely want *something*, but I'm not sure it's to help."

"It's possible. I'm not supposed to say this, but Arayallen is really upset with Axus for destroying her creations. When she's with the other gods, she acts like she doesn't care, but I've seen differently. She knows the prophecy, though. She knows there's nothing she can do that will change the outcome."

"Exactly. So why teach me to walk the paths?"

Aaslo couldn't have taken more than a dozen steps, and they were already at the end. Before him stood a blue door. Aaslo wiped his palms on his pants and secured his grip on his axe. He raised his fist to knock, and Myra grabbed his arm to stop him.

"Wait," she said. "Please, Aaslo, while I can touch you, let me give you a hug. It might be the only chance we get, and it would mean everything to me."

Aaslo's first instinct was to reject her, but the earnestness in her gaze caused him to reconsider. He nodded and opened his arms. Myra stepped into his embrace, wrapped her arms around him, and pressed her head to his chest. He could feel her shaking as though she were crying—or perhaps she was shivering, for she was cold as ice. Knowing time was not passing on Aldrea while they were in the paths, he let her have her moment. He held her until the shaking stopped, and they didn't speak after she pulled away.

He turned, opened the door, and stepped into fire—lots of fire. He raised his dragon arm against the flames, but he could feel the searing of his human side. The pain seemed muted, but he knew that if he didn't escape the inferno quickly, he would be a charred mess if he survived at all.

"Aaslo, look!" said Myra.

Then he saw that they were not alone in the fire. Cherrí was not only within the firestorm, she was its source. Aaslo turned and ran opposite her, managing to escape within five steps. Myra looked at him and gasped. His hand immediately went to his flesh that had become crisp and bubbly. He didn't want to look at himself. He didn't want anyone to look at him. The pain was meager for what he had endured, and he wondered if he had been burned so badly as to no longer be capable of feeling it.

He surveyed his surroundings. Lyksvight, magi, vights, and rublisks swarmed the area. Some were on fire. Others lay scattered in pieces across the lawn.

*"This looks like fun."*

Aria was surrounded by a short ring of fire and was struggling to hold off those who made it past the paladin. Aaslo could finally see the fiery monstrosity that had been consuming him the previous moment. The conflagration was the essence of a great serpent. Reared as it was, the beast's head rose nearly to the roof of the Vilusten. At the heart of it was the paladin encased in fire with blazing eyes and flaming hair.

"Cherrí!" he shouted, but she didn't seem to hear him. Aaslo turned to Myra just as she disappeared. He ran toward Aria, slashing through what seemed to be a never-ending stream of lyksvight and what seemed to be human recruits. Two such recruits looked at Aaslo and ran, only to be torn apart by their less-than-human comrades.

"Aria," he said as he dashed through the flames.

Her eyes widened when she looked at him. "By the gods, you're a mess. How are you still living? Or are you?"

"Of course I'm alive. Never mind that. We must get Cherrí. I can open another portal. The others are already away."

"I've tried already to get her to retreat. She won't come. Perhaps you can talk some sense into her."

Aaslo didn't fancy going back into the inferno. With any more burns, he'd have no flesh remaining. He looked down at his human hand where it gripped his axe and saw that the skin wasn't as burnt as he had thought. It gave him hope that perhaps he wasn't so ruined. The longer he stared, the less damaged his skin appeared.

"What's this?" said Aria. "I thought healers couldn't heal themselves." She looked away long enough to impale a lyksvight on her spear.

Aaslo brought his axe down on the fiend's neck before turning to the next. He said, "I'm not doing this."

"Well, there is no one else here."

He quickly devised a plan, one that he was sure to regret. Then he opened another rift. This time, it was much easier than the last. He said, "I'm going to get Cherrí. Stay here and guard the portal. If I don't return, you can take your chances in the paths or stay here and die. I don't know how long it will remain open after my death, and I don't know how you'll get back out."

Aria gave him a sidelong look. "This does not sound like a reasonable option. How about we just plan on you not dying?"

"I'll do my best," he said, then he leapt through the flames and back into the raging, viperous inferno. Aaslo wished he had a protection spell against flame. The fire bit at his skin like thousands of ants, and he hoped dearly that he would heal again if he survived. The air grew hotter as he neared the paladin. His eyes were so dry, it felt as if they were filled with paper. He looked down at his hands. His dragon scales glowed red with the heat but appeared unscathed. On the other, the skin had partially burnt away, exposing the muscle, tendons, and bones. If his face looked the same, he worried that Cherrí might try to kill him.

*"I would."*

"Cherrí," he said once he was within a few paces. Still, she did not respond as she focused on lashing out at the enemy. She danced and swayed with every movement of the serpent, raising her driftwood staff and swinging it to and fro. It appeared as if the spirit of Everon had completely consumed her.

"Cherrí," he said again as he reached out and grasped her shoulder with a scorched hand.

She turned to him, her eyes afire, her expression determined. "I see you, Dragon. Join me in this glorious destruction."

Her voice was strange, somehow larger, and Aaslo wasn't certain it was Cherrí with whom he was speaking. He said, "Come with me. I can get us out of here. Aria guards the portal."

"I cannot go," she said. "Look there." Her finger directed his attention to a point at the center of the Berruvian army. There, Pithor stood atop the nearly indestructible, house-sized taurini. *"He* is responsible for the death of my clan—for the deaths of all clans. He will pay."

"You are powerful, but you cannot defeat an entire army on your own. Even together, we could not. Come. We will fight another day."

Cherrí's face contorted into an expression of vicious contempt. "No, I will not go. Pithor will die!"

She thrust a hand toward Aaslo. A powerful wave of flaming-hot air blasted him from his feet. He landed with a crunch mere steps from Aria. He blinked up at what he presumed to be the sky and could see nothing.

"Dragon, are you alive?" said Aria.

"I think so," he grumbled, "but I can't see anything but red."

*"That's probably a good thing. You really don't want to see yourself."*

Aria said, "That's because your eye has burned away along with most of your face. The reptile one appears undamaged."

He blinked again and turned his gaze toward the chaos. He realized he was, in fact, seeing through the dragon eye. The brightly lit figures of men and creatures in varying shades of red and grey traversed his vision. He dragged himself to his feet to help Aria fend off the nearest creatures as he watched the paladin's dance with death. The magi with Pithor cast spell after spell at the viper of flame to no effect. The serpent lunged at the taurini. One of the magi fell from the beast, while the bulbous creature stomped and challenged the assault. Pithor raised his hands. In one, he held a talisman that glowed with power; and, in the other, he held a longsword. A young magus launched a cascade of spells, striking Aaslo in the side, causing him to collapse. He struggled for breath as he fell to his knees. Blood burbled up his throat and from his lips. He coughed and sputtered as he choked on his own blood. His head and chest throbbed with suffocation for what felt like an eternity. In an instant, air rushed into his lungs and after a few more coughs, he was breathing again.

The young magus's grin fell from her face as Aaslo pushed to his feet. His vision flickered, then he could see with human vision again. Her eyes widened, and he assumed from his recovery that the healing had kicked in. He bounded a few steps toward the magus, grabbed her with his dragon arm, and threw her as hard as he could. She crashed into a group of lyksvight, then was trampled by a rublisk that was rampaging unchecked. That was when Aaslo spied Myra again. She was battling the rublisk with flashes of bright light. The beast was smart, dodging, taking cover behind lyksvight, but it wasn't fast enough. One of the reapers' streams of light struck it directly in the face. The light wrapped around the creature like hundreds of grasping arms, and the beast was dragged into a rift in the air just narrow enough to consume it.

Aaslo grabbed his axe and turned back toward the bulk of the army. Pithor was responding to Cherrí's strikes with powerful bursts of his own. With each blast, Cherrí was knocked backward, but the flames grew larger. With his axe in one hand, and Mathias's sword in the other, Aaslo cut and chopped his way toward the hulking beast that carried the leader of the enemy army. He buried his axe in the taurini's leg that was at least thirty hands around. The creature jerked its leg away, then brought it heavily down, nearly crushing Aaslo. Although he had managed to heal from burns and cuts, Aaslo couldn't be sure the same would happen again *or* that he could contend with being crushed.

He grabbed hold of the axe handle and yanked it from the beast's hard, leathery skin. It came out clean without a hint of blood, and Aaslo realized he hadn't even damaged the creature.

*"That was disappointing."*

A stream of flame took care of the enemies closing on him, roasting his backside in the process. As he dodged the stomping beast, he searched for weaknesses in the typical places: the underbelly, the throat, and the eyes. All had thick folds of skin or protective bony protrusions that would make striking them difficult.

Aaslo was abruptly kicked from his feet as the creature reared away from the viper's incendiary strike. His back slammed into the ground, and he managed to roll out of the way just in time to avoid a deadly stomping. That's when he saw the fleshy, red patches of skin in the joints of each of the taurini's front legs and chest. The slits were narrow, far above his head, and difficult to access, but they appeared soft and tender, and they fluttered with each of the creature's exhales. Aaslo wished he had Aria's spear at that moment. What appeared to be some kind of gills or lung flaps could be the only weak points the monster had, and he couldn't reach them.

*"Don't be an idiot. You're a magus, remember?"*

Aaslo could have laughed if he'd had the extra breath. He knew he had power, but almost everything he did magically was accomplished with sheer luck. One magical attack he knew well was the release of the dark energy he had absorbed in the Ruriton blight. As soon as he thought it, the power surged inside him. It battered at his mental walls, demanding to be released. For once, Aaslo allowed it. Tumultuous, dark power surged from him in a tornado of inky snakes bound for the only soft flesh on the taurini. The creature inhaled the tendrils through the slits, then began coughing. Black smoke poured from its mouth and nose, and it choked on globs of the tar-like blight.

Aaslo ran from beneath the beast as it stumbled and listed to one side. When it finally collapsed, Pithor and his magus were both thrown from their perch. Aaslo was nearly buried in hard, leathery flesh. Thanks to Cherrí's incendiary serpent, Aaslo was saved from being overrun by Pithor's forces. The man, himself, quickly gained his feet, straightened his pristine uniform, and turned toward Aaslo.

"You!" he growled. "That woman will be the end of me! You should be dead already, yet here you are, a thorn in my side."

"I'm not so easily killed," said Aaslo.

*"That's an understatement. I fall on the first night, yet you just keep going and going."*

Pithor raised the talisman, a jade sphere bearing the carving of a lion's head. A light rushed down Pithor's arm to illuminate the sphere, where it appeared to be amplified to twice the brightness. Light spewed from the talisman as colorful beams in every direction. Then liquid-like black smoke suffused the sphere overcoming the light. The colorful beams turned dark like the brown-stained windows of a smoke shop. The ground began to shake and shift, and soon enough, skeletal remains and half-decomposed bodies began emerging from the dirt. Aaslo instinctually reached for the dead creatures with the dark power, summoning them to his side. They squirmed and squawked as they fought the opposing powers.

"You think to use my own power against me?"

"How?" growled Pithor. "Axus would not have blessed you. You have somehow stolen this power, and I will make sure you pay for it."

"You may try," said Aaslo as he hefted his axe and stormed the man.

Pithor dodged Aaslo's first attempt to cleave his head from his body and slashed at Aaslo with his sword. Aaslo sidestepped and was preparing for another attempt when what looked to be a long-dead cow charged them both. Aaslo realized the skeletal beast had broken free from control while they were preoccupied. After diving from the path of the cow, Aaslo lassoed it with a tendril of inky power. While he wrestled it under control, Pithor advanced on him. Aaslo quickly realized he had dropped his axe, so he raised Mathias's sword to meet the enemy's attack.

*"Now this is getting good. Stab him, Aaslo."*

"I'm trying," Aaslo gritted through his teeth. His blade met Pithor's overhead strike, and Aaslo pivoted to the left, flanking the man and placing Pithor between himself and the stubborn cow. Before the cow could trample him, though, a number of insects and rodents swarmed it. They gnawed at the beast's remaining ligaments, causing its bones to separate. As the cow buckled, Pithor attacked. Aaslo ducked beneath a slash meant to open his gullet and attempted to split the man's abdomen. Pithor dodged but was breathing heavily, and his intense concentration on both the fight and his control of the undead prevented him from foreseeing Cherrí's attack. The flaming viper struck him from above, consuming the enemy general entirely. Just when Aaslo thought Cherrí had succeeded, Pithor emerged from the flame unscathed and surrounded by a magical ward. Aaslo retrieved his axe and held it in his dragon arm's strong grip as he sheathed the sword. Cherrí screamed in dismay, and the flames separating Aaslo from the Berruvian force abruptly ceased.

As Aaslo backed away from the encroaching lyksvight, he shouted, "What are you doing? Cherrí, are you okay?"

"Take Aria and go, Dragon. Everon must have his revenge. Pithor will die by his flame."

"You cannot fight them all on your own. Come with me," Aaslo pleaded.

The viper's flaming tail abruptly struck Aaslo, casting him into the air above the battle. Burnt and with more than a few crush wounds, Aaslo slammed into the ground a few feet from Aria. He struggled to suck in a breath. Once his lungs finally expanded, he was able to sit up with Aria's help.

"Can you stand?" said Aria.

Aaslo couldn't feel his legs, and they didn't respond to any of his mental commands. In fact, he couldn't feel anything below his hips. "I think my back is broken," he said. "Hopefully, I will heal in a few minutes. I have to get back over there. She'll die if she stays here on her own."

Aria placed a hand on Aaslo's scaly neck and tilted his head toward her. Her tearful eyes held all the pain of her people as she said, "The paladin has made her decision. She will have vengeance for our people. I think, perhaps, she does not wish to survive this."

Aaslo looked up to see that a magus had turned his attention, and that of his lyksvight, on him and Aria. He made a quick assessment of the battle and found, in its futility, that Aria was right. The lyksvight sprinted toward them, and Aria began dragging Aaslo toward the open portal. He took one last look at the flaming serpent engaged in a vicious battle with the enemy general and then closed the portal behind them.

# CHAPTER 24

CHERRÍ'S HEART WAS AS HOT AS THE FLAMES THAT SURROUNDED HER. With every flutter she could hear the cries of her babes and the screams of her clansmen as the battle raged around her. She was no longer confined to that tiny trunk, though. The flames in her heart lashed out, splattering against the beasts and monsters responsible for ending her quaint but happy life. Her mind was no longer hers alone. She felt the fury of Everon pressing her every move. The purifying flames of vengeance sought every moving thing in the vicinity of the Vilusten. With Aria and the dragon gone, she no longer had to worry about containing her fury, which may have been greater even than that of Everon.

The saggy, grey cannibals; the little, black, toothy creatures; and the long-necked, horselike things weren't the worst monsters in this battle. That title belonged to the one called Pithor, the so-called Deliverer of Grace, His Mighty Light. There was nothing mighty or graceful about the abomination that took Cherrí's clan from her. As the dragon inclegantly flew over their heads, Pithor turned to her. He grinned and held his talisman aloft. A great gust whipped her flames into a frenzy, the once pristine lawn was aggravated into clumps of dirt, soil, and grass that struck her with unnatural force. As monsters closed on her from all sides, Cherrí's anger grew.

The grass was stripped away, and larger clumps of hardened dirt and fragments of rock began ripping from beneath the feet of Pithor's army. The monsters skittered, some caught by the wind, themselves, and tossed into clusters of gnashing fiends. They tumbled over each other, then turned on *her* as if they were blind to anything and everything else. Everon's flames heated, and much of the debris burned away, but as she struggled to turn her flame back toward the Berruvian general, the stronger projectiles began to penetrate her shield.

A rock, moving faster than a crossbow bolt, sliced her cheek. Another struck her in the chest. Slowly, the pain of the injury began to seep through Cherrí's rage. She pressed her fingers against the wound, and they came away bloody. With a thought, she seared the wound in flame, cauterizing the bloody leak. As soon as she was finished with one, she had another, though, and then another. Cherrí turned her attention from her own wounds back toward her target. She no longer cared if she survived. In fact, she relished the chance to join Runi and her babes in the Afterlife. She only cared that she sent Pithor to his precious death god before she went.

Cherrí took a step toward Pithor and realized her shoes had burned away. She didn't concern herself over the cuts to her feet as she stepped over fallen monsters and singed bones. As she closed on the general, her flames grew, and the whispers that had once accompanied them grew to wailing torrents. She managed to cast a whip of flame through Pithor's gale. It was caught in the whirlwind he used to protect himself, and as it swirled around him, it grew into a terrible funnel of fire that soared into the clouds. Human soldiers and lyksvight caught in the firenado were incinerated as they were swept into the sky.

Rocks continued to pummel Cherrí as she crossed the threshold of swirling flame. Once through, she was met not with calm but with a suffocating updraft. Pithor collapsed under the weight of his own lungs as they were deprived of his life's breath. His talisman fell from his hands and cracked in half upon striking the bedrock at their feet. He looked up at her as he reached for his throat, struggling to breathe. "Axus blesses me," he croaked. "You. Just. Die."

Cherrí knelt beside him, no longer cloaked in flame. Her skin, now bare, was shredded with cuts and riddled with punctures. All manner of debris clogged her wounds, and muddy rivulets of blood painted her body. She said, "I died with my clan. *Your* death was granted by the Great Spirit of Everon. Perhaps your god isn't as strong as he."

Pithor's last breath was torn from his lungs. His eyes rolled back into his head as he fell. The muscles and sinew of his neck were strained, the veins bulged through the skin of his face and hands, and his fingers and limbs curled in on themselves. His Mighty Light's death was as ugly and unremarkable as the fiends he had brought to her home.

Cherrí began to feel light-headed as she, too, struggled to breathe. The flames that were holding back the horde began to dwindle. Blood started to spurt from her wounds in great gushes, and the pain of her injuries struck her with a resounding blow that nearly claimed her consciousness.

Then it ceased. The pain was gone, and Cherrí was standing in the midst of the battle. Around her, the lyksvight, Berruvian magi, and Endricsian recruits swarmed like ants in a chaotic frenzy. At her feet lay a motionless woman in bloodstained white. She recognized herself, but her mind protested.

"It's time to go," said a gentle voice.

Cherrí looked up to see a lovely woman with long, dark hair and soft features staring at her. The woman's sleek, silky dress hugged her curves, and her bare feet and legs were exposed by a long slit in the skirt. She looked completely out of place and utterly unconcerned about it.

"Who are you?"

"My name is Myropa. I'm a reaper. I take the dead to the Sea of Transcendence, where they join the Afterlife."

"I really am dead, then."

"Yes, but you have done your world and Aaslo a great service."

Myropa nodded to a second body beside Cherrí's. It was Pithor. His bloodshot, sightless eyes stared at the sky, and no breath passed his purple lips. Cherrí thought she should feel some satisfaction with having exacted Everon's vengeance, but any resentment she felt seemed to have died with her.

She looked at the reaper. "You know the dragon?"

Myropa tilted her head. "I have heard you and your people refer to him as such. I suppose it's fitting. He was a handsome man before—well, that's no matter. Would you like me to give him a message?"

"You speak to him?"

"I do, but, more importantly, he hears me."

"I think I have said all that needs to be said in this world."

Myropa held out a small, clear sphere. "Then we go."

The next thing Cherrí saw was Runi standing over her. She said, "Cherrí, are you coming or not?"

"What?"

"We've been waiting. Our girls are eager to see you."

"Leyla and Ueni?"

"Of course, silly. Who else? Come. The others await you. Tonight, we celebrate."

"But how?"

"The beacon. You set the *sky* alight. Thank Everon we found you."

"Yes, thanks be to Everon."

# CHAPTER 25

MYROPA STOOD ON THE SHORE OF THE SEA OF TRANSCENDENCE, STARING out at the water that wasn't water as it lapped at her ankles. It did not take her as it did the souls she carried, and for that she was grateful. It was an odd feeling. For over two decades she had begged the Sea to take her; and now, when life on Aldrea was about to end, she was thankful she had not yet passed into the Afterlife. She watched as Cherrí's soul slipped into the illuminated abyss. Hers had been greeted by many others that glowed with warmth upon her arrival. Pithor had not been so lucky. Like hers, his soul had been rejected by the Sea. He was not destined to become a reaper, however. His soul was bound for Axus's maelstrom. It was a turbulent, dark place that had tried to claim her each time she visited but was, thankfully, unable. As with the Sea, she didn't know what happened to the souls once they entered the maelstrom, but she could only imagine it was terrible. She doubted it would be any better for Pithor. He may have been favored by Axus in life, but the God of Death did not abide failure.

Myropa's gaze turned to the turbulent eddy that had formed near the peninsula. The souls there were agitated, unlike anything she had otherwise seen in the placid Sea. The eddy had grown over the last several weeks, and at its center was a vortex—an emptiness that seemed to drain all the joy and serenity from the gateway to the Afterlife.

"This is the trouble of which you spoke?"

Myropa nearly fell into the surf upon hearing the unexpected, albeit glorious, voice. "Disevy, how are you here? The gods cannot come here."

"My strength is great, my dear Myropa, but even I could not, had Axus's exile endured."

"You mean he's been here?"

He tilted his head toward the whirlpool. "I think not as I am now, but he has certainly sent his power here—or, rather, he has pulled power *from* here."

Myropa balled her fists as hot anger threatened to crack the ice around her heart. "That's how he did it. He used the power of the Sea to draw the vights, taurini, and rublisks into Aldrea."

"His power has been growing with every death he claims. It does not surprise me that he was able to weasel through our ward."

"But why risk the wrath of the other gods for Aldrea?"

"This has never been about Aldrea. That little world is just a means to an end. I suspect Axus desires dominion over the pantheons."

"But he is not even the oldest. He couldn't possibly subjugate *all* the gods. Their combined power is vastly greater than his."

Disevy turned to her and brushed his warm fingers over her cheek. "Axus knows what you have yet to discern." He took her hands in his as he began to shrink to the size of a human man. He said, "Lovely Myropa, there is something I desire of you; but, for now, I cannot say it. Know that you are always in my thoughts, and promise me something? Promise me that when you understand, you will come to me without delay."

"When I understand what?"

"You will know. When you do, it is pertinent that you come to me right away."

She searched his gaze for the dominance and deception that always accompanied the other gods but could not find them. The power that suffused her previously frozen fingers delivered a soothing oath of sincerity, and she found herself falling for the power he held, not over the worlds, but over her heart.

Her mouth betrayed her sense. "I promise."

Sadness consumed his expression as he released her. "I must leave you now. You'd do well to report to Trostili before Arayallen or Axus find you. I'm afraid that in these brief moments I have enjoyed your company, events have overtaken us."

"What has happened?"

He took her hand again and kissed her fingers. He disappeared, and the emptiness of the space he had occupied seemed not only devoid of light but completely consumed in darkness. His voice, however, lingered for a breath. "Farewell, dear one—until we meet again."

After his departure, Myropa felt empty. Even the power of the souls at her feet could not compete with the chill of his absence. The icy grip spread as she considered her impending visit with Trostili. She tried to shake the feeling. She rolled her shoulders so that the ice between her shoulder blades crackled. Then she wiggled her toes, enjoying the sensual caress of souls slipping between them. Finally, she needlessly took a breath and crossed the veil into Celestria.

She appeared in the midst of a battlefield. A chaotic scene of men and women destroying each other played around her. Several soldiers wearing red tunics rushed by with a stretcher carrying half a man who was, unfortunately, conscious. Something detonated to her right, and a woman shouted orders to fall back. The woman, wearing blue, ran toward Myropa but never made it. She was exploded before Myropa's eyes, the pieces of the woman flying through Myropa insubstantially. Myropa was confused for a moment. She usually had form in Celestria—one that could interact with the things around her. Then she realized it was not she who was insubstantial. The people who fought around her were not really there. She was only slightly relieved, as it was entirely possible this was a real battle occurring *somewhere.*

Myropa didn't have to search for Trostili. He was only a few paces from her, and his voice boomed over the din of the battle. He stood head and shoulders taller than everyone around him, and he glowed with godly power. Myropa cringed. She hated when Trostili allowed his power to bleed into the space around him. It was a jarring, agitating power, completely unlike the soothing warmth and strength she felt from Disevy. The others could not see him, of course, but their hearts heard his commands.

"Reaper!" Trostili called. "Come here. Take this woman's soul. I'd like to keep it for later."

Myropa glided toward the woman, and it was only then that she realized the people in this battle were not quite human. Their eyes were larger, their lips thicker, their ears wrinkled, and their skin had a slightly pink hue.

"I cannot," she said. "I am not in their realm."

"You're not? Where are you?"

"I'm in Celestria. Are you not here?"

Trostili frowned. "Of course you are. Nothing can be easy."

He took a step toward her, and it appeared as if he were stepping from water to air, only the surface of the water sparkled golden with power. Myropa was suddenly socked in the gut with his power, and she crumpled to the ground. Trostili grunted, then abruptly pulled his power back into himself.

He said, "Get up. We don't have all day."

Finally able to move again, Myropa scrambled to her feet. The battle had disappeared, and she found that she was actually in the midst of a pool of water. Trostili walked upon the water without concern while Myropa trudged to the edge of the pool and climbed over the carved stone edge. She tugged at her dress, which clung to her legs and sent rivulets to pool at her feet. When she looked up, Trostili was staring at her with an inscrutable expression.

He seemed to remember himself and said, "What were you doing in there?"

She glanced back at the pool. "I didn't mean to. I was only looking for you, and that's where I ended up."

He stroked his clean-shaven chin. "I've never heard of a reaper doing that."

"Doing what?"

"Finding one of us in another realm. Hmm, must have been the Fates. . . ." He seemed to abruptly dismiss the subject as he turned and began walking toward his residence. Myropa followed, and they had not yet reached it when he began barking orders.

"You have several tasks. Firstly, there is a secret meeting of the Fifth Pantheon today. It is a private meeting for members only. You will distract Arayallen so she does not come looking for me."

"You want *me* to distract a goddess?"

"Yes, I know it sounds ridiculous, but I also know she has been spending time with you. I cannot ask another of the gods to do it because they will want to know why. You, however, are not important enough to know what's going on, so it will not seem odd."

Myropa tried to wrap her head around his reasoning, but it must only have made sense to the gods. She had no idea how she would accomplish what he asked. As if reading her mind, he said, "You will take her to see Olios. I have commissioned him to construct a microworld for her to play with. You may tell her it's an anniversary gift or some such."

"You have an anniversary?"

He furrowed his brow. "I don't know, but I doubt she does either, so it won't matter."

"What if she wants to come thank you for your gift?"

His laughter was completely unexpected, and, at first, Myropa thought him angry. "You obviously know nothing of Arayallen. She would never deign to be thankful. She will assume it her due."

"But what if—"

"Stop," he said, holding up a hand. "I don't have time for your blathering. Figure it out. Your second task—or, rather, your first—is to find out what Axus is planning. He is livid at the loss of his pet, Pithor. I understand you have his soul?"

Myropa held up the orange orb that dangled with the others at her belt.

He nodded with satisfaction. "Good. When you take it to him, you will remain in his company until the meeting."

"Um, aren't you allies?"

He turned and leaned down so that his eyes were level with her own. "He is being tight-lipped. You will *see* everything. You will *hear* everything. You will *remember* everything. I want to know *everything* that can be gleaned in his company. Do you understand?"

Myropa's mouth wagged soundlessly. She wanted to ask questions. She wanted to reject the order altogether. The last thing she wanted was to be in Axus's presence while he was angry. All that came out of her mouth was "Yes."

Trostili straightened and turned away. She could hear him muttering something about putting the fate of the pantheon in the hands of a human reaper as he entered his quarters. She couldn't imagine he would actually trust her with anything so important.

Myropa's fingers brushed the orbs at her belt. There was Pithor and five others. Disevy had entrusted her with the five plus one more, and she had betrayed that trust in giving one to Aaslo. She knew she wasn't deserving of the gods' trust, and she could not feel honored having it placed in her. Myropa truly could not claim loyalty to any of the gods. Arayallen wanted her to spy on Trostili, Trostili ordered her to investigate Axus, Axus expected her to report on Aaslo, and she had promised Aaslo information on the gods. Only Disevy had not asked anything of her except to care for his precious souls. Myropa would have cried had her tears not been frozen. Her desire for Disevy could not overcome her insurmountable feelings for Aaslo. What's more, she knew Disevy understood and accepted that. In that moment, the evidence of Disevy's adoration caused her feelings for him to grow, and she dearly wished she understood what it was he wanted her to know.

She shook the thought away and held the orange orb between her thumb and forefinger. She inspected the orb out of curiosity, a curiosity that had nearly escaped her over the past two decades. She marveled at how one tiny light could have such an impact on her world. Pithor had killed so many people. His life had been about terrorizing and destroying all in his path. Yet this blazing, little light appeared no different to her from any other that she had collected. It was a mystery to her how such a seemingly insignificant speck could be so treasured by the gods that they would fight over it.

The sphere clattered against the others as she released it, and Myropa stepped from Celestria into Hexus, the realm of Axus's maelstrom. Hexus was actually a subrealm—a realm within a realm. Although it technically existed within Celestria, it was an entity unto itself—one that was capable of freely holding the souls Axus claimed, not unlike a giant version of the orbs Myropa carried at her belt.

Standing on the cliff, the only entrance to Hexus, Myropa could feel the wind whipping her hair and dress but could not feel its temperature. She had often wondered whether Hexus was a burning desert of sweltering heat or a frigid gale of bone-splitting frost. She could not tell from the sight of it. All around her was darkness, but it was not like the black vastness of the heavens. It felt stifled, as though she were in the theater of a grand cave, only it was too dark to see the walls. The cliff upon which she stood was the only ground to be found, for the cave both descended and ascended into infinite, lightless depth. At its center was a tumultuous maelstrom of crackling power mixed with what looked like enormous serpents made of ash. The ashy tendrils continuously ebbed and flowed, twisting into themselves, while crackling bolts of lightning streaked from between them to briefly illuminate chunks of black, crystalline masses suspended unmoving around it.

Myropa felt a tug toward the maelstrom, and she knew it was once again trying to claim her. As usual, it was not strong enough to move her from the small sliver of rock upon which she stood. From its center, Axus emerged. He floated toward her, erupting angry power that felt strong enough to drive the entire maelstrom. His eyes glowed a golden orange, and the light that surrounded him nearly blinded Myropa to his practically naked form.

Axus's feet settled on the ledge next to her, and had he not pulled back his power, she might have crumbled into the abyss. As it was, she found herself barely able to speak or look at him.

"What are you doing here?" he boomed.

The obscene volume of his voice grated against her ears. "I've brought you a soul," she managed as she held up Pithor's orb.

A bolt of lightning snapped out of the god toward the maelstrom as he unleashed his anger. "Pithor. That . . . that . . . *human*," he growled, as though *human* were an epithet. "One cannot trust a *human* to do anything right, even one blessed with my power. I knew it the moment he failed, but I know not how he died."

An uncomfortable few seconds passed before Myropa realized it was a question. "He, um, he was killed in battle. A paladin blessed by Everon killed him. She died as well."

"A paladin? Everon? What is Everon?"

"I don't know," said Myropa. "I saw a serpent of fire."

Axus balled his fist and slammed in into the rock beside her, causing it to fissure so far above her that she could not see its end. "Trostili. He has betrayed me. I did not realize he was capable of bestowing such power."

Myropa hadn't considered that Trostili might be behind the paladin's power. Even after Axus had said it, however, it didn't feel right to her. She was not about to argue with Axus, though, so she kept her mouth shut. Axus narrowed his eyes at her with suspicion. Then he waved over his shoulder.

"Cast his soul into the maelstrom and follow me."

As she had suspected, Pithor was not to receive the godly rewards he had been promised. Instead, he would suffer Axus's wrath until such time that he was released. She had never been summoned to collect a soul *from* the maelstrom.

Myropa did as Axus bid and rid herself of Pithor before following him out of Hexus. The exit opened into a juxtaposed scene of beauty. Massive white, pink, and grey crystals—larger even than she—shimmered with specular and labradorescent light all around her. In the air were droplets, like chubby rain frozen in time, and each glistened with a rainbow of colors. As she passed through them, they tinkled to the ground to join their brethren in colorful ripples and dunes of sand. Some of the droplets stuck in her hair and to her clothes so that she carried their prismatic colors with her.

Axus stopped beside a rectangular clearing of level sand. A few smooth, opalescent boulders were placed within the clearing with intent, and the sand had been raked into intricate designs around them. Axus removed his sandals, a seemingly pointless action, since his feet still did not touch the ground. He hovered above the sand to sit upon one of the boulders. He crossed his legs so that his loincloth barely covered the parts she dared not observe, he laid his hands on his knees, and he looked at her expectantly.

Myropa shifted uncomfortably under his gaze. She didn't know what he expected of her, and she feared angering him by not providing it.

Eventually, he said, "You serve Trostili."

Again, she wasn't sure it was a question. She answered anyway. "Yes."

"Tell me what he is planning."

She was surprised that Axus would even consider that Trostili might take her into his confidence. "I don't know anything."

"No? You have spent time alone with Disevy. What are his thoughts on my assault on Aldrea?"

"Um, I don't know that either. He hasn't said."

She could see by the clenching of his jaw and hardening of his gaze that he was becoming angered, and she dearly wished he would ask a question she could answer.

"I know you have spoken with Trostili's pet forester. From where did he get his powers?"

Relieved, she said, "From a fae named Ina."

"Yes, I know about that. I mean his *other* powers."

"Well, I think maybe he got some of the dragon's power when he was fused with it."

"No, a dragon cannot do what he does. He has been stealing my souls. How?"

Again, Myropa was struck with an inability to answer. "I-I can only speculate—"

"Then speculate," he snapped.

"F-from you."

The sand in his rock garden suddenly erupted in a storm of fury. When it settled again, the lines it formed were jagged and disjointed. He shouted, "I did *not* bless that wretched human!"

Myropa wasn't about to say that she thought Axus's power of death had somehow been hijacked from *her* when she fell into Ina's transfer of power. Axus would be angry with *her*, and it wasn't her fault. After all, it had been Arayallen who had pushed her. Myropa had considered the incident to be an attack—or possibly a joke—on *her*; but, considering all that was happening between the gods, she now wondered if Aaslo's acquisition of Axus's power had been Arayallen's intention all along.

Myropa's thoughts were interrupted when Axus said, "What is my brother up to?"

"Up to?" she said. She hoped that if his question were more specific, she could avoid answering.

The lines in the sand began migrating into swirls around the god as he adorned the appearance of intense concentration. He balled his fist and said, "They are all against me. They hope to keep from me what is due. All these days they've been expending power, never concerning themselves over the loss. Can they not see it is in everyone's best interest that I reclaim it?"

Myropa anxiously stared at him, hoping it was a rhetorical question. Unfortunately, it appeared, by his burning stare, that he expected her to answer.

She hedged. "I could not say what the gods think."

"No, of course not. You would crumble under the intense complexity of our thoughts. You hear things, though. What has my brother said?"

"Um . . . that he desires a drawn-out war."

"I know that!" he growled. "What else?"

"I-I haven't spent much time with him. I've been busy gathering souls on Aldrea."

"I am well aware of that. You claimed my general. It's tiresome to train these human pests. Could you not have returned his soul to his body?"

She shook her head. "Oh, no. His body was badly damaged. It could no longer sustain life."

"I doubt you would have had you been able. You have been to the Sea recently?"

"Yes, I have delivered many souls."

"What does it look like?"

"It, um, has a massive whirlpool—a void."

"Then it is obvious. Have you mentioned this to Trostili?"

"No, he hasn't asked."

"Good. You'd best hope he doesn't. I will hold *you* responsible for the discovery."

"Me? But there are other reapers—"

"Only *you* serve Trostili."

"Yes," she said, fully aware that she had crossed into new territory by arguing with the disagreeable god. "I serve Trostili, and I cannot keep things from him if he asks."

"No, but why would he ask you anything unless you give him cause to? You are only a reaper—and a *human* reaper at that. You know nothing." He paused, then slid her a suspicious look. "Have you ever been in the pantheon vault?"

"I don't think so. I didn't know there was a vault."

"Only the oldest have access to it. You will get Disevy to take you there. Something is stored in the vault that I want. Figure out how to get it."

Questions and concerns swarmed Myropa's mind, but one stood out. "What is it?"

"I'll tell you once you know how to get in."

"Why would Disevy tell *me* how to get into the vault?"

"Do you think I am blind? It's obvious you have him wrapped around your finger. It's truly pathetic. I would never have thought that any of the gods would stoop so low as a human reaper, but Disevy least of all. It's just as well that he should be unseated." He stopped as though he had said too much, then said, "I have not seen him in days. No doubt he has been spending all his time with *you*. Just—tell him you want to see something shiny or whatever. I'm sure he'd love the chance to brag." With a wave of his hand, he said, "Go, begone from my sight."

Myropa felt herself being pushed from his home with urgency. She gathered her thoughts and power quickly lest she be propelled to a random location against her will. Her next step took her to the hall of Arayallen's lifeless menagerie. The goddess was standing on the squishy cloudlike floor and staring into a vacant display pod. She turned and saw Myropa approaching.

"Oh, it's you. Have you found it yet?"

"Found what?"

Arayallen snapped at her as though they'd been discussing the subject at length. "My stolen prototype. The *wind demon*."

Myropa had forgotten about the creature. She quickly thought back to her most recent experiences on Aldrea, particularly those with Aaslo, and came up blank. "No, I haven't seen it—or, um, figured out what it looks like."

"I don't like this at all," said Arayallen. "I'm sure it was Axus. There's no telling what he's using it for, but I'm sure your little dragon friend will receive the brunt of it."

"You mean Aaslo?"

"Do you know any other dragons?"

"But he's human—"

"If you paid attention, I think you'd find that he is less so by the day." She must have seen Myropa's alarm, because she added, "No, he won't completely change, but the dragon's composition is dominant over that of a human, as is its power and will. Let's hope Aaslo has acquired enough alternative power to compete."

"Is that why you pushed me into Ina's stream?"

Arayallen's smile was both innocent and malicious. "Did I? I don't recall." The smile dropped. "You need to find the wind demon."

"I really don't know how." Myropa remembered she was supposed to be distracting Arayallen. "Perhaps you could help me search?"

The goddess frowned at her. "Me? Help *you*?" She leaned down into Myropa's face and pressed her finger to Myropa's chest. "Remember that *you* are helping *me*." The goddess straightened, glanced back at the empty display, then said, "Let's go. This is very important." She waited a few seconds. "Well?"

"What?"

"You're my ride," said Arayallen. "Let's go."

"Oh! Where are we going?"

"To Aldrea, of course. We'll start with the forester. If Axus is responsible for this, the creature will be in play where it's important."

AASLO WAS CERTAIN HE HAD FOUND THE CORRECT DOOR. HE KNEW IT WAS so because he had managed to step in what was probably the only large, steaming pile of horse dung in the paths. He looked back at Aria, who had certainly seen better days. She leaned against a tree, appearing completely spent. Her eyelids were droopy, her wounds were angry, and her tongue frequently and ineffectually swept over cracked lips. Aaslo imagined he didn't look much better, but at least his wounds had healed on their own.

*"So far as looks go, your wounds were the least of your worries."*

Aaslo ignored the jab. He could barely have spoken anyway, and Mathias's taunts were hardly worth the trouble.

*"I'm the chosen one. I'm the only trouble worth enduring."*

"Arrogant much?" Aaslo croaked. He tried to swallow, but his tongue stuck to the roof of his dry mouth. They had been wandering the paths for what felt like days and had concluded that no bodies of water existed there. The trees weren't even real but figments of his imagination. As Enani had indicated, they were in a living metaphor, and he understood how people could easily die inside it.

Aaslo was hesitant because the door was already open, and it emitted darkness that glowed around the edges. It was ominous, and he began to question his conclusion that the dung belonged to Dolt. Was it possible that another ornery, frustrating, idiotic creature walked the paths?

*"Yes, it's you."*

"You may be right," Aaslo grumbled. "No one else would be stupid enough to drag you along for the ride."

"You're hardly dragging me," said Aria. "I've held my own. And what am I right about?"

"I think we've finally found it," Aaslo replied.

"I knew we would," said Aria as she reached out for him. She barely shivered when he grasped her hand with his claws. She pushed away from the tree and gripped his hand tightly as they prepared to step into the unknown.

They stepped through the doorway and became weightless—or, rather, groundless. Although they fell only for seconds, the impact was a painful reminder that walking the paths was unpredictable and dangerous. Aria screamed, and Aaslo looked over to find that her leg was bent where no joint existed. She cried out again as she tried to sit up, but Aaslo pushed back onto the flat roof.

"Don't move," he said. "You've broken your leg badly."

She whimpered and blinked away tears as her gaze sprinted around her. "Where are we? What is *that*?"

Aaslo followed her gaze to the sky directly over them. About fifteen feet up was a massive, jagged tear in the sky. Bursts of energy swirled around it, and as he watched, a scarlet, winged creature emerged. Aaslo recognized the raptor as one that had been following them in the paths.

"I think it's the rift in the paths."

"Why is it up *there*?" she growled. "And why is it still open?"

"I don't know," he said. "I didn't open it. It looks like we're on a roof. I can see the tops of a lot of old buildings. I'll investigate. Stay there."

With a whimper, she said, "I'm not going anywhere."

As she leaned back and began taking deep, steadying breaths, Aaslo approached the edge of the roof. Sure enough, they were in a city—an old one—and within it raged a battle. Peering over the edge, Aaslo could see people below on the street. They were barricaded behind a pile of stone rubble and broken wood. Although he didn't recognize the people, the uniforms on a few of them were familiar.

*"Hey, your buddies are here. What luck!"*

Aaslo snagged the broken spear Aria had dropped in her descent as he hurried back to her.

"We've found Dovermyer," he said as he knelt beside her.

She groaned in pain. "What is Dovermyer?"

"Well, Dovermyer is a city, but not the one in which we are presently located. I was actually referring to the Marquess of Dovermyer, or rather, his soldiers."

"Fantastic, I can die among humans," she said just before he shoved a leather glove into her mouth.

"You're not going to die. I'm going to set your leg and bind it to the shaft of your spear. Take a deep breath."

If the enemy wasn't aware of their location before he set Aria's leg, they surely would be afterward. He could hear shouts of men alerting each other to their presence. He knew it would be a matter of minutes before they came to investigate, and he hoped Aria came to before they arrived.

When he was finished securing her leg, Aaslo patted her face to no avail. He looked up as two men reached the roof via a set of stairs on one side of the building. One man trained a crossbow on him, while the other approached with a shield and sword. Unfortunately, Aaslo didn't know the men, nor did they wear the marquess's colors.

"What were you saying about luck?" Aaslo muttered to Mathias.

*"Oh, please. You always want things the easy way."*

"Before you, I didn't even know there was an easy way."

*"There was no before me. You're only a year older. You've been blessed with me your whole life."*

"Until now."

The two men closed to within twenty feet of him and Aria.

"What is it?" said the crossbowman.

"I don't know. Kill it," said the swordsman.

Aaslo hit the ground, barely avoiding the bolt. He rolled to his feet and shouted, "Stop! I'm with the marquess. I'm on your side."

"The monster speaks," said the crossbowman.

"Reload," replied the other.

"My name is Aaslo. I'm a Forester of Goldenwood. I'm not your enemy."

The first slightly lowered his crossbow and looked at Aaslo quizzically.

"Don't listen to him, Adok," said the swordsman. "He doesn't look anything like a forester."

"You've seen a forester?" said the crossbowman apparently named Adok.

The swordsman said, "Of course not, but I don't imagine they look like *that*. I heard they were like monkeys or some such. He doesn't even have a tail."

"Foresters don't have tails," Aaslo growled, much to Mathias's amusement. "We're not monkeys. We're just men and women."

"If that's true, then you ain't one," said the swordsman.

"No, Mink, look," said Adok. "In the stories Dovermyer's people tell, the forester is part lizard."

"I thought it was a dragon," said Mink.

"Right, well, he fits the bill," said Adok. "I don't imagine there's *another* dragon-man running around here."

"You never know in this place," said Mink.

"Good point," said Adok, raising his crossbow again.

"Men, listen to me," said Aaslo, slowly raising his hands. "This is Aria of Cartis. She's badly injured and needs help. I know the marquess has a field medic."

"Where's your healer?" said Adok, pointing the crossbow at him. "The forester travels with a healer."

"She was taken," said Aaslo. "I believe the rest of our people came here through a portal. It's just Aria and me."

"He's right, Mink. The others came through yesterday, didn't they?"

"Aye, they did, but not through *this* rift. Either way, it doesn't mean he's with them."

"Just find the marquess or Ijen. They'll tell you."

"We ain't got time for that," said Mink. "In case you didn't notice, we're at war. The damned lyksvight have overrun the city, and the natives are restless."

"What natives?" said Aaslo. "I thought Tohl Gueron was long abandoned."

"It was. But *things* have been coming through there for who knows how long," said Mink, pointing toward the massive rift with his sword. He finally sheathed the sword and came over to inspect Aria. "Let's get her inside," he said. When Aaslo didn't move, he looked up and said, "I figure if you were going to try to kill us, you'd have done it by now. We don't have time for anything else."

"Is it that bad?"

"Our numbers ain't a tenth of what they got, and they're vicious. If it weren't for those undead—"

"The wanderers," said Adok.

"Right, the *wanderers* and that magus who came through the portal, we'd have been done for by now."

Aaslo caught movement at the corner of his eye and tensed. Once he saw who it was, his muscles relaxed, but only a little.

"Not now, Myra. She's not going to die. I'm getting her help."

"I'm not here for her," said the reaper.

"Who for, then?"

"No one at the moment."

"You have a message?"

Myra glanced to her side, but Aaslo saw nothing that might have caught her attention. Then she turned back to Aaslo. "Um, not exactly. I was just wondering if you've encountered anyone or anything new lately."

Aaslo looked around. He motioned to the woman at his feet, the men on the roof, a strange creature in the sky, and then toward the sounds of battle in the distance. "Take your pick."

Aria started to rouse. She jerked when she saw the strange man standing over her and then jerked again when her gaze landed on Aaslo. Aaslo couldn't help but wonder if people were going to react that way upon seeing him for the rest of his life.

*"I think it's an improvement."*

"Your kindness knows no bounds," Aaslo muttered.

Mink said, "Nobody's ever accused me of excessive kindness. It's really a matter of necessity. Everybody counts."

"I'll not be much use now," said Aria.

"Your arms still work, don't they? You can use a bow? Or, at least, a crossbow?"

"Of course. I'm a Great Oryx."

"I don't know what that means," replied Mink, "but if it means you can kill lyksvight, I'm glad to help."

"How are we gonna move her?" said Adok.

"You keep that crossbow ready, and he and I can carry her."

"No," said Aaslo. "Ready your sword. I'll carry her." He carefully lifted Aria, and she buried her screams in his chest. "I'm sorry," he said. "Hopefully, we'll not need to move you far."

"It's just below us," said Adok, "but there's a lot of stairs and plenty of monsters."

"Give me the crossbow," said Aria. "You have other weapons, and I can cover our backs."

When they reached the stairs, what looked to be a giant salamander with slimy yellow skin and purple eyes was blocking the way. Although it was the size of a barrel, it didn't look particularly dangerous.

"Stay back," said Mink. "Don't let it fool you. That goo that's oozing from its pores is a powerful toxin, and it can project the stuff up to three feet."

"Is that so?" said Aaslo. He muttered a spell under his breath and released the tiniest amount of power. The salamander ignited, releasing the acrid smell of fever sweat as the mucus cooked. The creature squirmed wildly and fell from the stairs into a cluster of lyksvight in the street below. Upon impact, it burst, spewing flaming slime over the mass and igniting them as well.

Mink and Adok both looked back at Aaslo, appearing to have realized that could have been their fate had he been the enemy.

"Don't look so surprised," said Aria. "He's a dragon."

"I'm a man," growled Aaslo as he started down the stairs.

Aria's whimpers with each jarring step were mostly drowned out by the rising din of the battle that raged in the streets. Aaslo could finally see that the fight was not just between the Endricsian humans and Berruvian lyksvight but also between the strange creatures that infested the city and *everyone*. Mink led the way toward the blockade that protected the entrance to the building, Adok guarded their flank, and Aria kept her crossbow trained behind them as she watched over Aaslo's shoulder. In the fifteen paces it had taken them to reach the door, they had each taken down at least one threat.

As they entered the building and made their way through the groups of injured and resting, Aaslo's appearance elicited plenty of stairs and a generous helping of suspicion. The marquess's people who were already acclimated to him, and those who credited him with saving them from the blight reassured the newcomers that he was friend and not foe. In fact, many looked upon him with hope and reassurance, which somewhat soothed the sting of distaste from the others.

*"I never knew you to be so vain."*

"I'm not vain," he said. "I'm just uncomfortable with people."

"Get used to it," said Aria. "You're in the thick of them now."

*"You care more for their judgments than you admit."*

"I don't care for their judgment, only that they won't stab me in the back."

Aria huffed a pained laugh. "Few of them have the courage to approach you, much less try to stab you."

"Aaslo! Aaslo, it's you," called Mory with a joy-filled greeting and bearing a full waterskin. "I'm so glad to see you. You won't believe what's happened. I'm a hero and Peck is, too. If not for us, everyone would be dead. We wouldn't be here now." He looked at Aria, and his eyes widened. "Oh, she's hurt. Come over here. There's a place for her by the fire. Where's Teza? I'll be right back. I'm getting the medic."

Then he was gone, and Aaslo was finally freed from the weight of the woman. He was surprised that she was as light as she was, considering her height and strength.

"What?" said Aria after she had her fill of the fresh water.

"Huh?"

"You're staring at me."

"Sorry. I was marveling at my lack of fatigue. You're very light," he said as he took the waterskin.

"I'm not light. You're just strong."

Aaslo flexed his dragon arm, then looked at his human one.

*"Love yourself much?"*

"I wasn't being vain," he mumbled. "I feel different."

"Have a seat," said Aria. "We've been run ragged for days. You need a rest."

Aaslo scratched the scruff on his jaw and said, "I'm not sure that I do. I don't feel tired."

Aria released a husky, strained laugh. "That's the sleep deprivation talking. Now sit down before you fall flat on your face."

*"By all means, please keep standing. I'd pay to see that."*

"You wouldn't pay to see anything. You're dead."

"I most certainly am not, and I forbid you from planting me in the grave prematurely."

Aaslo glanced over to Myra, who had followed them from the roof and was hovering in his peripheral. He spoke loudly enough for the reaper to hear as he said, "No, you're not dead, and that's how it's going to stay."

"What are we looking for?" said Myropa.

Arayallen scanned the crowd. "It should be someone or something who has joined Aaslo since he garnered Axus's attention."

"But there are hundreds of people and creatures here. It could be any one of them."

"I will know it when I see it." Arayallen wasn't about to let Myropa appreciate their relative silence as they stood watching the crowd. She said, "Why does he call you *Myra*?"

"I told him that was my name. It's not a lie. My father called me that when I was young."

"Then he doesn't know?"

"No. I don't know how to tell him. I don't know if I want to."

"Why not? The fact that the Fates granted you this opportunity must mean something."

"What if he hates me?"

"Maybe he does, maybe he doesn't. You put yourself in this position. He deserves the truth."

Myropa was once again reminded of the terrible consequence of the last choice she made in life, and her shame could not be measured. She risked a glance at Arayallen, knowing the goddess's expression would hold only disdain and resentment for Myropa not appreciating her gift. Arayallen wasn't paying attention to her anymore, though, and her expression had nothing to do with Myropa. Hot anger suffused the goddess as she stared into a crowd of soldiers and refugees. Myropa tried to see what had captured the goddess's attention, but Aaslo's horse abruptly stirred everyone into a tizzy when he grabbed a chamber pot and began bobbing his head such that its contents sloshed over the lot of them.

"I have seen enough," hissed the goddess. "Their machinations go deeper than even I could have conceived. Disevy failed to rein them in, but they will not get away with this." She turned to Myropa, the wetness in her eyes speaking not only of pain but of betrayal. "You may tell Disevy, when next you see him, that the Fourth Pantheon is at war with the Fifth."

"But what of Trostili?"

"What of him?" Arayallen snapped.

"You love him."

"Those we love cause us the most pain. Remember that and know that your Aaslo is now at the heart of the gods' war."

Arayallen abruptly disappeared, and Myropa was left standing at a loss. She still had no idea who was the wind demon.

# CHAPTER 26

ALTHOUGH HE HAD ONLY BEEN SITTING FOR A FEW MINUTES, AASLO WAS becoming restless. He looked over at Aria and said, "They'll take care of you. I need to get out there and see how I can be of use."

Aria lay back against a pack. "Thank you. You're not as bad as I'd thought."

*"It's good for you the bar is set so low."*

"You're probably right," said Aaslo.

"Don't let it go to your head," replied Aria.

When Aaslo turned around, Dolt was standing behind him breathing into his face and looking none the worse for wear. Aaslo took a step back. "I see you made it out of the paths. I suppose I should thank you." Dolt merely stared at him as a horse might do.

A man behind him said, "Did you strike your head? You do realize you're speaking to a horse."

He recognized the voice. It was a man he would have been pleased to never see again. "Captain Lopin," he said without attempting to disguise his tone.

As Aaslo turned, the man's eyes widened. "I had heard you were changed. It's worse than I'd imagined." A pleased grin crossed his face, and he added, "I imagine Queen Kadia will not be so thrilled to see you now." Aaslo's gaze quickly roved the onlookers. Lopin lifted his chin and said, "She's on the other side of the hall."

"The queen is *here*?"

"Indeed. We met up with Dovermyer's convoy outside Tyellí while the city was overrun. The Berru came through the evergate after those accursed magi abandoned us. Rakith and the other princes held them off long enough for Prince Elirus and me to get the queen and the babe out of the palace. Elirus fell in our escape from the city."

"What babe?"

"Esmira, the girl-child of the king's consort. She went into labor during the assault. It was a difficult labor, but she might have lived under other circumstances."

"The queen is caring for the king's mistress's baby?"

"That's the right of it. Kadia has a big heart."

"You're on a first-name basis now?"

He grinned again. "Much has changed since last we met."

"The king is dead, then?"

"Indeed. He may have lost his nerve upon our failure to overcome the prophecy, but he went down fighting in the end."

"As captain of the royal guard, you've taken command of our forces?"

"No, the marquess has that under control well enough. My duty is to Kadia and Esmira now. I've not told the others who we are. If they knew what's left of the royal family was among the refugees, it would only upset things."

Aaslo stepped around the man and said, "Then you'll have nothing to say about my getting on with trying to save the world, then."

Lopin gripped Aaslo's arm as he tried to pass. He said, "You will say nothing."

"I don't care what you or the queen do. Fight or die."

Lopin nodded, handed Aaslo a wad of dark blue cloth, then walked away. Aaslo unfurled it to discover that it was a sleeveless tunic, the kind that was typically worn over another shirt. He had forgotten his half-naked state and had truthfully been unconcerned with it considering the dire circumstances. In fact, he contemplated storing the tunic until after the battle since it was unlikely to survive. He pulled it over his head anyhow, careful not to snag it on his scales and claws. Then he took Dolt's reins and walked toward the exit.

When he arrived at the barricade, Peck was waiting.

"Aaslo, I heard you were back. You have no idea how relieved I am. They put me in charge over here. Can you believe that? They've lost their minds."

"Mory said you saved them."

"Delayed the inevitable is more like it. The marquess went with most of the men to the front wall and are holding back the bulk of the lyksvight. Magus Ijen is on the south side dealing with the smoke dragon."

"Smoke dragon?"

"That's what everyone is calling it. *Wasp-monster* seemed more accurate, but it didn't catch on." As if to punctuate the point, an explosion rocked the city from the south. "Mory and I accidentally released the smoke dragon from an amphora. There's an amulet with a red stone that seems to control it, so we gave the amulet to one of the Berruvian magi."

"Why would you give control of the creature over to the Berru?"

Peck shook his head. "No, not like that. The smoke dragon goes after whoever's blood is in the amulet."

"I see. Where am I needed?" said Aaslo.

Peck looked at him as if surprised. He said, "Everywhere."

Nearly an hour later, Aaslo had made his way through a constant flow of strange creatures and lyksvight toward the front wall. Although saving lives was his primary goal, he knew he needed to find a way to claim the dead before the Berru turned them into lyksvight. He hadn't yet worked out the method, though, and it seemed he never had a chance to sit down and ponder it.

*"It's too bad you can't stop time."*

"Why quit at stopping time? It would be better to turn it back. I could prevent any of this from happening."

*"Are you distressing over what might have been?"*

"Foresters don't waste time on such frivolities. I was only responding to what you said."

*"Not really. What I said was realistic."*

"Realistic? How is stopping time real—" Aaslo nearly smacked himself in the face. Of course stopping time was possible. He had already done so several times. Each time he stepped into the paths, he stepped out of time on Aldrea.

Aaslo was roused from his self-reprimand when the hairs on the back of his neck stood on end. He had the feeling he was being followed. He led Dolt to one side and stopped just inside an alley. The wily horse nuzzled his hair as he waited for the soft shuffle of footsteps to grow closer. Aaslo ensured that his grip on his axe was secure, then abruptly rounded on his pursuer. The man didn't flinch. He didn't shout, run, cower, or attack. He simply stared at Aaslo with glowing green eyes.

"Shade," said Aaslo with a sigh of relief. "What are you doing here?"

The shade opened his mouth soundlessly and pointed at Aaslo.

*"Perhaps he wants to kill you."*

Aaslo scoffed. "That's his way of announcing it ahead of time? No, I think he wants to help me."

*"The pragmatist has become the optimist. It's your funeral."*

"There you are!" called a man.

Aaslo looked to his right and saw the marquess hurrying toward him. He said, "Greetings, Lord Sefferiah. It's good to see you alive."

"Alive or dead seems to matter less and less these days." He eyed the shade with suspicion and said, "Those who are gone aren't truly gone, and those still here will be gone soon enough."

"You didn't used to be so morbid."

"We came here hoping to find sanctuary, and it seems the city itself is trying to kill us. We're about to lose the gate. The Berru have already breached the walls in other parts of the city, as you well know, and nobody will be sending reinforcements. We're exhausted and out of time."

The marquess swiped a hand down his weary face, and Aaslo noted the signs of fatigue and sleep deprivation. It occurred to him that he hadn't slept in two days, yet he wasn't particularly tired. He had gone without food for much of that time as well. He wondered about the last time the marquess had sustenance and concluded that if any of his people were to survive, they would need rest and nourishment.

A piercing cry that sounded like metal scraping over rock resounded through the air over their heads, and the marquess pulled Aaslo back against a building. "It's returned!" he said.

Aaslo had no need to call Dolt to him. The horse had shoved open a door nearly in a panic and gone inside what looked to have once been a home. Aaslo turned back to the marquess. "It? What is it?"

"The smoke dragon. I don't know what it really is, but it's massive and it flies. It showed up in the city, then started attacking the Berru. I didn't get the full story from the scouts. It attacks anything that moves, though, Berru and Endricsian alike. It spews a horrible, choking smoke that melts the skin. The prophet had gone to contend with it. I hope this does not mean he's fallen."

"Ijen will outlast all of us," Aaslo growled.

He looked up just as a sleek, bluish-black creature passed over their heads. Its body had three lens-shaped segments, each with a pair of thin legs ending in a single claw. Long, insect-like wings tipped in spikes held it aloft, its head ended in a long, toothy snout, and a whiplike tail extruded from the rear. It looked like a cross between a wasp, a rat, and a snake.

*"It's your worst nightmare. Just say it's your worst nightmare."*

"So, we must deal with that in addition to the lyksvight and magi," said Aaslo. "Perhaps if we can keep its focus on the lyksvight, we may have a reprieve."

"So far, we've been fortunate. It's largely focused on them. How do you intend to keep it that way?"

"I don't know. You said it's attracted to movement. I wonder how it sees."

"I would assume with its eyes," said the marquess.

"That's not what I mean." He pointed to his dragon eye. "I've learned that different creatures see in different ways. Does it see color? Does it see light and dark? Does it see poorly and hunt by smell, listen for movement, or feel for heat?"

"I wouldn't presume to know, but you'd best do something soon. The gate has fallen."

He directed Aaslo's attention ahead of them, and sure enough, the gate had been smashed open. Lyksvight poured into the city entrance, and ten mounted magi followed. The wasp creature swooped down into the crowd of invaders, spewing thick black smoke into their midst. The unbreathing lyksvight, at first, seemed unaffected, but then their saggy skin began to erupt in bright yellow boils that grew until they burst, splattering their brethren with milky-white blood. They fell to the ground, twisting and seizing into unnatural poses before ceasing to move altogether like grotesque, macabre statues.

The marquess said, "Whatever you do, I suggest you avoid the smoke."

Dolt stuck his head through an open window, laid his ears back, and gnashed his teeth at the smoke dragon. Then he nudged Aaslo as if egging him into a fight with the creature. Aaslo pushed the mulish horse's muzzle away and focused on the so-called smoke dragon. He agreed with Peck—*wasp-monster* was a more apt description.

"Pull the men back," he said. "They'll do no good out there now."

The marquess placed two fingers between his lips and released a high-pitched whistle. The men that were anxiously hunkered down behind the barrier looked back and then quickly retreated while the smoke dragon's attention was on the lyksvight surging over the toppled gate.

As the men approached, the marquess called, "Fall back to the midway."

Aaslo was watching the smoke dragon cut a swath through lyksvight when a tear in the sky suddenly opened above the fiend. A silvery mass fell from the hole and landed directly on the smoke dragon's back. The smoke dragon immediately began contorting, lashing the mob of lyks-vight around it with its snaky tail and batting furiously at the air with its wings. Aaslo stared at the clump of metal until it finally took shape. It appeared to be a person who had been dipped in liquid silver. The silver person was noticeably small and lithe and definitely female, since nearly every curve was defined except for her face, which was missing. Where it should have been was a blank sheet of metal like uncarved stone on an otherwise finished statue.

The silver woman clung to a segment in the smoke dragon's carapace as it tossed about wildly. Her grip abruptly failed, and she tumbled to the ground in a graceless heap. Aaslo darted forward, but before he could reach her, the smoke dragon exhaled its toxic smoke over her. The wom-an's silver skin didn't bubble and pop as had that of the lyksvight. She scrambled to her feet and ran toward Aaslo. The smoke dragon looked, at first, as though it would follow but then turned back toward the horde of lyksvight as though it were looking for something else.

The silver woman didn't stop upon reaching Aaslo. She instead threw herself on him, wrapping her arms about him as though she never in-tended to let go.

"Aaslo, I'm so glad to see you. You won't believe what happened to me, and what is *that*?" The last, she shouted as she turned to point at the smoke dragon.

Aaslo pulled away from her. Although she looked the stranger, her sound was familiar. "Teza?" Before she could answer, he grabbed her wrist and pulled her back into the shade of the building where the mar-quess still waited. Once there, he said, "What is *this*?"

"Oh!" She reached up and tapped the side of her head. The metal visor slid back over her crown, and Aaslo could finally see her face. She danced backward and then spun so that he could see all of her. "Do you like it? It's amazing, isn't it?"

"But what *is* it?"

"It's armor, silly. It was supposed to be for you, but Sedi couldn't get you to follow her, so she gave it to me."

"*She does realize you aren't a woman, right? It would never fit.*"

Aaslo was more concerned with the source of the armor than its fit. "*Sedi* gave you armor?"

"Well, Bordecci gave it to me, but Sedi took me to him."

"Bordecci? The armorer Myra was trying to get me to see in Chelis?"

"That's the one. But, um, shouldn't we be doing something about that giant snake-wasp thing?"

"It's called a *smoke dragon*," said the marquess, who took her hand and pressed his lips against her fingers. The nobleman appeared smitten, and Aaslo could understand why. Teza might as well have been nude for all the armor hid, yet she showed no shame.

"*There's nothing about which to be ashamed.*"

"I didn't say there was."

"There was what?" said the marquess.

"A plan," said Aaslo.

"I don't see that we need one," said Teza, her gaze shifting to the havoc unfolding at the gate. "The smoke dragon seems to be doing a great job destroying the Berru."

"Eventually, it'll run out of lyksvight and come after *us*." His gaze traversed Teza's unblemished armor, and when they reached her face, she was frowning at him. "What?"

She pointed a silver finger at the smoke dragon. "More important things?"

*"Yeah, Aaslo, don't be a cad. Keep your head in the battle."*

"I wasn't—I was looking for damage. The dragon's smoke is toxic—worse than that. It melts flesh, and you took a direct hit. Your armor protected you against it."

"I'll consider myself lucky."

"I'll consider you bait."

Her eyes widened. "Bait?"

"You will be the distraction. Keep it from spewing smoke at me while I figure out how to kill it."

"I don't think I like this idea."

"Neither do I," said the marquess. "She's a lady. You can't—"

"She's not a lady. She's Teza." As soon as the words left his mouth, he knew his mistake. Teza's armored foot came down on his own, and pain shot up through his leg straight to his head.

"Ow! You know what I meant."

"Which is why I stomped on your foot."

*"It serves you right."*

Aaslo huffed with exasperation. "For what?"

*"For being you."*

"What about, um, *him*?" said the marquess.

Aaslo turned to see to whom he was referring and found the shade standing behind him staring at the smoke dragon. Its eyes glowed so brilliantly that Aaslo thought they might burn right through the monster. It shuffled its feet, wrung its hands, and licked its lips repeatedly. Then it barked. The bark wasn't like that of a dog. It was more like a tree trunk snapping, a window shattering, and thunder cracking all at once. Its mouth wagged silently, then it barked again.

Aaslo said, "I think it wants to fight."

It released two more resounding barks in quick succession, and that was it. The shade had successfully gotten the attention of the smoke dragon. The dragon turned from its monstrous prey and headed straight for Aaslo and his companions.

"Curse the gods, we're out of time," said the marquess.

Aaslo grabbed the marquess's shoulder and pushed him down the street. He said, "Fall back with the men. There is nothing you can do here. Teza, the shade, and I will face this."

"Very well. And, um, may you walk in the shade."

Aaslo smirked. "And your soil be rich."

As the marquess trotted away, Aaslo turned to face the monster. The shade had already stepped forward by several paces. It shrieked at the smoke dragon. In response, the monster's wasplike wings buzzed with agitation, and it rocked to one side. Its tail lashed at the shade but struck the ground several feet from its intended target. The shade released a wicked wail, causing the smoke dragon to list to one side. It smacked into a two-story building, partially collapsing the structure and trapping several of the smoke dragon's legs. While it struggled to free itself from the wreckage, Aaslo and Teza ran toward it. Teza stayed at the monster's front, while Aaslo attempted to sneak up on it from behind. The smoke dragon started to twist toward Aaslo in its struggles, so Teza smacked it in the face with a few powerful spell bursts. Although the spells did little damage, they were successful in keeping the beast's attention.

Aaslo paused for only a second to secure his axe to a strap he had slung over his shoulder and called out, "I'm going up!"

"What? No!" shouted Teza.

He was already on his way, though. He began climbing the joints and segments that made up one of the trapped rear legs of the creature. The leg began to shift as he reached the wasplike body, and he quickly grabbed hold of the edge of the carapace. The smooth exoskeleton lacked additional handholds, though, so he withdrew his axe and, using his right hand, he hacked into the hard shell. The sharp, strong claws of his left hand punctured the carapace enough to provide a handhold. And so he scaled the creature, hacking and clawing his way toward its back.

Mathias hummed in Aaslo's head. *This seems like a bad idea.*

"Of course it does. It's mine," growled Aaslo. "Everything I do seems like a bad idea to you."

The smoke dragon didn't seem to notice the chinks in its armor, but as it freed itself, its movements became erratic.

*You never take my advice anymore.*

"I'm kind of in the middle of something here. Can we talk about this later?"

*If there is a later.*

Aaslo clung to the beast with his considerable strength and eventually found himself atop the smoke dragon's thorax. He looked down at Teza just as the monster released its caustic breath over her. When the smoke cleared, Aaslo's heart leapt into his throat. Teza was collapsed on the ground, unmoving. Although it was still anchored to the building, Teza was close enough that the smoke dragon was able to grab her in its ratlike maw. She screamed as it flung her about like a dog with a rope, then tossed her into the air. Her fall was abruptly arrested by the ground.

Mathias hooted. *That's our girl! No one would ever accuse her of being graceful, though.*

Aaslo was just glad Teza still had the sense of mind to erect a ward around herself. While the smoke dragon lunged and snapped at the ward, Aaslo used his axe to crush the carapace, creating a couple of foot-sized holes. Just as he anchored his feet in the holes, the creature yanked itself free of the rubble.

The noise from the smoke dragon's wings was deafening. Fortunately, his footholds held him tight to the creature's back as he cautiously steadied himself at a stand. Then he gripped his axe with both hands and began chopping through the base of one wing. As the axe came down for a third time, the wing split, and the smoke dragon spiraled toward the ground. Before it hit, though, Aaslo heard an earsplitting shriek, and it didn't emanate from the smoke dragon. Aaslo thought his head might explode from the thunderous cry, and the monster he rode was, apparently, not immune. Aaslo was thrown from its back as it crumpled to the ground and began slamming its head into the overgrown paving stones. Aaslo, however, collided with the shade, who was standing only feet from the distressed smoke dragon.

The smoke dragon rolled about, fluttering one wing spastically as it tried to right itself. The injured wing smacked down onto several lyksvight that seemed oblivious to the commotion. The wing came free and trapped the lyksvight beneath it such that all they could do was lie there squirming and releasing slathering growls. The smoke dragon spied Aaslo coming up on its injured side. He thought he was done for when it abruptly belched its acrid smoke in his direction. At that moment, though, the shade released another of its terrifying wails. The wave of sound rocked the air and blew the smoke away from Aaslo back into the monster's face.

Suddenly, Teza was beneath the monster. She held her hands above her so that they pressed against its abdomen. Just when Aaslo thought she would be crushed, she released a concussive blast of power that burst the monster's abdomen and spewed green, caustic ooze over every monstrous creature in its vicinity.

An ample amount of the goo splattered over Aaslo. Although his dragon scales seemed resistant to the corrosive effects, Aaslo's human flesh wasn't. Aaslo collapsed under the pain as his skin burned and blistered. His muscles began to contract, and he could feel his body contorting. Something inside him reared up to confront the chemical attack, but Aaslo was too far gone to recognize what it was. Then he felt cool hands on his face. It felt like a fresh splash of water in the midst of a forest fire. He opened his eyes to see Teza staring down at him, and she looked surprised.

"Aaslo? Are you okay?"

"No, I'm dying," he groaned.

Her gaze was assessing as she surveyed his body. "Your tunic and trousers are total losses, but I think you'll be fine. You healed more quickly than anything I've seen. It was like your body took the spell and ran away with it."

Aaslo sat up and looked down at himself. His tunic was ravaged, but his flesh was unmarred, and his scales were glistening as though they'd been polished. "I seem to have developed the ability to heal myself. Your spell must have sped up the process."

"*Blah, blah, blah. Let's just sit around chatting while the enemy closes on us.*"

Aaslo glanced up with alarm. "What? Grubs," he growled.

"What about grubs?" said Teza.

"The Berru," he said as he stood. "What's left of them are nearly upon us."

Teza turned, but before either of them could prepare to meet their attackers, a rallying cry broke out down the street. A crowd of wanderers, soldiers, Cartisians, civilians, a prophet, and one ornery horse overtook the decimated square to meet the Berru in their stead. As the Berruvian and Endricsian humans fell, reapers appeared to claim their souls. Aaslo pretended not to see them but claimed those souls that he could. As the battle wore down, and mop-up actions were underway, he and Teza joined Peck, Mory, Ijen, and the marquess in a huddle of officers who were each sprawled on the ground or leaning precariously against anything that would support them. The days of fighting rift monsters, lyksvight, and Berruvian magi had taken their toll, and the officers who had slept less than their subordinates were drained.

The Cartisian elder Hennis looked at Aaslo. "Aria has not spoken of the paladin except to say that she is dead. What happened?"

"After you all crossed into the paths, I went back for Cherrí and Aria. Cherrí refused to leave. She was consumed with want of revenge. It was the three of us against Pithor's army. I tried to save her, but she was determined to die."

"And Pithor?"

"He's dead," said Myra, who suddenly appeared next to Aaslo.

"Dead," said Aaslo.

"Myra!" said Mory. "I'm so glad to see you. Look at the monster Aaslo and Teza killed."

Teza crossed her silver arms and smirked. "*We* fought it. *I* killed it."

Peck winked at her. "Yeah, you did; and you did it in style."

Teza flushed and then grinned.

"What now?" said the marquess. "If the leader of the Berruvian army is dead, we've won, right?"

Aaslo glanced at Myra, who didn't appear to share the marquess's optimism. "I think not," he said. "I doubt Axus will be deterred by the loss of one human general."

Myra said, "No, you're right, Aaslo. I need to give you something." She held out a handful of dangling orbs—five in all.

"What are these?"

"I don't know," she said. She appeared both anxious and embarrassed as she handed them over. "Like the other one I gave you, it was given to me for safekeeping by one of the gods. I'm sorry, Aaslo. I'm afraid you have a much bigger fight ahead of you. The gods are at war."

END OF BOOK TWO

*Aaslo will return in*
**Sanctum of the Soul**,
the Shroud of Prophecy series, Book Three

# ACKNOWLEDGMENTS

I thank my friend and fellow author Ben Hale for his support during the writing of this book, and, as always, to my daughter for her love and faith in me. Special thanks go to my agent and my editor for their patience and understanding.

# CAST OF CHARACTERS

Aaslo—forester from Goldenwood

Adok—crossbowman

Aen Ledrian—first prophet

Aria—Cartisian hunter, Great Oryx Clan

Bear—marquess's soldier in charge of training

Bordecci—Mouvilanian armor smith

Brenna—little girl in the community house

Broden—co-leader of Yellowtail Clan

Cherrí—Fire Serpent Clan

Cobin—head magus of the Berruvian army, Prithor's friend

Corin—little boy in community house

Daniga—leader of the scouts (seven points on her leaf)

Elirus—third prince of Uyan

Esmira—infant princess of Uyan

Everon—fire spirit

Hegress—cavalry and infantry leader of the marquess's army

Hennis—co-leader of Yellowtail Clan

Leydah—narrator

Leyin—Cherrí's neighbor

Leyla—Cherrí's youngest daughter

Lockry—Cartisian sentry, Salt Wave Clan

Lopin—captain of the Uyanian royal guard

Lysia—empress of Berru

Margus—general of Berruvian army, Pithor's friend

Maydon—Corin's older brother

Minea—Cherrí's neighbor

Mink—swordsman

Natu—Clan Father of the Black Rock Clan

Onlí—girl who escaped the Berruvians

Orb—lone traveler in Mouvilan

Pithor—leader of Berruvian invasion

Pongin (Pong)—Hennis's son

Runi—Cherrí's wife

Sedi Tryst—"ancient" magus

Skinny—Yellowtail Clan member

Traydan—boy running across the road

Ueni—Cherrí's oldest daughter

Vigold—the marquess's manservant

# DEFINITIONS

Amulet of Anthiyh—communication amulet

blauchney—alchemical potion for reducing pain

Endricsians—people from the continent north of the Endric Ocean

lyksvights—grey enemy creatures

rublisks—horse-sized, long-necked creature from the Alterworld

Sopora—sleep realms according to Magus Logan

taurini—bulbous, house-sized creature from the Alterworld

vight—small, black creature from the Alterworld

wind demon—stolen prototype creature from another realm

# NOTE FROM THE AUTHOR

I hope you enjoyed reading this second book in the Shroud of Prophecy series. Visit www.kelkade.com to sign up for my newsletter and receive updates and news. Please consider leaving a review or comments so that I may continue to improve and expand upon this ongoing series. Look for *Sanctum of the Soul*, SOP Book Three, in 2022! Also, check out my other ongoing series, King's Dark Tidings.

# ABOUT THE AUTHOR

KEL KADE is a full-time writer and geoscientist who lives in Texas with their teenage daughter, three wily cats, and three frustrating but totally lovable dogs. Thanks to their enthusiastic readers and the success of the King's Dark Tidings and Shroud of Prophecy series, Kade is able to create universes spanning space and time, develop criminal empires, plot the downfall of tyrannous rulers, and dive into fantastical mysteries full time.

Growing up, Kade lived a military lifestyle of traveling to and living in new places. These experiences with distinctive cultures and geography instilled in Kade a sense of wanderlust and opened a young mind to the knowledge that the Earth is expansive and wild. A deep interest in science, ancient history, cultural anthropology, art, music, languages, and spirituality is evidenced by the diversity and richness of the places and cultures depicted in their writing.